*Their passion would
ignite a scandal...*

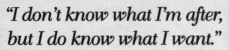

> *"I don't know what I'm after,*
> *but I do know what I want."*

He took her hand and lifted it to kiss her knuckles.

"Phin, don't—"

He drew her closer. Silently he placed a feather-light kiss on the right corner of her mouth, followed by another on the left. Then, as her heart hitched, he tilted her head up with his fingers and kissed her.

Shivering heat coiled down her spine. It would be so easy to simply float away on her fondest daydreams—

She pushed his chest. "What is it?" he murmured, running his fingers softly along her cheekbones.

Good heavens.

"You take too much advantage of an old friendship, sir," Alyse said with as much indignation as she could muster.

By Suzanne Enoch

Historical Titles

Contemporary Titles

SUZANNE ENOCH

Before the SCANDAL

THE NOTORIOUS GENTLEMEN

AVON

An Imprint of HarperCollinsPublishers

This is a work of fiction. Names, characters, places, and incidents are products of the author's imagination or are used fictitiously and are not to be construed as real. Any resemblance to actual events, locales, organizations, or persons, living or dead, is entirely coincidental.

AVON BOOKS
An Imprint of HarperCollins*Publishers*
10 East 53rd Street
New York, New York 10022-5299

Copyright © 2008 by Suzanne Enoch
Excerpts from *One Foot in the Grave* copyright © 2008 by Jeaniene Frost; *Your Scandalous Ways* copyright © 2008 by Loretta Chekani; *After the Kiss* copyright © 2008 by Suzanne Enoch; *Before the Scandal* copyright © 2008 by Suzanne Enoch
ISBN 978-0-06-145674-9
www.avonromance.com

First Avon Books paperback printing: August 2008

Avon Trademark Reg. U.S. Pat. Off. and in Other Countries, Marca Registrada, Hecho en U.S.A.
HarperCollins® is a registered trademark of HarperCollins Publishers.

Printed in the U.S.A

10 9 8 7 6 5 4 3 2 1

Chapter 1 _____

Lieutenant Colonel Phineas Bromley didn't expect paradise. True, after ten years spent fighting the French in Spain, anywhere seemed an improvement, but as he crossed the bridge over the River Ouse and onto Quence Park land, he felt more as though he were stepping into hell.

His friends, former soldiers now, had written him over the past two years and told him a little about the condition of his family's ancestral property, so he knew the fences would be in need of repair and the granary roof would leak. The estate, set in the middle of East Sussex, was still pretty enough, but he scarcely noticed the green of the grass or the crisp freshness of the air. Ten years away. The absence seemed both far too long and far too short.

The uneasiness that had been tangling through him

since well before he'd rented the only available transportation in Uckfield, grew into a hard-edged dread. It wasn't that he minded appearing on Quence's doorstep in a hay cart. The problem was what lay beyond the door.

Phineas reached into his uniform jacket and touched his sister's letter again. He'd memorized the correspondence from Elizabeth in the six days since he'd received it and taken an emergency leave from the First Royal Dragoons, but he continued to reread it anyway. According to his younger sister, their oldest sibling William, the Viscount Quence, was seriously ill. Haste was all-important, she'd said, if he wanted to arrive home before it was too late.

And so he put aside the thought of what he must look like, a crimson-coated army officer sitting behind an ancient gray nag in an ancient hay cart. And he put aside the way his breathing sped and his heart pounded as he trotted up the main road toward what had once been home. Whatever he felt at the moment didn't matter. At this point the only thing worse than setting eyes on his brother again would be arriving too late to do so.

White, with tall, narrow windows and the typical asymmetrical sprawl of a house expanded over several generations, Quence sat on a slight rise overlooking a pond and a large landscaped garden complete with faux-ruins and a moldering marble statue of Apollo. It had been a beautiful, half-wild place rampant with deer and foxes and, he'd been certain as a boy, a faerie giant or two.

For a moment he closed his eyes. Before he'd left, before the scandal, there'd been a princess there, too. Dark-eyed Alyse Donnelly. He hadn't heard a word about her in years, but if her plans had gone as intended she would have married a prince or a duke by now. For a spritely young lady of fifteen, she'd had a very clear idea of her future. Phineas smiled as he remembered her, then shook it off again. He had the present to worry about.

Other than looking as though it needed a coat of paint and some pruning done in the garden, Quence Park looked exactly the same as it had the last time he'd set eyes on it—which was strange, because he didn't feel at all the same. Except for the nagging guilt, of course. That had been his companion for the past ten years, and he imagined he would carry it with him to the grave. Now it sat like an old, not-quite-comfortable coat, loose enough to let him breathe, but tight enough that he had to make a conscious effort to do so.

He sent the cart up the curving road to the front of the mansion. A groom he didn't recognize trotted out from the stables at his approach, and Phineas climbed down from the seat. "This needs to go back to the hostelry at Uckfield," he said as the grizzled fellow took the bridle in one hand.

"Yes, sir," the groom returned, sending him a curious look before he escorted the cart, with his trunk on the back, around the side of the house.

Wide, shallow granite steps, a griffin perched on either side, marked the front entry. Keeping his pace steady, Phineas topped them to pause on the pillar-edged portico. The front door opened.

"Hello, Digby," he said to the ancient butler looking at him from behind a nose the shape of a hawk's beak. Digby had been old ten years ago. Now it looked as though all of the color had been leached out of him, part of his metamorphosis into a stern, efficient statue.

The butler blinked his pale eyes. "Master Phineas? Good heavens! Come in, sir!"

No black armband, no black crinoline draped anywhere—Phineas let out a slow breath. The worst of his fears hadn't come to pass. That didn't mean he wouldn't be in for it, or that he didn't deserve every bit of bile hurled in his direction, but at least no one had died. "Are William and Elizabeth to home?" he asked, still reluctant to step through the front door. He'd lost that privilege, if not in their eyes, then in his own.

"They are in the dining room. I shall have a plate set for you, sir."

"No, that won't be necessary. I . . . may not be staying."

"But sir—"

"You might go and tell them I'm here. Give them a moment before I barge in." The butler nodded, but before he could do more than turn around, Phineas grabbed his arm. "Wait. On second thought, I'd best barge in." Otherwise he might not have the chance to see them at all.

"As you wish, Master Phineas."

Squaring his shoulders, Phineas strode through the front door. It felt more momentous than it undoubtedly looked, but his insides were rattling about so loudly that he wouldn't have been able to hear anyone else's opinion.

He still remembered precisely where the dining room lay down the long hallway, and he stopped outside the half-open door. Inside, low conversation touched his ears, enough that he could hear the voices but not the words being spoken. His younger sister and his older brother. The only family he had.

Just get it over with, he ordered himself. For God's

sake, he'd faced down cannon fire with less trepidation. Death, though, was likely easier than this. All that entailed was giving up. With a last shallow breath Phineas pushed open the door.

And he realized two things: One, William didn't look even close to being on his deathbed, which meant Elizabeth had lied to him; and two, once he'd heard that they were sitting down to dinner he should have asked whether or not Lord Quence might be entertaining. Bad form for a soldier, and even worse for a prodigal son.

"Hello."

Considering the amount of time he'd had to compose a cunning, dry, witty, or cynical greeting upon his return, Phineas thought he probably could have done better. But seeing his brother seated at the head of the table with a fork in his hand and color in his cheeks simply . . . stunned him. He felt thankful to have squeezed out that one coherent word.

The slender, ginger-haired young lady seated closest to William shot to her feet. "Phin!" she screamed. Almost before he could move she flung herself on him.

"Elizabeth," he muttered, recognizing her only because of her resemblance to their late mother.

"I knew you'd come!"

"You asked me to."

"Did she, now?" the figure at the head of the table said quietly.

Phineas extracted himself from his younger sister's embrace. "William. I—"

"I wrote and asked him to visit," Elizabeth broke in, refusing to relinquish his hand. His younger sister had the strength of a Titan. "I didn't tell you, because—"

"It's no matter," the viscount stated. His face had

paled since Phin's entrance, but no one could blame him for that. "Lord Donnelly, Mrs. Donnelly, Miss Donnelly, will you please excuse us for a moment?"

The light-haired man at the opposite end of the table nodded. "Of course, William. I believe we can entertain ourselves for a few moments."

Another jolt went through Phineas. *Miss Donnelly? Alyse?* Before he could do more than glance in the direction of wide brown eyes and swept-back dark hair, the servant standing behind William pulled backward on the viscount's chair, and the wheeled seat rolled away from the table. Abruptly his brother had every ounce of Phin's attention again.

"The morning room, Andrews," William said in the same cool voice he'd used a moment earlier.

Elizabeth practically dragged Phineas with her as she followed William and his wheeled chair. He looked at her again. *Good God.* Ginger curls, laughing hazel eyes—an attractive young woman no matter how he assessed her. And the last time he'd seen her, she'd been seven years old.

Andrews wheeled William close by the fireplace, then without being told left the room, shutting the door quietly behind him. For a moment Phineas considered fleeing behind the servant, but then he would never discover what the devil was afoot.

William gazed at him in the ensuing silence, then abruptly turned his attention to their sister. "Why did you ask him to visit?"

"Because it's been ten years," she replied, her chin high.

"She told me you were on your deathbed," Phineas supplied.

"You wouldn't have come home otherwise." She

scowled, abruptly looking more like the child he remembered. "And don't the two of you yell at me just to avoid talking to one another."

Phineas narrowed his eyes. "If this is meant to be some sort of ill-conceived family reunion, I have duties elsewhere."

"Ah," his brother said, "you're disappointed that I haven't shuffled off the mortal coil, then."

"No." Phin frowned, then buried the expression again. "I was worried."

"Don't be. You'll inherit eventually. I haven't cut you off."

That actually surprised him. Phineas took a breath. Approaching a battle from a position of weakness was something to which he wasn't accustomed, and after a decade as a soldier that realization left him even more nettled than he would have been otherwise. "Shall I stay, then? Or do I go?"

"You stay," Elizabeth stated, clutching his arm again.

He sent her another look, softening his gaze only when he saw her tense expression. She wasn't the source of this trouble, however much he wished to blame her for bringing him back home. "Why the devil would you write me that William was dying?" he grumbled. "I don't appreciate being made to look like a fool."

William raised a brow at that, but was wise enough not to comment. Elizabeth, though, dug her fingers hard into his sleeve. "I did it because you need to be here," she stated.

Phineas searched her gaze, looking for any clue. He knew how to assess a man's character in the briefest of moments, and it didn't even take that long to see that his sister was worried. And not just about whether he would stay the night. "Care to elaborate?"

"I don't think Beth and I are the ones who need to be answering questions, Phin."

Phineas blew out his breath. Anger was easier, but as Elizabeth had said, it had been ten bloody years. "Look, William, I've been traveling for nearly a week. I'm tired. We can fence tomorrow, if you'd like, or I'll leave tonight if you wish it. I was asked to come, and I came. That's all I know."

"I have a bit of skepticism regarding you doing as you're asked," his brother said in his low, quiet voice.

Abruptly Phineas felt as though he were seventeen again, facing a dressing-down from his then-twenty-four-year-old brother. He pushed back against the sensation. He wasn't that stupid boy any longer—though convincing his family would obviously take some doing.

Stating that he'd been through things his family couldn't imagine wouldn't serve; not when William sat in that chair. "All I can do to demonstrate that I'm not here out of any ill will is to leave again," he said slowly. "As I said, I was worried. That is the sum total of my motivation."

William faced him, hazel gaze to hazel gaze. "I don't want the neighbors thinking we've turned away family," he finally said. "I'll have Digby set a plate for you, and you'll sit down to dinner."

Dinner. That stirred another thought—one that thankfully had nothing to do with guilt or suspicion. Of all the things he'd been prepared to face on his return to Quence, he hadn't expected *her*. He nodded. "You said your guests were the Donnellys," he ventured in an even voice. "Kin of the viscount?"

"His heir. The fellow, anyway. Richard, Viscount Donnelly. The older woman is his mother, Ernesta. And you know Alyse. She's keeping Ernesta company."

"Alyse," he mused. "I haven't seen her . . . in years." He fumbled over the last bit, cursing himself. Distraction wouldn't serve at the moment, but Alyse Donnelly had been his closest friend. Not that he would have called his affection for her brotherly.

"Yes, I would imagine she's thinking the same thing about you," his brother returned, clearly lacking the ability to read minds. "Beth, fetch Andrews for me, will you?" Phillip continued. "And tell Digby—"

"I shall." Sending Phineas a glance that he couldn't read, she hurried out of the room. Wisely she left the door open behind her.

"She's nothing like I remember," Phineas said.

"Be kind to her," William commented as Andrews returned to the room. "She worships you. Don't make her regret it."

Phin remained where he was as his brother, propelled by Andrews, returned to the dining room. That had gone swimmingly. For the devil's sake, the ball he'd taken in the arm had been less painful.

For as long as William indicated he should stay, though, he would. He owed his brother no less. The unkempt lands were sign enough that he'd let his guilt keep him away for far too long. But it was more than that. Elizabeth's letter, the looks she'd kept sending him, the small tidbits of information he'd intentionally overlooked in her previous correspondence—he needed to be here. And he needed to figure out why.

Chapter 2 _____

Phin Bromley. Alyse Donnelly had never thought to set eyes on him again. Her hands had begun shaking the moment he'd walked into the room, and she folded them into her lap.

She knew he'd joined the army, but he didn't wear his uniform like a soldier on parade along the Mall. He wore it like a second skin, as if he'd ceased to notice it a very long time ago. And—

Richard jabbed her in the shoulder. "Who is he?" her cousin hissed.

Alyse shook herself. "Their brother," she answered in the same low tone he'd used. "The middle sibling."

"You never mentioned another brother."

"He's been away for a very long time."

"Even so, I would call failing to mention that Lord Quence has an heir a somewhat significant omission."

"Yes, of course," she said hurriedly, hoping to avoid a dressing-down. "But it has been ten years or more." She smiled a little, remembering. "I haven't set eyes on him since I was fifteen."

"Well, this could be an opportunity for you, then, Cousin," Richard murmured. "After all, if he hasn't come up in your conversation, perhaps you haven't featured in his."

Her face heated; she couldn't help it. After five years she should have been used to the insults, direct or implied, but obviously they still had the power to cut her. "Thank you, Richard," she said softly, "but I prefer to make his acquaintance first." To renew it, rather, since she doubted he still accepted pond-jumping challenges or dumped frogs in unsuspecting young ladies' laps.

"I suggest you speak to your cousin with less sarcasm, Alyse," her aunt cooed. "You are not who you once were."

And no one in her family ever let her forget that fact. "I remember, Aunt Ernesta."

"Then have someone fetch me a blanket. My legs are cold."

Carefully hiding her annoyance, Alyse motioned to the nearest of the footmen and passed on her aunt's request. Things in the Bromley household might have taken a turn for the unexpected, but her life progressed with the predictability of a clock. An endlessly ticking clock. And to think that once, before the scandal, she used to look forward to the future.

The dining room door opened again. Lord Quence entered first, being wheeled in on his chair and a somber look on his face. Beth followed a heartbeat later, her expression tense. The door closed again, but Alyse kept her gaze on it.

Phineas Bromley. Phin. The last person she ever would have imagined joining the army. Clearly neither of their lives had turned out as they'd intended. She didn't know what the insignia on his shoulder meant, but he was clearly an officer.

A moment later he walked into the room, his gaze touching on the rest of the occupants, and then finding her. Alyse blushed again at those clear hazel eyes, wondering what she looked like to him. Other than his eyes, she wasn't certain she would have recognized him. His dark brown hair was a little long, as though he'd been too busy to seek a barber, and his face leaner than she remembered. A narrow scar dissected his right eyebrow and touched his cheek, giving his appearance the rakish bent that he'd always seemed to have inside. He'd been pretty as a boy, and he'd become a strikingly handsome man.

"Alyse," he said, and took the newly placed seat across from her. "Miss Donnelly. William told me that your parents passed away. I am truly sorry."

"Thank you. It was . . . unexpected."

Richard leaned sideways to cover her hand with his. "I'm only glad that we've been able to give Alyse a place in our household."

Phineas glanced at her cousin as he would an annoying fly, and then returned his attention to her. "Do you still like to ride?" he asked.

It felt odd, these days, to have someone pay attention to me, and especially at the expense of her titled cousin. "I haven't had much opportunity," she hedged. "My aunt is unwell, and I sit with her a great deal."

"If I stay long enough, we should go riding," he pursued.

Alyse smiled. "I would like that."

"How long *will* you be staying?" Richard cut in again.

This time Phin glanced at his brother. "As long as I'm needed. I have several months of leave coming, if I require it."

"Where are you serving?" Alyse asked, disliking when that gaze left her.

"The north of Spain, at the moment. I'm with the First Royal Dragoons."

"A . . . lieutenant, is it?" Richard asked, eyeing the crimson and blue uniform.

"Lieutenant Colonel," Elizabeth corrected, pride in her tone. "Phin's received five field promotions."

"That's extraordinary." Richard lifted a glass not in Phin's direction, but in his brother's. "You must be very proud of him."

"Yes," Lord Quence said, returning to his meal. "Very proud."

Clearly all was not well at Quence Park, though Alyse had known that before. But for Richard to poke a stick into the tension—it was so unlike him in public, though in private he did little else. "When we were all children together," she said into the air, "we had the most hair-raising adventures."

Phineas sent her a short smile. "I can face cannons fearlessly after surviving the infamous pond-jump dares."

Alyse snorted, then quickly covered her mouth with one hand and made the sound into a cough. "You were fearless well before then."

"The First Royal Dragoons," her cousin said slowly. "You're the ones who rode on Maguilla several years ago."

Phin winced. Alyse opened her mouth to change the

subject, but before she could do so, he nodded. "That was an ill day," he said calmly.

"I would have to agree with that. You lost, what, a quarter of your company?"

"Phin didn't lead that charge, Richard," Beth contributed stoutly. "And his dearest friend was wounded, saving his life."

"Good heavens," Alyse breathed, not even aware that she'd spoken aloud until Phin looked at her again.

"No worries," he drawled. "Sullivan and I both survived." He returned his gaze to her cousin. "I'm not likely to forget the loss of one hundred and ninety-seven men, but thank you for reminding me."

Now that was the Phin she remembered, always ready for a confrontation, willing to spit right in the devil's eye just for the sake of annoying him. The hothead. The bit of him she'd missed the most and the least.

Richard pushed to his feet. "Clearly this is a night for family," he said to William. "We shan't intrude further."

"You are always welcome here, Richard. My brother has been at war for ten years; his manners are a bit blunted."

"I didn't begin the conversation," Phin muttered, shoveling a thick slice of roast pig onto his plate.

"I do understand, William, and I take no offense. Beth, may I take you driving into Lewes tomorrow?"

Elizabeth blushed. "That would be delightful, Richard."

Muttering her own apologies at their early departure, Alyse rose and hurried out to the foyer to collect her wrap and her aunt's from Digby the butler. Keeping the frown from her face, she placed the shawl around Aunt

Ernesta's shoulder and then took the place of her aunt's walking stick as they left the house and descended the shallow front steps.

Once the claws dug into her upper arm had left and she'd helped her aunt into the coach, Alyse rolled her shoulders. Beth and Phin stood in the doorway, and she sent them a smile that she hoped didn't look too disappointed. She wanted to stay. Phineas looked utterly . . . magnificent, tall and lean and brave. That wild boy with whom she'd played, and about whom she'd dreamed and then hadn't spared a thought in years, had returned. And he'd spoken with her as though they had been the dear companions that she recalled.

She climbed into the coach herself, and they rumbled down the long drive and onto the main road toward Donnelly House, perched on a hill a mile away. In the long-distant past she'd enjoyed the ride, the return home after an evening of charades or whist or hide-and-seek. Now, though, it only meant that the cage doors were swinging shut again.

"You didn't waste much time, did you?" Aunt Ernesta commented, scowling at her.

"What?"

"Don't presume to think you were fooling anyone, Alyse," her cousin took up. "You were practically drooling on him."

"I was not," she exclaimed. "He's an old friend whom I haven't seen in a very long time."

"And it didn't look as though he was any more welcome in that home than you are in ours," Richard said coolly. "If you are looking for an escape, dear cousin, you should be looking to the viscount."

"That is mean, Richard."

He shook his head. "It is logic. You know the way of

the world by now, Alyse. And to be perfectly blunt, you'd fare much better wed to a titled cripple than to his estranged younger brother."

Alyse closed her lips over her retort. However much she valued her friendship with the Bromley family, Lord Donnelly directed the affairs of *her* family. And Lord Donnelly was no longer her fond, warm-hearted father. It was now in her own best interest to be agreeable—to their faces, at least. The money she'd been slowly and painstakingly saving wasn't yet enough for her escape. While she couldn't be grateful that Richard and Aunt Ernesta had taken her in, she did have a roof over her head, and food to eat—and a shilling or two to hold back whenever they sent her out on errands.

"I thought that might clear your vision," Richard murmured. "Now. Tell me what you know of Lieutenant Colonel Phineas Bromley."

She drew a breath. "As I said, I haven't seen him since I was fifteen years old. The siblings were very close, but Phin . . ."

"Phin what?" he prompted.

"He had a wild streak," she said reluctantly. It had been very public knowledge at the time, though. Nothing Richard couldn't discover elsewhere. "Women, wagering, drinking, anything he could do, he did. And then there was an accident, and he left. I haven't seen him since."

"'An accident'?" Richard repeated, sitting forward. "William's accident?"

She nodded. "It was some sort of horse race. Everything became very chaotic once William was injured, and I don't know the details."

"That explains some things," her cousin mused. "If I'm to marry into that family, I would like to know the identity of all the skeletons. The last thing I want is a scandal."

"Then ask Beth about him. I'm certain she'll tell you." Alyse sank back into the corner of the coach. The night might be early, but she still had a great many duties to attend to. Seeing her aunt put to bed would take another hour, and then she had mending and tomorrow's breakfast, luncheon, and dinner to plan out.

And then she could, with luck, find some sleep in the small room they'd granted her, a floor above where her old bedchamber had used to be. And if she slept, she knew of whom she would be dreaming. Phin Bromley was back.

As soon as the Donnellys left the house, William vanished into his office. He claimed to have some ledgers to go over, but he needn't have bothered making excuses. Phineas hadn't expected much of a homecoming, but neither did he deny that a tearful embrace wouldn't have been unwelcome. Elizabeth had asked him to return, after all.

"I'm so pleased you're here," Elizabeth said again, hugging his arm in both hands as they walked to one of the upstairs sitting rooms.

William had another wheeled chair placed at the head of the stairs, and it looked like a third one rested on the floor above that, each one ready and awaiting the viscount's use. Phineas shut his eyes against a new surge of guilt. "You told me he was on his damned deathbed," he said in a low voice.

She hauled him down beside her as she sat on the couch. "Would you have come if I'd written that I miss you? Because I've done that before."

He eyed her. "So this is merely your way of arranging a social visit?"

"No."

"I'm glad to hear that, at least. I think." Sinking back into the soft cushions, he stretched his booted feet out toward the fireplace. "I can't believe how . . . grown up you look, Elizabeth. You're the very image of our mother."

"My friends call me Beth now. And it has been ten years, Phin. I was seven when you left."

"I remember quite well, thank you."

She looked toward the fire, then cleared her throat. "I saw your friends a few months ago," she said abruptly, clapping her hands together. "Lord Bramwell and Sullivan Waring. You heard that Sullivan's just gotten married, haven't you?"

Phineas nodded. "I received his letter the week before yours arrived." The letter had spoken of a great deal, but nothing that seemed relevant to his present location or circumstance—except where it had noted that William had recently suffered a fever and looked more frail than previously. If anything, it had made his sister's letter even more plausible. "If you weren't tricking me into a visit, then why am I here? Obviously William doesn't want me about."

"That's not true, Phin. He was surprised. And so was I. I wasn't certain you would come, whatever I wrote to you."

Rather than explaining the panic that had touched his heart when he'd read her letter, or the speed with which he'd arranged to take an extended leave and then galloped across half of Europe, Phineas unbuttoned the stiff top button of his jacket. "You still haven't answered my question, Beth. Why am I here?"

The sitting room door opened. "Because of a young girl's silliness," William said, releasing the door handle as Andrews rolled him into the room. "You couldn't even wait until you had time for a chat with us before you were back to it, could you?"

Phineas scowled. "Back to what?"

"Fighting with a guest, and flirting. With poor Alyse, this time. You can't be content unless you're ruining yourself or someone else."

"That is not tr—"

"I was informed you actually arrived on a hay cart. How did you manage that?"

"I begged a ride from Dover with Malcolm Pepper, a solicitor from Uckfield. Once I arrived there, the hay cart was the only transportation available until tomorrow. I thought speed to be of the essence, if you'll recall."

"How long do you intend to stay?" William cut in again.

"I have no bloody idea." He sent a glare at Beth. "I didn't expect a warm welcome, but I *was* asked. I'll leave in the morning." Standing, he made his way around the wheeled chair to the doorway. "Sully has a house in Sussex now. I'll pay him a call and then head back to the Peninsula."

"William," Beth grated, then pushed by the viscount to grab Phineas around the wrist. "We will all go to bed," she continued more loudly. "And in the morning we will sit down for breakfast at eight o'clock, and we will all be very civil and cordial to one another. Is that clear?"

William's expression softened as he gazed at their sister. "While I dislike your methods, I suppose I can't fault your motives," he finally said. "Andrews."

The chair wheeled past Phineas and back through the door again.

"I will see you both in the morning," the viscount continued over his shoulder. "Beth, a word with you?"

"Of course." With an apologetic smile at Phineas, she left the room as well.

Abandoned, Phin returned to his seat. Whatever he'd been tossed into, Beth wanted him about, and she wanted to tell him something. Something that William clearly preferred he not know. Considering his brother's opinion of him, it could be nothing, but he'd learned to pay attention to the tickle along the back of his skull. It had saved his life on several occasions.

At least William still knew how to cut into him. Women, fighting, drink—the recipe had always sounded the same, whichever vice his brother chose to rail at. If William thought that nothing had changed over ten years, Phin might as well leave. Because in his own soul, he knew that from the moment William had fallen from that horse, everything had changed. Himself the most of all.

Aside from all that, damn it all, he hadn't been flirting with Alyse Donnelly. They'd always gotten along well, and for God's sake she seemed to be the one person of his acquaintance in the house who wasn't trying to bite his head off or didn't have some sort of secret agenda behind his return. Of course he'd spoken with her.

Alyse. Dark-eyed Alyse. They were only two years apart in age, and just about the time he'd left he was beginning to realize that his very good friend was becoming a very lovely young lady. The other lads in Lewes had realized it first, and he had no idea how she could be five-and-twenty and still a miss. As he recalled, her plan had been to marry either a duke or a prince. He smiled. Back then he'd grown just enough wit to be disappointed that he was neither.

The sitting room door swung open again, and Beth slipped back inside. "Apologies," she whispered, her cheeks pale.

"I assume he told you not to discuss anything with me," Phineas commented, lowering his voice out of deference for her rather than because he didn't want William to overhear him.

"He's only surprised," she pointed out for the second or third time. "I should have informed him that you might be returning home."

Phineas shook his head. "None of this is your fault, Beth. All of the 'should haves' belong to me."

"Even so, you are part of this family. A very big part. And I don't like secrets."

Neither did he, though he'd long ago seen their necessity in both war and peace. "I shall take your advice and go to bed, and then be civil in the morning. If William wants me included in family business, I imagine he'll tell me so."

As he climbed to his feet, his younger sister flung her arms around him again. "I'm so glad you've come back, Phin," she said, her voice muffled against the front of his coat.

He would have been more glad if he knew *why* she'd summoned him home. William might not want him to know, but that had never stopped him before. He had every reason now to behave, he supposed, except for one: Things were amiss, and he owed his brother a debt that could never be repaid. If William wished to continue railing at him, then so be it. In the meantime, though, he had some information to discover, and he didn't intend to be patient about it. "I'm glad to be back," he returned belatedly, knowing she expected some sort of response. He patted her on the shoulder.

"I had your trunk brought up to your old bedchamber. It's been kept exactly as it was when you left."

He refrained from asking if it had at least been dusted in the interim. "I shall see you in the morning, then, Beth."

Elizabeth kissed him on the cheek, then released him. "Good night, Phin."

Once she'd left, Phineas walked the house. Knowing the surrounding terrain had saved his life on more than one occasion, but this had at least as much to do with trying to grasp hold of his past—and Quence Park's present—as it did with survival. Nothing much had changed since he'd last lived there—other than a few new rugs and a vase here and there, he might have been transported back in time.

When he finally pushed open the door to his old bedchamber in the middle of the house's east wing, the fire had been lit and his trunk lay open at the foot of the large bed. "I took the liberty of unpacking for you," Andrews said as he walked out of the attached dressing room.

Phineas hid a flinch. "Thank you," he said aloud. "Did Lord Quence ask you to see to me?"

"No, sir. But as you have no valet, I thought to offer my assistance."

"My thanks again, Andrews, but I'll manage." He had his own man, Sergeant Thaddeus Gordon, but he'd left the fellow in Spain with the remainder of his kit. And he didn't like other people meddling with items that were responsible for his safety. "Good evening."

Andrews nodded. "Good evening." Moving past Phineas, he left the room and closed the door behind him.

Of course William had sent the valet in, probably to

determine what Phin had brought with him and hence how long he meant to stay. Blowing out his breath, Phineas sat on the edge of the bed to pull off his boots and then remove his scarlet and blue coat. He would have to wear the uniform again tomorrow, and at least until he could flatten the wrinkles out of some of the civilian clothes he'd thrown into his trunk.

The thought of being out of uniform made him nervous. He'd been a soldier for ten years, and it was the one thing at which he excelled. He knew how to be an officer. He was hell on horseback, and a dead shot. With him at the head of the battalion, his men had accumulated an impressive roster of accomplishments, despite the disaster at Maguilla. But he'd joined the army because he'd been a failure as a civilian, and as a brother. Now that was something he could no longer afford to be, in or out of uniform.

Phineas rose again. "Damnation," he muttered, walking to the window and throwing the curtains open, then pushing open the glass. Cool air brushed by him, making the fire spit.

He took a deep breath, then walked over to the writing desk in the corner. William might not be willing to talk to him, but he had other sources of information. He had two friends, two former comrades, who had been sending him tidbits about his family for the past two years. And they could damned well let him know what was going on now.

Taking a seat, he pulled out paper and inked his pen, then began to write. Sullivan Waring and Lord Bramwell Lowry Johns had best be cooperative, because he didn't plan on sitting still for an ambush, no matter who intended to fire on him.

Chapter 3 _____

For a moment as Alyse awoke, everything seemed perfect. With eyes closed she could just make out the early morning light at the edges of the curtains in the window. In the distance, sheep baaed and a rooster or two crowed, and the covers pulled up to her chin left her in just the coziest state of warmth she could imagine. It was all like it had been before, as if nothing ill had ever happened.

Then the bell began ringing. No, not ringing. Jangling. Every high-pitched, fast-paced clang stabbed into her ears and her comfort. For a few seconds she ignored it—or tried to, though she certainly wasn't fooling herself. For those few seconds, though, if she pretended, concentrated, hard enough, she could be Alyse Donnelly, daughter of the Viscount and Viscountess Donnelly, the diamond of East Sussex and the most sought-after waltzer in two counties.

"Alyse!"

At the same time as the muffled female voice yelled her name, a thud came from the middle of her floor. She sighed as the sound repeated. For an invalid, Aunt Ernesta was fairly spry with her walking cane. And how she could reach the ceiling while lying in bed, Alyse had no idea.

As she shoved down the covers and sat up, perfection faded away again. Now she was daughter to the deceased viscount and viscountess, and cousin to the present lord. And now she rarely waltzed. Waltzing was difficult when her aunt insisted on having a companion seated at her elbow for the entirety of each soiree—when they attended them.

"Alyse! You lazy girl!"

Alyse stomped on the floor. "I'm coming!" she shouted back.

For heaven's sake. Her aunt had set up residence in her old bedchamber, though whether that had been out of spite or because she liked the view from the windows, Alyse didn't know. She did have her suspicions. Her new bedchamber, on the drafty third floor, had been her old governess's room. If she'd had any idea how chilled Mrs. Garvey must have been in the winter, she would have insisted that the kindly woman be lodged downstairs.

Throwing on a green morning dress, Alyse knotted her hair and pushed a few clips into it, then left the room and hurried down to the second floor. "I'm here, Aunt," she panted, giving a perfunctory knock on the door with one knuckle and then pushing it open.

"Don't you dare stomp at me," Aunt Ernesta said, her dour face even less friendly than usual. "It's bad enough that you go clomping about up there at all hours, without you intentionally making noise."

"Apologies," Alyse returned tightly, joining her aunt's maid, Harriet, beside the bed. They each took an elbow and hauled.

"Be careful! I am not a sack of flour."

No, sacks of flour didn't complain nearly as much as her aunt did. Alyse kept that thought to herself, however. There were worse things than being an unpleasant woman's companion. There were even degrees of unpleasantness. And she knew that firsthand, because she'd personally experienced half a dozen aspects of it.

"I'm going into Lewes today to look for gown material," Aunt Ernesta announced as her maid dressed her. "We have several soirees just in the next fortnight, and I'm beginning to think I haven't brought enough evening gowns with me."

That meant that Alyse would be going into town, as well. It was better than sitting in the drawing room and embroidering, and it meant a good chance to increase the amount of her hidden-away funds. Her escape money, as she'd come to think of it. "What time shall I have Winston bring the coach around?"

"Don't be so eager," Mrs. Donnelly snapped. "I haven't had my breakfast yet."

"Neither have I, Aunt. I merely inquired so you wouldn't be kept waiting when you were ready to leave."

With a sniff, Aunt Ernesta nodded. "Ten o'clock. And I want to take the barouche. The fresh air may do me some good."

"Very well. I'll see to it."

Before anyone could change their minds or put her to brushing out her aunt's hair, Alyse left the bedchamber and hurried down to the foyer. "Saunders," she said to the tall, spindly butler, "Mrs. Donnelly would like to take the barouche into town at ten o'clock."

The butler nodded. "I shall inform Winston." He pursed his lips. "I believe there to be a very limited quantity of early summer strawberries available in the breakfast room."

Strawberries. She adored strawberries. "Thank you, Saunders," she murmured, "but for heaven's sake don't risk Richard overhearing you."

"I'm surprised to still be here as it is, Miss Alyse. And I haven't forgotten how you always liked strawberries."

With a quick, fond smile Alyse put a hand on his arm. "Thank you," she whispered again. "I—"

"Alyse!" Aunt Ernesta's strident bellow could peel paint from the walls.

Unwilling to risk Saunders being blamed for her absence, Alyse rushed into the breakfast room to hide three strawberries beneath the toast and then returned upstairs. "Yes, Aunt?" she asked, skidding back to the doorway of Mrs. Donnelly's bedchamber.

"You're dawdling again. Find my gold earbobs."

"Yes, Aunt."

As she finished dressing, Aunt Ernesta turned from the dressing mirror. "I have decided that I shall ask Mrs. Potter and Lady Dysher over for luncheon tomorrow," she said. "Send out the invitations, and select a half dozen passages from Milton. You shall read them to us for discussion."

"Milton?" Alyse repeated, inwardly cringing. "That

seems a bit . . . heavy for luncheon. Are you certain you wouldn't prefer Shakespeare or Chaucer?"

"Shakespeare is far too risqué, and I wouldn't be caught dead reading Chaucer, you silly girl. It's to be Milton." Mrs. Donnelly waved her back out the door. "And formulate some questions to guide the discussion."

"Yes, Aunt." Scowling now that no one could see her, Alyse went into the library for *Paradise Lost* and then headed for the stairs and the breakfast room.

"Ah, good morning, Alyse," her cousin said from his seat at the head of the breakfast table. The carcasses of what looked like the remainders of all the strawberries save her hidden three lay piled to one side of his plate.

She sent out a silent thanks to Saunders. "Good morning," she returned, accepting a plate from Donald the footman and heading for the toast.

"How is my mother this morning?"

"Well, I believe. She wishes to drive into town." Her strawberries were still where she'd hidden them. Swiftly she bit into the plumpest of them and placed the other two on her plate. Strawberries tasted like summer. More significantly, they tasted like the summers of her youth, warm and moist and overflowing with sweet flavor.

"Come sit beside me," Richard prompted, before she could take her usual seat halfway down the length of the breakfast table.

Suspicious, she did as he asked. "Thank you."

"Of course. Tell me, Cousin, why do you think it is that Elizabeth Bromley never mentioned her other brother to me?"

Alyse shrugged. "He's been away for quite some time. I don't suppose she thought to discuss him any more than you thought to ask whether there might be another sibling about."

Richard nodded." Well, he's about now, isn't he? Why do you think that is?"

Alyse edged her plate away from him. "You know as much as I do, Richard."

"Yes, well, give me your opinion, anyway. He seemed to know you quite well." Her cousin finished off his sliced ham, then reached over and plucked one of the strawberries from her plate.

She didn't say anything about the theft. He would only remind her how lucky she was to have relatives who were willing to provide for her, and then he would take the other berry. He would probably do so anyway. Before he could, she plopped it into her own mouth. *So there.* "In my opinion," she said after she'd chewed and swallowed, "he may have come home because of Lord Quence's health. You know the viscount has scarcely left the house since they arrived at the end of the Season."

"I agree. It didn't seem that William had any inkling he might be returning, however. I would wager that Beth sent for him."

That made sense. Richard was nodding to himself, though, so apparently her further opinion wasn't required. As far as she was concerned, the fact that Phineas Bromley was back in East Sussex held far more interest than wondering why he'd journeyed there.

"How close are you and Colonel Bromley?" Richard asked abruptly.

Alyse shook herself. "We used to be great friends. As I said, though, I haven't seen him for a good ten years. I know nothing about him, these days." She drew a breath, weighing whether having her curiosity satisfied would be worth the verbal lashing she was likely to receive in return. Curiosity won out. "Why so interested in Colonel Bromley, Cousin?"

He pinned her with his pale blue gaze. "I'm pursuing his sister," he said flatly. "I would be foolish to ignore the presence of a man who might have a different agenda. Is there anything else about which you'd like to question me?"

"No. Of course not."

"I thought not." Her cousin gestured for Donald to fetch him a cup of coffee. American coffee. She detested it. "I imagine," he continued after taking a swallow, "that when he spoke with you last night, the colonel thought you were still a diamond. I wonder if they've told him yet that you're made of cheap paste."

Aunt Ernesta cackled from the doorway. "We'll know the next time we encounter him."

Alyse's cheeks heated. "There's no need to be cruel," she said quietly, pushing away from the table.

"We aren't cruel," Ernesta countered. "If it weren't true, it wouldn't hurt. They do say that pride goes before the fall."

True or not, Alyse didn't want to hear it. For God's sake, she detested these people. Even at her most self-absorbed, she didn't think she'd ever been cruel. "Excuse me."

"Yes, dear. Go read the Milton until time for us to leave for town."

Not bothering to reply, Alyse retreated to her bed-chamber. She'd been looking forward to going into Lewes, but now she wasn't as certain. What if Phineas was there, as well? Would he look at her with the same gloating pity as her so-called friends had after the scandal?

Last night all she'd seen in his eyes had been surprise and relief at seeing her. To him she'd been a friendly face from a kinder past. She recognized that look because she'd felt the same way herself. Once he learned what had happened, how her fortunes had fallen, he wouldn't smile when next they met. Or worse, he would smile behind her back.

Frustration, anger, loathing at her so-called relations all mingled thickly in her bones and her blood. For five years she'd attempted to make the best of things, learned to be grateful for small kindnesses that scarcely would have reached her notice previously. And finally began making plans to escape them altogether. Still every day ended a little worse than it had begun. Until last night. But feeling hope or anticipation only meant that she would hurt more when they passed her by, pausing only to laugh at her.

She closed her eyes for a moment before she opened *Paradise Lost*. Just to herself she breathed a silent prayer. *Please don't let Phineas Bromley laugh at me.*

Chapter 4 ─────────────

Phineas awoke before dawn. He was still accustomed to the early hours he kept in Spain, and given how his greeting at Quence Park had gone thus far, he didn't see much use in adjusting his regimen for East Sussex. With a yawn he lit the lamp at his dressing table and sat down to shave.

They truly had left his room as it was when he'd last been there, though if he had to guess whether it had been out of deference or because they wanted as little to do with him as possible, he would choose the latter. At any rate, he hadn't yet begun shaving when last he'd slept there. Thankfully he'd thrown all of his necessities into his trunk before he'd left his regiment.

He sat back to look at himself in the mirror, shirtless, barefoot, and wearing an old pair of trousers to sleep in as he'd taken to doing in case the French attacked in the middle of the night. He bore a nice selection of scars from being shot and stabbed and having a horse or two fall on him, but nothing that could compare with what he'd done to William. He had the use of all his limbs, after all.

Dark brown hair that was past due for a trim, his face leaner than it had once been and well tanned from long days in the Spanish sun. Even his eyes seemed different than the last time he'd sat there—still hazel, but . . . older.

His door rattled with the force of a knock. Phineas jumped. "Come in," he called, deliberately setting aside the razor. The only war here was the one of his own making.

The door opened. "Good mornin' to you, Colonel."

For a moment Phineas simply stared. "Gordon?" he finally managed. "What the devil are you doing here?"

"That's a bit of a tale, it is," the stout Scotsman drawled. "That bloke downstairs took me bags. Hope he's employed here."

Phineas sank back in the dressing chair. "Tall fellow, old as Methuselah?"

Thaddeus Gordon snapped his fingers. "Aye, that's him. Bit of a temper, too."

"Did you call at the front door?"

"Aye. I couldnae climb in through one o' yer windows. Wouldnae be polite, that."

"That's what annoyed him."

The Scotsman lifted a craggy eyebrow. "That I didnae climb in through a window?"

"That you called at the front door. You, Sergeant, are uninvited. Even worse, you're my man." When Gordon continued to eye him, Phineas grinned. Thank God for stubborn Scotsmen and their unflagging loyalty. "You use the back door."

"Oh. Right, then. Grand houses, back door. Ye might've said something before."

"You weren't supposed to be here." Phineas stood. "Which brings me back to my original question—why *are* you here?"

"Ye answered that yerself, sir. I'm yer man. Couldnae stay behind and leave ye to fend for yerself."

"You're in the service of His Majesty, Sergeant. You can't simply leave when the mood strikes you."

"I didnae. I told Captain Brent that ye'd sent for me. And I stowed yer kit with the captain, in case ye was wonderin'. It's nice'n safe."

Phineas blew out his breath. Under other circumstances, Gordon's disobedience would have annoyed him greatly. After last night, though, he was happy to see an ally. "As long as you're here, then, help me dress."

"In yer uniform, or are ye a civilian now?" the sergeant asked dryly.

"Considering the current state of my civilian clothes, I'm still a soldier." He cocked an eyebrow. "As a matter of fact, I believe I have some ironing for you, as well."

"Oh, grand."

He might have dug through his old wardrobe, but at four inches taller and two stone heavier he wouldn't be able to wear anything in there, anyway. Thanks to some vigorous shaking and the strategic application of a hot iron Gordon procured from somewhere, his uniform managed to remain parade-worthy even after a week of hard use.

"Very fine, Colonel," his man commented, stepping back as if to admire a painting he'd just completed. "Though yer boots could use a polish."

"They'll do." Phineas checked his pocket watch.

Time to go down to breakfast and be civil, as Elizabeth—Beth—had requested. And time to see whether he could decipher what the devil beyond the general disrepair had happened to cause his sister to lie to get him to return to the estate he'd once called home.

Sergeant Gordon pulled open the bedchamber door for him and then followed him out of the room. "I do believe I smell roasted chicken," he crooned, rubbing his hands together.

Phineas stopped. "At the moment, *Mr.* Gordon, you are not a member of my military staff. You're my . . . valet."

"Well, don't that sound elegant," the Scot chortled.

"Valets eat with the household staff in the kitchen. And they don't make trouble, drink, or gossip."

"Bloody 'ell! Who would ever want t'be a valet, then?"

"You, apparently, since you followed me here. Take the back stairs down to the kitchen. No trouble, Sergeant." He hesitated. "Find yourself some civilian clothes, as well. Anything you might hear about Quence Park in general, I would appreciate knowing."

Thaddeus Gordon straightened, offering a crisp, precise salute. "Ye have my word, Colonel."

Phineas could only hope the sergeant meant it. His own presence was bad enough. He didn't know how William would react to a rather unorthodox part of his younger brother's life making an unasked-for appearance. Frankly, Phin didn't want to find out. "I'll hold you to it."

The morning still lacked a few minutes of eight o'clock when he started down the main staircase. From the sounds around him the house was well awake, though he hadn't seen or heard either of his siblings yet. A wheeled chair sat empty at the foot of the stairs, and he paused.

His brother, who'd loved to go fishing and ride horses, was confined to that straight-backed cloth and wood and wicker trap—because of him. And that complicated everything. Delving into his brother's affairs would be difficult enough, but to do so when he owed a debt he could never repay—he needed to be two people. The one with whom William could comfortably be at odds, and the one who could uncover Beth's mystery without ruffling his brother's pride or walking all over his responsibilities.

A heavy tread sounded on the stairs above him. Startled, he looked up. Andrews descended, William cradled in his arms. The viscount had one arm around his valet's shoulders, the other holding up the loose blanket tucked around his legs. Being carried like that, William looked broken and frail, much older than the thirty-four years he had to his name.

"I—"

"Not planning to stay long, then?" William interrupted, as Andrews carefully settled him into his chair.

Phineas shook himself. He couldn't ask for forgiveness. It had to be offered. "Beg pardon?"

"You're still in your uniform."

"Ah. Nothing else I own was quite . . . shipshape this morning," he said, brushing at his sleeve.

"Andrews tells me you have a valet after all."

Andrews apparently knew everything that went on in the house. Phin would keep that in mind. "Yes," he said aloud. "Gordon. My sergeant-at-arms. He . . . followed me here."

"Are all your soldiers so well disciplined?"

Damnation. "Gordon's hardheaded, and he worries about me. If you don't want him here, I'll knock him over the skull and ship him back to Spain."

William looked at him for a moment, his expression unreadable. "If you're here as a gentleman, you should have someone attending to you." As he finished speaking and on some unseen signal, Andrews turned the chair and rolled the viscount into the breakfast room.

Phineas fell in behind them. "I thought I might go into Lewes today, if you'll lend me some transportation."

"Bored with Quence already, are you?"

Swearing again under his breath, Phineas went to the sideboard and looked over the selection of breakfast items. The spread seemed less lavish than he remembered, but after ten years of stale bread and meats of uncertain origin, he wasn't about to complain.

"Yesterday when I arrived I expected to see you bedridden," he said slowly, choosing his words as carefully as he could. He'd become used to taking action, to making a quick assessment and reacting. Feeling his way without knowing any of the pertinent information necessary for even a conversation—he wasn't accustomed to it, and he didn't like it. But he would tolerate it. "Today I'm being civil and cordial and as unobtrusive as possible."

"I'll have Warner find a mount for you," Lord Quence said in the same even tone he'd used before.

"Thank you."

"Good morning, my two handsome brothers." Elizabeth swept into the room, her smile bright enough to challenge the sun. She kissed William on the cheek, then danced forward to do the same to Phineas.

"Good morning." He returned the kiss, noting that her smile was a touch too bright, and her voice a shade too determined. If she wanted a morning of harmony, then he would attempt to do his part. "You look very fetching, if I may say so."

She fluffed a rose-colored sleeve. "Yes, you may. I'm going out to the garden to pick some flowers, and then Richard is going to be by to take me driving."

Phineas set down his plate and took a seat at William's left elbow. "Mm-hm. Are we delighted that Richard is calling, or should I be armed?"

Beth chuckled. "*I* am delighted. William hasn't yet threatened anyone, and you may do as you please." She sent him a mock scowl. "Within reason, of course. No shooting or stabbing him."

"You have my word, subject to future observation."

"Very well."

"Phin is going in to Lewes this morning," William commented.

Beth frowned, but wiped the expression away so quickly that Phineas wasn't certain if he'd imagined it. "Are you?"

"Unless you have another suggestion for me." One he would welcome, and wasn't likely to receive. She'd apparently given her own word, and to William.

"No, of course not. You're home. You should become familiar again with your surroundings."

"Any particular surroundings?"

Beth forced another chuckle. "Of course not. For heaven's sake."

Very well. He wouldn't force her into anything, and certainly not in William's presence. "Is there any good gossip to be had, then?"

Her expression relaxed again. "Oh, I know cartloads

of gossip." She sat forward. "They say, for instance, that Lord Roesglen has been taking to the roads at night to retrieve and return his new mistress to her home. No one's yet discovered who she might be."

Phineas chuckled. "For a moment I thought you were going to say that Roesglen was roving the night as a highwayman. I wouldn't have minded seeing that, considering that the last time I set eyes on him he weighed over twenty stone."

"I don't think he can even ride a horse any longer." With a laugh, Beth dumped three lumps of sugar into her tea. "That would definitely be a sight. Do you remember the stories Papa used to tell us about The Gentleman?" She sighed. "We haven't had a decent highwayman in thirty years."

"And thank God for that," William put in. "We don't need any more trouble."

"*More* trouble?" Phineas pounced on the word. Perhaps he couldn't interrogate Beth, but if William volunteered anything, that would certainly save him a great deal of effort.

A muscle in the viscount's cheek jumped. "Go for your ride, Phin. Lewes has become a great deal more sophisticated. I'm certain you'll find enough opera singers and actresses to satisfy even you."

His face heating, Phineas pushed to his feet. So this was the game they would be playing. "I didn't come here to find someone to share my bed," he grunted.

"The inns and taverns open early as well, then. Andrews?"

"Yes, my lord."

The wheeled chair backed away from the table and then rolled out of the room. Phineas sat down again, trying to rein in his growing frustration.

"Phin, he—"

He shook his head at his sister. "Don't make excuses for either of us," he said. "Are you going to tell me why you sent me that letter, or am I on my own?"

To his surprise, her hazel eyes filled with tears. Beth shook her head. "All I can do," she whispered, "is ask you not to let him drive you away."

"Beth?" William's voice echoed from somewhere down the hallway. "Magpie, you have some mail."

"I'll be right there," she called back, rising. As she crossed behind Phineas she touched his shoulder. "Please stay," she continued almost soundlessly.

That settled that. The devil himself couldn't drag him out of East Sussex now. The next step was to gauge the lay of the land—and then prepare for battle, whether he knew what he was about to come up against or not.

"Alyse, carry my reticule."

Alyse closed the small distance to her aunt and took the older woman's bag from her drooping fingers. It felt nearly empty; undoubtedly Aunt Ernesta was more interested in having someone tote her things than in relieving herself of a burden.

She shook the reticule a little. A few coins, but she would wait to see whether she could lighten it by a shilling or two. Heaven knew she'd learned to be patient, at about the same time she'd realized that she felt perfectly content to slowly gather funds that, if her cousin had had any heart at all, would have been hers to begin with. Her father had tried to provide for her, but he'd been forced to leave it to his heir's discretion. And Richard had declined to abide by the former viscount's wishes.

"And stay close by," Ernesta continued. "You know I detest when you wander off."

"Yes, Aunt."

They waited for a milk cart to pass by and then crossed the street to Daisy Duvall's Dress Shop. The shop was practically a decade behind the current fashion, and seemed much more popular with the grand dames of Lewes than with the younger set. Alyse had never purchased a stitch there, had never even crossed the threshold until a year ago. Not that she had any ready money to spend at the establishment, but she meant never to do so regardless.

They spent nearly an hour inside, Mrs. Duvall and her shopgirls hovering and fluttering around Aunt Ernesta and Lady Hestley once the baroness joined them. Alyse sat to one side, pasted an interested look on her face, and let her mind wander.

Her mind wandered a great deal these days, since her shoes were unable to do so. Left to her own amusements she would, for example, have begun the day with a visit to the sweet shop. She loved hard candy, and Mr. Styles had always used to keep some aside on Tuesdays, the day she and her friends usually ventured into Lewes for shopping and luncheon. Aunt Ernesta disliked candy, though she would go so far as to dance for biscuits. The closest Alyse had come to any sweets lately was the strawberries she'd hidden from Richard.

"Alyse!"

She blinked. "Yes, Aunt?"

"I said, please go to the bakery and fetch me a half dozen biscuits. And you would do well to pay better attention. For heaven's sake."

The viscount's mother handed her a shilling. Alyse stood and walked outside, ignoring the muttering and giggling going on in the shop behind her as she left. Her aunt didn't need to remind her that her life had irrevocably altered; all she had to do was open her eyes in the morning to know that. How unfortunate that Aunt Ernesta wouldn't be receiving any change for the biscuits. She hadn't in nearly a year.

"Good morning, Miss Donnelly."

She looked up as a gray-muzzled chestnut mare crossed in front of her and stopped. Her heart skittered as she recognized the low drawl of the rider. "Colonel. Good morning."

He dismounted smoothly, taking the reins in one hand and reaching for her fingers with the other. Alyse studied him as he bowed over her knuckles. The tall, thin boy had become a lean, hard, and well-muscled man. And so, so handsome, with that dark, wild hair and half-smiling, sensuous mouth, and that blue and scarlet uniform. Hazel eyes lifted to gaze at her face as he straightened. He seemed pleased to see her, and he wasn't laughing.

She took a quick breath as she withdrew her fingers from his. "What brings you into town this morning?"

"What if I said it was you?"

Alyse felt her cheeks warm. "I would say, Phin Bromley, that ten years haven't erased my intelligence. You didn't know I would be here."

"Witty and beautiful," he drawled, clearly undaunted. "I nearly embraced you last night, Alyse. To find you here . . ." He cleared his throat. "It's good to see you again."

Her heart shivered. "And you," she returned, seeking the wit on which he'd just complimented her. "What brings you to Lewes, again?"

"Back on the trail, are we? Then the wish for fresh

air brings me here," he replied. Alert eyes scanned the street around them. "I swear this town has grown again by half."

"I think it has," she agreed, more at ease now that she was no longer the subject of the conversation. "That's Warner's mare you're riding, isn't it?"

His grin deepened. "Yes. Daffodil. I would have arrived in town earlier, but I'm afraid sending her into a trot would cause her to drop dead. Apparently Warner travels everywhere very slowly."

Alyse smiled back at him. She couldn't help herself. "That uniform suits you."

"It is a universally acknowledged fact," he drawled, his gaze lowering to her mouth, "that given the choice of two otherwise equal gentlemen, a woman will choose to flirt with the man in uniform."

There was something disconcerting about the attention he paid her. With a laugh she shook her head at him. "You've made a scientific study of this, I assume?"

Miss Jane Austen has. *I* am a simple soldier, Miss Donnelly."

"You've never been a 'simple' anything, Phin. Or rather, Colonel Bromley."

"Phin, please," he returned. "You've put mud down my back, after all."

She laughed. "Ah, yes, but I was nine years old at the time. And you were, what, eleven?"

"Good God. Yes, I believe so." He glanced past her at the busy shops along the street. "Are you here with friends?"

He truly didn't know. For a moment she wished she could keep it that way. "No. I'm with my aunt. She's sent me to the bakery after biscuits."

Swiftly he held out an arm to her. "Allow me to accompany you, then."

"That's not necessary."

"Which makes me amazingly gallant, I think." He shook his fingers in her direction, and with another smile she hoped wasn't too wistful, Alyse wrapped her hand around his arm. It had been nearly five years since anyone had troubled themselves to be gallant on her behalf.

"If I may be so bold," she ventured as they strolled along the street, Daffodil in tow, "your family seemed surprised to see you."

"A miscommunication," he said promptly. "I thought I was expected."

"Is it true, what Beth said, that you've received five field promotions? You must be quite heroic in addition to being gallant."

He chuckled. "Thus far I've excelled at not being killed." Abruptly he sobered. "Again, I'm sorry about your parents. No one informed me, or I would have written."

Would you have? "Thank you. They both caught that awful fever going about five years ago, and never recovered. I am glad they went together, though. For their sakes."

"Your cousin inherited the title, then?"

She nodded. Richard had inherited much more than the title of Viscount Donnelly, but she wasn't going to regale Phin with her tale of woe. Certainly not when she hadn't seen him for ten years.

"It's good that you didn't have to leave Donnelly House."

He really did know nothing. Torn between wanting to pour out her troubles and laughing, Alyse released his arm. "Thank you for your escort, Phin," she said aloud, trying to keep her voice steady, "but my aunt hates to be kept waiting." With a half smile she continued down the street.

After a half dozen steps his hand came down on her shoulder, bringing her to a halt. "Alyse," he said again, his voice lower and more intimate, "might I ask you a question? Just between us. It can go no further."

Alyse frowned. Evidently she wasn't the only one with troubles. The realization surprised her a little. "What is your question?"

His shoulders rose and fell as he took a breath. "Do you know of anything that my brother might find . . . troubling?"

" 'Troubling'?" she repeated. "Do you mean something like the Quence east pasture flooding? That happened a fortnight ago. Richard—my cousin—has been helping to put in a new irrigation dam on the creek, since William can't oversee it himself."

"Yes, something like that," he murmured. "Thank you. If you can think of anything else, please inform me. In fact, may I take you driving tomorrow?"

That was the second time he'd suggested such an outing. Her heart hammered, but she attempted to ignore it. He only wanted information, and thought she might be able to supply it. "I'll ask my aunt."

He cocked his scarred eyebrow, attractive and dangerous. "Though I'm not looking to be slapped, are you not five-and-twenty? And I can't remember you ever asking permission to do anything, regardless of your age."

She shrugged free of his grip. "As I'm certain you're aware, things change. And not just for you."

Keeping her chin up and her shoulders square, she

walked into the bakery. Phin might not know what the past four and a half years of her life had been like, but she wasn't about to forget. And his abrupt reappearance reminded her of other things she hadn't forgotten.

Phin Bromley had always been equal parts trouble and excitement. The last thing she needed was either of those. No matter how handsome the face bringing it, or how fond the memories she had of him.

Chapter 5 _____

Phineas watched as Alyse Donnelly disappeared into the bakery. Clearly he'd said the wrong thing, but what? Had someone broken her heart, turned her into one of those frightening, man-hating females? That made sense considering her spinsterhood, but it also unsettled him a little.

When he'd left, she'd been a fresh spring bloom just beginning to blossom. He'd given up any claim to her almost before he'd realized she could be more to him than a dear friend. Seeing her now—she was his Alyse and at the same time someone else completely. And the thought that some man might have hurt her . . . angered him.

He shook himself. Puzzling out Alyse would have to wait. She'd given him a clue, and he needed to follow it. He swung back into the saddle. "Walk, Daffodil."

At the best pace the mare could muster, it took him nearly thirty minutes to reach the boundaries of Quence's large, low-lying east pasture. In the past sheep would be scattered across the low grass, inviting some artist or other to paint the pastoral scene. Now, though, it was empty, with shimmers of light reflecting from between the blades of grass and dragonflies skimming the wide stretches of wet. "Good God," he muttered.

There had to be three inches of water covering the entire pasture. At the upper end he spied several men, and encouraged the reluctant mare through the ankle-deep marsh to the higher bank of the stream.

Three of the men stood arguing with a fourth, who was better dressed and on horseback. "Good afternoon, gentlemen," Phineas drawled, stopping beside a cart full of rocks.

They stopped bickering to look at him. "Who're you?" the stoutest of them asked, stabbing the end of a shovel into the wet ground and resting his crossed arms on the handle.

Phineas gazed at him steadily, unmoved by the show of aggression. "Colonel Phin Bromley," he said, crossing his own wrists over the saddle's pommel. "Who are you?"

"Brown," the fellow retorted.

"And what are you doing on my land, Mr. Brown?" Technically the land belonged to William, but it had been in the Bromley family for generations, and he was still a Bromley.

Mr. Brown spat into the mud. "If it was your land, you'd know why we was here, Colonel Bromley."

Hm. He *did* know, but that was only because Alyse had told him. And now that he'd identified himself as a Bromley, he had to behave in a relatively civilized manner. That could be a problem, and not just here. If Beth was unwilling to be communicative, he could only imagine what he might face with the rest of the citizenry. "I only ask because you seem to be talking rather than working."

"Tell that to bloody Mr. Stuggley there." The fellow gestured at the still angry-looking man on horseback on the far side of the stream.

The name was familiar, and unusual enough that Phineas was willing to risk being in error. "Stuggley," he repeated aloud. "Not John Stuggley."

The tall man's expression eased a little. "The same, Colonel Bromley. My father retired a year ago now. I've been seeing to the stewardship of Roesglen since."

A few years older than William, John Stuggley hadn't been part of the Bromley circle of friends. His father had been well respected by the Marquis of Roesglen, and Roesglen had been close friends with the former Viscount Quence, Phin's father. A rather roundabout connection, but Phineas felt more inclined to listen to him than to the sullen Brown.

"Perhaps you could enlighten me, then, Mr. Stuggley," he said. "What's the difficulty here?"

"The difficulty is that if a new irrigation dam goes in here, it might save the Quence east pasture, but the backed-up water would flood the Roesglen north pasture and overflow the fish pond. Lord Roesglen wouldn't take the news of the demise of his favorite fishing pond well at all."

"This stream is on Quence land," Brown countered. "And Lord Donnelly says the dam goes here."

"This is robbery, sir," Stuggley snapped. "You will set Roesglen and Quence at odds."

Phineas took in their wet surroundings and the

Roesglen land off to the northeast in the distance. "What kept this pasture from flooding before?" he asked, wishing he'd paid more attention to land management in his youth. That had been William's duty, though. He'd had other interests.

"The old dam half a mile upstream, just south of the east tributary," Stuggley said promptly. "It collapsed a fortnight ago."

"Then perhaps the new dam should stand where the old one did," Phineas stated. "It did serve for better than twenty years."

"Lord Donnelly already decided against that." Brown spat again, just missing Daffodil's near hoof.

"Another day won't make any difference. Stuggley, do you have a terrain map of the property?"

"Aye."

"Bring it by Quence in the morning, will you?"

"Of course." The steward glanced in the direction of the workers.

"And you lot," Phineas continued, "go home."

"What about our wages? We ain't mucking about here for nothin'."

Phin lifted an eyebrow, but kept his voice even. "See Lord Donnelly. He hired you."

"Damned soldier's got a ramrod up 'is arse," Brown sneered.

If Phineas hadn't had the uniform on, if he didn't have William's reputation currently in his hands, he would have been quite willing to show Brown just how flexible he could be where legalities were concerned. He'd never wanted to be two separate people so badly before.

Riding away at a brisk trot would have put a good period to the conversation, but Daffodil falling down dead in the mud would not. He needed a more sound damned mount. As he clucked at the mare and turned her around, he caught Stuggley's grateful look. At least someone appreciated his presence.

He slogged out of the pasture and rode back to the broad white manor house. The flooded pasture was ill luck enough. But the way Donnelly had chosen to resolve the matter troubled him even more. With one carelessly designed and easily prevented dam mistake, the viscount might have set two allied families at odds. And since Donnelly had shifted the dam from its original location, Phineas had to wonder whether it could have been intentional.

Beth liked Lord Donnelly, and William likewise seemed to consider him a friend. Phineas scowled. If he was going to be conjuring and pursuing conspiracies, he needed to be cautious about it. His footing in the household was uncertain enough without him accusing friends and neighbors of misdeeds—especially when he had no evidence, and no real reason to do so. No reason but a soldier's hard-learned instincts. And he needed to use those instincts to figure out how he could get to the bottom of what troubled Quence and his family without causing William to boot him back to Spain.

"Welcome back, Mr. Bromley," Warner said, meeting him at the front of the house. "Daff's got a gleam in her eyes; she must've enjoyed the ride."

"Thank you for the loan."

"There's something you should—"

The front door opened, and Gordon charged onto the drive, a practically apoplectic Digby on his heels. "Colonel, ye have—"

"That is *my* duty, you upstart," the butler interrupted, actually swiping at the sergeant.

That wasn't the wisest move old Digby could make, considering Gordon's skills as a soldier. "Enough, Gordon," Phineas cut in, before anyone could exchange blows.

"Indeed," the butler echoed, and held out the silver salver he carried in his other hand. A folded missive lay roughly in the center of it. "You have a letter, Master Phineas."

"My thanks," he said, taking it. The sprawling hand across the front read "Colonel Phineas Bromley" in a familiar hand. "It's from Sullivan," he said aloud, breaking the wax seal.

"Beggin' yer pardon, Colonel," Gordon broke in again, "but ye need to come to the stable with me."

The man was red-faced and practically vibrating, so Phineas gestured his valet to lead the way around the side of the manor house. "This had better be good, Gordon, or you're going to find yourself a private without privates."

Gordon pushed through the wide double doors and stood aside. "Oh, it's good, sir. Bloody good."

Phineas stepped inside the stable—and stopped dead. "Good God," he breathed.

"I tried to tell you, sir," Warner put in from the stall where he was removing Daffodil's saddle.

"No worries," Phin said absently, his gaze on the monster that snorted at him from beside the post in the center of the floor. Black and sleek and clearly a thoroughbred, the beast looked at him and stomped.

"Now that's a horse," Gordon said reverently.

Abruptly Phineas remembered that he still clutched Sullivan Waring's missive in one hand. He opened it hurriedly.

"'Phin,'" he read aloud for his sergeant's benefit,

" 'Welcome home. I thought you could use a good horse. His name is Ajax.' "

"Ajax," Gordon repeated. "Aye. Captain Waring always did know his blood-horses."

"He has a stable in Sussex," Phin said, walking forward to take a closer look at the animal. Sullivan was arguably the best horse breeder in the country, even with the four-year absence he'd taken to serve with the First Royal Dragoons in Spain. Reluctantly he looked away from the horse and down at the note again. " 'I hope your brother and sister are doing well, and that Bram's and my concerns have been unfounded. If you need anything—<u>anything</u>—I'm but a few hours distant. Sullivan.' "

"Now that is a good friend," Gordon commented, then stirred. "What concerns?"

"I'm still determining that," Phineas replied, running his free hand along the stallion's withers. "You are a handsome lad, aren't you?" he murmured, and the black nickered at him.

Ajax was hardly the horse a fellow attempting to do some subtle investigating should be riding. Of course, that same fellow probably shouldn't be bringing attention to himself by wearing a shiny uniform, either. *Hm.* No, he shouldn't be riding about on Ajax, unless he could somehow use the animal's striking appearance to his advantage. A plan began to curdle through his brain.

He glanced over his shoulder at Warner. "You're a local fellow, yes?"

"Yes, sir."

"Do you remember the stories about The Gentleman?"

The groom grinned. "Aye. A highwayman, from about thirty years ago. My grand drove one of the coaches he held up." With a chuckle, he gestured at Ajax. "Rode a horse very like that, as I recall."

"Yes, he did supposedly have the swiftest animal in the county, didn't he?" Phineas agreed, half to himself.

Gordon looked from the groom to Phineas. "And what happened t'this Gentleman, if I may ask?"

"No one knows," Warner returned. "Retired with one of the pretty young things he robbed and charmed, I would imagine. He stole as many hearts as he did coins."

"Might I have a word with ye, Colonel?" the sergeant said gruffly.

"Certainly." Phin walked to the stable door, then looked back at Warner. "I would appreciate if no one else learned about Ajax here for the moment."

The groom looked curious, but nodded. "Aye."

As soon as they were outside, Gordon rounded on him. "Ye came back home to become a highwayman? What the devil is—"

"I suggest you think very carefully before you continue, Sergeant," Phineas interrupted darkly.

"But ye—"

"What have you noticed since your arrival here?"

"Noticed?" Gordon frowned. "If I'm to be in trouble, it won't be for insulting ye or yer family, sir."

"I appreciate that. But I want you to be honest. What have you noticed?"

"Some fields could use plowing, too few servants, but one carriage, only four horses in the stable—five, now—and a handful of burned-to-the-ground tenant cottages."

Phineas looked at his so-called valet for a moment. He'd noticed the rest himself, but he hadn't known about the tenant cottages. And that was after only a single day in residence. He drew a breath. "My sister admits that she lied about my brother's health to get me here," he said slowly, "but she's apparently given her word not to involve me in anything further. All I know is that something is wrong, and that I'm not leaving until I discover what it is and make it right."

"I think that's fine an' noble of ye, Colonel, but I don't see how bein' a highwayman can—"

"I need information, without drawing suspicion to my family or to me. And under the circumstances, I . . . welcome the opportunity to obtain some answers that I might not be granted as Phin Bromley." He cocked his head. "Are you with me, Gordon?"

"Always."

"Explain it to Warner, there. For the moment, no one can know that Ajax is here."

"Aye. But if ye become a highwayman, Colonel, yer goin' to be risking getting yer neck stretched."

"It's a risk I'm willing to take."

Digby, still looking annoyed that Gordon had galloped through his territory, opened the door for him as he topped the shallow front steps. "I trust everything is well, sir?" the butler asked.

"It is. Has Beth returned yet?"

"No, sir. I don't expect her for another hour, at the earliest."

"Where might I find William, then?"

"Lord Quence is in his office. Do you req—"

"I remember where it is," Phineas interrupted, leaving the foyer for the main hallway and the rooms at the back of the house.

The office door stood open, but he stopped to knock, anyway.

"Enter."

"Good afternoon, William," he said, strolling into the office and pasting a friendly look on his face. Andrews stood to one side of the room, immobile as a statue but obviously ready at any moment to become the viscount's legs.

"Phin." William closed the ledger book on which he'd been working. "How was your ride?"

Was William attempting to keep the condition of Quence from him? Or was there something else in the air? "It was interesting," he answered aloud. "Might we speak in private for a moment?"

A muscle in William's gaunt cheek jumped. "This is as private as I get."

Phineas clenched his jaw, but nodded. If his brother wanted Andrews there, then the valet would remain. He had long ago realized that he didn't have much skill at diplomacy; he left that to others more qualified. Where he excelled was charging in after the diplomats failed.

He drew a breath as he closed the door. New situations, new tactics. "I rode by the east pasture."

William continued to gaze at him. "And?"

"The site where Donnelly wants to put the new dam will flood Roesglen's north pasture and his pond."

His brother rubbed a finger against the silvering hair at his temple. "And?" he repeated.

"And so I told his men to wait a day. John Stuggley will be here in the morning so the two of you can decide where best to locate the dam."

"Very well." William opened the ledger again.

Phineas blinked. " 'Very well'?" he repeated. "That's it?"

With a breath the viscount shut the book for the second time. "What would you like me to say? 'Thank God you returned to Quence in time to keep Lord Roesglen from losing his fish pond'?"

"Didn't Donnelly mention that he was moving the dam's location, and that it might cause friction between you and Roesglen?"

His brother scowled briefly, then smoothed his expression over again. "I didn't think to ask."

"Where's your estate manager? Where's . . . what's his name? Boling. Where's Mr. Boling?"

"He married a young lady whose father owns a mill in Darbyshire. He runs the mill, now."

"Why haven't you hired someone to replace him?"

William's eyes narrowed. "You're not actually questioning my governance of this property, are you?"

"No. Of course not. But—"

"You reappear after ten years, and because you happen across a dam being constructed in the wrong place you've, what, become the family's salvation?"

Phineas straightened. "I said no such thing. I was only concerned that Donnelly's decision might harm this family's friendship with Roesglen. That is all—"

"Richard Donnelly has been unendingly helpful since his arrival here last year," William interrupted. "And he requests nothing in return. No acknowledgment, no money, noth—"

"Nothing except for Beth, perhaps."

"Beth likes him. He's become a part of this family."

Phineas understood that. "You mean he's taken my place in this family," he said stiffly, turning his back and heading for the door.

"Someone needed to."

"Insult me all you like, William. It's nothing less than I deserve. But it won't make me leave."

His jaw clenched, Phineas stalked back down the hall. He'd expected to find a fight ahead of him, and he certainly had never thought William would greet him with open arms. But not to have a place at all—that had never occurred to him. It should have.

Swearing under his breath, he lengthened his stride and turned up the stairs to his bedchamber. In the past he would have paced and sulked, or climbed out the window to head into Lewes and find trouble. Tonight he meant to become someone else entirely and, as a stranger, venture into places that the new and hopefully wiser Phin Bromley could no longer afford to go.

"Milton," Alyse grumbled, setting the book down on the library table with a thud. It had used to amuse her that Aunt Ernesta tended to select for her silly discussions pieces rife with heavy-handed morality and themes of eternal damnation. After a year of it, though, she'd come to realize that irony lost its bite when its intended victim didn't see that she was being targeted. So her aunt went blithely along discussing sin and hubris and not realizing that she committed those very same acts on a daily basis.

She dragged the step stool over to the correct shelf and then retrieved the book from the table, replacing it between equally dull tomes where it could gather age and dust until Aunt Ernesta circled around to it again. Personally she hoped to be long gone before then.

Out the tall, narrow windows, the moon was past full, but still bright and silver over the leaves in the pretty garden. At least Richard hadn't seen fit to dig up the roses and replace them with something more to his taste—though she couldn't imagine what that might be, as money trees were solely the stuff of myth.

Heaven knew she could use one of those right now otherwise.

In the drawing room her aunt and cousin were playing whist and carrying on a criticism of everyone who wasn't themselves. Sighing, Alyse slipped past the half-open door and down the stairs.

"It's a bit late for a stroll, Miss Alyse," Saunders commented, turning from putting out one of the pairs of candles lighting the hallway.

"Yes, but it's also very nicely quiet out there," she returned, lifting her shawl off a hook and wrapping it across her shoulders. "If my aunt should ask after me, would you mind telling her I'm looking for some thread to decorate her hat for the soiree on Thursday?"

He sketched a bow. "Don't be too long, miss."

"I shan't."

In her youth, in the days before the scandal had ruined everything, she'd loved the garden at Donnelly. Alyse smiled as she took a seat on the stone bench placed beneath the old crooked elm tree—the best climbing tree in England, according to Phin. Of course that had been well before he'd turned seventeen, before her father had asked her not to spend time alone with him any longer, before the rumors that he'd taken up with actresses and married ladies and begun drinking. And before he'd disappeared for ten years.

Movement beneath the study window caught her attention. Her heart jumped even as she told herself that it was a rabbit or a hedgehog. Except that the shadow was larger than that. A dog? A deer?

Her fingers tightened convulsively around the edges of her shawl. *Oh, heavens.* It was a man. A large one, despite the utter silence of his movements along the base of the wall.

Abruptly he froze. Slowly his shadowed face turned in her direction. Alyse shot to her feet, a scream rising in her throat. With a rush he was on her, pressing her back against the tree trunk, a gloved hand pressed over her mouth. "Shh," he whispered softly, gentle despite the speed of his movement.

She couldn't see his face. He wore a mask, she realized, beneath an old-fashioned tricorne hat and a greatcoat with the collar turned up and shadowing his mouth. For a brief, amazed second she thought he must be The Gentleman. That fellow would be beyond ancient by now, though.

"Je ne vous lésez pas," he murmured in a deep voice. *"Comprenez vous?"*

He said he wouldn't hurt her. Frightened as she was, she believed him, not that she wished to argue the point. Slowly she nodded.

His hand left her mouth. He took her fingers in his and drew her back to the bench. She sat, grateful for its solid support. The dark shape retreated farther into the shadows, then reappeared, a red rose in his black-gloved hand. *"Merci, ma belle mademoiselle,"* he said quietly, and handed her the flower. He bowed with an old-fashioned flourish, then vanished into the night. A moment later she glimpsed him heading into the trees, a huge dark horse beneath him.

Alyse sat where she was for a long moment. Her hands shook, the spicy scent of the rose soft in the evening air. Who was this Frenchman? Had he come to burgle the house? Whoever he was, whatever he wanted, he'd gone out of his way to demonstrate that he had no intention of harming her.

Had this man followed Phin to East Sussex? After all, Phin had spent the last ten years fighting the French.

If one of them had come to exact revenge on him, though, he'd ended at the wrong manor house.

No, something else was afoot. And even as she stood and returned to the house, the rose in her hand, she knew that she wouldn't be informing Richard or Aunt Ernesta that anyone had been lurking outside Donnelly House. He hadn't carried off the pianoforte—or anything else, as far as she could tell. And as far as she was concerned, her relations deserved a bit of ill luck.

If she ever came across this Frenchman again, then she would worry about him. For now, she would call it an odd, not entirely unpleasant experience, and put the red rose in a vase. Neither would she be informing Colonel Phin Bromley that a masked Frenchman had stumbled across her in the night. She had enough trouble in her life. At this point causing bloodshed would do no one any good, herself least of all.

Chapter 6 _____

Phineas deliberately delayed heading downstairs for breakfast. He wanted time enough for the rumors to spread.

He'd intended to be seen last night, though Alyse had been the very last person he'd expected to encounter. And her presence had altered his plans. He'd intended to break a few windows, roust some of the stableboys, and make the appearance of a masked stranger obvious. If he could rattle some cages as a supposed burglar, he would have the opportunity as Phin Bromley to see what might fall into the open. A guilty man reacted differently than an innocent one. But he absolutely hadn't wanted to frighten Alyse. She'd literally turned him into a gentleman just by sitting in her family's garden last night.

"Good morning," he said as he finally entered the breakfast room at half past nine.

Beth and William were bent over a pamphlet of some kind, and both looked up as he walked in. "Good morning," Beth said, greeting him with a kiss on the cheek.

"What's so interesting?" he asked, gesturing at the paper and prepared to show the appropriate amount of cynical surprise.

"We're going to the theater tonight," his sister said with a grin. "An opera. Please say you'll join us, Phin."

He blinked. "Of course."

"Don't answer too hastily," his brother commented. "This is an entire evening's commitment."

Phineas clenched his jaw. It was only words, just William attempting to drive him away. Why, he didn't know yet. But he supposed the worse the attacks became, the closer he must be getting. At the moment he clearly had barely a clue. "I expect it is the height of excitement in Lewes," he returned, hoping one of his siblings would contradict him with the story of how Alyse had just last night encountered a masked intruder.

"The very height," Beth said, giggling. "What are your plans today?"

He'd intended to go see the burned-out tenant cottages. Now he needed to see Alyse. And not just because he'd wanted to kiss her last night. "I sent Sergeant Gordon into town this morning to fetch me a horse that won't drop if I try for a trot. I thought I might take Alyse riding when he returns."

His sister frowned. "But—"

"Don't make trouble for Alyse," William said, returning to the remains of his breakfast. "She's seen enough."

Taking his seat and digging into the pile of sliced ham, Phin looked up. "Care to elaborate?"

"I don't gossip. Andrews?"

Silently the valet stepped forward and took the handles of the wheeled chair. In a moment both the viscount and his servant had left the room for the office. "Splendid," Phineas grumbled. He glanced at Beth. "And what are your plans for the day, since you won't tell me why I'm here?"

"I can't tell you, Phin, but that doesn't mean we don't need you here." She stood up and left the room.

"Bloody wonderful."

Before he'd finished breakfast, Gordon reappeared. "I used the blasted back door," the sergeant grumbled as he walked into the breakfast room. "Came to the front of the house and walked all the way around. Bloody English customs."

"Here," Phin said, tossing him a peach and rising. "What did you find for me?"

"Ye said nothing too fine," his valet commented, falling in behind as Phin made his way to the front door. "Lewes ain't precisely the center of thoroughbred breeding, is it?"

"No, it's not. This is sheep country."

"Aye. I've noticed that fact."

Digby opened the front door for them, managing to send Gordon an annoyed look at the same time, and Phineas left the house—and stopped dead. "What, pray tell, is that?" he asked, staring.

"That's yer horse."

"It's yellow, Sergeant."

Gordon passed him to pat the gelding on the withers. "He ain't yellow. He's a butter chestnut."

Phineas looked from the horse to the Scotsman. "A 'butter chestnut'? Who fed you that cartload of turnips?"

"How else d'ye explain his color? It ain't as though he's been painted."

"What color is the horse you got for yourself?"

The sergeant edged away from him. "Ye said a bay or a chestnut fer me. Somethin' no one would notice. So Gallant's a scraggly bay, Colonel. I wouldn't want to be caught ridin' a more bonny horse than my commanding officer."

Tempted as Phin was to argue the point, the yellow horse did serve a purpose; no one who owned another horse like Ajax would be caught dead riding this one. "What's his name, then?" he asked, checking the gelding's cinch and then swinging up into the saddle.

The sergeant cleared his throat. "He's yer horse. Ye call 'im whatever ye like." He slapped the animal on the haunch.

Obviously the move was meant to send horse and rider galloping down the road, but with a precise move of his knee and a light tug on the reins, Phineas sent the animal in a tight circle around Gordon. "Name, Sergeant," he ordered.

Gordon straightened. "Saffron, sir," he said, saluting.

Saffron. At least it wasn't *Jaundice* or some such thing. "I'm going to the theater tonight," he said. "I want that to be the last event I have to attend wearing my uniform. Make me an appointment with a damned tailor. And shine my dress boots for tonight."

"Aye, Colonel."

He kicked Saffron in the ribs and headed for the main road and Donnelly House beyond. The gelding had an off gait and a hard mouth, but he had to count it as an improvement over walking everywhere on

Warner's mount. And he supposed his uniform would survive the dubious honor of riding a yellow horse. He'd caused his career enough potential damage by riding about the countryside as a highwayman.

"You know I don't show well in green," Aunt Ernesta snapped, tossing her half-finished hat onto the table. "What in the world made you select green?"

Alyse stifled the answer she wanted to make. "You admired the green ribbon in the shop, Aunt. I thought—"

"Yellow. I want yellow flowers, and a yellow ribbon. I won't have you attempting to make me look foolish. We could send you back to your great-aunt, you know."

"I beg your pardon, Aunt Ernesta," Alyse sighed. "I'll fetch the yellow ribbon."

"I thought you would."

As she stood up, Saunders knocked and leaned into the room. "Mrs. Donnelly, Miss Donnelly, Colonel Phin Bromley."

Crisp, precise, and commanding, Phin strolled into the room and sketched a shallow bow. "Good morning, ladies."

Aunt Ernesta stood. "Colonel. What in the world brings you here today?"

"I thought I would take Miss Donnelly riding, if you can spare her for a time."

Alyse's heart skipped a beat. He'd said he wanted to go riding with her, but she hadn't realized that he'd meant it. "I . . . I'm mending my aunt's h—"

"You will return her by luncheon," her aunt said, and motioned at her to leave the room. "I'll never have a decent conversation out of her if she doesn't get her way."

Well, that was uncalled-for. And a lie. But arguing would be worse than pointless, since she'd never be allowed to go riding if she reacted. "Thank you, Aunt Ernesta."

"Humph."

"I took the liberty of asking that a horse be saddled for you," Phin said, offering his arm as they left the morning room.

"I have to change my dress," she said, rushing her words and half worried that he would change his mind.

"I'll wait outside, shall I?"

"Yes, please."

She hadn't worn her sea-green riding dress in over three years, but luckily it still fit. Swiftly she buttoned it up the front and stomped into her riding boots, then hurried down the stairs again.

Saunders opened the door for her, and she took a breath to steady herself. "I shall return shortly," she said, and walked onto the front portico. And burst out laughing. "Oh, my."

Phineas lifted his scarred right eyebrow. "I will assume my mount amuses you," he said dryly.

"The poor dear. What's his name?"

"Saffron. He's reputedly a butter chestnut. Shall we?" With a glance at the groom holding the bridle of the bay that had been saddled for her, Phin turned Alyse to face him and then lifted her up into the saddle.

The sensation of being lifted effortlessly into the air left her breathless. No one did such things for her any longer. Heavens, no one had even given her flowers in over four years—except for last night.

Phin led the way down the drive, and she urged her mare up to keep pace with the striking Saffron. Belatedly she noticed the groom falling in behind them. A chaperon. It had been years since she'd warranted one of those.

"Two conversations within two days," she said aloud, trying to collect herself. "You're not becoming infatuated with me, are you?"

"I've always been infatuated with you," he returned easily, his gaze focusing on her mouth. *Trouble*, she repeated to herself as he looked away again. He was trouble, and that was something she couldn't afford.

"I suppose that explains the plethora of frogs I received." Alyse was relieved that her voice sounded level and amused. She had learned some things over the past few years about hiding her true feelings.

"I can safely promise there will be no more frogs." He looked over at her again. "After all, you're not twelve any longer."

"Not for thirteen years."

"I'm long past being seventeen, myself." He hesitated. "How is it that you're unmarried, Alyse? Even at fifteen you had every lad in East Sussex following you about."

She snorted. "You don't mess about with chitchat, do you?"

"I'm not a chit. And as a soldier I've found it wise to speed to the heart of the matter as swiftly as possible."

"Why do you wish to know?" she asked, not certain what she wanted to hear him say.

"Because I've made a great many mistakes in my life, and I've begun to think that leaving here just when . . . just when I did was the largest of them." He headed them down toward the narrow path along the river.

"After you hear what happened, you may count yourself grateful." She couldn't stop the abrupt bitterness in her voice. Oh, she'd been so young, and so stupid.

"Technically, I believe you and I may already be married," he said unexpectedly, "considering the ceremony that William performed for us. We might have been only eight and ten, but I do think it's a possibility."

Alyse laughed reluctantly. "You only pretended to marry me so that you could pretend to go off to war and be killed in battle to leave me a grieving widow."

"In hindsight it was probably more entertaining for me than for you." He stopped Saffron and dismounted, circling around to slide his arms around Alyse's waist and lower her to the ground. His warm hands stayed where they were for a moment too long. "Wait here," he instructed the groom, and offered her his arm.

She wrapped her fingers around his crimson sleeve, and side by side they made their way down to the willow-edged riverbank. "I don't want to tell you what happened," she said slowly.

"Then don't. I intend to find out, though, and I prefer to hear it from you. If it helps, I'm nowhere close to perfection myself, and I don't expect it from anyone else."

Blowing out her breath and pretending to be more annoyed than worried he would turn around and simply leave her there, whatever he might say, she shrugged. "Very well, then. To touch on the plot points of a very long tale, I had a wondrous debut Season in London. Four proposals of marriage within a fortnight. But I wanted to fall in love, so I waited." So foolish, she'd been, thinking that she would love and be loved and that everything would be daisies and waltzes. She should have married the first man to ask her.

"You were set on marrying a prince, or a duke at the very least, as I recall."

"Yes, well, I was a silly girl."

"Go on."

She liked the way he said that, as though he were truly interested in hearing what she had to say. "At the beginning of my third Season, I met him. Phillip Ambry, the Marquis of Layton."

Phin scowled, the muscles in his arm tightening. "But he—"

"Yes, he rather famously married Roberta Engles, that American heiress." She paused, but her pride didn't sting as it used to—too many other things had given her a better perspective on the relative importance of her heart. "He asked Papa's permission to marry me, and my father refused to grant it. Phillip was a fortune hunter, you see, and everyone knew it. Everyone but me. Or I suppose I did know, but I thought that he hadn't pursued me because of money. He was so very dashing, you know."

"I believe I know the type."

"When he suggested that we elope to Gretna Green, it was the most romantic thing I could imagine. I was to pack a bag, and then halfway through the Windicott soiree he would whisk me away in his coach and no one would be able to stop us."

"Something stopped you."

"A fortnight before the ball, Papa died, and Mama four days after that."

"I'm so sorry, Alyse," Phin murmured.

"Thank you," she returned automatically. "I miss them."

"Layton begged off because your parents died? That's—"

"A few days after the funerals, my father's solicitor called on me. Everything—all of the Donnelly property—was entailed. Everything—the paintings on the walls, the furniture, my clothes, even—was to go to my cousin Richard. I panicked, tried to find Phillip and tell him that I wanted to leave with him immediately. I couldn't stand the thought of seeing Richard take possession of my family's home and title and . . . everything. But I couldn't find him."

"You went to the soiree, didn't you?"

She nodded. "With my bag packed. He was there, dancing with that awful Roberta Engles. At first he pretended that he didn't even know me. Then he took my bag and threw it onto the floor and said that I was mad and should stop following him about before he had someone deliver me to Bedlam."

Phin muttered a word that she couldn't quite make out, but that sounded exceedingly rude. "What about a stipend for you? An inheritance?"

"It was to be up to the discretion of Richard."

" 'Was to be,' " he repeated. "What happened?"

"I had ruined myself. I couldn't stay in London with everyone laughing at how stupid and blind I'd been, so Richard sent me to Cornwall to live with an aunt." She couldn't quite suppress her shudder as she remembered the overpowering smell of cats and mildew. "We weren't compatible. And I . . . still had far too much pride to suit everyone, including myself."

"Alyse, you were never proud."

She gave a humorless smile. "Yes, I was. Remember, I wanted a prince. And love. I thought I deserved them. After all, as you said, half the young men here wanted to marry me. Half the men in London did, too—until my fortunes turned and I made a complete fool of myself.

And the women to whom I should have been nicer weren't quiet about their satisfaction with my new circumstances. That proverb about pride and a fall is very true, you know."

Her voice quavered a little, but either he didn't notice or he pretended not to. She thought it was probably the latter. When he stopped at the edge of the slow-flowing water it seemed quite natural for her to keep her fingers gripped into his arm, and they both gazed out at the river and the hovering dragonflies as she continued to speak.

"I wrote to Richard and asked him to please let me return to London, but he wrote back that I wouldn't find anything more pleasant there. Instead he sent me to a second cousin, but she and her husband couldn't afford to keep me there. After several more changes of address, Richard brought me back to Donnelly House here. As a bachelor he wanted someone able to serve as hostess while he set up a household, and his mother, my aunt, is frail."

"You're her companion," he said slowly.

She nodded. "I'm her companion."

Well, he knew her story now, knew that to the amusement of a great many of her acquaintances she'd been pushed off her pedestal—or jumped off it herself, rather—and then made to clean it. She watched his expression and waited to see how long it would be before he began searching for an excuse to return her to Donnelly House. After all, she wasn't the sought-after daughter of a viscount any longer. She was a seven-Seasons-unmarried companion to a viscount's mother with absolutely no prospect of her situation ever improving.

"However much you thought you deserved happiness, Alyse," Phin finally commented, his gaze turning from the water, "you weren't wrong." He drew a breath. "I should never have left here."

"And what in the world would you have done?" she asked, though she had the feeling that he wasn't talking about her as much as he was his own family.

His hazel eyes met hers, and then he took a single step forward. Taking her face in his hands, he leaned down and kissed her. Warm lips touched hers, soft and seeking and not the least bit comforting. The sensation . . . lit her on fire. A long moment later he lifted his head away from hers a few inches.

"If I'd stayed, Alyse, at least neither of us would have been alone," he murmured.

It took several tries for her breath to return. Good heavens, he'd learned how to kiss since the peck he'd given her during the faux-marriage game and the infrequent occasions after that. But she'd learned some lessons about life, as well—none of them as pleasant as that kiss. "What do you want of me, Phin?" she asked, keeping her voice fairly steady. "We both know you didn't return to Quence Park because of me."

He smiled fleetingly. "What do I want of you?" he repeated. "Perhaps you'll grant me more than two days back to figure that out. For both our sakes. And no, I didn't return because of you. Because I didn't know."

"I know how you like adventure and strife, Phin. Don't make trouble for me."

"I will try not to make any more trouble for you. But I don't frighten easily." He glanced back in the direction of the horses. "There's an opera tonight in town and a public ball tomorrow night, I believe. Will you be attending either of them?"

Did he actually intend to court her? Phin? "Not the opera. Aunt Ernesta finds it dull."

"The ball, then."

"I don't know yet. It depends on whether she wishes to go."

"Perhaps I should try to persuade her."

She blanched. "Don't you dare."

"Very well," he said, chuckling probably to ease her obvious alarm. "I shall attempt to behave. Save a dance for me if you do attend, dark-eyed Alyse. Because I want to see you again."

They stood there for another few moments, then returned to the horses and continued their ride. It wasn't until he'd returned her to Donnelly House that she recalled what he'd said—he would try not to make *any more* trouble for her. Had he done something already? Or perhaps he'd simply referred to that kiss. Because from they way her heart had pounded, that in itself could signal a great deal of trouble.

Phineas handed Saffron over to Warner and trotted up the front steps of Quence just as Lord Donnelly left the house and climbed aboard his fine chestnut gelding. "Donnelly," he greeted, nodding.

"Colonel Bromley," Donnelly said, circling his mount to face Phineas, "I don't know whether you noticed or not, but the sky is clouding up. If it should rain heavily before the irrigation is repaired, Quence might lose the east pasture for the remainder of the season."

"It's unfortunate to see that your concern for Quence doesn't extend to Roesglen," Phin retorted, descending again to the front drive and inwardly cursing himself. Damnation. He'd forgotten about the meeting with Stuggley. And he had no one to blame but himself, because he'd wanted to see Alyse, and he'd wanted to discover why she hadn't told anyone she'd encountered a masked Frenchman last night.

"It's unfortunate to see that you have no concern at all," the viscount snapped. With a kick of his heels he sent his mount into a gallop and left the drive.

"That doesn't even make any sense," Phineas muttered, sending the retreating Donnelly a rude gesture and heading up the front steps.

Digby pulled open the door as he reached it. "Good morning again, Master Phineas."

"Good mor—"

"Phin?" William's voice echoed from down the hallway.

He didn't sound amused. *Bloody wonderful.* "On my way," he returned, moving past the spindly butler.

"Phin!"

"Christ," Phineas muttered, striding down the hallway to his brother's office. "Apologies," he said as he walked through the open door. "I meant to return in time for the meeting with Stuggley."

William, seated behind the desk with Andrews a statue at his shoulder, clenched his fist around a full cup of tea. For a bare moment Phineas thought his brother would throw it at him.

"Digby and Andrews looked for you," the viscount said tightly. "In case you meant to be present for the meeting."

"I did mean to be. I apologize, William. Were you able to resolve the issue?"

"Yes. It was a misunderstanding between Richard and the men he'd hired. You might have simply come to me first, before you swept in and arranged for meetings and to send angry men away."

Phineas hid his frown. It hadn't been a misunderstanding. If Richard Donnelly wanted to save his pride by saying so, that was one thing. But Phin didn't like being kicked in the arse for another man's sake. "I apologize again, then," he said anyway. Protests wouldn't do him any good.

"Where were you?"

"Riding with Alyse."

William blew out his breath. "Phin, a great deal has transpired in your absence. Alyse is not—"

Someone rapped on the closed door behind him. Andrews remained unmoving behind William, so Phineas pulled it open. Gordon stood there, a wide grin on his face.

"Beg pardon, Colonel," he drawled in his Scots brogue, "but I got ye in to see Mr. Murdock the tailor, if ye can get yer arse there by one o'clock."

Phineas winced. "Thank you, Gordon," he said. "I'll be with you in a moment."

"Oh, no, Phin," William interjected. "Mr. Murdock is quite popular with the gentry. You'd best ride your new mount into town and keep your appointment. And close the door behind you, if you please."

Phineas closed the door. With a glare at Gordon, he led the way back to the front door. "Damnation, Sergeant," he grumbled, "what did I tell you about barging into rooms?"

"I knocked, Colonel."

"Allow me to add, then, that you shouldn't barge straight into conversation, either."

"I beg yer pardon, then, but what, precisely, is wrong with sayin' I did as ye asked me to?"

Yes, how could he explain that without delving into

the sad story that was his youth? "Tell *me*, then. No one else."

"Bein' a valet is a damned pit o' vipers, Colonel."

"So it is. Shine my dress boots while I'm gone, will you?"

Gordon nodded, indicating they should step into the sitting room off the foyer. Another faux pas, but Phineas ignored it as he entered the room and closed the door after the sergeant.

"What is it?"

"Did ye find out why no one's talking of the highwayman's appearance last night?"

"Yes. I showed myself to someone who didn't wish to admit that she'd crossed paths with a stranger. If I want to upset the local gentry, I'd best make a more . . . spectacular showing."

"Oh, aye. We can't have ye being subtle."

"*I* will be subtle. Our highwayman will not. That is the point, Thaddeus."

"Far be it from me to argue with a madman."

Phineas grinned. "Exactly."

Chapter 7 _____

The process of transporting Viscount Quence to a night out in Lewes was more complicated than Phineas had realized. First Andrews rolled him to the foyer in his chair. Then the valet lifted William in his arms and carried him down the front steps to the waiting coach. After carefully seating him where he could hold on to a wall strap for balance, Andrews returned for the chair, which he also carried down the steps and then tied on to the back of the coach.

They had the system perfected, which made sense after ten years of practice. Phineas didn't comment on their efficiency, and instead kept his mouth shut and climbed into the carriage to sit beside Beth.

"Do you like opera?" Beth asked, hugging his arm. She wore a pretty blue and yellow silk gown, with matching ribbons tied through her curly ginger hair.

"I should have discovered that before I asked you to join us."

Us. He wasn't back to being one of the family yet, then. Not that he truly expected it. "Nonsense," he said aloud. "Of course I enjoy opera," he returned. In the face of her hopeful, pleased expression he would face a firing squad before admitting that opera left him indifferent at best, and asleep at worst. "Do you attend often?"

"We try to go to the theater for every new production during the late summer and early fall. They almost never perform opera, so I'm quite excited. I've been learning Italian, so I will translate for you, if you wish."

"Thank you. I can ask for directions to the nearest inn in Italian, but that's about as far as my knowledge goes." That wasn't entirely true, but he liked seeing her happy.

"What a surprise," William said into the silence. "Now that you're here, pray determine which of the *local* inns and taverns the nobility frequent so that you don't embarrass the family by entering a bawdy house."

"I'm not going to any tavern," Phineas retorted. "I'm going to the theater with you and Beth, and during intermission I'll be chatting and behaving in a pleasant and gentlemanly manner."

"Tonight, anyway. Forgive me if I otherwise remain skeptical."

At the word "forgive," Phineas flinched. He had a hunch that William had used it intentionally. "You may be correct," he grunted. "If I find someone willing to purchase me a glass of bitters, I may lose all bearings."

Beth cleared her throat. "You look very handsome tonight, Phin," she said, too loudly. "And very rakish, with that scar."

He'd nearly forgotten about his scar. Absently he touched the right side of his face where the old, thin line dissected his eyebrow, skipped over his eye, and ran for an inch down his cheek. "If the fellow had been a feather closer when he swung his saber at me, I'd be looking rakish with an eye patch. Thank goodness for ground squirrels and their well-placed burrows."

"Yes, thank God for them."

Phineas glanced again at William. The words sounded sarcastic, but his brother's tone seemed almost . . . sincere. As far as *he* was concerned, if he'd lost an eye it wouldn't be anything he hadn't deserved.

"I thank goodness that nothing worse happened to you," Beth went on.

Nothing except for being shot twice and having a horse fall on him. But his family didn't know about any of that. Nor did he want them to. "I was lucky," he said aloud.

"Lord Bramwell said you were clumsy and generally fell down at the right moment."

"Bram's an idiot."

"He's very nice," Elizabeth argued, her color rising, "in a dangerous, naughty sort of way."

Phineas sat forward. "What do you mean, 'naughty'? If he's put a hand on you, I'll castrate him."

"Good heavens!" Beth's cheeks darkened to scarlet.

"Bram has done everything possible to avoid being in the same room with our Magpie," William said, humor entering his voice for what seemed like the first time since Phineas had returned. "It couldn't hurt to pass your sentiments on to him, though."

"No! No, no, no! You will do no such thing! Because if you do, I will die from embarrassment!"

"I thought you were being courted by Lord Donnelly." Phineas eyed his sister. Under other circumstances he might have pursued this topic more delicately, but he and William seemed to have momentarily become allies. He couldn't allow that to pass by without doing anything to encourage it.

She lifted her chin. "Clearly it would be very silly of me to continue to participate in this conversation."

"But how will I know who I'm supposed to threaten if you don't tell me which gentlemen you find interesting?"

"Richard has been a great help to us," she retorted, "so please do not threaten him simply because he takes me driving."

Phineas's amusement faded. He'd brought up the topic of Richard Donnelly, but not to be slapped with the reminder that the man had stepped into the place within the Bromley family that had been his. Had been and would have continued to be, if he hadn't been such a fool.

"Did you write Lord Bramwell to tell him you're here?" Beth asked, either realizing that she'd trodden on sensitive ground, or unable to overcome being a seventeen-year-old young lady with a very ill-placed infatuation.

"I've written both Bram and Sullivan. I didn't ask them to come, however, so don't expect to see either of them." He refrained from mentioning that he'd already received a very substantial gift, in the form of Ajax, from Sullivan.

"I didn't ask anything about whether anyone would be visi—"

The coach jolted sideways. Beth shrieked as with a tremendous crack the vehicle pitched forward into the road. Phineas felt the sickening roll begin as the top-heavy vehicle started over onto its side. Not even taking the time to think, he shoved Beth against the sinking wall to keep her from falling that way, and then launched to the other side of the coach to grab William, bracing himself beneath his brother.

With Beth's screams in his ears the coach rocked onto its side and continued on toward the roof before it settled back again. "Beth! Quiet!" he snapped.

She subsided with a surprised whimper.

"Are you hurt? Beth! Are you—"

"No. No, I don't think so."

"William?"

"Intact, as far as I can tell."

Thankfully the oil in the coach lamp had drowned out the flame, but all of them were covered with the slick substance. Inside the toppled coach it was dark as pitch, but looking up he could make out the overcast sky through the trio of windows he'd been sitting beside a moment ago. He could hear the horses neighing and stomping, and crickets, but nothing of the two men who'd been seated on the driver's perch. "Warner? Andrews?" he called.

"Here, sir!" Warner's voice came. "Is anyone injured?"

"No."

"Give us a moment, then, to free the horses so they don't drag the coach."

"What happened?" Beth quavered, crawling over to grasp William's hand.

"I would guess that we lost a wheel," Phineas supplied. William was heavy across his chest, but he wasn't about to complain. As his eyes adjusted to the dark well enough for him to make out his siblings, the tension in his muscles eased a little. They were all bumped and bruised, but thankfully nothing worse. And he couldn't detect any trace of the distinctive metallic scent of blood. He'd smelled that often enough to recognize it anywhere.

"I want to get out."

He also recognized the beginnings of panic in his younger sister's voice. "I'll see what I can do. William, I'm going to shift you to my right."

"I can manage." His brother gripped the edges of the facing seats and bodily lifted himself high enough for Phineas to scramble out from under him.

"Remind me not to arm-wrestle you," he muttered, unbuckling his sheathed saber and setting it aside. He stood to shove hard at the door above his head. It lifted up and over, falling open with a creaking thud. He offered a hand down to his sister, pulling her carefully to her feet in the cramped space. "I'll lift you," he said, putting his hands around her waist. "Rest your elbows on the frame, and then stand on my shoulders to climb out."

She reached up as he lifted, and within a few seconds she made it out onto the skyward-pointing side of the coach. "What about you two?" she asked, leaning her head back in to look down at them as Phin handed her up his saber.

He sank back onto his haunches. "We'll wait for Andrews and Warner. And you stay up there until one of them can help you down. Don't stab anyone unless it's strictly necessary."

As she nodded, clutching his weapon against her chest and sitting back out of his sight again, Phineas realized this was the first time he and William had been alone in ten years. No Beth, no Andrews—and he didn't know what to say.

"I'm sorry you won't be able to go into town tonight," William said into the silence.

"I don't give a damn about going into town," Phineas retorted, keeping his voice low.

"What do you give a damn about?"

"You and Beth. My men, my friends. Or was that supposed to be a rhetorical question?"

William took a breath. "I don't want to fight with you, Phin. I just don't know why you're here."

"Beth wrote me t—"

"Yes, I know what Beth did. But I'm not on my deathbed, and I think you know you can't just . . . step back into this life. Things have changed over ten years."

"I shouldn't have stayed away for so long," Phineas returned slowly, on guard against another insult from his brother. How could he explain why he had stayed away? How did his shame and . . . cowardice compare against William, who hadn't had any choice but to face what had happened? "I don't expect everything to be as it was," he continued. "But perhaps—"

"My lord?" Andrews looked down through the open door above, his usually stoic expression folded into one of clear concern.

"I'm perfectly fine," William returned.

"The chair is flattened, I'm afraid," the valet commented.

William's jaw clenched briefly. "No matter. We'll manage."

Andrews swung his legs through the door. As he gathered himself to jump down into the coach, Phineas stood again. "Stay there, Andrews. I'll hand him up to you."

The valet paused. "My lord?"

"I don't care how you do it," William commented, his voice tighter. "Just get me the bloody hell out of this hole."

He must hate it, being completely dependent on others not just for his rescue, but for everything. Did he hate the person who'd done it to him? How could he not?

Later, Phineas told himself. He could contemplate his stupidity and damnation afterward. "If I lift you," he said, squeezing behind William again and wrapping his arms around his brother's chest, "can you hold on to Andrews's legs while I shift my grip?"

"Yes."

Phineas lifted William beneath the arms. His brother was solid and his legs nothing but dead dragging weight, but Phin refused to stagger or to give any indication at all that he was struggling. The viscount clutched on to his valet's ankles, and Phineas let him go just long enough to grip him around the waist and lift again.

With some pushing and pulling and some swearing on William's part, they got him out through the sky-facing door. Once he was clear, Phineas jumped up, gripping the doorframe, and hauled himself out as well.

"May I suggest that you ride on my back, my lord?" Andrews asked, climbing down so that Phineas could lower William into the valet's arms and from there onto the road where he could lean back against the coach's undercarriage.

"We'll take turns," Phineas said, clambering down

and then squatting to eye the half-buried front axle. It had snapped like a twig, but he couldn't tell much more than that in the dark.

"I don't know what happened," Warner was saying to Beth from where he held the nervous horses. "I check the coach every morning. I didn't see anything unsound about it, or I would never have—"

"Calm yourself, Warner," William said from his seat in the dirt. "It was an accident. No one's blaming you."

"Thank you, my lord. Shall I ride to Lord Donnelly's and bring back a coach?"

Phineas could sympathize with the groom's wish to make amends. But leaving William sitting on the ground for at least another thirty minutes while the clouds gathered seemed a supremely poor idea. "Returning to Quence straightaway seems more prudent," he said, trying not to give orders so that William wouldn't feel the need to contradict him.

"Yes, home," the viscount agreed.

They helped William up onto his valet's back, and then the lot of them started for Quence. In the dark, with two miles to walk, and Beth wearing her thin slippers, Phineas figured it would take them at least forty minutes to get back to the manor house. He glanced at the lowering sky again. They would be lucky to make it back before the rain began. And luck seemed to be in short supply for the Bromley family.

A hand gripped his. "I'm glad you were here tonight," Beth said quietly.

For a moment she looked like the wide-eyed seven-year-old he remembered. He squeezed her fingers. "I'm glad I was here, too," he returned, "whatever the reason you wanted me back at Quence Park."

Her lips tightened. "Phin, he made me promise."

"Let me give it a try, then," he muttered back. "If I'm right, squeeze my hand."

With a quick, guilty glance ahead at William clinging to Andrews's back, she nodded.

"Quence Park has seen a string of ill luck lately."

Squeeze.

"Over the past year or so there's been fire, flood, and some money issues."

Squeeze.

"William's worried that another instance or two of bad luck could cost the family the estate."

Squeeze.

"He doesn't want me here because he's concerned that I'll get in the way and make things worse."

Nothing. Phineas glanced sideways at his sister. She kept her gaze straight ahead, picking her way through the rutted road. Hm.

"William doesn't want me here because he's still angry with me."

Nothing. That made his heart pound with something oddly like hope, but he pushed back the resulting questions for later. This wasn't about his demons; it was about Quence's.

With that in mind and instead of continuing with aimless guesses, he decided to alter direction a little. "*You* wanted me here," he said slowly, lowering his voice further, "because you think I can help."

Squeeze.

She thought he could help. So she suspected that something more than ill luck was afoot, just as he did. Who, though, would want to drive the Bromleys off their property? Asking her that wouldn't do any good, because neither she nor William knew the answer. If they did, they would have done something about it already.

That made resolving this problem his responsibility. He was a soldier, a trained officer, and he arrived in East Sussex with certain skills and a certain mind-set. This was what he excelled at. War. Even if he didn't yet know the identity of his opponent.

He should probably stop the questions now and go relieve Andrews, but there was one more thing he wanted to know first. In the grand scheme it was probably inconsequential, but it mattered to him. "William doesn't want me here because he's worried I'll be hurt."

Squeeze.

That night Phineas slept better than he had since he'd received Beth's letter in Spain. But he rose early, digging out some of the civilian clothes from which Gordon had managed to press the worst of the wrinkles, and dressed before the sergeant arrived to roust him from bed. He was pulling on his boots, in fact, when his so-called valet knocked on the bedchamber door and opened it.

"Well, yer up with the roosters this mornin', ain't ye?"

"I know we've only discussed knocking, but you're supposed to wait for an answer before you open the door."

The sergeant frowned. "How d'ye answer, Colonel, if yer asleep?"

Phineas glared at him for a moment. "Never mind. Come along." He headed through the open door.

"Come along where?"

"I want to take a look at that coach in daylight."

The ancient butler hadn't yet assumed his post at the front door, so Phineas unlatched and opened it himself. He closed it quietly, and the two of them walked around to the stable to saddle Saffron and Gallant.

Sergeant Gordon chattered about the foggy morning and about the coloring of a good beer, and then about one of the house's upstairs maids who apparently had fiery red hair and a temper to match. Not paying much attention, Phineas instead wondered how he could best use the highwayman to discover who happened to be encouraging the ill luck that had beset Quence Park.

He hadn't been there in ten years. He didn't know old neighbors or friends any longer, and he had no idea at all who might be a stranger, let alone who might bear a grudge against William or Beth or the family in general.

It had rained overnight, and his boots were well spattered with kicked-up mud by the time they rounded the last curve in the road. "Company," Gordon muttered.

Phineas looked up. Through the fog he could make out three riders, two men and a woman, stopped beside the overturned coach. They were all well dressed and wearing the latest fashions, and one of the men had dismounted to climb up onto the vehicle.

"I don't see any corpses," he called out, straightening.

"Charles, that's gruesome," the young woman said with a delicate shudder.

"I said that I *don't* see any—" The fellow stopped as his gaze found the two men approaching on horseback. "Any *dead* people," he continued, hopping to the ground. "Good morning, gentlemen."

The other two moved around to view them, as well. "Good morning," Phineas returned, automatically noting that Gordon had sent Gallant a dozen steps to his right. *Spread out possible targets; make it more difficult for the enemy to wipe out your forces.*

"You wouldn't know what happened here, would you?" the one on foot, Charles, continued.

"That depends," Phineas said, stopping. "Who are you?"

"Lord Charles Smythe," the fellow said. "That's Lord Anthony Ellerby, and the lovely lady is his sister, Lady Claudia." He cocked an eyebrow, confident and arrogant. "And who might you be?"

As an officer, Phineas had learned to assess people quickly; his life, and the lives of his men, depended on his being correct. And he didn't like this Lord Charles Smythe. He would reserve judgment regarding the other two. The Ellerby name, though, sounded familiar. "Ellerby," he said aloud. "Any relation to Edward Ellerby, the Duke of Beaumont?"

The mounted man nodded. "Our grandfather. We're visiting."

Beaumont had an estate southwest of Lewes. He and the previous Lord Quence, Phineas's father, had entered into some sort of dispute over who had priority at the local granary, but that had been twenty years ago. He didn't know of anything more recent, but he preferred to keep on the side of caution until he had more details about what was going on.

"You still haven't introduced yourself, friend," Lord Charles commented. He dipped his right hand into the right pocket of his greatcoat.

He was probably armed, then. Phineas wasn't, except for the knife stuck into his right boot. As far as he was concerned that made the odds about even, but he didn't know nearly enough to push for a confrontation. Not yet. "Phineas Bromley," he said, intentionally excluding Gordon from the introductions. The less the others thought about the sergeant, the freer he would be to make a first move unopposed.

Lord Anthony blinked. "Bromley? Are you a relation of Lord Quence?"

Phineas couldn't read anything more than surprise in his expression. "His brother."

"The army fellow?"

"I'm on leave." As he supplied that, he noted that despite the fact that they were standing beside an overturned coach with the Quence coat of arms clearly emblazoned on the door, no one had asked anything other than the most general of questions about it. Did any of them have reason to be less than surprised to see the aftermath of the accident?

Lord Charles strolled closer, his gaze taking in the yellow horse and the old jacket Phineas had donned for their investigation. "The army, eh? You look more like one of those gypsies who wanders the countryside, robbing people."

"Charles," Lady Claudia chastised again, though she sounded more amused than troubled on his behalf.

"I meant no offense, Sergeant," Smythe continued.

"Colonel," Gordon burst out, his face reddening.

"Lieutenant Colonel, actually," Phineas said easily. "No offense taken, Lord Charles."

"Well, Colonel Bromley," Lady Claudia said, flicking the ends of her reins against her thigh, "I hope to see you at the public ball tonight. It's been rather dull here."

"I shall do my utmost," he drawled. "My coach does seem to have suffered an accident."

Lord Charles Smythe swung back onto his horse.

"And we'll suffer an accident if we don't return to Beaumont in time for breakfast."

Phineas watched until they vanished behind the hedgerows. Then he dismounted, moving over to the undercarriage of the coach and squatting down. "Take a look at this," he said.

Gordon moved in and bent down beside him, resting a hand on one of the airborne wheels. "That's a terrible clean break," he observed.

"Yes, it is." Phineas had seen malicious destruction before, and this looked like it. Nothing he could prove, of course, but he added it to the list of bad-luck items he'd compiled thus far.

"So what d'ye plan to do about it?" his sergeant asked.

Phineas straightened, wiping his hands on his thighs before he clapped his valet on the back. "What we're going to do, Thaddeus," he said smoothly, "is ride into town and see what we can do about getting another carriage. I want to go to that ball tonight."

"I should've stayed in bloody Spain. It would've been safer, I'm beginning to think."

"You're likely correct. But this is turning out to be much more interesting."

Chapter 8 _____

Phineas hired the resident blacksmith and a team of heavy work horses to pull the Quence coach upright and render the broken vehicle capable of limping into Lewes for more permanent repairs. While Gordon oversaw that, Phin rode to a local coach house, where he rented a curricle. He would have preferred a coach, but most of the gentry had returned to the country from their Season in London, and none were available. And he needed to attend the public ball.

He drove back by the blacksmith's to collect Gordon. "What are the damages going to be?" he asked, as the Scotsman tied his horse to the curricle and climbed onto the seat beside him. Never mind that a servant would be expected to sit on the narrow perch at the back. Sergeant Gordon wasn't precisely a typical servant.

"Replacing the axle and three wheels, and the left-hand door—Carter says twenty quid, give or take."

"He agreed to do the work?"

"I gave 'im a fiver." Gordon looked over at him. "Ye are goin' to pay me fer bein' yer valet, ain't you, Colonel?"

"I didn't ask you to follow me here, but yes, I suppose I will. Though five quid seems a bit generous."

"What the bloody h—"

"Did you volunteer the money, or did he ask for something before he began the repairs?" Phineas interrupted.

"He asked."

Phineas nodded. The locals knew, then, that Quence was suffering money troubles. Otherwise a commoner would never have asked for any payment from a noble's household before providing a service.

Gordon squinted one eye at him. "Ye told me not t'gossip, but does it count if I hear things'n tell ye about 'em?"

"No, that doesn't count," Phineas agreed swiftly, turning the curricle down the road toward Quence.

"Then there's been some speculation as to 'ow long the Bromleys can hold on to Quence Park, what with the bad luck they been havin'."

"Was this from the blacksmith?"

"Aye. And with nods from the tanner and Fred the innkeeper."

"And how did you respond?" Phineas queried.

"With outrage, tempered by respect fer my gentlemanly master."

"Hm." That was as well as could be expected, he supposed, but rumor could do as much damage as any flood. "How much ready blunt do you have to hand?"

The sergeant sighed. "Near about forty quid, I would wager. The rest of me pay I sent home to me poor mum."

"You were found under a rock, Thaddeus."

"All right, ye cruel man. Sixty quid. But that's me drinkin' money."

"After Saffron and Gallant I've got about two hundred still to hand, and another five hundred or so I can draw from the bank on short notice." He had more, but it would take longer to get his hands on it.

"That's a fair sum, Colonel. What d'ye intend to do with it?"

"Turn the rumors to our favor, and see if I can figure out who's trying to drive the Bromleys out of Quence Park."

"I foresee some mayhem comin', then."

"I should think so."

"Excellent." They rode in silence for several minutes. "How much trouble are ye willing t'cause here?"

"I'm becoming convinced that someone is doing this to my family," he returned, for once letting his anger at this unknown foe temper his voice. "I mean to flush him from hiding and bury him. And whatever I can't do, our masked friend can. Beginning tonight."

"That's plain enough, then. This fellow's begun a war. We'll end it fer 'im."

Phineas drew a breath. War. He knew war, but once he'd set eyes again on Alyse, this had become much more complicated. He'd kissed her, and he wanted to do so again. He wanted to go riding with her, and chat with her—and he wanted those things he'd sought with other women because he'd never thought to be able to experience them with Alyse. He wanted to feel her warm skin beneath his hands, feel her shudder with pleasure.

". . . help in the stable, don't ye think?" Gordon was saying.

Phineas shook himself. If he was to be fighting a battle, the distraction Alyse presented could be dangerous. He'd turned his back on his old life. Some of it he frankly was glad to leave behind. But other parts, he wanted again—and with a yearning he'd never expected. He placed Alyse firmly in that category.

"Are ye listenin' t'me at all?" the sergeant complained.

"You think we need an additional stableboy. I agree. See to it. Someone we can trust, Sergeant."

"Ye couldnae have decided this before we drove halfway back to Quence?"

"Apologies. Take Gallant, and see what you can do."

Gordon sighed again as he hopped down from the curricle. "Next time ye tell me t'stay put in Spain, I'm goin' to listen to ye."

"Then I'll consider the lesson well learned. And if you return home before I do, I'll be at Donnelly House to take Miss Donnelly driving."

The sergeant eyed him. "The lady'll be thinkin' ye have an infatuation with her, sir."

"I do."

Gordon blanched. "In the middle of a fight, Colonel? Can ye—"

Phineas raised a hand. "I believe I can govern my own affairs, Sergeant. And today, I'm only after information, anyway." And another kiss, if the lady was amenable.

"What do you think, Richard?" Aunt Ernesta asked, tilting her head this way and that to examine her yellow-decorated hat in the mantel mirror. "It's not too fussy, is it?"

Alyse tried to ignore the preening as she pulled a half dozen stitches from the embroidery her aunt had supposedly completed yesterday. Either the new proverb was "Cleanliness us Next to Goodliness," or Aunt Ernesta couldn't spell. And considering that the piece was meant to be a throw pillow for Lady Dysher's birthday next week, she had no time to waste in "putting on the finishing touches," as Aunt Ernesta had instructed her to do.

"You have all the makings of a milliner, Alyse," Richard observed from behind his newspaper. "Or a dressmaker, perhaps."

Alyse would have stuck her tongue out at him, but her aunt would have seen the gesture. The woman could detect both sin and ungratefulness from five hundred yards. "Thank you, Cousin," she said instead, pulling out more stitches.

The butler walked into the morning room. "My lord, you have a note from Quence Park," he intoned, holding out the silver salver.

Richard set aside the newspaper to pluck the missive off the tray. "Damnation," he muttered as he read through it. "Saunders, have Raleigh saddled."

"Right away, my lord."

"Is William well?" Alyse asked as the butler exited the room again.

"Yes. Their coach overturned last night. His damned brother no doubt ran it into a ditch."

Alyse just managed to stifle her gasp. "Is that what the note said? Is Phin unhurt?"

He glanced at her as he exited the room. "Mind your own business, Alyse."

Alyse sat back. What in the world was Phin doing? He'd become reckless and angry and self-absorbed as he'd gotten older, but he seemed to have changed since his return. If he'd done as Richard had said, though, perhaps he hadn't changed at all.

"Alyse, make certain Cook knows that Mrs. Potter will not tolerate cucumbers."

She shook herself. "Mrs. Potter?"

"For luncheon. Have you forgotten that Eloise will be dining with me today?"

Blast it. "Of course not. I'll remind Cook immediately."

Oh, she'd completely forgotten. Phin was very distracting. Setting aside the embroidery, she hurried out of the room and down the succession of hallways to the kitchen. "Mrs. Jones," she said into the general chaos, "I'm to remind you not to serve cucumbers."

The cook nodded. "Yes, Miss Donnelly. I won't be serving anything off a vine for luncheon."

"Thank you," Alyse said with a smile, then spied the berry tarts cooling on the table.

"Help yourself, miss," Cook said, grinning. "I know how you like berries."

"Oh, bless you, Mrs. Jones."

Berry tarts. A small piece of heaven on Earth, as far as she was concerned. Taking small bites to make the treat last longer, she strolled back to the front of the house. Her aunt wouldn't touch the tarts, so she would be expected to abstain, as well. Now at least she could do so without any unsightly drooling.

As she reached the morning room again, she heard her aunt speaking, and then a deep male voice answering. Saunders was in the dining room supervising the luncheon preparations, but as a shiver ran down her spine she knew it wasn't the butler or a footman speaking. Straightening her shoulders, she strolled into the room.

Phin Bromley, smartly attired in a blue jacket and trousers with Hessian boots, was seated in the chair she'd vacated. As his hazel gaze caught her, he stood. "Miss Donnelly," he said, inclining his head.

Goodness. No one bowed to her anymore except as a jest. But she saw nothing in his lean face to make her think he was teasing. Belatedly she gave a half curtsy. "Colonel Bromley."

"The colonel," her aunt declared, "thinks to convince me that I can do without you for an hour so that you can show him about the valley."

"I wish to become reacquainted with the area around Lewes," Phin said.

"What about your sister? Isn't she available to conduct a tour?"

Aunt Ernesta was going to send him away. Alyse stepped forward. "I imagine Beth wanted to be home to greet Richard."

Her aunt opened and closed her mouth again. "You will return Alyse here within one hour, Colonel. I am expecting a guest, and I require her presence."

Phineas offered Alyse his arm. "I will have Miss Donnelly home by noon, then. I give you my word."

"Have one of the maids go with you, Alyse."

Stunned at being allowed to leave her aunt's side for the second day in a row, much less at her aunt suddenly demanding propriety from her, Alyse nodded and pulled Phin toward the door. Aunt Ernesta could change her mind as long as they were in earshot, so she grabbed a passing maid with her free hand. "Mary, come with me," she said, and the three of them practically ran through the front door and down the front steps.

"I assume we're to leave quickly," Phin murmured, putting his hands on her hips and lifting her onto the seat of the curricle. The sensation left her pleasantly breathless. Every time he touched her, she seemed to lose all bearings.

He helped Mary onto the carriage's small rear bench, then came around and climbed up beside Alyse. With a whistle he sent the team down the drive at a brisk trot. Once they'd rounded the hedgerow, Alyse finally let out the breath she'd been holding.

"Thank goodness," she sighed, belatedly setting aside the bonnet she'd snatched on the way out the door.

"That was quick thinking, saying that Beth was occupied. Where *is* your cousin?"

"Your brother sent for him," she returned, surprised that he didn't know. "Something about you overturning the coach."

A muscle in his jaw jumped. "I did no such thing," he muttered. "The coach broke an axle and overturned on the way to the opera last night."

Phin stated it so matter-of-factly that the import of what he'd said took a moment to sink in. She reached over to touch a scratch on his chin. "While you all were in it?" she gasped.

"Yes. More ill luck for Quence Park."

"Everyone's well, though? Beth? William?"

"A bit knocked about, but no additional damage done."

No *additional* damage. Alyse badly wanted to ask him what precisely had happened that day ten years ago, but it had been enough to cause him to flee once, and she liked having him back in East Sussex. Best keep to safer topics, then. "Did you have a destination in mind for us this morning?"

"I thought perhaps the Quence tenant cottages."

She smiled. "I haven't been there in ages. Do you think Mrs. Hutchens still makes that wonderful sharp cheese?"

He glanced sideways at her again. "You haven't heard? My valet informed me that half the cottages were burned to the ground last year."

Alyse stared at him. "What?"

"At the moment it's a rumor, since I haven't seen them yet myself, but I'd like to amend that. You wouldn't happen to know whether any other estates have been . . . troubled by misfortune, would you?"

"What are you implying?"

"That Quence's misfortune is deliberate."

She felt as though she'd been punched in the gut. And to think, a few moments ago she'd been anticipating another kiss. "You're mad," she stated. "Either that or you're trying to make trouble for me by deliberately entangling me in some . . . conspiracy. Stop the carriage, Phin."

"No."

Blast it all. She should have known better. The first man to pay serious attention to her in better than four years, and he wanted something from her. "You promised that you wouldn't make things worse for me."

"I'm not—" He stopped, taking a deep breath. "There are four people in East Sussex whom I trust, Alyse. Two of them won't talk to me because they're afraid of what could happen. The third arrived here when I did. And then there's you. This isn't the sort of conversation

I want to have with you, but honestly, there isn't anyone else."

"Is that why you kissed me?" she asked quietly, trying to keep her voice steady. "Because you need my help, and you're, what, attempting to charm me?"

"I kissed you because I've been wanting to kiss you for the past ten years," he growled. "I never claimed to have any sort of timing."

That stopped her for a moment. If he was attempting to confuse her, he was doing a brilliant job of it. She gazed at his profile, at the line of the scar dissecting his right eyebrow. "How long will you stay at Quence?" she asked.

"I don't know yet. Apparently there's a fine line between stopping trouble and causing it."

"You shouldn't have left like that. Of course no one knows what to make of you now."

He turned to look full at her, his hazel eyes glinting with a steel that he hadn't possessed as a youth. "If you think you can say anything that I haven't dwelled on endlessly, you are very much mistaken."

"Why did you go?"

"Because I couldn't stay."

"My father said you made him promise that he would look after William and Beth. He said you gave him every penny you had."

Phin shrugged. "It wasn't much. I was seventeen. I'd probably stolen half of it from William to fund my escape from here."

Alyse looked down at her hands for a moment. He'd made his escape ten years ago, and she was trying to make hers now. The only difference was that she had no intention of ever returning to her so-called family. "Why did you stop the work on the dam?" she asked again, refusing to be thrown sideways by the realization that they had more in common now than they'd had as children.

"Because they set it downstream, where it would have flooded half of Roesglen. I didn't see a need for that."

She didn't, either. "Why would William do that in the first place?"

"I doubt William knew the particulars."

Frowning, Alyse elbowed Phin in the ribs. "Are you going to stop being deliberately obtuse?"

"I am not—"

"You said you wanted help. Then stop dancing about and say that this person you suspect of . . . of malicious destruction, I suppose, is my cousin."

"Because I don't know that for certain, and because we have company." He indicated Mary seated behind them. "Company employed by Lord Donnelly."

Alyse looked over her shoulder at Mary, who sat swinging her legs out over the edge of the narrow seat. Mary hadn't been at Donnelly House long; she'd been one of the new servants Richard had hired once he'd decided to take up residence in East Sussex. In the past, Alyse might have trusted the maid to keep any overheard conversation to herself. Over the past few years she'd seen precisely how easily gossip could spread and how damaging rumor could be.

"You ask sharp questions," Phin said after a moment.

"I'm trying to figure out where I stand in your little plot. I haven't seen you in ten years, Phin. Things aren't the way they used to be."

His gaze took her in from toes to the top of her head. "So I've noticed."

Her cheeks heated. "Stop that."

"Stop what? Looking at you?"

"You know very well what I mean. I may have been spoiled, Phin Bromley, but I was never stupid. And for your information, Richard only took up residence full-time at Donnelly a year ago, so perhaps he wasn't aware of the particulars of water flow."

Phin drew the curricle to a stop and jumped to the ground. Bypassing Mary, he walked around to Alyse. Before he could put his hands around her waist again, she made her own way down. He hesitated, then offered his arm. "We'll be back in a moment," he said over his shoulder, otherwise ignoring the maid.

"What is it?" Alyse asked, putting her hands behind her back so she wouldn't be tempted to touch him and fall prey to his charm.

"I thought you were less than happy with Lord Donnelly and your current situation."

"That is to be kept between us," she said, abruptly worried that he would mention it elsewhere. "And my 'current situation,' as you call it, is much better than my previous one. Or the one before that. Take me back to Donnelly, Phin. Whatever it is you're after, I can't provide it. And I won't trade information for your affection."

Hazel eyes met hers. "You have my affection, anyway." He stepped closer.

"Phin, don't—"

Phin drew a hand around her waist. Silently he placed a feather-light kiss on the right corner of her mouth, then another on the left. Then, as her heart hitched, he tilted her head up with his fingers and kissed her.

This was precisely what her mother had been worried about back before Phin had left, but she'd been only fifteen, and he couldn't possibly have kissed as well as he did now. Shivering heat coiled down her spine. Oh, it would be so easy to simply float away on her fondest daydreams—except for that one nagging bit of logic that said he hadn't come back to see her. He'd come back to see to his family, and she'd been . . . some sort of coincidence.

She pushed his chest. She might as well have pushed a stone wall, but he lifted his head. "What is it?" he murmured, running his fingers softly along her cheekbones.

Good heavens. "You take too much advantage of our old friendship, sir," she said with as much indignation as she could muster. "I was once engaged to be married. I know very well what men do to get what they want."

For a long moment he gazed down at her. Then, a muscle in his jaw clenching, he nodded. "Of course." He gestured her back toward the curricle. "My apologies."

Alyse was relieved that he'd given in. Because more troubling than his kisses was the realization that, previously engaged or not, no one had ever kissed her like that before. And she liked it very much.

Chapter 9 _____

"Did you rise early, or have you been out since last night?" William asked from his chair, placed behind the desk in his office.

"I rose early," Phineas returned, fighting against the sensation that he was seventeen and being dressed down by his older brother. "I had the coach righted and brought into Lewes for repairs, and I rented a curricle."

"Interesting." His jaw working, William flipped open his ledger book. "How much will the coach repair and curricle rental cost me?"

"I made the arrangements," Phineas answered.

William looked up at him. "You paid for it."

Phineas settled for nodding, though he was tempted to point out that, late to the game or not, he wasn't completely useless.

"Ah," William said. "So the accounts that've been run up for the past weeks in Lewes remain outstanding, while Quence has paid for more recent services. That should go over well."

Damnation. "That is not my fault. We couldn't leave the coach lying in the middle of the road. And I had Gordon pay the blacksmith; I didn't do it directly." He took a frustrated breath. "And if Quence is suffering money problems, you might have said something. I have blunt to hand if y—"

"Quence's business is none of yours," his brother retorted. "You can't reappear after ten years and jump straight into the middle of everything."

Phineas folded his arms across his chest. "Then why don't you tell me what's going on?"

"Nothing is g—"

"Flooded pasture, burned cottages, wrecked coach, servants going elsewhere—have I missed anything? Oh, and Warner mentioned something about ruined horse feed and you losing two animals and selling off four others."

William closed his mouth. For a long moment Phineas's brother gazed at him. "Quence has suffered through some ill luck," he said finally. "We've done so before, and managed to pull out of it without your assistance."

That hurt, but it was no more than he deserved. "I'm here now," he returned slowly. "And I would like to help."

"Then pay your visit and go back to Spain without causing any more trouble. Moving the dam again to accommodate Roesglen's fish pond has already cost me an additional twenty pounds."

One thing Phineas had learned in the army was the

wisdom of seeing when it might be more prudent to fall back and regroup rather than keep pushing ahead in the face of imminent defeat. "Very well," he said aloud, "but we're not finished with this conversation, William."

However much he wanted . . . peace between himself and William, he had more to worry over than family harmony. Someone was trying to hurt Quence Park, or her owners, or both. And as far as he could decipher, no local farmer would have either the means or a reason to vandalize the Bromleys.

That left the gentry. *His* people. And tonight he would be meeting all of them. The highwayman would take the reins from there. He paused. The highwayman whom Alyse seemed to find intriguing. Perhaps that fellow could coax a kiss from her.

"Oh, heavens," Aunt Ernesta said, digging her fingers into Alyse's arm. "I had no idea there would be such a crush tonight. Perhaps we should return home."

Alyse forced a smile. "All of your friends are here, Aunt. They will be so disappointed if you cry off."

Her aunt sent her a sideways glance. "Don't pretend you're concerned over me, Alyse. You've already gone riding with him yesterday and driving today. Being seen panting after him will hardly aid your reputation."

"I'm not panting after anyone," she retorted. Particularly someone whose motives she couldn't begin to decipher. "I think tonight will be enjoyable for both of us."

Ernesta pulled her closer. "Watch how you speak to me, Alyse. I might have had Harriet accompany me and left you at home."

"Nonsense, Mother," Richard unexpectedly put in, removing the claws from Alyse's arm and placing them over his own. "Alyse has few opportunities to dance and chat these days. We shouldn't begrudge her one of them."

The unexpected support immediately made her suspicious, even laced as it was with the usual touch of condescension and cruelty. "Thank you," she said tentatively.

"Of course. But you shouldn't be disappointed if your dance card is less than full. In fact, I'll partner you for the evening's first quadrille. That way you'll have at least one opportunity to dance."

The idea of dancing with Richard made staying behind at Donnelly House sound very reasonable, but she smiled anyway. "I'll save it for you, then," she returned.

Richard's gaze moved beyond her. "Excuse me, ladies."

She turned around as he moved past her. The Bromleys had arrived. For a moment she allowed herself to forget that she was angry and frustrated with Phin; in a dark gray jacket and lighter trousers with a cream-colored waistcoat, he looked so handsome she literally forgot to breathe.

Was she being an idiot to be suspicious of his kindnesses and his attention? After all, own agenda or not, at least he paid attention to her. No other man had in over four years—except for the masked French burglar who'd taken nothing that Richard had noticed. An abrupt thought left her cold. What if the Frenchman was the vandal Phin sought, and she'd said nothing about his presence? They were at war with France, after all.

"Good evening," Lord Quence said, as Richard led the Bromleys over to the side of the room where she and Aunt Ernesta waited.

"Good evening, my lord," her aunt replied, smiling. "And don't you look lovely, Beth. I have to say that yellow is definitely your color."

Beth curtsied. "Thank you, Mrs. Donnelly. It looks well on you, also."

"Oh, please, my dear. How many times must I ask you to call me Ernesta?"

Alyse stood back a little and watched the display. Familiar as this scene had become over the past weeks, in a sense it was even more familiar than that—a few years ago, it had been with her that Aunt Ernesta had been trying to ingratiate herself. Before her parents had died, and before the scandal.

"Are we speaking?" Phin's low drawl came from beside her.

She shook herself. "Of course we're speaking. I've never trusted you overly much, but we are still old friends."

"That's better than a punch in the eye, I suppose." He glanced about the crowded room before his hazel-eyed gaze returned to her. "Do they waltz in this part of England?"

"They do. There will be two waltzes tonight."

"I'm claiming one of them, then."

She liked the way he said that, as if he were ready to fight for the chance to waltz with her. Clearly he hadn't noticed that no gentleman other than Richard had even spoken to her.

"How long do you intend to make me wait for an answer?" he prompted, rocking forward on his toes.

"I would be pleased to waltz with you, Phin. Should I pencil in your name now, or do you wish to scout the rest of the guests present and look for evildoers before I force you to commit to anything?"

"I want to dance with *you*," he returned quietly, then flashed his most dazzling smile. "For the remainder of the evening, though, I might as well mingle."

"You should have worn your uniform this evening, Colonel," her cousin commented. "Ladies do love a uniform, whoever happens to be wearing it."

"I've never had to resort to bragging about my position to attract a lady's attention," Phin returned, then flicked a finger at the diamond pin pushed through Richard's cravat. "You look very fine, by the way."

Alyse fought the abrupt urge to smile. Seeing her overly confident cousin set back on his heels was both a rare and not-unwelcome sight. When she glanced again at Phin, he was looking at her. At her mouth, more precisely. She blushed. Wary of him and his motives or not, she had to admit that he was handsome as the devil and kissed like sin. After the loneliness of the past five years, how could she not be affected by his attentions? He knew it, as well. She would keep that in mind, and she had learned to look after her own interests first. No one else would.

Richard claimed the quadrille with her and the evening's first waltz with Beth. Just as Alyse was beginning to wonder whether Phin might request a second dance with her, he stirred again and offered his arm to his sister.

"I wonder if you'd dare introduce me to your friends and our neighbors," he said with his easy smile.

Beth grinned back at him. "Of course," she returned,

tugging him toward the refreshment table. "But I do intend to tell everyone that you've purchased a yellow horse."

"You've doomed me, Magpie."

"Clever fellow," Richard commented, looking after the siblings. "He's managed to make off with the most beautiful scenery in the room."

Alyse rolled her eyes. "May I fetch anyone something to drink?" she offered, making certain Lord Quence knew he was included in the question.

"A glass of claret would be splendid," the viscount said, smiling up at her. If his brother and sister walking off troubled him, he didn't show it.

"Madeira," Aunt Ernesta put in, and Richard echoed William's request.

With a nod she strolled away to find a footman. The partygoers mingled and chatted and laughed around her, but no one approached to include her in their conversation. By now she knew better than to attempt to insinuate herself into one or other of the groups, because they would only stare at her and then find they needed to be elsewhere.

At the already-familiar sound of Phin's laugh she looked sideways. A charming smile on his face, he had his head bent over some young woman's dance card while he penciled in his name. The pretty blonde thing giggled, holding out her hand for Phin to bow over. *Oh, please.*

"Miss Donnelly?"

She started, turning so quickly she nearly knocked down the man who stood behind her. "Yes? Oh, Lord Anthony. You startled me."

The Duke of Beaumont's grandson smiled. "I do

apologize. I saw you, and thought I'd best move in before you were swallowed by the crowd."

"Well, you've caught me," she said, smiling back at the tall, light-haired man. "What may I do for you?"

"I was wondering if you might have a place on your card for me."

Alyse managed to keep her expression open and friendly. But this man was a friend of Richard's—they'd even gone to Oxford together—and she couldn't think of a single reason why he would wish to dance with her. Oh, for the days when she hadn't had to consider motives and repercussions. "Certainly," she answered, pulling the card from her reticule. "You may have your choice."

He took it and the pencil from her fingers. "Ah, I see you've given a waltz to Colonel Bromley."

"You know him?"

"We've met," he returned. "He came upon us surveying Quence's overturned coach. For a moment I thought he might be the ghost of that local highwayman of yours. What was his name? Grandfather was always telling us tales about him. The Frenchie."

"The Gentleman?" Alyse supplied, fighting a blush. She'd half managed to convince herself that she'd dreamed up his appearance—until someone else mentioned highwaymen.

"Yes, that's him. He'd be a bit better dressed than Bromley was, though, and I don't think The Gentleman would have been caught dead on a yellow horse."

"Yes, he was a notorious horseman, if I recall my local history." Curving her lips in another smile, Alyse indicated her dance card. "Do you wish a dance, my lord, or were you merely looking for an excuse to chat?"

He looked down at her card. "You still have a waltz," he said, ignoring the fact that she also had four country dances and three quadrilles available to let. Lord Anthony penciled his name in beside the evening's second waltz and then handed the card and pencil back to her. "Thank you."

"You're welcome."

Hm. First Richard, and now one of his cronies saw fit to be . . . pleasant to her. When Lord Charles Smythe approached a few moments later and requested a quadrille, she had no idea what might be afoot. The old Alyse would have expected men to approach her for a dance. The Alyse she was now knew enough to be suspicious of gift horses—and gift gentlemen.

"If I had known such beauty awaited me in Lewes, I would have returned sooner," Phineas drawled, circling Lady Claudia Ellerby.

"I believe you're attempting to turn my head," Beaumont's granddaughter returned with a coy smile, her light blue eyes meeting his boldly.

"Is it working?"

"I couldn't possibly reply to that and still remain a lady."

He chuckled. They circled one another again, and he took her hand as they proceeded down the length of the ballroom floor. Beth was dancing, as well, and he caught sight of his brother seated with Andrews standing behind him, at one side of the room. An old man who looked half blind and three-quarters deaf was his nearest companion.

So that was how it was for William. Reduced to chatting with other invalids at the edges of the room where the wheeled chair wouldn't get in anyone's way. Without Beth present beside him, not even Donnelly could be bothered to remain at the outside of the crush of guests.

Of course, he wasn't precisely doing anything differently himself. In his own defense, William seemed to prefer him elsewhere. Aside from that, he had a vandal to discover. If there was a source other than nature, coincidence, or God for the ill luck at Quence Park. Every bone in his war-tempered body, though, felt a human touch in the mix.

"You must tell me," Lady Claudia said, "how it is that you dance so well."

"Practice," he returned. "Even during wartime, we have to celebrate what it is we're fighting for."

"So you fight for the quadrille?"

"I fight to be able to enjoy a dance with a lovely lady."

She smiled again, prettily. "My grandfather warned me that you were charming, and a danger to every respectable lady's reputation."

Beaumont remembered him from his previous residence at Quence, then. And the duke wasn't the only one. He'd been receiving sour looks from a handful of husbands since he'd entered the assembly rooms. And he'd caught the looks from their wives, as well. Several mothers looked ready to produce chastity belts for their unmarried daughters.

Good God, he'd been an idiot ten years ago. Given his relative lack of experience as a sixteen- and seventeen-year-old, he was surprised half the women present weren't laughing at him. Then again, he supposed he'd had a good share of anger and enthusiasm to make up for what he'd lacked in skill. Over the past ten years he'd managed to take care of the skill bit.

"How long have you been in East Sussex?" he asked Lady Claudia.

"Practically since the end of the Season. Anthony and Charles enjoy the hunting here, and Grandfather likes for us to visit."

Phineas nodded. "And how does a young lady fresh from the London Season spend her days when her brother and his friend are riding about the countryside?"

"Heavens, Lewes may not be London, but it's not cloistered, by any means. I have friends here."

"Ah. You must introduce me to them."

Her smile deepened. "Perhaps I wish to keep you all to myself, Colonel Bromley."

"Call me Phineas."

"Phineas, then."

The music ended, and he joined in the applause as he led her off the dance floor. That had been useful. A few minutes of dancing, and he'd already discovered that Anthony Ellerby and Charles Smythe regularly rode about the countryside, which made them suspects—at least as far as he was concerned. Added to that their uncaring manner when they'd encountered a neighbor's overturned coach, and they'd already earned a place at the top of his list.

At the moment everyone in and around Lewes was on his list of possible suspects, in fact. As for a motive, he hadn't yet determined that. When he did, he had the feeling that the other bits would fall into place.

"Phineas Bromley."

The feminine purr lifted the hairs on his arms, the same sensation he got just before he discovered an ambush. Imminent danger. He turned around. The tall, red-haired woman looked familiar. The generous curve of her breasts at her low neckline stirred definite memories, among other things, but for the life of him he couldn't recall her name.

She lifted a straight eyebrow. "I would be offended that you don't remember me, except for the fact that if I hadn't heard your name, I wouldn't have recognized you, either." Her green gaze drifted upward from his boots. "You were quite a boy. And you've definitely grown."

Her name, along with some rather heated memories, snapped into his mind. "Lady Marment."

Ruby lips curved into a smile. "Rebecca," she breathed.

Phineas nodded. "It's good to see you again. How have you been?"

"I'm much better now."

As he recalled, she was four or five years older than he was, the very bored wife of the bookish Earl Marment. They'd spent some interesting evenings in her downstairs sitting room while her husband slept just upstairs. "Lord Marment is well, I hope," he said aloud.

"You never used to care about that."

He forced a smile. "As you said, I've grown."

"I would like to hear more about th—"

The music for the evening's first waltz began. "Excuse me," he said, sketching a quick bow. "I'm engaged for this dance."

When he turned around he caught sight of Alyse. She stood a foot or two behind her aunt and was clearly looking about the large ballroom for him. The muscles across his shoulders, tight and wary since his dance with Lady Claudia had begun, relaxed a fraction. If there was one person in East Sussex he knew to be innocent of any offense against his family, it was Alyse Donnelly. He strode over to her.

"Shall we?" he asked, holding out his hand to her and touched by the abrupt relief in her eyes. Had she expected him not to appear?

"Yes," she said with a smile, gripping his fingers.

When they reached the polished dance floor he faced her, slid an arm about her slender waist, and stepped into the waltz with her. "How has your evening been?" he asked.

"Pleasant," she returned. "Aunt Ernesta is in a good mood."

"That's a rare thing, I assume?"

Alyse cleared her throat. "You have no idea."

"I have several commanding officers. I probably have a very good idea of the rarity and importance of a pleasant mood."

"I could argue that, but frankly I'm too happy to be waltzing."

He started to reply, then changed his mind. He'd been absorbed with unearthing clues, and she'd been hoping to dance. Somehow that seemed to speak better of her than of him. "Do you have more partners for tonight?" he asked, finding that while he wanted her to be able to dance, he would be at least as happy to be her sole knight in shining armor this evening.

"Yes. Richard and his friends are feeling charitable tonight."

"Is this a good thing, or should I make off with you?"

A laugh erupted from her chest. He liked the sound; it reminded him of summer . . . and innocence. And it made him want to kiss her again. He'd lost some of her trust with his questions, though. If he pressed her now, for kisses or for information, she would likely wash her hands of him entirely. And whatever else might happen, he didn't want that.

"I hardly think a kidnapping, friendly or not, would aid my cause, but thank you for the offer."

Unable to resist, he pulled her an inch or two closer. "You're welcome, Alyse."

She held his gaze for several surprisingly hard beats of his heart, then visibly shook herself. "Lord Anthony said that when he saw you riding up the road this morning through the fog, he thought you were the ghost of The Gentleman."

Phineas snorted despite the internal jolt to his gut. He needed to tread carefully here. "I think I was more mud-splattered than dashing." For a moment he put aside the thought that she knew Anthony Ellerby well enough that they chatted—even when she claimed that almost no one spoke with her. "And he's accused me of being a damned lawbreaking Frenchie."

She hesitated. "He probably forgot that you've spent the past ten years fighting Bonaparte and the French."

Still she hadn't mentioned her encounter with the masked Frenchman. "Yes, well, in all fairness I wasn't in uniform this morning." He took a breath, praying that he hadn't already pushed her too far. "I missed you, Alyse."

"I'll wager you barely gave me a thought between the day you left and the day you returned."

"I did, but that's not what I mean."

"Then what do you mean, Phin?"

He frowned. "That I missed you."

Her soft lips pursed. "Is this how you defeat the French? By attacking in such a nonsensical manner that they become dizzy and fall down?"

She still showed flashes of that keen wit and fierce spirit he'd enjoyed when they'd been children together. Even with a brother seven years older than himself, he'd still found her at two years his junior to be his most fearless companion and friend. And it could have been more, if he hadn't destroyed everything and fled.

He smiled at her. "The cynicism's new, isn't it?"

"It's a lesson well learned, Phin. Which is why you make me nervous."

He tugged her still closer, aware both that the waltz would end any moment and that he didn't want to release her back into the callous, judgmental crowd. "*I* make you nervous?" he murmured. "Why?"

"Because I know you're trouble, and I still want you to kiss me again."

Phineas nearly missed a step and took them both to the floor. So much for a career begun as a blackguard and followed by ten years of battle-tried soldiering. "I neglected to add forthright to your attributes," he drawled quietly.

"Did I frighten you just then?" she murmured.

"A little."

"Good. Then you know how *I* feel."

The music crashed to a close, and they both joined in the applause. Still obviously amused at herself, Alyse wrapped her fingers around his arm as they made their way back to her aunt.

Behind Mrs. Donnelly, her son shook hands with Lord Charles Smythe. A second later, Smythe slipped something into his coat pocket. In itself it was nothing, but Phineas had become very good at deciphering people—his life had frequently depended on it. From the swift glance Smythe sent around him, he was nervous. And Phineas abruptly wanted a look at what the fellow had in his pocket.

Whether he'd burned his bridges or not, if his family needed protection, he would give his life to do it. And it seemed he had his quarry for the evening sighted.

Ellerby, Smythe, and Donnelly were all approximately the same age, and while Richard had only become a viscount by luck, he was still of aristocratic stock. They might very well have attended school together, and Alyse had called them cronies. That wasn't a surprise, but it did raise a question: If Ellerby or Smythe or both were maliciously vandalizing Quence, did Donnelly know about it?

No, that made no sense. Donnelly had been spending a great deal of his time and energy helping repair the various mishaps that had befallen Quence. In fact, the other men's friendship with Richard made their involvement in this mess less likely.

If he could discover what it was that Lord Charles had put into his pocket, he would know why the fellow had been uneasy. He might even be able to rule him out as a suspect. Or in as one.

"You look very serious, Phin," Beth commented as she strolled up with Lord Donnelly.

"Do I? I'm trying to remember the steps for the next quadrille," he improvised.

"I know for a fact that you attended a great many soirees on the Continent," she returned, "because you wrote and told me so."

"There weren't exactly a great many. You shouldn't believe everything I write, Magpie."

"Of course I believe everything you write," she retorted. "Though I could tell there were things you left out. The worst things, I think." She wrapped both hands around his arm. "I'm going to be tired and need to leave now," she whispered, "because William will never admit when he's fatigued. You should return home with us."

Clenching his jaw, he nodded. He could at least see them home, no matter how badly he wanted to do more investigating. "Of course."

From the well-rehearsed way Beth claimed fatigue and William agreed to see her home, Phineas could see they'd done this countless times before, probably at countless events. Had Elizabeth ever been able to stay for the end of an opera or a soiree?

"Stay if you wish, Phin," William said as Andrews settled him on the curricle seat. "You seem to have partners aplenty."

Phineas swung up on Saffron. They didn't all fit on the curricle, but he could at least look as though he were performing his brotherly duties. "Always leave them wanting more," he drawled. "That's my motto."

When they'd returned to Quence he handed Saffron off to the new stableboy and untied William's chair from the rear of the carriage while Andrews lifted him down from his perch and up the front steps.

"Welcome home, my lord," Digby wheezed, pulling open the front door for them.

"Thank you, Digby."

"I'm a bit fatigued, myself," Phineas commented, heading through the foyer for the stairs. "Good night, all."

"Good night," Beth called after him, her voice a touch wistful.

He would have to forgo a game of cards or chess with her; as clearly as he wanted to see her happy, keeping her safe was more important. He found Gordon waiting for him in his bedchamber and swiftly shrugged into his old breeches, retied his cravat, and then pulled on his military greatcoat. The mask waited in his pocket. "Ready?"

Gordon pulled an old tricorne low over his eyes and handed over the similar hat Phineas had uncovered in the attic. "Aye."

They slipped down the back stairs and around the house to the stable. Once the horses were saddled, he swung up on Ajax. "Good lad," he murmured, patting the stallion on the neck. "Let's see how you run." He jammed the ancient tricorne hat onto his head. Then, ducking as he passed through the stable doors, Gordon and Gallant on his heels, he kneed the big black.

They were off like the wind. This was more like it. With barely a tug on the reins they went pounding down the main road at a full gallop. Phineas leaned down along the black's neck, barely catching his hat before it blew backward off his head.

He laughed, and Ajax's ears flicked back at him. For a long moment he was tempted just to keep riding, to run until he'd put anything resembling trouble and a past far behind him.

"Bloody 'ell, Colonel, slow up a bit!" drifted up from well behind him.

He might be able to outrun trouble, but he had little doubt that Sergeant Thaddeus Gordon would sooner or later track him down. With a sigh he slowed to a trot.

"I always said you was hell on horseback, Colonel," Gordon panted as he drew even. "And if that's so, and I say it is, that horse there must be fire'n brimstone."

Several vehicles passed by them as they waited in the shadows. Then another coach rounded the turn toward them, the yellow crest on its side showing faintly in the moonlight. Beaumont's. "There it is," he hissed, turning up the collar of his greatcoat and tying the mask across his eyes. "Remember, speak only French."

"I never thought I'd die banded a Frog," the sergeant muttered.

Phineas pulled his pistol from his pocket. Stories about The Gentleman were rampant locally, and had clearly been on Lord Anthony's mind this morning. And a highwayman wouldn't have to show restraint toward Quence's neighbors. *Let the games begin.*

Chapter 10 _____

Lord Anthony shifted his hip closer against Alyse's, and she just as carefully moved away, or as far as she could do so, on the crowded coach seat.

"Stop smothering me, Alyse," Aunt Ernesta complained.

"I apologize for the confined conditions," Lord Anthony said easily, not giving back an inch of the space he'd taken over.

"Nonsense," her aunt returned. "It was very generous of you to offer us a ride home."

"And it was equally generous of you to offer your coach to Lord and Lady Bagston," Lady Claudia, seated between Lord Donnelly and Lord Charles, said as she placed a hand on Richard's knee. "I can't imagine what might have befallen them if they'd allowed their coachman to drive them home."

"The man was nearly too drunk to find the ground,"
Lord Charles commented. "I imagine when he sobers
up he'll be quite annoyed to discover that he's lost his
employm—"

A shot rang out, thunderously loud in the quiet evening.

"Stand and deliver!"

Claudia shrieked. Richard might also have screamed,
but with the crowded coach lurching and sliding to a
halt and everyone bumping into one another, Alyse
couldn't be certain, because her own heart had stopped
beating altogether. It *couldn't* be the masked Frenchman, though. It couldn't be.

"Sortez de la voiture!" a deep voice shouted. *"Ouvrez la porte!"*

"Good God, it's The Gentleman," Lord Anthony
gasped, paling. "I should never have mentioned his
name."

"Nonsense," Lord Charles snapped. "Ghosts don't
have pistols."

"What's he yelling about?" Richard muttered, peer-
ing through the curtained window. "There are two of
them."

"Sortez vite!"

"Oh, dear, does anyone know what he wants?" Aunt
Ernesta quavered.

"It's French. I only speak Greek," Anthony supplied.

It *was* the Frenchman. Despite being both mortified
and frightened half out of her wits, Alyse had the abrupt
urge to laugh. As high and mighty as her companions
considered themselves, they couldn't communicate
with a French highwayman. "I think he wants us to get
out," she offered aloud.

"I am not about to step out there and get shot," Richard hissed. "You do what you like, Alyse."

The door wrenched open. *"Sortez!"*

This must have been the second fellow—his voice wasn't as commanding as the first. As he motioned with his pistol, not even her French-impaired fellows could mistake his meaning.

One by one they squeezed out of the coach. Alyse looked up—and up—to see the first highwayman. He sat on that monstrous black horse, his greatcoat collar turned up again, the dashing, old-fashioned tricorne hat pulled down and a mask across his eyes so that she could only make out shadowy, glittering slits. There was no mistaking the straight, steady arm with the cocked pistol pointed at the coachman, though. It was the same fellow. And he knew what he was doing.

For a bare moment the shadowed eyes seemed to bore straight through her. Alyse shivered.

"Videz votres poches."

"Alyse, what's he saying?" Lady Claudia whispered.

"Apologies, my good man," Richard said in an overly loud voice, "but we don't speak your language."

She thought she heard a very quiet, very bad French curse. "Open your pockets," he said, in heavily accented English. *"Vite.* Now. Quickly."

"You'll never get away with this, you brigand." Lord Charles began pulling his snuffbox and pocket watch and handkerchief and an ivory-toothed comb from his pockets.

"Mon ami, the saddlebag," the Frenchman said.

The other fellow hurried up to him, and he handed down a worn leather pouch with his free hand. The beast stood motionless beneath him, apparently guided only by his rider's heels. With the faint moonlight behind him, he looked . . . stunning. Legendary, even.

"*Vite*," the other fellow said, stopping in front of Lord Anthony and shaking the bag at him.

"You damned Frogs," Richard snarled, dumping his pocket watch and a handful of coins into the bag when it stopped in front of him. "We'll have the army down on you for this. I hope you fancy getting your necks stretched."

The rider dismounted in one fluid motion, the pistol swiveling until it pointed squarely at Richard. Alyse held her breath as with long, booted strides, his coattails flapping out behind him, the highwayman closed the distance to her cousin. "How to protect the ladies when you are dead, monsieur?"

"Oh, heavens," Aunt Ernesta gasped. "They mean to ravage us!"

The highwayman made a dismissive sound. "*You* are safe, madame." He angled his face toward Lady Claudia. "Your necklace, mademoiselle. And the . . . *boucles d'oreille*."

"The what?" Claudia asked shakily, unfastening her necklace and half-tossing it into the bag.

"Your earbobs," Alyse translated.

The shadowed face turned to her again. "*Parlez vous français?*"

He didn't intend to give away the fact that they'd already met. Thank goodness. "*Oui.*"

"Then I take your baubles, myself." Pocketing the pistol, he took her hand in his gloved fingers, drawing her closer and then turning her to face away from him. His fingers at the nape of her neck made her shiver again.

"*S'il vous plaît, monsieur*," she said quietly, "*c'est de ma mère. C'est precieux à moi.*" The pearl necklace was one of the few things of her mother's she'd managed to keep.

"Then I shall keep it close to my heart, *ma chère.*" He turned her around again. Gently brushing her hair aside, he removed her matching earbobs one by one and pocketed them. "*Merci, mademoiselle.*" He took her hand, bowing to gently kiss her knuckles. Alyse swallowed hard.

"That is enough, sir."

The pistol reappeared, this time aimed at Lord Anthony. "Turn your pockets. All of you."

That produced various notes and coins and another two pounds from Richard, everything going into the bag. Finally the highwayman motioned, and his companion shouldered the bag and climbed up onto a sturdy bay. The Frenchman backed away until he reached his mount. In another graceful move he swung into the saddle, the pistol never wavering from its target.

He touched the brim of his hat in a mock salute. "*Merci*, ladies and gentlemen. *Bon soir.*" With that he nudged the black in the ribs and they vanished into the night, the bay pounding behind him.

"Oh, my," Aunt Ernesta breathed, and fainted dead away.

"So th' high'n mighty hereabouts don't speak French, eh? That was a bit of a surprise."

"They're too busy hunting and dancing, evidently."

"Th' next time we rob a coach, could ye let me know in enough time so I can at least have a loaded pistol?" Gordon handed the spent one back over.

Phineas pocketed it, his fingers curling around Alyse's pearl necklace as he did so. "You should have brought one," he returned, pulling his gloves off with his teeth and then holding out his hand again for the saddlebag. With Ajax at a walk beneath him, he dug through the contents. They'd recovered three notes. One of them had to be the missive Lord Charles had stuffed into his coat.

"So are we rich beyond imaginin', now?"

"What? Oh." Pocketing the notes and tying down the flap, he tossed the bag back to the sergeant. "Spread the blunt about, and do what you want with the rest. Just be cautious about it," he said.

"So this was all about those letters?"

"One of them. Hopefully."

"Well, this's been a fine evenin', anyway. What of the pearls?"

"I'll take care of those. Gordon, make certain Warner and the new boy Tom understand that we're helping my family, and that Ajax is not to leave the stable during the day for any reason. He's difficult to mistake."

"Oh, aye."

They rode in silence for a long moment, crossing the bridge back onto Quence property. Taking the long way around made sense, and Phineas hoped it was precaution enough.

"Colonel?"

"Yes?"

"Ye know I'd follow ye straight through th' gates o' hell itself, but what exactly did we accomplish?"

"I'm trying to find a vandal. As soon as I know more, I'll tell you." He paused, looking over at Gordon. "And thank you, Sergeant. You're a good man."

"Fer a French highwayman."

"For anything."

The Scotsman blushed. "Thank ye, sir."

Once they'd returned to Quence he led Ajax into the stable himself, and gave the fellow an apple. When this was finished he'd have to send the black back to Sullivan or risk being discovered as a highwayman, but he hoped the escapade would be worth the loss of a very fine animal.

Digby seemed to have retired for the evening, so Phineas let himself into the house. He quietly climbed the stairs and closed himself into his bedchamber. Once he was assured of some privacy, he dumped the pair of pistols onto the bed, then pulled Alyse's pearls from his pocket.

"Damnation," he said quietly, studying them in the candlelight as they lay across his palm.

He'd wanted Smythe's paper. If he'd had any idea before he stopped the coach that Alyse and the other Donnellys would be inside . . . He probably would have robbed it, anyway. It didn't make sense to delude himself on that count, whether he wanted to be a kinder man than he was or not.

Once this was resolved he would see that her mother's jewelry was returned to her. Until then, he would do as he'd promised and keep her things safe. Going to his trunk, he opened it and pressed the knot on the inside of the lid. A loosened panel slid aside, and he carefully slipped the pearls inside to rest beside his three medals for bravery and the letter of commendation he'd received from Wellington himself.

He closed it up again, and only then pulled from his pocket the three pieces of paper he'd liberated. Shrugging out of his greatcoat, he flung it over a chair and sank down in the opposite seat before the fire dying in the hearth. Settling in, he opened the first missive.

It was an invoice from the same tailor he'd used.

Apparently Lord Anthony had expensive taste. With a frown he leaned forward and tossed it into the fire-place. He had no intention of hanging over a clothing bill.

The second missive was larger, and made of very thin rice paper. As he unfolded it, turning it this way and that, Phineas abruptly realized that the haphazard lines and dots on the paper were a map. Or rather, they were meant to be overlaid on a map. The question was, what map? And what would he see if and when he matched them together?

Setting it aside for the moment, he opened the third folded paper and snorted. Lord Donnelly fancied him-self a poet. And apparently "Elizabeth" was meant to rhyme with "fine, turned earth," for her eyes. Well, the viscount was going to have to begin this effort over again. It followed the invoice into the fire.

He examined the marked paper again. No words had been written on it, so he couldn't tell whether he was looking at a single garden or an entire county. It was rural, but even that was more of a feeling than a logical conclusion. Several circles seemed to mark areas of importance, while one small *X* looked very piratical.

Well, he'd wanted a clue, and this certainly felt like one. A clue to what, though, he had no idea. Asking, especially after the way he'd acquired it, was out of the question. Ajax would have to stay on at Quence for a while longer.

He sat back, staring into the fire. He'd managed to abuse his friendship with Alyse and caused her to mis-trust him, but he could still do something kind for her. Or rather, The Gentleman could.

Before he could regain his sense of logic, Phineas pulled his greatcoat and mask and hat back on, pocketed the pearls he'd hidden away, and crept back out-side to the stables. Warner and young Tom had both turned in for the night, and he swiftly saddled Ajax himself.

Avoiding the main road in favor of the pastures, he made his way to Donnelly House. The windows were dark, so however upset Donnelly had been by the rob-bery, he appeared to be managing a night's sleep. He remembered where Alyse's bedchamber had been, and stopped Ajax beneath the small stand of trees to the west of the house to go the last few yards on foot.

Swiftly he climbed the trellis, leaned out, and pulled open the window with his fingertips. He'd never snuck into Donnelly House before, since in the past he'd al-ways been welcomed there. Things had changed, and not just because he was currently disguised as a dead highwayman.

Putting one boot on the windowsill, he shifted his weight and then silently stepped inside. As he pushed through the closed curtains, it occurred to him that he didn't know what to say to her. Over the past ten years he'd become accustomed to the idea of deception; it was a necessary part of war. But deceiving Alyse, especially when she'd been deceived by a man before—one who'd promised to marry her, yet—felt wrong.

And still he stood there, in her bedchamber, in the costume of a highwayman. Of course, after tonight he supposed that he *was* a highwayman. Leaving the cur-tains parted just enough to let in a sliver of moonlight, he moved silently closer to the bed. She stirred, turning onto her back—and let out an indelicate snore.

With a silent curse, Phineas backed away a step. Her damned aunt. Fighting the urge to cast up his accounts, he moved quickly and quietly to the door and slipped out to the hallway. Christ. That had fairly much frightened any thoughts of romance out of him.

If Alyse wasn't in her old bedchamber, then where was she? As her aunt's companion she was likely within easy earshot, but the rooms on either side of Mrs. Donnelly's quarters were empty. Likewise the one across the hallway seemed to have become an auxiliary wardrobe of dowdy clothes.

He turned a slow circle in the dark. Now that he was here, he was damned well going to see her. Hm. Her governess had used to room on the third floor across from the storage attic. Taking a breath, he climbed the back stairs to the top floor of Donnelly House.

The door was latched, but the hinges were so loose that all he had to do was lift up on the door and push. She'd left the curtains in the small window open, and he could clearly see her curled up on the narrow bed. Phin clenched his jaw. The diamond of East Sussex, and her own family kept her locked up in the attic room. Well, not locked up, but expected to stay there.

For a long moment he simply gazed at her, at her hand curled beneath her cheek and her long chestnut hair half covering her face. Good God, she was lovely. Just looking at her left him feeling protective, possessive, and filled with longing for something that might have been. Perhaps still could be, if he didn't get himself hanged or completely disowned by his family.

"Monsieur?" she whispered, her dark eyes opening wide. She sat up, clutching her blankets to her chest.

He shook himself. How could he do this without lying to her? *"Je regrette,"* he apologized in a murmur, and withdrew the pearls from his pocket, holding them out to her. *"Pour un baisser."*

She reached out, then pulled her hand back again. "You'll give me back my pearls in exchange for a kiss? And that's all you want?"

Phin nodded. "*Oui.*"

"A bit of honor from a *voleur de grand chemin*?" she whispered, her cheeks darkening.

"*Un peu,*" he agreed. A very little bit of honor from a highwayman.

Alyse took a breath, then nodded. "Very well. For the pearls."

His heart hammering, Phin sat on the edge of her bed. Gently he tilted up her chin with his gloved fingers, and touched his mouth to hers. They'd kissed before, but he'd never been able to take his time, to know the softness of her mouth, to feel the passion she held deep within her. He did so now, advancing, retreating, deepening the kiss until she moaned.

He wanted all of her. Whoever he was pretending to be at the moment, though, he'd given his word that he wouldn't make more trouble for her. He was already treading a very narrow road. The old Phin, before he'd joined the army, wouldn't have realized there was even a road to cross. He'd thought only of himself. Now all he could think of was Alyse.

Regretfully he pulled back, stroking his fingers along her cheek. "*Merci, mademoiselle,*" he murmured, turning her hand to place the pearls into her palm. "*Votre bassier est bien valoir son prix.*" Yes, her kiss had definitely been worth the price. And more.

He stood again, taking a rose from the bouquet beneath the window, and placed it across her lap. "*Merci,*" she whispered.

Phin nodded, opening her door to slip out back into the black hallway. "*De rien.*"

It wasn't nothing, though. He doubted he would ever be the same again. And for tonight, at least, he welcomed the change.

"Good morning," William greeted as he rolled into the breakfast room, Andrews as usual behind him.

Phineas deliberately finished chewing his bite of ham and eggs. "Good morning."

"I trust everything is well? Andrews tells me he saw your valet head out to the stables last night."

Mentally crossing his fingers, Phineas put a grin on his face and nodded. "Gordon wanted to try a new pair of dice. He won five quid off Warner."

"He gambled out in the stables," his older brother said quietly, no trace of emotion in his voice. "Your servant."

"I wanted to join them, but I drank a bit too much port at the soiree."

"I see. Andrews, Digby, excuse us for a m—"

"Good morning, my sweet brothers," Beth sang, twirling into the room, her ginger curls bouncing. She kissed William and then pirouetted around the table to give Phineas a sound hug from behind.

William smiled. "You're chirping quite merrily this morning, Magpie."

"Why shouldn't I be?" she returned, going over to the sideboard to select her breakfast. "It is a very lovely morning, and I'm going riding with a very handsome man who's promised me a very pretty poem."

Phineas had his doubts about that. About the poem bit, anyway. "That sounds very nice."

His sister laughed. "And what are your plans for today?"

"I thought I might go into Lewes and visit one or two

of the taverns William suggested the other day." Or
visit the surveyor's office to take a look at some local
maps and compare them with the puzzle he'd acquired.

The tavern nonsense was another black mark against
his character, but if he admitted that he was still stepping into the middle of Quence business against William's wishes, he would probably be asked to leave.
While he wasn't certain whether being directly disowned was better or worse than the disappointed look
in Beth's eyes and the . . . nothing coming from William, being banished wouldn't serve his purpose. Not
yet. And not after last night.

"Perhaps you'd care to go riding with Richard and
me," Beth suggested, her happy expression fading.

"No worries," he said breezily. "I'll amuse myself. Do
you think Lady Marment might be seeing callers?"

A knife clattered onto William's plate. "May I have a
word in private with you, Phin?" he grated.

"I've no wish to have my ear chewed off," Phineas
returned. "You told me to mind my own affairs, William, and so I am."

Elizabeth opened and closed her mouth. "But—"

"What did you think, Beth, that I would gallop back
to Quence and set everything to rights again?" Finishing off his tea, he pushed away from the table and
stood. "If you'll recall, I'm the one who set everything
wrong in the first place. Excuse me."

He took the stairs two at a time. Inside his bedchamber again, he leaned back against the door and took a
deep breath. Ten years ago that had been who he
was—angry, defiant, and without an ounce of subtlety.
If he needed to appear to be that hellion again in order
to stay near his family while he discovered what the

devil was going on, then so be it. But he didn't have to like it. Not one damned bit.

No one was surprised, of course; as far as his siblings were likely concerned, he'd never stopped being that foolish boy. Shaking himself, he grabbed up his great-coat, choosing to leave the military one for whatever late-night activities might still be required.

As he headed downstairs again, he paused. He'd intended to go straight out to the stables for Saffron and then into Lewes. From the raised, excited voices in the breakfast room, though, they had a visitor. One who'd apparently been robbed. Steeling his expression to one of reluctant curiosity and hoping that Alyse had come along as well, he pulled open the breakfast room door.

". . . bloody Frenchman made off with my poem!" Richard, Lord Donnelly, was exclaiming, his color high.

"A Frenchman stole your poem?" Phineas broke in, furrowing his brow. No Alyse. "The very fine one you promised to Beth?"

"Phin," she muttered, blushing.

The viscount faced him. "The very same."

"Begging your pardon, but I have it on good authority that we're at war with France. Where were you, that a Frenchman could steal anything?"

"You missed the first part of the conversation," William said, his own face pale.

Bloody wonderful, Phin. Kill your own brother. Finish the job, rather. "Clearly," he said aloud. "What's going on?"

"A highwayman held up the Beaumont coach last night," Beth supplied.

"Two highwaymen. Both of them Frogs."

"And they took your poem."

"For God's sake, Bromley, keep up, will you?" Donnelly snapped. "You're the officer here. You should be out protecting us from the damned French roaming the countryside."

Splendid. If everything continued with its usual irony, he could well end up chasing himself across East Sussex. "Perhaps you should begin the tale over again," he suggested.

"I don't have time for that," the viscount returned. "I only came to warn William and to beg Beth's pardon for not taking her riding this morning. I'm on my way to the constabulary." With that he bent over Beth's hand, nodded at William, and brushed past Phineas into the hallway, Digby on his heels.

The three siblings looked at one another. *Say something*, Phineas ordered himself. "Perhaps The Gentleman's more spry than we thought," he offered.

"We haven't had a coach robbery for a dozen years," William replied. "Obviously someone is using the local legend to their benefit."

"No doubt." Phineas shrugged into his greatcoat. "Did Donnelly say anything else?"

"He said the leader rode a huge black stallion and that he made everyone empty their pockets. He even took Claudia and Alyse's jewelry. The only one he left alone was Mrs. Donnelly."

Phineas looked at his sister. "He took Alyse's jewelry?" he repeated, allowing a little of the anger he had felt at himself to seep into his voice.

"Just be thankful no one was shot," William said.

"Two Frenchmen shouldn't be difficult for the constabulary to find, should they?" Beth asked.

"No, they shouldn't," William agreed. "In the meantime, however, you are not going anywhere without an armed escort, Magpie." He turned his head to eye Phineas. "And you shouldn't, either."

"I've been killing Frenchmen for ten years," Phineas commented. "I believe I can manage two of them." He saluted his siblings. "It might even be a bit of fun to see if I can hunt them down."

"Leave that to the authorities," his brother said sharply.

"You've given me nothing else to do here."

"I would rather you go do whatever it was you had in mind before you heard about this."

Phineas lifted an eyebrow. "Is that an order, Lord Quence?"

"It's a damned suggestion."

This was going well. Now, in addition to Quence's land troubles, William had a highwayman and an errant brother to worry over. Phineas went out to the stables for Saffron. The hole he was digging was so deep now that he'd never be able to climb out of it if he fell in.

Chapter 11 _____

"Thank you, Jones," Alyse said, stepping down from Richard's barouche. "We'll be back in a moment."

The driver doffed his hat. "No hurry, miss."

With Mary behind her, Alyse entered Daisy Duvall's Dress Shop to retrieve the two new gowns for her aunt. Ernesta had intended to supervise the errand herself, but the encounter with the highwayman last night had overset her. Whether that was because of the pistols and threats or because the dashing fellow hadn't troubled to take her jewelry Alyse didn't know, but she had her suspicions.

Richard, despite his anger at being robbed of six pounds, a watch, and a poem, didn't seem overly concerned over anyone's safety. He certainly hadn't objected to his female cousin going out in an open coach with only a maid and an old groom for company.

As for her, she didn't know what to think. For heaven's sake, she'd kissed a highwayman—a man whose name she didn't know, and whose face she'd never seen. A responsible member of the household would have screamed for assistance and fled upon seeing him. True, she didn't feel much loyalty to her cousin or her aunt, but that didn't quite explain it. It wasn't even that she found a robber . . . irresistible, though she did like the sound of his voice. She could think of no one who lived more freely than a highwayman. And in kissing him, she'd felt it, too. A spark of fire. A spark of life. And she liked it.

The story of the robbery was already spreading through Lewes, and she had to recount it twice just in the dress shop. The half dozen ladies present had already come to the conclusion that The Frenchman, as he'd been dubbed, unless he was the ghost of The Gentleman, must be a disenfranchised French nobleman who'd barely escaped Bonaparte and was now trying to gather enough funds to purchase back his lands and title.

"You never said all of that," Mary whispered from behind a stack of hatboxes as they left the shop.

Alyse hefted the heavy dresses draped across her arms. "I didn't know any of it," she returned. "They've made that all up among themselves." It did sound very attractive, though.

"But—"

"Miss Donnelly."

Alyse turned around as Phin Bromley hopped down from his horse. Her lips twitched with a smile she couldn't help. "That is a yellow horse."

He grinned. "You've admired him before."

"Yes, but I thought I must have been dreaming."

Phin patted the horse on the withers before he left the animal to approach. "Poor Saffron. He's too exquisite to be believed."

"Too vivid, you mean."

Without asking, he took the gowns from her arms and led the way to Richard's barouche. "Donnelly came by this morning," he commented, setting the dresses across one seat. "Are you well?"

"Yes. I'm fine. It was quite exciting, actually."

He faced her. "He took your jewelry."

The serious, concerned expression on his lean face surprised her. She hesitated. In a day or two, though, she could say she'd found the necklace abandoned in the garden or something. "I will miss Mama's pearls," she said, "but I'm glad no one was hurt."

"I doubt your fellow passengers reacted as charitably."

Alyse covered a brief smile. "No, they didn't."

Phin held out his arm. "Do you have time for a cup of tea and a biscuit?"

She shouldn't. Aunt Ernesta would be angry if she didn't return immediately, and by way of punishment she would probably end with another basket of mending to do this evening. But Phin was the only person she'd encountered who'd asked about *her* losses. And the highwayman wasn't the only man she'd kissed lately. Oh, for goodness' sake. People wrote morality plays about women like her. She couldn't even honestly say that Phin was any safer than The Frenchman. Just the opposite, more likely.

Alyse wrapped her fingers around his gray sleeve. "I have a few minutes," she said.

"Good," he said, as they crossed the narrow street to the corner bakery. "What did this fellow take from everyone?"

"He had the men turn out their pockets, and he took Lady Claudia's jewelry as well. A few pocket watches and twenty or so pounds."

Phin opened the door for her, then pulled out a chair at one of the dozen tables in the small open area at the front of the shop. "Donnelly said they were French," he commented, taking the seat opposite her and signaling for tea and biscuits to be brought to their table. "In fact, he seemed to think it was my fault for allowing a Frog into Britain."

She snorted. "From the way he and Lord Charles were ranting, it almost seemed as though Bonaparte himself had fired on us." His hazel gaze met hers, and her breath stilled. "I'm glad you weren't there," she said quietly.

He lifted his scarred right eyebrow. "And why, pray tell, is that?"

"Because you wouldn't have been content with cursing at the Frenchman after he disappeared. You would have fought him, and then he would have killed you." The thought chilled her to her bones.

"Doubtful," he said dryly.

"Don't scoff. I know you're a trained officer, but he seemed very deadly." And very enticing, though surprisingly not as much so as Phin. She stopped talking as a girl brought a teapot and cups, along with a plate of warm biscuits, to the table. Once they were alone again, she sat forward. "What I don't understand," she said in a low voice, "is why a man whose country is at war with ours would risk notice by robbing English noblemen on their own soil, and for such a small reward."

"Perhaps he was anticipating a greater reward," Phin suggested, biting into a biscuit.

"Two dozen coaches left the assembly within an

hour," she countered. "I'm just thinking aloud, but it seems to me that he and his friend could have made off with a great deal more if they'd wanted to."

Phin brushed the back of her hand with one finger. "I'm just glad you're unhurt," he murmured.

A pleasant shiver traveled down her spine. "I might be more inclined to believe your . . . attentions if you hadn't vanished without a word for ten years."

He looked her straight in the eye. "I didn't leave because of you."

"You didn't come back because of me, either."

"You know, every time I say something decent to you, you needn't throw it back in my face."

Did she do that? "Perhaps it's because I witnessed you slipping away during house parties on innumerable occasions, and always in the company of an older and generally married woman. I'm neither."

"That was ten years ago, Alyse. For God's sake."

"Yes, but since your return you've kissed me twice."

He frowned. "And why shouldn't I have? You're . . . remarkable. Body and soul."

Alyse fought her blush. "Thank you, but I'd feel less troubled if you had fewer ladies of your acquaintance with whom to compare me."

"Fine." Phin pushed away from the table and stood. "You don't trust me. Join the vast herd of those who never forget and never forgive." He tossed several coins onto the table, more than enough to pay the baker. "But I have never said, or thought, one unkind thing about you. Ever."

She watched as he left the bakery and crossed the street again. With one unreadable look back at her, he swung onto his yellow horse and trotted down the street. "Oh, bother," she muttered.

If he still wanted something from her, she didn't know what it might be. If he didn't, if he was seeking her out solely because he wanted to—could she let herself believe that? And what would it mean? He was on leave from the army, and clearly already spending his days away from his family. He would go away soon enough, back to the Peninsula. And then she'd be alone once more. The Frenchman kissed well enough, but he simply wasn't Phin Bromley. The Frenchman's life expectancy was even shorter than her old friend's.

"What do you want, Phin?" she murmured under her breath. He probably wouldn't answer even if he could. As for what *she* wanted, that question was becoming more complicated by the moment.

That had been close. Alyse Donnelly had a sharp mind and a keen sense of logic. And while distracting her from her line of thought had been necessary, turning their conversation into an attempted—and failed— flirtation had not been. No, that had been . . . stupid. All he needed was to enter into a competition against himself for Alyse's affections.

"Muggins," Phineas muttered.

In his defense, the moment he set eyes on her, he wanted to be close to her. It was becoming an obsession. He wanted Alyse. And his . . . lust was beginning to interfere with the business of discovering who was vandalizing the property and putting a stop to it. Hell, he was risking his disguise just by kissing her.

He left Saffron around the corner from the surveyor's office. It would have been helpful to at least know the name of the man in charge of the county's property tax assessments, but he couldn't very well ask anyone for an introduction. William and Beth couldn't know what he was up to, and he didn't trust anyone else. Except for Alyse, that was.

"Hello?" he called, pushing open the door.

The office was lined with books and maps, while the floor was covered by barely visible tables which in turn were sagging with the weight of still more rolled maps. Phineas sneezed.

No one appeared. It took less than a minute to peer into the corners and make certain no one had been buried in the rubble. If the office were well-organized he would have considered some time alone in there a bounty. As it was, he would be lucky if *he* didn't end up smothered beneath the chaotic stacks.

Shrugging out of his greatcoat and his jacket, he rolled up his sleeves and dove into the closest stack of rolled maps.

If his suspicions were correct, Smythe's overlay had something to do with the area around Lewes, and more specifically with Quence Park. The problem, though, was scale. An exact match would be nearly impossible, but the surveyor's selection of maps seemed his best chance.

Of course, first he needed to find a map that covered Quence. Thankfully over the years he'd spent a great deal of time perusing various terrain maps and battle schematics, and he eliminated an entire table in short order. That only left another two hundred or so rolls of maps before he even got to the back room.

The door rattled and opened. Phineas pasted a bewildered smile on his face and turned around. "Thank God. Please tell me this is your office."

A tall, white-haired man, a pair of spectacles pinching the bridge of his nose, squinted at him. "This is my office," he returned raspily. "Who are you, pray tell?"

Phineas picked his way over and stuck out his hand. "Phin Bromley. And you are?"

"Artemis Spyres." They shook hands. "Bromley. Quence Park?"

"The very same, Mr. Spyres. Can you assist me?"

"That depends, sir. I'm the only one what should be putting my hands on the maps. It's for the government, you know. All very precise."

Ah, a bureaucrat. Easy to spot, and easier still to work with, if one knew how to encourage them properly. "Splendid," Phineas said aloud. "We're having some difficulties replacing our irrigation dams," he continued. "My brother the viscount disagrees, but *I* thought that you would have the most accurate maps we're likely to find anywhere."

Mr. Spyres squared his shoulders. "I should say I do, or I haven't been doing my work. Now let's see what we can see."

Over the next two hours they found six maps of Quence—one of all East Sussex, one of the area north of Lewes, one of the land bordering the River Ouse, two featuring Donnelly, Beaumont, Quence, and Roesglen, and finally one solely showing the Bromley family estate. With an assessing glance at Spyres, Phineas went over to his jacket and pulled the rice paper map overlay from his pocket.

"A friend sketched this for me," he said, unfolding it, "but I'm having the devil of a time trying to decipher what he was trying to tell me."

With a frown Mr. Spyres set it over the map, sliding it this way and that while Phineas clenched his fists to keep from interfering. "What scale was he using, your friend?"

"I haven't a clue."

"Well, I would guess that your friend's map wasn't of Quence Park. These lines here look like a road, and there's no lake or pond of that shape on the property." He gestured at another of the squiggles. "And unless you've put up a sheep barn or other walled structure—which would require an additional tax assessment—there's no outbuilding here."

Phineas looked at the overlay. "May I have a look?" When Spyres stepped back, he turned the rice parchment forty-five degrees. If he slid it a little to the north and west, there were bits that intersected with the actual map—a bridge, the old tumble of ruins in the south pasture, one corner of the river where it passed from Donnelly to Quence property. "What scale is this map?" he asked.

"One inch to a quarter mile," the surveyor said promptly.

This was not good. Low uneasiness ran through his gut. It was a feeling to which he'd long ago learned to pay attention. "Thank you, Mr. Spyres," he said easily, folding the overlay again and returning it to his pocket. "You've been a great deal of help."

"Glad to be of service, Mr. Bromley."

Shrugging back into his jacket and greatcoat, Phineas left the office. Saffron still stood where he'd been left. For appearance's sake he would have to go to one of the local taverns for luncheon, at least, though he would have paid a fair sum to avoid all of his old haunts. And then he needed to go take a look at the pasture where someone evidently thought there was or should be a road.

He'd barely sat down at the Caesar's Ghost for a mug of bitters when Gordon rushed inside. Spotting him, the sergeant hurried forward. "Thank Christ I've found ye, Colonel," he panted.

"What's happened?" Phineas asked sharply, his first thought going to William and his brother's uncertain health.

"It's dogs, sir. A dozen of 'em got into the west pasture and tore up the sheep somethin' awful."

Phineas dropped some coins on the table as he pushed to his feet. "Let's go."

In a moment they were galloping back down the road toward Quence. "Did you see the animals?" he asked.

"Aye. Mr. Bibble the shepherd came up th' road screamin', and me'n Warner rode straight back. Shot two of the curs meself, and th' rest tucked tail'n ran."

"How bad is it?"

Gordon worked his jaw. "Ye know how dogs'll work themselves into a blood frenzy, Colonel."

"How many sheep?" Phineas asked again.

"Nigh half th' flock, would be my guess."

Phineas cursed. Quence ran three flocks of Southdown sheep. This was the smallest of them. If Gordon's assessment was correct, and he had no reason to think otherwise, they'd just lost ten percent of their stock. Under good conditions Quence could weather the blow, but these were not good conditions.

As they rode up on the pasture, he slowed. Half a hundred white and red-splashed bodies lay scattered amid the soft green grass. At the far end of the pasture, among the trees, he could make out the remainder of the flock. Mr. Bibble stood in the middle of the carnage, openly weeping.

"Where are the dogs you shot?" Phineas grunted, his jaw clenched hard against the useless soldier's profanity he wanted to spew into the air.

"This way, Colonel."

Gordon led him over to one edge of the mess. As he

spied the two large brown bodies, Phineas kicked out of the stirrups and jumped to the ground. "Wolf-hounds," he said, squatting by the nearest and checking the insides of the beast's ears and then lifting its upper lip to peer at the red-stained gums.

"Anything?" the sergeant asked, walking up beside him.

Phineas straightened, wiping his hands on his trousers. "No, damn it all. No tattoos. No marks at all."

"Just a pack gone feral, ye think?"

"No. If twelve wolfhounds were running wild through here, we would have heard about it before this."

"Who would do this on purpose, then?"

"I damned well mean to find out, Sergeant."

It was late afternoon when he stepped back through the mansion's front door. "Digby," he said, gingerly handing over his greatcoat, "where's William?"

"Dear heavens," Beth gasped, hurrying down the stairs. "Phin, please tell me you're not hurt."

He pushed her away with one elbow before she could grab on to him. "It's not my blood," he grunted.

A tear ran down her cheek. "The sheep?"

Phineas nodded. "Where's William?" he repeated.

"Going over accounts," she returned, her voice still shaking. "Try not to upset him."

"I'll do my best."

Outside the office, Phineas paused. He looked liked he'd been on the losing side of a brawl, but neither did he want to wait until he'd washed and changed his clothes. Taking a breath, he rapped on the door.

"Come in."

He opened the door to find his brother surrounded by ledger books and almanacs. "William."

"Digby said that your Mr. Gordon went to find you," his brother said, looking up from his scribbling.

"He did." Digging into his pocket, Phineas pulled out thirty quid and set it on the desk. "Forty-seven sheep. We carted them into town and sold them to the butcher. They'll likely end up as feed for the same dogs that killed them."

"You found out to whom they belonged?"

"No ownership marks at all. But they were well fed and healthy-looking. I don't suppose anyone else has been bothered by packs of roving dogs?"

William looked at him for a moment, then shook his head. "Thank you for cleaning things up."

"Is that it? No anger, no frustration? Only 'thank you for toting my slaughtered sheep out of the pasture'?"

"What would you have me do, Phin? Scream and stomp my feet? Run away and join the army? It's done. Now we move forward."

"You move forward," Phineas murmured. William knew precisely how to strike the most painful blow. "I'm going to make certain the way remains clear." He turned on his heel.

"Phin!"

Keeping in mind that he'd been asked not to overset his brother, Phineas stopped his retreat. "I'll leave as soon as I'm finished here," he said, turning around again. "But I'm not going anywhere with things as they are."

"I apologize," his older brother said quietly. "I shouldn't have s—"

"No," Phineas cut in sharply. "Do not apologize to me. Ever."

Chapter 12 _____

"Oh, I detest foreign histories," Aunt Ernesta said, setting aside Richard's book on ancient Rome. She lifted her gaze to Alyse, trying to embroider over a hole in a handkerchief. "Fetch my knitting, Alyse."

Keeping her expression still, Alyse nodded and slipped down the hallway. No one had handed her any additional mending yesterday, but that still left her with several hours of work. She *had* had to listen to a twenty-minute lecture on timeliness and her high degree of selfishness for keeping her aunt waiting on her. Even with the way Phin had left, it had still been worth it. For a short time she'd been a pretty young lady in the company of a handsome gentleman interested only in her.

She descended the stairs and retrieved her aunt's

basket of yarn. On the way back down the hall she paused before the wide mirror there. This was her portrait now. Clothes clean but every day falling a little more behind the current fashion, light brown hair in the simple twisted bun she could manage without a maid's assistance and wisps of it already coming down, a load of items fetched on someone else's behalf in her arms.

She had thirty pounds put aside now. That would get her to London and into a rented house for a time, but it wasn't enough. She needed to be able to earn a living once she got there. Open a shop, perhaps. But that would take more funds, which would take more time. An unexpected tear ran down one cheek. Swiftly she wiped it away, but the basket tipped and three balls of yarn bounced onto the floor.

"Drat," she muttered, shifting the basket awkwardly beneath one arm and hurrying after the escaped yarn.

She scooped up the first ball and scrambled forward. All she needed was for her aunt to decide she was being defiant and lazy again. Because unpleasant as she found her present circumstances, they could always get worse.

". . . lost forty-seven, and made thirty quid," she heard from Richard's office. It sounded like Lord Charles, though she hadn't been aware that he'd come calling.

"That was quick thinking, really," Richard returned. "Hold a moment."

The door opened directly in front of her. Alyse straightened, nearly dropping the yarn basket. "Richard," she squeaked. "You startled me."

He squatted to retrieve the other two balls of yarn. "Apologies," he said, straightening again to hand them to her. Pale blue eyes regarded her for a moment. "You should get that to my mother," he continued.

"Yes. Yes, I shall. Thank you." With a quick, forced smile Alyse headed for the stairs and hurried back up to the sitting room.

Low uneasiness ran through her as she delivered the yarn and then went up to her bedchamber to retrieve her basket of mending. Thirty pounds and quick thinking. What did that mean? Perhaps Phin's insistence that something was afoot had tickled into her mind more than she'd realized. Alyse shook herself. The only thing worse than trouble would be looking for it where none existed.

"Miss Donnelly."

She jumped again. Someone was going to give her an apoplexy today. "Lord Anthony. I hadn't realized you were here."

He stood in her bedchamber door, gazing at her. Counting The Frenchman, she'd now had two men in her bedchamber over the past three days. "Charles and I came to go shooting with Richard." The duke's grandson shifted his attention to her tiny room. "This is . . . cozy," he said after a moment.

"It's convenient if my aunt should need my assistance during the night."

"No doubt." Slowly he wandered into the room and over to the window where she kept her books. "I saw the Marquis of Layton during this past Season," he said offhandedly.

Her heart dropped. "Did you?"

Lord Anthony nodded. "That American wife of his brays like a donkey when she laughs." He sent her a sideways glance. "You read Donne?"

"I read whatever is available. I really need to return

to my aunt. Feel free to borrow any book you like. Excuse me."

"You spent your childhood here at Donnelly House, didn't you?"

She paused on her way out the door. "Yes, I did."

"How long have you known Lord Quence and his family?"

"All my life. We haven't been as close in recent years, however."

"No doubt. Colonel Bromley seems a friendly enough fellow."

Friendly. "Charismatic" seemed a more apt description, but she nodded anyway. "Yes."

"Has he said how long he intends to stay on at Quence?"

"He doesn't confide in me, Lord Anthony. Excuse me."

Leaving him alone in her bedchamber felt unsettling, but she simply added it to the overall oddness of the day. Keeping Aunt Ernesta waiting any longer would be worse than any feeling. She was certain of that.

Twice in a handful of days, Lord Anthony Ellerby had sought her out. The old Alyse would have been flattered—he was a handsome young man, only a year or two older than herself, and he would one day inherit a substantial fortune. As things were now, she had to wonder what his motives were, and why he seemed so interested in Phin.

And if her cousin and his friends were going shooting this late in the day, she couldn't help but think they might be hunting after something other than pheasant or quail. Specifically something that spoke French and rode like the devil.

Especially now that he'd returned her mother's pearls,

she wasn't certain she wanted them to find The French-man. It would be a bit like being caught, herself.

She passed Saunders outside the sitting room door, and he sent her a fond nod. "A note arrived from Miss Bromley," he whispered before he descended the stairs.

Aunt Ernesta was still reading it as she entered the room and took her seat again. "Where have you been?" her aunt demanded, looking up from the missive.

"Lord Anthony wanted to borrow a book," she improvised.

"You do not want to be known as a bluestocking, Alyse."

"I'm not a bluestocking. I simply enjoy reading when I have the chance."

"Hm. Don't argue with me, for heaven's sake. And the Bromleys will not be joining us for dinner tonight. Lord Quence has a fever." She refolded the note and set it aside. "I shouldn't wonder if that unmanageable brother of his will be the death of him."

"What a terrible thing to say," Alyse exclaimed before she could bite it back. "Phin only returned home," she continued in a calmer voice, "to help his family."

"So *you* say. *I* think he's returned home hoping to inherit the title. With Quence ill, it's only a matter of time."

Alyse felt ill, herself. Her aunt spoke about losing William the same way she talked about . . . pudding. It was hurtful and it was wrong, and she didn't dare say anything about it. Not yet. One day she planned on telling Aunt Ernesta precisely how she felt.

If she knew one thing, it was that Phin wasn't after an inheritance. He'd never been comfortable with the idea of being the family's spare son. And aggravating as he could be, it was nice to have him back. More than nice, actually. Since he'd returned, she felt . . . cared for. And hopeful. Both were sensations she'd missed terribly. Almost as much as she'd missed Phin himself.

"This isnae a good idea," Gordon muttered, settling his hat low over his eyes.

"We have to rob someone else, or they might figure out that it's us," Phineas returned, his gaze on the deep gloom of the valley below them.

"Or we could rob no one, and they'll forget aboot it."

"I need something more from Smythe. This will throw them off the trail. And I'm not ready to put all my blunt on one horse, anyway."

"If I might ask, Colonel, throw *who* off the trail?"

That was a damned good question, and one he wasn't particularly in the mood for. "Smythe and whoever else might be assisting him."

"To do what?"

"I am not going to explain myself to you, Sergeant," Phineas snapped. "Join me, or don't."

"I'd never abandon ye. If we're to hang, I'd just like to know what for."

"Because someone is attempting to destroy Quence Park and my family, and I intend to find out who, how, and why, and stop them. By whatever means necessary."

Gordon looked at him for a moment. "Well, then. Find us a coach to stop, Colonel."

It was a tricky process, he was beginning to realize, deciding who to rob. It couldn't be anyone who couldn't afford a modest loss of valuables—he was here to solve one problem, and he didn't want to create another for someone else.

Finally he spied the bouncing lanterns of a coach heading toward Roesglen. "There," he said, pointing, and kneed Ajax.

This time they each carried a pair of pistols, all loaded. He didn't intend to shoot anyone, but he'd long ago learned the effectiveness of confidence and the appropriate application of aggression.

They cut in front of the coach, selecting a narrow, tree-lined point in the road to stop it. Phineas pulled a pistol. He waited for the coach to round the curve, then fired into the air. "Stand and deliver!" he bellowed, lowering his tone and assuming a French inflection.

The driver pulled the team up so quickly he nearly went forward over the animals' heads. "Don't shoot! For God's sake!"

Considering that only one out of six passengers had spoken French the last time, Phineas opted again for broken English. "Out of the coach! Slow!"

From the whimpering inside, at least one female was present. Considering that Roesglen was both of advanced age and a widower, that was interesting. Could it be the mysterious mistress about whom Beth had been gossiping?

"*Ouvrez!* Open," he repeated. "Now!"

Gordon shifted farther to the rear so he had a good look at both doors. The sergeant knew not to kill anyone, but neither of them was above delivering a flesh wound in self-defense.

Finally the near door, propelled by a plump male hand, pushed creakily open. "We're unarmed," came the marquis' quavering voice.

"Out," Phineas ordered. "*Sorti.*"

The rotund Stephen Orville, Lord Roesglen, emerged, climbing awkwardly to the ground. Phineas frowned.

The marquis looked distinctly . . . disheveled, his cravat pulled sideways and his trousers only partially buttoned.

"H-have pity, for God's sake," Roesglen stammered, his hands raised as he looked back inside the coach.

"Out, or I pull you out," Phineas returned. "*Vite.*"

A much more slender arm than Roesglen's reached out of the coach and clasped the marquis' hand. For a moment he thought she might be completely naked. She'd managed to wrap her cloak around her from head to toe, however—which he found disappointing. Whoever she was, she was tall, and slender, with a build similar to . . .

A stab of black anger dug into his chest. "Show your face, mademoiselle," he ordered, sending Ajax a step closer.

She pushed back the blood-red hood of her cloak, revealing bright orange hair. The tight muscles across his gut relaxed a little. Lady Marment. Apparently her tastes ran from slightly younger to much, much older men.

Why he'd thought it would be Alyse, he had no idea, except that he seemed to be thinking of her almost constantly. She had no reason to debase herself with a goat like Roesglen. But just the idea of it twisted him up inside. It was a damned unpleasant sensation, and he didn't care to feel it again.

"Open your pockets," he said, and Gordon dismounted with a cloth bag.

"You won't get away with this," the marquis returned, apparently bolder now that his purse was being threatened.

"And you, mademoiselle, are you wearing anything of value?"

"See for yourself, monsieur." Slowly she undid the tie at the top of the gown and then pulled it open.

Gordon whistled, a sound that somehow managed to sound French. Even Roesglen, who'd presumably already tasted the delights of her nude form, couldn't seem to tear his gaze away.

"Only the gifts God gave you, I see," Phineas said in his heavy French accent. "You may keep them, then."

"Are you certain, monsieur? I am at your mercy."

Resisting the urge to clear his throat, Phineas dipped his hat lower. "Perhaps another time."

Rebecca remained a beauty, but he was no randy sixteen-year-old any longer. They had business to see to, and it wasn't her that he wanted. He had Gordon relieve Roesglen of sixty or so quid, his pocket watch with its diamond fob, and a ruby necklace that was no doubt meant for Lady Marment.

"You'll hang for this, Frenchman," the marquis growled. "They've already put a hundred pounds on your head."

That hadn't taken long. "*Merci.*" He gestured at Gordon, who nodded and remounted Gallant. "*Adieu, monsieur, mademoiselle.*"

Kneeing Ajax, he led the way back up the road and into the trees. After two or so miles they turned back south, in the general direction of Quence. In a suitably gloomy glade he pulled up to lower his greatcoat collar and pull off the half-mask.

"God in heaven," Gordon rasped. "Did ye see that? Not a stitch of cloth on that gel. Naked as mornin'."

Phineas grinned. "I've seen it before."

"By Christ, I want t'be you, sir." Shaking his head, he hefted the bag. "Do ye want any o' these treasures, Colonel?"

"No. Do what you will with them. Just—"

"Be cautious," the sergeant finished. "Aye. I will."

"We'll head back separately."

Gordon nodded. "Mind yerself. There're those'd shoot'n stuff ye for a hundred quid."

"Keep your own head down."

"Always do."

The sergeant turned east toward Lewes, no doubt to hide or distribute their newfound wealth and probably to buy himself a drink while he was at it. Phineas, though, remained restless. No one could say now that The Frenchman was targeting any particular nobleman, but other than that tonight's efforts had netted him precisely nothing.

He set off at a canter through the back meadows of Roesglen and then Donnelly, staying close to the trees for cover and enjoying the crisp night air. Ajax was a damned fine animal, and it was a bloody shame that he would have to give him up within a few days.

Just before they would have crossed the bridge onto Quence land he pulled the black up again. In the relative quiet of the night he heard it again—the rhythmic jangle of bridles and tack. A coach was approaching. Through the hedgerows he spotted it—Beaumont's coach again, apparently leaving Donnelly House.

"What do you think, boy?" he murmured, patting Ajax on the neck. Swiftly he reloaded his spent pistol and turned up his collar again.

Without Gordon there to watch his back he was taking a considerably larger risk, but with the occupants of this coach he at least had a chance of discovering something usable. And with William's fever and worry over the slaughter of the sheep, he had the sobering realization that he could very well be running out of time.

"Let's go, Ajax." With a gathering of the black's muscles they charged onto the road. Phineas fired into the air. "Stand and deliver!"

The coach didn't slow. With his knees Phineas urged Ajax forward, directly into the middle of the road. At the same time he drew the second pistol and aimed it straight at the driver's head.

"Stand and deliver," he repeated clearly.

The driver yanked back on the reins so hard that the left-hand horse skidded nearly onto its haunches. At the same time the lantern inside the coach went out, leaving the interior completely dark.

Damnation. Phineas stayed toward the front of the coach. He dumped the spent pistol back into his pocket to free one hand. "Out of the coach!" he called.

The long muzzle of a musket pushed out the window, aimed straight at him. With a curse Phineas fired into the door, sending splinters flying. The barrel swiveled sideways wildly. Not knowing how many occupants were inside or how many might be armed, he kicked Ajax hard in the ribs. With a grunt of exhaled air the black leapt forward, through the hedgerow and into the trees.

A musket fired. A half smile touched Phineas's face as he ducked lower along the horse's neck. As far as battles and fighting went, this barely qualified, but he couldn't deny that it was . . . fun.

And it was more than that. Whoever rode in Beaumont's coach had anticipated that The Frenchman would return. The odds of that were fairly minuscule—except to someone who felt they had something to protect and to hide. For *that* person, threats existed everywhere.

The question became, then, which of the previous

passengers had been inside Beaumont's coach? As much as he wanted to circle back around and drag whoever it was out onto the road, he was outnumbered at least two to one, ineffective a defense as the driver seemed to be. No, he would have to be a little patient, and with luck the gossip—or better yet, Alyse—would tell him tomorrow.

Chapter 13 _____

"But if he's not feeling well, he would probably appreciate *not* having guests," Alyse said, carefully balancing the pot of hot soup on her lap.

"Nonsense," Aunt Ernesta protested from the opposite seat of the barouche. "Everyone looks forward to visitors. And at the least we might raise the spirits of his sister. Isn't that true, Richard?"

Her cousin turned from gazing at the countryside they passed. "Hm? Yes. I imagine Beth, at least, could use something to distract her from William's illness."

It was more likely that Richard didn't want Beth too distracted *by* William's illness. Alyse kept her gaze on the jostling soup. It had been just a few days since she'd last seen Phin, but she didn't know how to describe the tightness in her chest as anything other than anticipation.

And considering the rumors traveling across the valley this morning, she couldn't wait to hear his reaction. Generally she abhorred gossip, but Roesglen had reported it all to the constabulary. How long had Lady Marment been . . . redesigning the interior of Roesglen Abbey—and why was she apparently doing so in the middle of the night? She knew Phin and Rebecca Marment had once been lovers. In her opinion, Lady Marment had lowered her standards rather significantly since then.

Digby pulled open the front door of Quence as they left the coach. "Good morning, my lord," he intoned in his reed-thin voice. "Mrs. Donnelly, Miss Donnelly."

"Digby." Richard brushed past the butler. "How is Miss Bromley this morning?"

"Quite well, my lord. You will find her in the morning room."

"Very good."

No one asked where Phineas might be, and Alyse couldn't help a glance toward the stairs before she was swept into the morning room. Did he rise early or late? She had no idea, but she supposed the question made her as selfish as the rest of her family. None of them had asked after William.

Beth set aside a book and stood as they entered the bright room. "Richard, Alyse, Mrs. Donnelly!" she exclaimed with her usual warm smile. "What a lovely surprise!"

Richard pushed forward to take her hand and bring it to his lips. "How is your dear brother this morning? We've brought a broth that my cook especially recommends for feverishness."

"He's much improved," Beth returned. "Thank you for your concern, and for the broth." She gestured at her maid, who had risen at the same time as her mistress. "Meg, will you take the broth to the kitchen, please?"

"Allow me," Alyse broke in before the maid could respond. "I daresay I know the way to the kitchen by now."

When no one protested, she left the room. They wouldn't miss her until Aunt Ernesta needed a pillow fluffed. And it gave her a moment to breathe, and a better chance of encountering Phin. She managed to surreptitiously peek through every doorway between the morning room and the kitchen, but all of the rooms were empty of Bromley family members.

"Miss Donnelly," Cook exclaimed as she entered the wide room, "I recognized you straight off. Haven't set eyes on you since you and young Master Phin used to sneak biscuits straight from the oven."

Alyse smiled. "I burned my tongue on several occasions, as I recall." She handed over the pot of soup and repeated the instructions given her by the Donnelly House cook. Then she took a breath. "You don't by any chance know if Colonel Bromley might be about somewhere, do you?"

"I saw him heading for the stables not ten minutes ago, miss," one of the cook's helpers said.

"Thank you." After a brief hesitation she headed outside through the servants' entrance at the far end of the kitchen.

The stables were attached to the manor house only by an old overhang where coaches could stop to let out passengers during foul weather. She passed beneath it as she had a hundred times before, and what seemed like a hundred years ago, to emerge into the cobbled stable yard at the side of the house.

The yard was much quieter than the one at Donnelly, but the stables' wooden double doors stood wide open to allow in the fresh morning breeze. She put a hand on the nearest door and leaned in. "Hello?"

Boots echoed beneath the wide overhang and skidded into the stable yard behind her. "Alyse!"

She turned around as Phin strode up to her. "There you are. I was told you were at the stables."

"I was," he replied. Hazel eyes, rich and earthy green in the sunlight, gazed at her. "What brings you here?"

"We came to inquire after William. How is he?"

"Much better. His fever broke last night. I imagine he'll be out of bed by noon."

"That is good news."

"Yes, it is." He held out not his arm, but his hand to her. "Take a stroll with me."

She had already risked her aunt's anger by leaving the morning room. Being away for another few minutes would hardly make things worse. Not by much. She took his proffered hand, wrapping her fingers around his warm ones.

The silence, their hands entwined, made her not nervous, but . . . unsettled. "Did you hear that The Frenchman has struck again?" she blurted. "Twice."

He frowned. "Not you, I hope."

"Oh, no. Lord Roesglen and Lady Marment, and Lord Charles and Lord Anthony again."

"But you said he struck twice."

"Lord Roesglen and Lady Marment were together. According to the report he gave the constabulary, she is helping the marquis redecorate his manor house."

Phin looked sideways at her. "You did that very well. Not a hint of salacious enjoyment, or even any indication that you don't believe their tale."

Alyse shrugged. "Gossip doesn't amuse me the way it used to."

They reached the overhang. "Tell me something, Alyse," he whispered, stopping. "Did you come out here just to tell me about a highwayman?"

Oh, my. "What if I didn't?"

Tugging her closer, Phineas closed his mouth over hers. Alyse shut her eyes, sensation shooting all the way to her toes. He backed her until she was pressed against the wall, all the while molding his mouth, his lips, against hers.

She dug her fingers into his shoulders, grateful for the solid strength of the wall behind her. His own hands breathlessly brushed the sides of her breasts, then settled at her hips. "Alyse," he murmured, shifting his attention to her throat and the line of her jaw, "dark-eyed Alyse."

Good heavens. She'd been engaged once, and Phillip had never kissed her like this. The highwayman had come close, but exciting as that had been, no one had ever kissed her like this, so that the whole of her felt ready to burst into flames. And for it to be Phineas—she didn't want him to stop touching her, ever.

Alyse shook herself. Words like "ever" and "forever" simply weren't compatible with the Phin Bromley she knew. "Stop," she muttered, pushing at his shoulders and very aware of his lean body pressed hard against hers. "Stop it, Phin."

She shoved harder, and he backed away all of an inch or two. "Why?"

"Because you shouldn't be kissing me."

His scarred eyebrow arched. "You'd rather be kissing someone else, then?" he asked, his voice low and rumbling. "Who would you rather be kissing, Alyse? Tell me. I'll fetch him for you."

Jealousy? The idea thrilled her over and above the mortifying thought of what would happen to her if anyone discovered that The Frenchman had kissed her. No one would care that it had been done in exchange for her pearls. "No one," she said truthfully. "I just don't wish to be seen."

His expression eased. "We won't be seen."

"How—"

"And besides," he continued, moving in again, "I like kissing you." He ran a finger along her left collarbone. "You taste like—I don't know, but it's very compelling." He nibbled at her lower lip. "You're very compelling, Alyse."

The sensation made her knees weak. "Compelling, or convenient?" she made herself ask.

He gazed at her from inches away. "Definitely not convenient," he murmured. "And I wouldn't recommend teasing me."

"Me? Teasing you? I don't—"

"You came out here to find me. And when I see you, I want . . ." With a scowl he blew out his breath and backed away. "Let's get you back to the house before we begin arguing again. Or kissing."

He wasn't convenient, either. Goodness knew her life would be simpler without him back in it. Even with that in mind, though, she couldn't wish him gone again. Phin was like . . . fire—warm, bright, compelling, and without proper precautions, extremely destructive.

This time he offered his arm, but she pretended not to notice. Touching him right then would be unwise, considering that her heart still beat so fast and hard he could probably hear it. Instead she folded her hands behind her and started back to the main part of the house. A moment later he fell in beside her.

"So Smythe and Ellerby were held up for the second night in a row? That must have been embarrassing."

"The Frenchman wasn't successful," she returned, grateful for the change of subject. "Apparently they were expecting trouble. Lord Charles shot at him. He swears the ball struck home, but I have my doubts."

"Do you? Why is that?"

"The Frenchman seems to know what he's doing. I would think that he would have anticipated trouble, stopping the same coach twice."

She felt his gaze on her. "You don't fancy this Frenchman, do you?"

Alyse blushed. "Of course not. He stole my pearls. It's just that he seemed . . . dashing."

"Hm."

" 'Hm' what?"

"I just gave you what I consider to be a fairly proficient kiss, and you're consumed with thoughts of a highwayman."

She snorted, beginning to wonder whether he could read minds. "I am not consumed with anything. I said his manner was dashing." And Phin's kiss had been much more than fairly proficient. She wasn't entirely certain she was walking straight.

They reached the servants' entrance, and he pushed open the door for her. Without looking, even when he stood behind her, she knew how close he was to her. Unsettling, indeed. And arousing in ways she'd never anticipated.

"There you are," Aunt Ernesta said, sending her a glare as she walked back into the morning room.

"It's my fault," Phin said easily. "I asked Alyse to help me convince Cook to make a cinnamon cake. I've always had a weakness for them."

Goodness. He lied so easily, and with such convincing charm. Yes, it had probably saved her from being yelled at later, but if he lied so well, how could she know if he was lying when he said he found her compelling or attractive or interesting or inconvenient?

"Beth was telling me that you had some trouble with dogs the day before yesterday," Richard said, standing as they entered the room. Alyse didn't think the gesture was out of deference to her; Phin seemed to make her cousin nervous. She counted that as a point in Phin's favor.

Phineas didn't seem to have the same difficulty as Richard, since he gestured her to a seat and then took one himself. "Yes, we did," he answered. "A dozen or so wolfhounds got into the west pasture. Killed forty-seven sheep."

Alyse gasped. "That's awful!"

"It is indeed," Richard agreed. "Shall I send some men to help dispose of the carcasses?"

"I took care of it," Phineas returned. "Thank you for the offer."

Forty-seven sheep. With everything else that had befallen Quence Park of late, the loss of so many animals could be devastating. No wonder William had come down with a fever.

"What did you do with them?" her aunt asked, shuddering delicately.

"The dogs? We shot two of them. We've been trying to track down the rest of the pack, but no luck so far."

"Heavens! Richard, what about *our* flocks?"

"I'll put some additional men out to keep watch." Richard sat again, taking Beth's hand in his. "I'm so sorry, my dear. If you require anything, please let me know."

"How is it," Phin said slowly, flicking a piece of dust off his dark sleeve, "that you're just hearing about this now?"

Richard frowned. "What do you mean?"

"It would be irresponsible of us to keep the news of a roving pack of dogs to ourselves, don't you think?"

"I wouldn't have phrased it that way, but—"

"I informed the constable myself, the day before yesterday," Phineas went on. "The news of that damned Frenchman seems to have circulated, but you hadn't heard anything about our losses until now?"

Richard's color deepened. As she watched him, Alyse remembered her uneasiness the other day when she'd overheard a conversation between William and Charles Smythe about . . . forty-seven something. *Forty-seven sheep*, she realized, her blood going cold. Good heavens. He *had* known. Why had he pretended ignorance, and why had he happily informed his mother and cousin about the exploits of the highwayman, but said nothing about sheep-killing dogs?

Gulping a breath, Alyse glanced at Phineas. He was looking directly at her, his expression unreadable. A heartbeat later he chuckled, turning his gaze to Richard. "Obviously the local wags are far too taken with that bloody Frog, if they can't be bothered to mention anything else," he said, grinning. "It's a sorry state of things."

"Indeed it is," Richard agreed, smiling as well. "And I hate to mention something so frivolous at such a time, but if William is feeling up to it, I do hope you'll attend our house party evening after next. If you wish to stay the night and allow William to rest before and after, or even to make certain he's well during the party if he doesn't wish to attend, I think we all could use a distraction."

"I don't know," Beth said slowly, looking at her older brother. "William is our first concern, and I'm not—"

"You're certain you wouldn't mind the lot of us staying overnight?" Phineas interrupted, sitting forward. "Because from what I've heard, your new cook is the finest in Lewes. I would hate to miss it."

Alyse caught Beth's frown, quickly covered. Privately, she agreed with Beth's concern. The viscount's health had been bordering on delicate since the accident ten years ago, and with a fever now, transporting him even just a mile down the road so that his siblings—his brother—could eat pheasant seemed the height of selfishness.

Of course, knowing this new Phin as she was coming to, he likely had a reason for wanting to be at Donnelly House. She took a quick breath. Could *she* be the reason? If so, she needed to do some thinking. Being discovered dallying with him could ruin the plans she'd been putting together. Would it be worth it?

". . . hope they shot him dead," Beth was saying. "I keep worrying that Phin will put on his uniform and go after the man simply because he's French."

"He needs to be shot simply for being a highwayman," Richard returned. "Being a Frog only makes him more offensive."

Alyse glanced at Phin, but thankfully he didn't seem inclined to announce to everyone that she thought The Frenchman dashing. Richard had been increasingly venomous at the mention of the highwayman, and she didn't relish the thought of being locked in the attic to polish silver because she felt more charitable than the rest of the family did toward the thief.

She continued feeling more charitable toward Phin, as well. And that could be much more problematic than fancying a thief she would likely never set eyes on again. The Frenchman had only wanted a kiss. Judging by their last embrace, Phineas wanted *her*.

Warmth swept down her spine. Being the focus of Phin Bromley's attention, even when they were children, had been an exhilarating experience. Now, though—

"Penny for your thoughts," Phin said, sitting on the couch beside her.

"What do you want from me?" she murmured, pretending to take a sip of tea to cover her words.

"Ah. You were thinking of me. I should pay double the price, then—once for the information, and once for the flattery."

"It's not flattery when you worry me. What do you want?"

"From you? I don't know yet," he returned in the same tone, more serious now.

"I'm not comforted."

"I like being close to you." He offered her a plate of biscuits, brushing her fingers as she selected one, and nearly making her drop it. "I like touching you, Alyse."

She closed her eyes for a moment to concentrate on breathing. "You will ruin me all over again if you don't stop this."

He shook his head. "Do you think me that much of a blackguard?"

"I don't want to, but the last time I saw you, you *were* that much of a blackguard. Should I ignore that because you protest now that you're . . . benevolent?"

His lips twitched. "I never said that."

"Phin."

For a moment he sat still beside her. "I know you said

you couldn't help me, but answer this: Richard already knew about the dog attack, didn't he?" he murmured even more quietly.

"My cousin is not the one hurting Quence. Look at him. He's courting your sister."

"That's not what I asked. He knew, didn't he?"

Alyse started to her feet. Before she could rise, Phin put a hand on her arm, keeping her seated. "Let me go," she hissed.

"Very well. I won't make you choose, yet. Eventually, though, you'll have to take a side." Making the touch on her arm another caress, he stood again. "If you'll excuse me," he said at normal volume, "I have some things to see to."

Mostly Phineas needed a moment to himself so he could catch his breath and his scattering wits. He started out the door, but Donnelly stood before he could escape. "Would you inquire if your brother will see me?" the viscount asked. "I need to discuss a few things with him."

Phineas kept his expression pleasant and mild. So Lord Donnelly was still trying to make himself indispensable to Quence Park. He nodded. "I will." If that was what William wished, then so be it. For now. Until he had some proof.

Climbing the stairs to the first floor, he stopped outside the master bedchamber and knocked quietly. "Enter," came William's voice.

He pushed open the door. His brother was seated in his wheeled chair just beneath an open window, a blanket across his lap and a ledger book atop that. "You're out of bed."

"Your skills at observation continue to amaze."

"And your sense of humor continues to surprise," Phineas returned dryly. "How are you feeling?"

"I only slept in, for God's sake."

"Mm-hm. Donnelly asked for an audience, if you're up to it."

"I'll see him."

Phineas stifled his frown. "I'll go tell him." He headed back out.

"Phin?"

"What is it?" He stopped to face his brother again.

"You did well with the sheep. Thank you again."

"You lost nearly fifty head. Don't thank me for cleaning up the carnage after the slaughter."

"You still handled it well."

With every fiber of his being Phineas wanted to tell William not to trust Richard Donnelly, that he suspected the viscount of at least some of the ill things that had befallen Quence. And just as strongly he knew that William wouldn't believe him, and that he would be accused of looking for trouble or excitement or some other daft thing. In addition, he would lose whatever incremental amount of his brother's trust he'd been able to gain.

"Thank you, then."

"And Phin?"

"Yes?"

"My window here has a very nice view. Over the back of the stables and the archway, in case you wished me to clarify."

Damnation. Bloody hell. "I—"

"I warned you not to make things worse for Alyse. She's paid enough for one moment of foolishness."

"I'm not trying to make things worse. I . . ." It didn't

seem like the time for honesty. What would he say, anyway? That he'd charged out to the stables to keep her from seeing Ajax and that Alyse—her presence, her taste, her voice—filled a chasm in him that had been open and dark and empty for a great deal longer than ten years?

"Leave her be, Phin."

"I won't ask for your trust, but I will say that I'm not playing." He turned around again. "I'll send Donnelly up."

When he returned downstairs he leaned into the morning room and informed the viscount that William would see him. The three women remained behind, Beth attempting to chat with both Alyse and Mrs. Donnelly, and the older woman doing all of the responding.

For a moment he contemplated returning to the conversation, but he needed to make some plans for the next few days to be certain no further ill luck befell Quence Park. So instead he went to track down Gordon. His so-called valet was in the stables, feeding Gallant an apple. "You're supposed to be starching my cravats and polishing my boots," he commented, selecting an apple for himself.

"I already starched yer cravats, and yer wearin' yer bloody boots, Colonel."

Phineas bit into the apple, then pulled the knife from his boot and sliced the remainder in half, giving one section to Saffron and the other to Ajax. "Donnelly claimed not to know about the dogs," he said offhandedly. "What would you do if you owned several valuable flocks of sheep and suddenly heard that a pack of dogs had just killed half a hundred of your neighbor's animals?"

"I'd get home, collect me weapons and me men, and go huntin'," Gordon returned promptly. "No question."

"As would I."

"Ye think the hounds are his, then?"

"His or Smythe's, would be my guess."

The sergeant strolled over to lean against the stall door beside him. "I heard some rumors of me own this mornin'."

Phineas scratched Ajax behind the ears. "What rumors?"

"That The Frenchman got 'imself shot last night, stoppin' a second coach."

"Rumors are nasty things, Gordon. You simply can't trust them."

"Don't ye go enjoyin' this too much, Colonel. Yer family wouldnae come out well, were ye found t'be a highwayman."

"I know that." Phineas gave Ajax a last pat and walked away from the stall. "The problem is, they're not doing well under the present circumstances." Another bad fever or two for William, or another overturned carriage, and he might never have a chance to make amends.

"What's next then, sir?"

"We go to Uckfield and see whether we can purchase fifty or so Southdown sheep. And we order lumber and hire workers to repair the burned cottages. And we hire some . . . gamekeepers, we'll call them, to travel the property and keep an eye on things. And tonight we go out and try to discover who owns a pack of wolfhounds."

It would just about wipe out his ready funds, but it would also put Quence back close to where it had been before its disintegration had begun, and at no additional expense to William. In the grand scheme of things it was little enough, but it was a start.

"That takes care o' today," Gordon commented. "What about tomorrow?"

Phineas smiled grimly. "Tomorrow depends on what we find out tonight."

Chapter 14 _____

"Where are you going?"

Covering his flinch, Phineas turned away from the front door and faced the landing above. "It may be late for you, Magpie," he drawled with a grin he didn't feel, "but for me the night's barely begun."

"If you're not ready for bed, come and play whist with me. Or billiards, even."

He shook his head. Thank the devil she'd never encountered The Frenchman, or she might have recognized the army greatcoat he carried draped over one arm. "Not the kind of amusement I'm looking for, Beth."

"But you—we—"

"Come along, Beth," William said from the stop of the stairs above her. "My billiards game is a bit rusty, but I think I can manage whist."

"Phin," she murmured, her tone making the single word into a plea.

"Don't wait up," he said, opening the door and slipping outside.

As soon as he was out of earshot, he began cursing. English, French, Italian, Spanish—the language didn't matter, as long as it was black enough to suit his mood. What if he was wrong? What if he had invented some sort of conspiracy to avoid facing the fact that his family didn't need him after all?

"Saddle Saffron," he snapped as he entered the stables.

Gordon, already mounted on Gallant and holding Ajax's reins, looked at him. "Beg pardon?"

"Beth might be watching." He stepped back as Warner walked over to collect the butter chestnut from his stall.

"Then what—"

"Wait five minutes after I leave, and meet me in the glade just southwest of the bridge. The one with the lightning-struck oak. Do you know where that is?"

"I know. Don't be doin' anything foolish without me."

"I'll hold off on being foolish until you join me."

"Fair 'nough."

A moment later Warner led over Saffron. "Master Phineas?" the groom intoned.

"Yes?"

"Mr. Gordon says this highwayman business is to help Lord Quence and Miss Beth. Is that so?"

God, he hoped so. "Yes, that is my intention."

The groom nodded. "Then keep your head down, sir. You can trust me and young Tom here."

"Thank you, Warner." With a nudge of his heels he

sent Saffron through the double doors and out into the stable yard.

On the chance that Beth or William might be watching him ride off, he headed in the direction of Lewes until he was beyond view of the house. Only then did he turn south and east toward the River Ouse. He dismounted beside the old shattered oak tree and led Saffron into a thicket that held a patch of good grazing. Once he'd tied off the yellow gelding where no one would stumble over him accidently, he donned his highwayman attire.

He heard a low, two-toned whistle. Whistling back, he slipped out of the thicket to join Gordon in the glade. "Let's begin at Beaumont's," he said, swinging up on Ajax. "We can take a look around Donnelly on our way back."

"Aye. Any idea what ye want t'do if we come across ten or so wolfhounds partial to sheep?"

"Shooting them comes to mind."

"I don' think The Frenchman'd care about dogs."

No, he wouldn't. Not unless they were chasing him. And it could link the highwayman to Quence, which he couldn't afford. "Then if we find them tonight I'll make plans to discover them again tomorrow as Phin Bromley. And I'll have the constabulary with me."

It wouldn't be the most satisfying way to deal with the trouble, but it was the way William would want it resolved. And therefore, however aggravating he found the idea of allowing someone else to determine the outcome of this malicious destruction, he would do so. To a point.

Once they'd crossed the bridge, they left the road, cutting through the pastures and meadows and scattered stands of trees belonging to Quence's neighbors.

No flooding here. No fires, no slaughtered sheep or poisoned feed—just peaceful, sleeping flocks and the occasional sheepdog or deer or startled pheasant. That alone should have been enough to convince William that Quence Park was being targeted. His brother, however, seemed to believe either that his fellow landowners were as honest as he was, or that he had to expect a certain amount of ill luck. After all, ill luck had found William ten years ago, and it hadn't left him since.

"What d'ye think, Colonel?" Gordon asked from a little behind and to his right. "Start at th' stables?"

"We'll take a look, but I doubt anyone would keep sheep-killing dogs where all the servants would know about them. East Sussex owes its prosperity to sheep, after all."

"Aye. Yer sayin' those dog's'd be difficult to keep secret."

"Exactly." Kicking out of the stirrups, he jumped down from Ajax. "But I'm a cautious fellow, and we will therefore check the stables and all of the outbuildings here and at Donnelly and anywhere else I can think of until we find them."

"This could be a very long night."

Phineas ignored the comment. "Let's get moving. And remember to be French."

Lights still showed in a few of Beaumont's upstairs rooms, and though the stables were quiet he was unwilling to wager that all of the grooms and stableboys were asleep. Motioning Gordon to stay outside and keep watch, he pulled open one of the tall doors and slipped inside. Sixteen or so horses, but no dogs. Nor any sign that dogs had ever been housed in the stables. Beaumont didn't have a kennel—not at the main house, anyway.

He made his way back outside. "Nothing. Let's try the outbuildings."

Gordon, his eyes nothing more than glittering slits behind his black mask, nodded. "Divide'n conquer?"

"It'll go more quickly that way. I'll take the west side."

They searched the gardener's shed, the small hothouse, the grain barn, the outlying cottages, and the small estate manager's cottage. Growing frustration tightened Phineas's muscles as they continued to find nothing.

An hour after they'd begun, he caught sight of a figure on horseback heading away from the manor along the private path that wound around the small lake and up the hillside. Though the Beaumont and Quence estates and families had never been friendly, he did recall some stories of the present lord going on drunken binges at his family's small hunting lodge during his youth.

"Damn," he muttered, striding for Ajax. A hunting lodge could mean a kennel. He gave the two-toned whistle to summon Gordon, but, not wanting to risk losing his prey in the dark, he mounted and rode off after the horseman.

They wound through the trees, turning away from the lake and into the rolling hills. Phineas stayed back as far as he dared, listening both for the rider in front of him and for any sign that Gordon was following behind.

A light flared up ahead, and he pulled up sharply. At the same moment he heard the muffled sound of dogs barking. Large dogs. Sending Ajax forward at a walk now, he approached the light through the trees.

The small cottage was long and low and dark. The light emanated from a lantern hung on the back of a railed wagon. The vehicle was stopped alongside a large kennel, and several men removed hounds to lift them up into the bed of the wagon. *Bloody hell.* By tomorrow the dogs would be gone.

He pulled out a pistol. No one could be allowed to remove the only evidence he had. Phineas gathered the reins in his left hand.

Something slammed into his left shoulder from behind. A heartbeat later he heard the shot, thin-sounding amid the trees.

Trying to keep from pitching forward out of the saddle, Phineas fired back in the general direction from which the shot had come. The reins dropped from his hand, pain belatedly tearing into him. Shoving his spent pistol back into his pocket, he grabbed the reins again with his good hand and kicked Ajax hard. In a second they were muscling up the hillside.

A muzzle flashed below him, and then another. "Come on, Frenchman!" Smythe's voice, shaking with barely suppressed excitement, came from the direction of the woods. "Rob us now! *Vite, vite!*" Voices laughed, also excited at the prospect of blood. "Find him!"

Hoping Gordon had heard the commotion and gotten away, Phineas sent Ajax straight west at a gallop. Shot and in near-total darkness, if he hadn't spent most of the past ten years of his life in the saddle, he never would have been able to do it. Thankfully he doubted that Smythe and his cohorts could match either him or Ajax.

For a moment he thought they might set the hounds after him, and he intentionally rode through the middle of one of Beaumont's flocks, scattering it. Once a dog had killed sheep, it would go after them again at every opportunity.

Cutting back toward the lake, he listened, but couldn't make out anything aside from the half dozen men and horses pounding after him. No dogs, then. They came to a fairly level stretch, and he took the reins into his teeth so he could dig the second pistol out of his left pocket. Abruptly the black veered sideways. A figure loomed out of the darkness directly in front of them.

"Don't move," Phineas hissed, lifting the pistol.

"Colonel!" Gordon's voice rasped back at him.

Phineas didn't take the time to ask what the devil the sergeant was still doing there. "Come on," he grunted instead, tucking the pistol into his right pocket and grabbing the reins again.

"Ye've been hit," Gordon said abruptly, his voice tense.

"A graze," he grunted.

Another pistol fired, and a ball whistled past his ear. Their aim was improving, or his luck was failing entirely. Every thud of Ajax's hooves against the ground jolted his shoulder, and sticky warmth crawled down his back.

The sergeant turned in the saddle to look behind them. "Six," he panted, facing forward again. "How'd they know we were comin'?"

"They didn't. Not specifically. The dogs are up at the lodge. Smythe's moving them."

"Then—"

"Bad people expect bad things to happen."

"What does that say aboot us?"

Phineas smiled grimly. "We can debate that later."

They plunged across a stream. Pain screamed through his shoulder as they pounded up the far bank. He swayed, gripping the pommel to keep from falling out of the saddle.

"Colonel." Gordon edged closer, putting out an arm to steady him.

This was not good. They'd crossed onto Donnelly land, and were only about half a mile from the manor house. On any other night, he and Ajax could have ridden circles around their pursuers. Now, though, he was fast running out of time. "Gordon, take Ajax and lead these fools away from Quence. I'll meet you back home."

"And how is that?"

"It's only a mile or so to Saffron. I can walk it, but I don't think I can ride it. Not at this pace."

"Then we stand'n fight."

Phineas shook his head, tossing the end of the reins to the sergeant. "I want proof before I begin killing people. Wait for me in my bedchamber."

He kicked out of the stirrups and jumped. The ground was damp, but it still stole his breath as he slammed into it knees first and rolled. With difficulty he came up onto his feet, and ran at right angles to the path Gordon took as the sergeant veered away from him.

Crouching against the fallen trunk of an elm, cradling his shoulder, Phineas held still as the riders passed by, close enough that if it had been daylight they would have seen him in an instant. He stayed where he was until the pursuit passed out of earshot. Then he stood, staggering a little and putting out his free hand for balance. If he couldn't stop the damned bleeding, he wasn't going to make it back to his blasted yellow horse.

Phineas looked over his shoulder. Just at the top of the rise he could make out the darker bulk of Donnelly House against the night sky. Not precisely friendly territory, but much closer than his horse and another mile home beyond that.

Lord Charles Smythe was an enemy. Whether he could prove it or not after tonight was another matter, but he knew it to be true. He could and did suspect further involvement, but he still found himself short of facts. If he approached Donnelly, who'd been so helpful to his brother, would the viscount help him, or finish what Smythe had begun?

There was, though, another course of action, something that wouldn't involve a direct confrontation before he was ready for one. There was one person in that household whom he could trust. He hoped.

Alyse awoke abruptly. After her heated, half-coherent dream about doing the wash and about Phineas and a very large bathtub, the air of the attic felt still and cold. She turned onto her side, pulling the blanket up to her chin.

Then she heard it again, the slow lowering of the door handle. Her heart skittering, she sat bolt upright. *Him.* Oh, this was too much. However mysterious and charming The Frenchman might be, this could not continue. She and Phin might not have any kind of understanding, but he was the man she wanted in her life.

Slowly the door swung open. Shaking, Alyse climbed to her feet. She would simply tell him to go away, and no one need know he'd ever been in the house. She hoped her French was proficient enough to explain that. As she watched, the tall figure in his tricorne hat and turned-up greatcoat stole into the room—and then stumbled to his knees.

Good heavens. "What—what are you doing?" she hissed.

He lifted his head, his shadowed eyes glittering. "Shot," he whispered.

Oh, no. "You've been shot?"

When he nodded, all of the protests she'd been ready to utter fled. No one could be allowed to catch him. Not like this. She hurried around him to the door, closing and latching it again.

Moving back to her bedstand, she lit the lamp there. The Frenchman stayed where he was, crouched forward on his knees and one hand, the other arm braced closely against his chest. Alyse wiped her palms against her thighs, abruptly aware that she was dressed only in a thin nightrail. Quickly she grabbed her dressing gown off the foot of the bed and pulled it on over her shoulders.

"Let me see where you're hurt," she whispered, setting the lamp down on the bare wood floor in front of him and tentatively kneeling beside it.

"You should know something first," he murmured, no trace of French in his very familiar voice.

Her heart stopped. *Phin?* All the blood drained from her face. "*You?*"

He lifted his head. Even with the hat and mask on, in the flickering lamplight she could tell. With shaking hands Alyse reached and pulled the coverings from his head. The light illuminated dark brown hair, damp with sweat and laced with dirt and bits of grass, and definitely, unmistakably, belonging to Phin Bromley.

"Apologies," he said quietly, reaching up his right hand to turn down his greatcoat collar. "I didn't—"

Alyse slapped him. Hard. "Get out of here," she hissed. "You liar! You thief! How could you? You stole from me! You *kissed* me!"

She lifted her hand to hit him again, but he caught her wrist. "Let me expl—"

"No!" She jerked free of his grip and shot to her feet. "I am not going to listen to you any longer. Get out!" Alyse shoved his shoulders, pushing him backward toward the door.

Phineas flinched away from her, gasping, and went down flat on his back. How much of it might be real pain and how much might be him trying to gain her sympathy she had no idea. Neither did she care. He'd pointed a pistol, if not directly at her then certainly at her cousin. He'd stolen from her, and then listened with apparent compassion and sympathy when she'd told him about it later. And he'd tricked her into a kiss. Oh, and then she'd practically admitted to him that the mysterious Frenchman intrigued her. He'd played with her, apparently for his own amusement.

She reared back her foot and kicked him. "Liar," she repeated, and did it again.

Faster than she could blink, Phineas caught her bare ankle in midstrike, twisted onto his stomach, and pulled her down hard onto the floor beside him. "Stop that," he grunted. "It hurts."

"Good. Why should I stop?"

"Because I've been shot, damn it." He hauled her closer, looking down at her face from inches away. "I need you to help me stop the bleeding."

She pushed aside the niggling worry that he might actually be badly injured. "What if I refuse?"

"Then you'll have to explain my being in your bedchamber in the middle of the night. And . . ." He dragged her beneath him. "And I'll tell anyone who'll listen that you knew what I was up to all along."

Alyse looked up at his lean, serious face with the rakish scar across his right eyebrow and gaped. "You wouldn't."

"Only if you leave me no choice. Now. Are you going to help me?"

"I suppose *I* have no choice."

"No, you don't. Help me sit, and unbutton my coat."

For a long moment she glared at him, before she pulled away again and sat up herself. "Very well. But you and I are no longer friends."

Wrapping her arms around his good one, she pulled. With a grunt he brought his legs back under himself and sat. As she looked at his face more closely she realized that he was pale, except for the red mark on his cheek where she'd slapped him. With an exaggerated humph, she scooted closer and began unbuttoning his heavy, coarse greatcoat.

There was something . . . unsettling about undressing him, even if it was just his outer coat, and even if she was furious with him. "Where are you shot?" she asked grudgingly, having to move nearly into his arms to reach the last buttons.

"The back of my left shoulder," he rasped, leaning his forehead against her neck as she pushed the coat off his arms and down to the floor.

She swallowed. "Why did you come here?"

"I was being chased, and I didn't think I'd make it home." He glanced up at her face. "And because of you."

"Oh, please." Raising up on her knees, Alyse looked over his shoulder to see his back. Dark blood stained through his jacket, spreading from a hole just at the edge of his shoulder blade. "Oh, my goodness."

"You need to stop it from bleeding before I pass out, in which case I won't be able to leave here. Take off my jacket. Carefully."

At least she didn't have to unbutton it first. Sliding

her hands along his collarbones, she first pulled his right arm free, then gingerly lifted it down his left. As she glanced down at his face, she was disconcerted to realize both that her breasts were directly at his eye level, and that he was gazing at them. Her chest tightened. "Who shot you, anyway?"

"I can't tell you that if we're not friends. My waistcoat."

Goodness. That meant moving even closer to him, balancing herself between his bent knees as he leaned back on his good hand to give her access to his clothes. "It would serve you right if you bled to death, you know."

"No doubt. If I do, push me out your window so no one will know I was up here."

"You'll fall into the rosebushes."

He made an almost-amused sound. "I won't mind, as I'll be dead."

She felt flushed and embarrassed and confused, as though her mind wasn't working entirely correctly. "I was worried for the roses."

"Ah."

Once she had his waistcoat off, she sank back. "I suppose you want me to remove your shirt and cravat now?"

Hazel eyes met hers. "I can manage them, if you'll fetch some water and some clean cloths."

For the briefest of seconds she was disappointed. It was rather like tearing the paper from a present and then having to leave it in its box. She had no intention of letting him know that, though. Alyse stood, walking over to her dressing table for the basin and pitcher of water there. "If you can manage your shirt, why have me do the other bits?"

"I couldn't unfasten the buttons one-handed."

That actually made sense. "Oh."

When she turned to face him again, she stopped. She'd been to the museum, and she knew a magnificent figure of a male when she saw one. She was looking at one. *Good heavens.* Most fascinating of all was the light dusting of dark hair across his chest and the way it narrowed down his flat belly to disappear into his trousers.

Only when he curled forward again, cradling his left shoulder, did she shake herself and move back to his side. "What do you want me to do?"

"Firstly, is it still bleeding?" he asked, craning to look over his shoulder.

"Yes."

"I have a reason for doing all of this, Alyse. And it wasn't to hurt you."

She did her best to ignore the soft words. "What's second?"

He hesitated. "Clean it off so you can see what you're doing, then run your fingers around the hole."

"Beg pardon?"

"I need to know if the ball's close enough to the surface that you can dig it out."

And she used to be squeamish at the thought of attending a boxing match. *Steady, Alyse,* she ordered herself. Clearly he had come to find her out of necessity. He had to know that she would be furious with him. Taking a deep breath, she dipped the corner of her washing cloth into the basin and began stroking it gently along his skin.

"The bleeding is slowing, I think," she observed after a moment.

"Good. If the ball had hit a major blood vessel I'd be dead by now. I don't think there's too much damage."

When she'd cleaned it as best as she could, she set the cloth aside. "I'm going to try to find the ball now," she announced.

He nodded, his shoulders rising and holding as he took a breath.

Carefully she pressed two fingers together on one side of the wound. "Does that hurt?"

"Yes. Continue."

"How will I know if I find it?"

"You'll feel a bump beneath my skin."

Of course she would. Ninny. She continued around the wound until she pressed just beneath it. "I think I've found it," she exclaimed unsteadily, barely remembering to keep her voice down. Aunt Ernesta slept just below her, after all.

"Good," he rasped between clenched teeth. "You need to hurry, then, so you can bandage it up. You don't happen to have any whiskey or brandy up here, do you?"

"Yes, I keep it in my pocket."

"You'll need it to clean the knife and the wound."

Her heart skittered again. "I don't have a knife, either."

He reached for the cuff of his right Hessian boot and drew a long, slender blade out from along his calf. "I do."

Fighting the abrupt urge to panic, Alyse stood again. "There's brandy in the billiards room. I'll be back in just a moment."

"Remember, if you're caught, we're both finished."

Fresh anger brushing through her, she nodded. "I remember."

As she left her room and then crept down the stairs to the first floor, Alyse reflected that he'd probably made her angry intentionally. Otherwise she would have been terrified, both at the thought of what would happen if Richard caught Phin in her room, and at what she was going to have to do if he didn't.

Cut someone open. Cut Phin. She closed her eyes for a moment. If it needed to be done, she would do it. There was no one else. And over the past few years she'd learned how to stand on her own two feet. Once she found the brandy decanter she clutched it to her chest and hurried upstairs again.

Back inside her bedchamber she held the knife over her washbasin and splashed brandy over it. Likewise she dashed some onto Phin's back, holding her breath as he hissed in pain but didn't lose consciousness.

Alyse knelt behind him, raising up on her knees and putting her left hand on his bare upper arm to steady herself. "Are you ready?" she asked, once he'd told her how to proceed.

"Yes. Do it."

Chapter 15 _____

Phineas blew out his breath at the sound of the lead ball clanking into the porcelain basin behind him. Then Alyse pressed a brandy-soaked cloth against his shoulder, and he flinched, cursing.

"You didn't make a sound while I had a knife stuck in your back," she observed, her voice much calmer than it had been a few minutes ago, "but you scream when I touch you with cotton?"

"Cotton and alcohol," he pointed out, wiping an unsteady hand across his brow. "You didn't warn me. And that wasn't a scream. Trust me on that."

"Mm. Lean back against the bedpost, and I'll fetch some bandages."

So she was still angry with him. He could hardly blame her for that. Sidling backward, he let her guide him back so that the cloth stayed pressed between his shoulder and the oak bedpost. He watched as she found a bedsheet in what looked like a pile of mending, and proceeded to tear it into strips.

She kept mending in her private room. Her life *had* changed. She'd told him that, but seeing spirited Alyse Donnelly reduced to being a glorified maid—it . . . angered him.

"Explain something to me, Phineas," she said, kneeling in front of him again. "You're robbing people. Whatever the devil you think you're doing for your family, you're the villain of this piece." She folded one of the bandages into a square, then put the end of a second strip into his hand. "Hold this."

"I am not the— Ow."

Alyse pulled him forward, replacing the cloth with the folded bandage, then pulling the other end of the long strip across the back of his shoulder. "Don't begin crying now," she said shortly, taking back the end he'd anchored and tying it across his chest.

She smelled good, of soap and brandy. Now that the ball wasn't grinding against his shoulder blade any longer and he could actually move without much pain, ignoring her nearly naked presence was becoming more and more difficult. When she leaned against him to wrap another strip of bandage around his back, he couldn't resist brushing his lips against her ear.

"Stop that."

"Stop what?" He twisted a strand of her light brown hair around his fingers.

"Stop touching me." She pulled back to eye him. "I'm angry with you."

"Yes, but I'm grateful to you. Angry or not, you're risking a great deal by helping me."

"No one will know. And if you attempt to tell anyone, I'll say that you cried and sucked on your thumb."

A chuckle rumbled from his chest. He couldn't help it. "Be my friend again, and I'll tell you what I know."

"When we were friends, you robbed me and pretended to be French. I fail to see the advantage of an alliance."

"Look more closely." Phineas took her chin in his fingers, drew her closer, and kissed her softly. "However poorly it ended, I'm glad you didn't marry Layton," he murmured, kissing her again, noting that her mouth softened and molded against his. "Given his character, he never deserved you."

Her fingers tangled into his hair. "You never even met him. You don't know his character."

"I know yours. And I know what he did to you."

"He wasn't the only one to abandon me."

Of course she meant him. He took her free hand and placed it on his chest. "Can you feel my heart? You're the reason it's beating so hard."

"Phin."

"You were always going to marry someone important and fabulously wealthy," he continued. "I was neither."

"Why did you leave?" she breathed, her kisses growing in urgency to match his.

"I was never anything," he replied, shifting sideways so that he could sink down onto the floor, drawing her up across him so he wouldn't have to stop kissing her. "The last thing my father said to me was that if I didn't move off the path I was on, the best he could hope for was that I broke my neck before I could hurt anyone else."

Her fingers paused in their trek across his chest. "He didn't mean those to be his last words to you, I'm certain. And it was a warning; not a condemnation. Surely you see that."

"I see it now. Then, I was fairly certain I needed to stay on that very crooked path and do as much damage as possible in whatever time I had."

"You should have talked to me. We were friends."

"Your father told me to stay away from you before I dragged you into hell with me."

She kissed his throat, and he shuddered. This was bad. He needed to leave, before he did what her father had warned him away from and ruined her remaining reputation. And yet to be able to . . . unburden himself after so many years—he wasn't certain he could make himself walk away now.

"I would have gone with you into hell," she whispered.

Wrapping his arms around her, he twisted them so that she lay beneath, looking up at him. He dipped his head and kissed her again, letting her know with his mouth what his body wanted of her. Before she answered, though, he needed to tell her everything. "That day, the day William . . ." He stopped, clearing his throat. "I came home at midmorning, probably stinking of whiskey and whatever else I'd been doing the night before. William stopped me in the doorway and said he'd allowed me to be stupid long enough."

"Good for William."

"Not really. I was still three sheets to the wind, and I told him that the only way I would listen to him was if he could beat me on horseback to the old ruins. Because if I could outrace him drunk, then he couldn't offer me anything sober. I goaded him into it."

"It was an accident."

"No, it wasn't. I had the lead, and then at the last hundred yards or so he caught up and started to pass me by. I sent my horse into his. They both went down. I kept going until I circled around the ruins. I was taunting him when I came back around, except that he was lying on his back across one of the old masonry stones and he wasn't moving. I thought I'd killed him."

The dawning horror in her eyes, the realization that whatever romantic reason she'd made up for his flight was terribly, awfully wrong, was too much. He pulled away from her, climbing stiffly to his feet.

"So now you know. As soon as the doctor said he would live but never walk again, I secured a promise from your father to help manage Quence, packed my things, and left. If I was going to hurt anyone else, it wasn't going to be someone I cared about." Carefully he bent down to pick up his shirt.

Behind him, he heard her stand. "You shouldn't go yet. You need to rest a little. There's time."

He shook his head. "I'm not staying. I want you. If I stayed, I would ruin you."

She yanked on his uninjured arm, turning him to face her again. "I'm already ruined," she muttered, and pulled his face down to hers again.

Phineas could dispute that, since at the moment she could at least dance at country soirees, but her sweet mouth, her slender body in his arms, were too much too argue against. With a groan he pulled her closer, dropping his shirt again.

He swept his hands down her shoulders, shoving off her dressing robe as he went. His cock ached already, but he ignored it as he lifted her backward onto her bed and followed her, sliding up her body to kiss her again, openmouthed. With the lamp on the floor, their shadows against the far wall looked huge and misshapen, his looming over and consuming hers.

Cupping her left breast through the thin fabric of her night rail, he moaned again as he felt her nipple harden beneath his palm. With swift fingers he undid the two buttons down her breastbone and pulled the material aside to run his hand along her bare, soft skin. Then he licked.

Alyse gasped, writhing beneath him as he tasted her breasts, sucking at her nipples. "Phin," she breathed, arching her back.

He heard the urgency in her voice, mostly because he felt it himself. It had been weeks since he'd had a woman, but that had nothing to do with this. This was Alyse, and everything else melted away. Raising up onto his knees, he found the bottom hem of her night rail and pushed it up, bending down to follow its rising trail with his lips and his tongue.

Twisting a little, he plied off his boots, using one against the other. When one of them hit the floor, though, Alyse froze. "Quiet," she hissed, pushing him aside to grab his second boot and lower it carefully.

"Apologies," he murmured back, pushing her down again and resuming his kisses along her inner thighs. "If it helps, I could hear your aunt snoring very loudly as I came up the stairs."

"She does sleep soundly," she said, her voice unsteady and breathy.

The sound of her excitement aroused him further. "I'll keep that in mind." As he slipped a finger through her curls and pressed against her, he sucked in a sharp breath. God, she was damp for him. For him. Even knowing what he'd done both ten years ago and to her personally just a few nights ago. "Alyse," he whispered, replacing his finger with his lips.

She bucked, digging her fingers into his scalp as he tasted her. He sent his free hand up to tease at her breasts again, and she nearly brained him with her heel. Though he'd hate to be found unconscious with his head between her legs, he would have to admit that it was worth the risk.

He crept upward again, pausing at her flat belly to nip at her skin. Finally he pulled the night rail off over her head, so that she lay, naked and breathless, beneath him. "I mean to have you, Alyse Donnelly," he murmured, unfastening his trousers and shoving them down, watching as her eyes lowered past his hips and widened.

"I want you to have me, Phin Bromley," she returned, pulling him down over her again.

Phineas settled himself between her thighs, kissed her again, and slowly angled his hips forward. The sensation of entering her hot, tight flesh was nearly enough to send him over the edge, and he fought for a measure of control. Alyse. His Alyse. His friend, and now his lover. And tonight neither of them had to be alone.

Alyse dug the pads of her fingers into his shoulders as he pushed through her barrier. She didn't cry out, but then Alyse wouldn't. "Now you're mine," he murmured, dipping his head to place another kiss on her achingly soft mouth.

The clutch of her fingers hurt where she neared his wound, but he didn't care. With a smile Phineas kissed her again. As she relaxed a fraction he moved once more, beginning a slow rhythm against her, inside her. William had said to leave her be. How could he, though, when she was the best part of his memories here?

"Alyse." Nibbling at her throat, he sped his pace, then slowed again, relishing in her obvious pleasure.

"Phin, Phin, this is too much," she breathed, arching her back, pressing against him.

"There's more," he whispered, deepening his thrusts.

As she gasped something he couldn't make out, he shifted a little, moving faster when he felt her draw tighter and tighter and then break with a breathless pulsing that pulled him over with her. He convulsed against her, shuddering.

When Alyse could breathe again, all she could do was hold on to Phin as he climaxed inside her and hope that she hadn't screamed her own release aloud. *Good heavens.*

She didn't have the words to describe how . . . wondrous that had felt. And to be with Phin, to feel his desire and his pleasure—it could mean more trouble, worse even than she'd known before, but with his weight on her, her fingers on his skin, she couldn't regret it. Not now. Not tonight. She could be worried and logical tomorrow.

With a soft sigh Phin kissed her again, then rolled onto his good shoulder so she could curl across his chest. She never wanted him to leave her bed. Alyse ran her fingers lightly over a jagged scar just above his waist on the right side. "What happened to you?" she asked.

"A horse fell on me," he answered easily. "Broke a few ribs, but it wouldn't have been so bad except that the fellow panicked and tried to stand up on me."

"So this is a hoofprint," she said, tracing the ragged half moon.

"Yes, it is."

She shifted her attention to the meaty part of his

right shoulder. "This looks familiar. How many times have you been shot?"

"Including tonight, three." He bent his right knee and jabbed a finger into his lower thigh. "Here's the other one."

Alyse touched it, feeling the round pucker of flesh, then reached up to run the tip of her forefinger down from his forehead across his eyebrow, and down to his right cheek. "You nearly lost your eye."

"Very nearly. French officers are good swordsmen."

His low voice reverberated into her, a private, intimate sensation that she liked very much. How close had he come to dying tonight? How close had she come to never being able to feel this way with him? "Who shot you, Phin?"

He lifted his head to gaze at her. "Are we friends again?"

After this? Only a man would ask such a question. "Yes, we're friends again."

"Lord Charles Smythe."

Alyse gasped. "What? Why would—"

"Because I came upon him removing a pack of wolfhounds from Beaumont's kennel."

The implications of what he was saying stunned her. "Beaumont likes to hunt. Why shouldn't he have hounds?"

"No reason."

"And what—you were dressed as a highwayman. I would have shot you, as well." Unless she was too occupied with kissing him, but she didn't say that aloud.

"That's good to know," he said dryly.

"You know what I mean. You're saying that Lord Charles is responsible for the attack on Quence's flock of sheep. Why would he do such a thing?"

"I don't know. Not yet. I intend to find out. Did Smythe have wolfhounds with him when he came down from London?"

"No."

"If they did belong to Beaumont, can you think of a reason that Smythe would be moving them after midnight, and with half a dozen armed men for company?"

"Phin, you've tried to rob him twice."

He blew out his breath, shifting a little to twine a strand of her hair around his fingers. The sensation made her shiver all over again. "I need help, Alyse," he murmured. "Something is afoot. In the past year Quence has been hit with far more than a coincidental share of accidents. I know Smythe is part of it. If I knew why, I might be able to put a stop to it before William is forced to sell the estate. It's affecting his health now, too. Do you know *anything* that might help me?"

For a second she wondered whether all of this had been part of a plan to charm her into becoming a cohort of some kind. Allowing himself to be shot, though, seemed more than a little extreme. The ball might have killed him. "I heard Charles talking with Richard the other day," she said slowly. "All I could make out was the number forty-seven, and then thirty quid. After we found out about the sheep, I realized that was the number you'd lost."

Phin nodded. "I sold them to the butcher for thirty quid."

"It doesn't mean anything, you know."

"It means that Richard knew about the attack before I told him about it."

Alyse lifted her head to look at him. "I'm not particularly fond of Richard, but he has allowed me to have a roof over my head. And over the past year he's spent a great deal of time helping your brother."

"And he's courting my sister. We've discussed this. I just . . . I don't know how much time I have to resolve this, Alyse. I don't want you to betray your family, but if you should happen to hear anything you can tell me, please do so."

She nodded. "I'll do what I can."

"Thank you."

His breathing slowed, his fingers slipping from her hair and relaxing on her shoulder. For a long time Alyse listened to his heart beating, felt his chest rise and fall as he slept. Promising she would do what she could was one thing; if she heard nothing, then her word would be easy to keep. If she actually discovered something, though . . .

She'd been staying with her hideous Great-Aunt Stevens in Hereford when Richard had appeared to remove her from the house. At first she'd thought that he would simply turn her out, at best giving her a reference as a governess or a companion. At worst, he would just tell her to leave. He'd had some questions about Donnelly House, though, and she'd been able to answer them.

She'd been eager to demonstrate that she could be useful to him. When he'd decided she might serve as a companion to his mother, she'd been relieved—Aunt Ernesta was arrogant and spiteful, but staying with her and Richard meant that she could return home. She could live at Donnelly House again, even if it was in the attic and at her relations' beck and call. It gave her a place from which to plan an escape on her own terms.

Minding her manners was difficult enough; actually

carrying tales about them to Phin could well put her beyond any chance of seeing another Christmas in East Sussex. It might put her beyond any chance of seeing another Christmas, period. She needed another year. That was what she told herself every time she had to bite her tongue against speaking her mind to Richard or Aunt Ernesta.

Phin, though, overwhelmed her. Above his handsome appearance, she simply liked him. She liked talking with him, and listening to him, and she very much liked kissing him. But he was in a hurry to assign blame for Quence's misfortunes. And when he'd satisfied himself on that count, wherever it left her, he would go back to Spain. He was only on leave, after all.

Whatever happened, she would be alone again. The only question was over how much damage she was willing to see done to herself before then, and how much silence her conscience could bear.

Chapter 16 _____

"Phin. Phin, wake up."

Phineas sat straight up, in the same motion grabbing for the pistol he kept beneath his pillow. It wasn't there. Abruptly he realized that this wasn't his bed, and that Alyse stood a few feet from him, a startled expression on her face.

"You're dressed," he said, disappointed.

She brushed at her dressing gown. "I'm back in my bedclothes," she corrected. "It's nearly five o'clock."

Five o'clock. In the morning. Phineas blinked. *Concentrate*, damn it all. He'd lost blood, but not enough to prevent him from having some very nice sex—with Alyse. The stiffness in his shoulder caught up to him, and stifling a groan he rotated his arm. Slowly he swung his bare legs over the side of the bed. "Why'd you let me fall asleep?"

"Because you were shot. How do you feel?"

He looked at her, beginning at her feet and taking his time to reach her pretty eyes. Her cheeks darkened, and lust stirred through him again. "I feel hungry," he said, standing.

"Hm. You'll have to take care of that on your own. Get dressed."

Crouching, Phineas picked up his trousers and pulled them on. "Are you angry?" he asked offhandedly. After all, last night he'd told her some things that she more than likely didn't want to hear.

She shook her head, apparently occupied with gazing at him dressing. If he didn't get his trousers buttoned immediately, he wouldn't be able to do so.

"Frightened?" he suggested.

"Why did you stop the coach and take my pearls in the first place?"

"Ah." He found his shirt, sticking a finger through the blood-lined hole in the back, then pulled it over his head. "At the assembly I saw Smythe put something in his pocket. I wanted to get a look at it. I had no idea you would be inside that coach. If I hadn't . . . taken something from you, the others might have suspected something about me."

Phineas reached out and caught Alyse's hand, drawing her up against him. Slowly he brushed the hair from her face, then kissed her again. His heart stopped beating until she began kissing him back.

"I came to see you as The Frenchman," he whispered, sliding his hands down to her hips, bending her back so that she had to wrap her arms around his shoulders to keep her balance, "because I had to give them back. I know how much they mean to you."

"Why demand a kiss for them, then?" she returned in the same quiet voice.

"Because I wanted to kiss you," he countered, releasing her again to retrieve his waistcoat. "Why the questions now?"

"I'm still trying to decide where I figure into this after you've rescued Quence."

Phineas scowled. That same thought had been troubling him. "Did you sleep at all, or did you spend the night looking for reasons not to trust me?"

"I didn't have to look very hard. I even had time for a nap."

He shrugged into his jacket, wincing as the tight material pulled at his wound. Next he swept up his greatcoat and jammed on his discarded hat. The mask went into his pocket. He didn't intend to be seen. "Give me everything with blood on it," he said shortly, tossing the pillows off her bed and removing her stained bedsheet. He appreciated the evidence that he'd been her first, but he didn't want anyone else to know what had happened. He'd broken his word not to make trouble for her, but he could minimize it as much as possible.

She bundled various cloths and bandages into the sheet and wrapped them all up into a solid lump. His blood and her blood, together. For some reason that seemed . . . significant to him. *Later*, he ordered himself. He could consider it later. "I'll burn them when I get back to Quence."

Finally he sat on the stripped bed and pulled on his boots, careful not to stomp them against the floor. As he stood she went to the door and unlatched it, leaning out to look up and down the short attic hallway. "It's clear," she whispered.

As he passed her, he leaned down and kissed her again. After the night he'd had, it seemed vital to do so. "I know you don't entirely trust me," he breathed. "But you will."

"I hope so."

It was barely audible, and he pretended not to hear it, but he did. And quiet as it was, or perhaps because it was so quiet, it troubled him. Alyse enjoyed his company, but she didn't quite believe he knew what he was doing. He wanted her to. In some ways, that became as important to him as helping his own siblings. And the price of failure could be just as high.

He slipped down the staircase and out the side door through the orangery. Fog hung close to the ground, rendering earth and sky the dull gray-blue of fading moonlight. Pulling his greatcoat closed against the chill, Phineas hurried through the garden and down along the river through the trees.

Smythe and his riders had probably given up the hunt hours ago, but he kept to the thickets just in case. Saffron still stood in his glen, snoring softly. Phineas clucked at him, not wanting the gelding to spook and draw the attention of anyone who might be about. Shifting the bundle of bloody rags beneath his coat, he climbed stiffly into the saddle.

"Let's go home, boy," he muttered, urging Saffron into a trot. The motion jolted his shoulder, but he clenched his jaw and kept going. Back at the Quence stables he woke Tom to tend the gelding, then made his way inside the house and up the stairs to his private rooms.

"Where the devil have ye been, lad?"

He jumped as Gordon practically leapt on him. Pinning the sergeant with a raised eyebrow, he stepped away. "Beg pardon?"

"I mean t'say, where've ye been, *sir?* I nearly paced a trench in th' floor, worryin' over ye."

Phineas went to the fireplace and tossed the bundle of cloth onto the flames. "I had to get myself bandaged up before I could make it back. Any trouble with Smythe?"

The sergeant shook his head. "Nae. Led 'em on a merry chase. They could be halfway to Wales by now."

"I hope not. I want him close enough that I can wrap my hands around his throat." He pulled off his greatcoat. Sticking his finger through the hole at the back of the shoulder, he tossed it to Gordon. "Can you mend this?"

"Swate Jasus," the Scot ground out, dropping the coat and striding forward to grab Phineas's shoulder. "Ye call this a graze?"

"Ouch," Phin snapped, twisting away. "I've dealt with it. You'll have to dispose of these clothes for me, though. A pity I could only wear them once."

"Bandaged or not, Colonel, ye can't leave the ball in there."

"It's not. Now help me out of my jacket, will you? I need some damned sleep." He looked sideways at Gordon. "And no one—*no one*—can know I was hurt. Everything depends on that."

"Aye. What of Lord Charles'n his hounds?"

"The dogs will be well away from here or drowned by now." His jaw clenched as he spoke; he'd found the easiest, most straightforward way of proving that intentional mischief had been done, and he'd lost it just as swiftly. He'd blundered badly last night, and more than once. The best way to demonstrate that he cared for Alyse would have been to stay as far away from her as possible.

"What do we do next, then?"

"Smythe doesn't know it's me who discovered him with the dogs. The Frenchman and I may each have an advantage of sorts—if I can figure out how to use it."

"And how not to get one 'r the other of ye killed."

"That, too."

The sergeant checked his bandage and reluctantly declared it fairly done. As soon as Gordon left the room, Phineas collapsed on the bed. He fell asleep with the scent of Alyse soft on his skin.

Alyse sat back on her heels, examining her handiwork. The wood floor of her bedchamber was damp, but in the growing light from the window she couldn't make out any particularly interesting patterns or stains. Luckily most of Phin's blood had soaked into his clothes.

Luckily. She stood, stretching her back, and then opened the attic window to throw the rest of her wash water out the window and onto the rosebushes. Then she turned to look back at her small room. Clean, tidy, the bed with fresh sheets and already made—just as it always was. Except that it wasn't. She wasn't. Phin had been there, and she could still see him, feel him on her, inside her.

Warmth spun deliciously down her spine. She was far too old for an infatuation, especially when she'd seen—and now knew—the worst about him, but she didn't feel infatuated. Her eyes had been wide open, and she'd seen in him the same loneliness and frustration that she felt every day. And for a time last night she hadn't felt lonely.

Her floor thudded. "Alyse, you lazy girl! Come down here!"

She blew out her breath. If Phin had said it was Aunt

Ernesta who was terrorizing Quence, she might have believed it. Slipping into her shoes, she unlatched her door and hurried downstairs.

"Good morning, Aunt," she said, offering a bright smile. "Might I fetch you some tea?"

"I will take my tea downstairs at breakfast. I want you to go into Lewes with Cook right away and make certain she purchases everything we need for dinner this evening."

Dinner. She'd nearly forgotten that the Bromleys would be joining them for dinner tonight. A shiver ran through her muscles. She would see Phin again. "Of course."

"Richard has also invited Beaumont's guests, so remind Cook that there will be nine of us."

Oh, dear. Phin and Lord Charles, dining together. "But Beaumont and Quence have never dealt well toge—"

"We are aware of that," Aunt Ernesta cut in. "That is why Richard only invited the young people. They are his friends, after all."

"Will they be staying the night, as well?"

"No. Only the Bromleys will be. Though why that awful brother of theirs can't ride a mile home at the end of the evening, I have no idea."

"Perhaps he prefers to stay with his siblings," Alyse suggested, glad she could keep her voice steady at the thought of Phin spending a second night at Donnelly House.

"It seems to me that his siblings were doing quite well before he decided to return from the Continent."

"Hm," Alyse responded. She certainly couldn't say anything aloud about it.

After she and Harriet had helped her aunt dress and

gotten her downstairs to breakfast, Alyse made off
with a buttered roll and headed to the back of the house
to find Cook. As soon as she left the breakfast room,
though, she literally crashed into a tall figure coming
from the foyer.

"Ph— For goodness' sake," she muttered, staggering
backward. Phin certainly would not still be lingering
about the house at this hour.

A hand grasped her elbow, steadying her. "My apologies, Alyse," Lord Charles Smythe said with a faint
smile.

Once she'd regained her balance, she shrugged free
of his grip. "Oh, no, it's my fault," she managed, stifling the abrupt urge to strike the man who'd shot Phin.
"I simply didn't expect to see any visitors up and about
this early."

"It certainly wasn't my idea." Lord Anthony brushed
past his friend to take her hand and bring it to his lips.
"Saunders said Richard would be in his office."

"I don't know. I haven't seen him yet today." She
dipped a curtsy, nervous in their company, and blaming Phin for that, too. "Excuse me."

"Certainly." Lord Anthony smiled at her.

"Alyse," Lord Charles countered, capturing her arm
again before she could escape, "be cautious if you leave
the house today."

She frowned. "What? Whatever for? You don't think
The Frenchman would strike by daylight, do you?"

"That would depend on how desperate he is."

Oh, she didn't know how to play this game. She didn't
want to have to play this game. Naming Phin Bromley
as The Frenchman, though—she simply couldn't do it.
"Desperate for what?"

"Help, I would imagine. I shot him last night."

Alyse gasped, hoping she sounded convincing. "You—"

"Are you certain about that, this time?" Richard asked, as he stepped out of his office. "Because I'm fairly certain you made that claim before."

"But this time I found blood," Charles replied. "We need to talk."

"Breakfast first." Richard gestured them toward the doorway. "Have you eaten yet?"

"Absolutely not," Anthony commented. "Will you be joining us, Alyse?"

She lifted the roll in her left hand. "I've an errand," she said.

"I think any errand can wait until you've eaten." Her cousin stepped back to allow her to return to the breakfast room.

"But your mother—" she muttered.

"Don't worry about my mother. Come and sit with us."

Aunt Ernesta glared at her, but didn't say anything as she led the way to the sideboard and selected a breakfast. After the night she'd spent she was absolutely starving, but since she wasn't supposed to have been there to eat breakfast at all, she chose sparingly. No sense risking having her aunt say she was eating more than she was worth.

"Did Richard tell you that dogs attacked one of Quence's flocks two days ago?" her aunt asked conversationally once the men were all seated around her.

Alyse sent a quick glance in Lord Charles's direction, to find his gaze on Richard. "Yes, he did. Horrible."

"It was probably that highwayman's doing. He's going to kill all of us in our beds—I'm certain of it," Aunt Ernesta continued.

"I shouldn't be at all surprised," Richard supplied.

"There were certainly no wild packs of dogs roaming about before he appeared."

Oh, dear. "But where would he keep them?" she ventured, trying to be the voice of reason. "He must be hiding out somewhere during the day. A pack of dogs is hardly conducive to silence."

"Aren't you the smart one?" her aunt said. "If you have it all figured out, then where is this Frenchman?"

"I'm certain I haven't the slightest idea. I'm only saying it's unlikely that he would have a pack of barking dogs with him."

"And I'm saying that he's already hiding that monstrous black horse somewhere, you silly girl. A few dogs wouldn't be much more difficult."

"Alyse, you're more familiar with the local geography than the rest of us," Richard said with a smile. "Can you think of anywhere he might be stashing himself?"

She was absolutely going to kill Phin for making her a party in this mess. "Not off the top of my head. I didn't do much hiding from the authorities as a child."

"Richard said you used to play in some old Roman ruins," Lord Anthony put in. "Tell us about those."

"The ruins? They're on Quence land, but they're right in the middle of a huge meadow. No one could hide a horse there." She glanced at her aunt. "Or any large dogs."

"Then what was their attraction?" Lord Charles asked, as he buttered a thick slice of toasted bread.

"We think it was an old Roman bath," she answered. "At least that's what we used to pretend. The water in the spring was certainly warm enough."

"I rode by it just the other day," Richard took up between sips of tea, "checking on the irrigation system for Quence. Steam rises from the ground all around it still. It looks to have been a fairly large complex, nearly twice the size of the Great Bath at Bath."

"You and those hot springs," Aunt Ernesta said, snorting delicately. "You talk about them so much, you would think they're on Donnelly land."

Richard's smile deepened. "I can't help being fascinated."

"If they're so wonderful," her aunt went on, "why hasn't Quence done something with them?"

Alyse frowned. "We used to play in them," she repeated. "The ruins are pretty enough, but I'm certain William's barely thought of them in years." Except for the fact that he had lost the use of his legs there—which was undoubtedly part of the reason the family ignored them. Of course she hadn't learned that until last night, but it made sense.

"I believe Lord Quence has enough matters on his plate for just about anyone," her cousin seconded. "And that's without his brother stepping in to counter all of the decisions we've already made."

"He is a part of their family." *And you're not*, Alyse added, not daring to do so aloud. For heaven's sake, they made it sound as though Phin were not only unhelpful, but detrimental to his family's well-being. While she might have doubts about his methods, he'd certainly gotten the attention of Lord Charles—and his two friends.

"Alyse, we shouldn't keep you from your errands any longer," Richard said. "And once you return, you'll need to air out the guest rooms and prepare fresh bedding for Lord Quence and Beth."

"And Phin."

"Yes, and Colonel Bromley."

Eyeing her half-eaten breakfast regretfully, Alyse excused herself and left the table. All speaking up for Phin got her was dismissed from the conversation. No one here liked him—except for her, and she still had to measure her growing affection against an expanding quantity of trouble.

Chapter 17 _____

"It's a bit early in the evening for a highwayman," Phineas drawled from his corner of the newly repaired coach. "And we're fifty yards from Donnelly's front door. I'd wager we're safe."

Beth turned away from her anxious gaze through the half-curtained window. "If I were a highwayman, I would rely on rigid thinking like yours in order to amass my fortune."

Phineas chuckled. "I hadn't realized that you'd studied the tactics of outlaws so closely."

"I'm only being logical."

"Ah." He looked at his older brother, who sat across from him, one hand looped through the hanging wall strap. "Are you certain you're feeling well enough for this?"

William shrugged. "It's important to Beth that we attend this dinner, and so we shall do so."

"Important to Beth how?" Phineas looked from one sibling to the other, taking in Beth's pretty ivory and green gown, the way she sat on the edge of the seat. The realization hit him like a slap in the face. "You're only seventeen," he stated.

"You joined the army at seventeen."

With a scowl, he turned to his older brother. "You approve of this?"

"Richard is very fond of Beth. He'll see her well taken care of."

"*We* will see her well taken care of."

William lifted an eyebrow. "Forgive my skepticism, but you've been away for more than half her life."

"I'm sitting right here, you know," Beth put in, her own expression annoyed.

"What about Lord Bram Johns?" Phineas suggested, a touch desperately. "A few months ago you were mad for him."

"You sent me more than a dozen letters warning me to stay away from him," she said succinctly. "And he's *your* friend. That's hardly a sterling recommendation."

"Perhaps not. But I swear—*I swear*—that you will never have to settle for someone to see you safe." His voice shook a little, but her present situation was also his bloody fault. William had to consider not only Beth's current well-being, but her future. And he'd done his equations without figuring in his errant younger brother. That was going to change. It had to, for all of their sakes.

Beth abruptly scooted across the seat and threw her arms around him. Her fingers dug into his injured shoulder, but he only clenched his jaw, otherwise refusing to flinch.

When he caught William looking at him again, he lifted an eyebrow, daring him to comment on anything. It was their opinion of him that needed to alter—or not. He wasn't precisely showing them his best side, but he was doing as he needed in order to help, when he'd been asked—ordered—not to. Regardless of that, he was not the stupid, callous boy he'd been ten years ago.

Upon their arrival at Donnelly House, he handed Beth to the ground and then stepped back to let Andrews manage William. He had the excuse of being considered a self-absorbed cad, but it still irked him to stand aside. Worse, though, would be trying to lift William and tearing open his wounded shoulder again, and then having to explain that.

"Welcome," Lord Donnelly said with a smile, meeting them in the doorway.

"Thank you for having us," William returned, sitting back as a pair of footmen joined Andrews to lift him and his chair up the front steps.

"I'm just pleased you're feeling recovered enough to attend."

Phineas followed the group into the large foyer, where Mrs. Donnelly stood to second her son's greeting. He nodded to her, but kept his gaze moving. She wasn't who he wanted to see.

"We've all been chatting in the drawing room," Mrs. Donnelly announced, "if you'd care to join us. Lady Claudia has been telling the most amusing tale about a dress shop in London."

They weren't the only guests? Willam hadn't mentioned anything about that. From his brother's quickly covered expression, though, he hadn't expected it, either. "Who's dining with us tonight?" Phineas asked.

"Lady Claudia and Lord Anthony, and of course

Lord Charles. I don't know what I shall do, with all of you handsome young people surrounding me," Mrs. Donnelly said, tittering.

Lord Charles Smythe. Clenching his fists, Phineas forced a return smile. "Without you present, the ratio of young ladies to young men will be sadly out of balance."

"Oh, heavens."

As the group of them clumped down the hallway, Phineas leaned over and grasped William's arm. "Do you wish to stay?" he murmured.

"If I didn't, I would be perfectly capable of making my own excuses."

He straightened again. Well, that had been a nice slap in the face. And considering that his brother had been making his own excuses for the past ten years, it was a much-deserved one. *Idiot.*

In the drawing room, the three guests were gathered on one side of the room, chatting amiably. Across from them, her gaze out the window, sat Alyse.

His breath stilled. He'd never lacked for lovers, but the warmth that trailed out from his chest to the tips of his fingers, the abrupt yearning to touch her—that was new. Her dark eyes lifted to meet his, and desire flooded through him.

"I don't think we need to make introductions," Richard said, motioning a footman to bring around glasses of wine.

"No, indeed," Lady Claudia took up. "We're all friends here."

Phineas shook himself. Lusting after Alyse was dangerous enough, but the man who'd shot him last night stood just a few feet away, laughing at something Lord

Anthony said. He hadn't expected his clearest enemy to be present. Now that Smythe was, though, he could not afford to be distracted tonight.

He might as well have asked the moon not to rise. Everyone still milled about, chatting, and he found himself standing in front of Alyse. "Hello," he said quietly, not trusting himself to take her hand.

"Hello. How are you?" she asked, sending a pointed glance at his shoulder.

"Quite well, thank you." Phineas took a slow step closer. "And how are you?"

Her cheeks colored a soft rose. "Very well," she murmured.

God, he wanted to kiss her soft mouth. This was torture, standing so close and not allowed to touch. Then Beth grabbed his shoulder, and his eyes nearly rolled back into his head.

"Isn't that so, Phin?" his sister was saying.

Swiftly he grabbed her hand, making a show of kissing her knuckles. "Isn't what so, Magpie?" he asked with a smile.

"That you speak four languages. Lord Anthony doesn't believe me."

"I never said I didn't believe you, Miss Beth," the duke's grandson returned, chuckling. "I said we should count ourselves lucky that our highwayman was French. If he'd been The Turk or The Russian, no one at all would have comprehended what he was babbling."

Smythe gazed at Phin. "Which languages do you speak, Colonel?"

Damnation. "Ah. I speak the language of cards, of wine, of women, and of song. That's four, isn't it?"

Richard burst out laughing. "Well said, Colonel."

"And French, and Spanish, and Italian," Beth insisted, frowning at him. "Don't jest about your own accomplishments."

He kissed her knuckles again, his mind racing for a way out of this stickiness. He'd never counted on his sister having so much faith and pride in him. "I've served on the Continent for ten years, Beth. One does tend to learn the rougher parts of the language of the people one is killing or cheating at cards."

"Is that your polite way of saying you've learned all of the unrepeatable words?" Alyse contributed unexpectedly.

"And how to ask for directions," Phineas added with a nod, trying not to let his sudden gratitude show on his face.

"But you—"

"I'm sorry to have exaggerated, Beth," he muttered, squeezing her fingers before she pulled away. *Please let me be able to explain myself later.* William had said he'd been her hero; there was likely a special place in Hades for brothers who dashed the dreams and hopes of their sisters—and right after he'd sworn she would always be looked after.

The number of people who believed in him seemed to be dwindling down to naught. He took a breath. At the moment, he would settle for blaming this all on Lord Charles Smythe, and make himself ready to expand his anger to Richard Donnelly. "Did I hear you correctly?" he continued, speaking to Lord Anthony. "Did you say the highwayman *was* French? Did someone help him on his way to the afterlife?"

"That would be me," Lord Charles said with a grin. "Put a ball right between his shoulder blades. Or perhaps his neck. It was dark, so I'm not entirely certain.

At any rate, I'd wager a hundred quid that he's deceased by now."

Beth clapped. "Well done, Lord Charles. Though I admit, it might have been exciting to see a highwayman."

"I would have preferred to see one hang," Richard put in, drawing Beth's arm around his. "But at least we're done with that nuisance."

Phineas nodded. "In a way, it's a shame. I would have liked to try some of my inappropriate French on him."

They stayed in the drawing room while Donnelly's servants brought their overnight bags upstairs. It didn't look as though the other guests would be staying the night, which would make things easier on him when he went . . . exploring later. Everyone might think Richard Donnelly practically a saint, but he had his doubts. And until they were satisfied, he was not about to stop hunting—whatever the cost.

Alyse couldn't help looking at Phineas every few minutes as they ate dinner. She'd never doubted his courage, but to hear him calmly talking about the supposed demise of The Frenchman, to hear him chuckling over the way Lord Charles had lured the outlaw into an ambush and then finished him off—it gave her the shivers. And not the usual pleasant ones she felt when she thought about Phin. It was the difference, she supposed, between seeing a man in uniform waltzing in a ballroom and seeing him in action on the field of battle. Phin was a soldier, and clearly possessed nerves of iron.

At the same time that his mettle impressed her, though, it worried her. She'd tried to tell him that his wasn't the only life that could change if his actions were discovered, and yet he continued to press on, un-checked. Didn't he realize that there were more impor-tant things than being proved correct?

"I took a ride around the countryside yesterday after-noon," he was saying, from his place between Lady Claudia and Lord Anthony, "and I was a bit surprised to find that no one seems to own wolfhounds. Have they gone out of favor lately?" He chuckled a little. "Of course, if they've been killing sheep, I can see why no one with any sense would want them about."

"I think they're more popular farther north," Lord Charles said, his voice a little stiff. If she hadn't known, if Phin hadn't told her that the hounds were his, she wasn't certain she would have noticed.

"Ah, perhaps that's the problem. We should look into any visitors in the area who've come from the north to go hunting."

"You know, I think Lady Matthews's niece is from York," Aunt Ernesta contributed.

"I don't think Miss Harper is much of a hunter," Richard countered. "And I'm afraid that just about every visitor and houseguest in East Sussex is from the north."

"Or from Brighton," Beth said. "More and more every year, it seems."

"Yes, well, we can thank Prinny for that." William picked at his dinner. "Where he goes, everyone fol-lows."

"I'll admit, my acquaintance with Prinny helped convince me to take up residence here," Richard said.

"I shouldn't wonder that the Romans stopped at your baths on the way to Brighton, my lord," Aunt Ernesta declared, sipping at her third glass of wine.

"I believe Brighton's a bit more recent than that,

Mother." Richard shifted. "Tell me, Colonel Bromley, how much longer do you think Wellington intends to chase after Bonaparte?"

"Until Bonaparte's dead or captured, I would imagine."

"But the baths are right on the way to Brighton," her aunt blurted again. "Something must have been there, or why bother to build here in the middle of East Sussex?"

"There was some kind of fishing pavilion, no doubt," Lady Claudia said, smiling. "What baths are you talking about?"

Phin showed no sign that talk about the ruins made him uncomfortable, and she could rarely tell what William might be thinking. Still, though, Alyse would have preferred that they discuss something else.

"Some old ruins on Quence," Richard said, motioning for more wine. "With five field promotions, I thought perhaps you might know the duke personally."

"Ah. We've met, then. I just don't like to brag about it."

Oh, dear. "I see you had your coach repaired," she said into her plate. "I'm glad the damage wasn't too extensive."

Richard leaned forward. "Are you accusing me again of being a braggart, Colonel? Because I assure you, I'm nothing of the kind."

"I merely made a comment. You're the one who concluded I must be discussing you."

"Phin," William said. "That's enough."

Richard had begun it, but of course no one would censure him. No one ever did. It always made Alyse want to scream, or to punch him in his nose. Phin must be so frustrated, knowing he was attempting to do something to help his family, and with no assistance, no one else to believe in—

His toe kicked against her ankle. Alyse jumped, looking across the table at him. Phin lifted his scarred eyebrow and subtly angled his head toward the dining room door.

She ignored it. Very well, so being embarrassed didn't . . . embarrass him. She wasn't going to leave the room with him.

"These baths," Lady Claudia said into the awkward silence, "are they like the ones at Bath? Those used to be terribly fashionable."

"Used to be, indeed," William returned. "Now you'll find mostly old ladies playing loo and cripples like me taking the waters."

"Don't call yourself that," Beth broke in, frowning.

"Have you taken the waters?" Phin asked abruptly.

His brother looked at him. "I'm not ill," he said slowly. "I don't see the point."

"But—"

"We can discuss my health regimen later, if you wish," the viscount interrupted, no trace of anger in his face.

Did he blame Phin for what had happened? Phin certainly did. Alyse shook herself. Getting tangled in Phin's troubles was the last thing she wanted to do, no matter how much she enjoyed the man himself.

Kick.

She glanced at Phin, subtly shaking her head.

Kick.

He might as well be burning her with a hot poker. Every time they touched, lightning coursed down her spine, hot, and intimate, and welcome. "Stop it," she breathed.

Phin pushed away from the table. "Excuse me for a moment," he said, and left the room without further explanation.

The table conversation went on without pause, leaving her sitting in the middle of it while no one spoke to her. "Aunt, are you cold?" she asked abruptly.

"What? No. I'm fine."

"I'm a bit chilled. I think I'll fetch a shawl."

No one seemed to care, so she stood up and walked out to the hallway, shutting the dining room door behind her.

Phin stood across the hallway, vanishing into the morning room as she appeared.

Her breath speeding, she followed him. As soon as she crossed the threshold he caught hold of her arm, pressing her back against the wall with his body and seeking her mouth with his. With his free hand he reached over and quietly closed the door.

He moaned, tilting her chin up with the force of his kisses. "Alyse," he whispered, taking her other wrist and drawing her hands up over her head. The only way she could reach him was with her mouth. It both frustrated and thrilled her.

"Let me go," she muttered against his lips.

"No." He turned his attention to her jaw and throat.

Oh, heavens. "I thought you would be spoiling for a fight with Richard after that conversation," she managed, feeling warm and boneless.

"I wanted to kiss you," he returned. "I don't give a damn about your cousin, except where he affects my family."

She knew what would come next; he would ask if she'd been able to discover something to support his hunt. When she tugged again he released her hands, and she twisted them into his lapels as his coursed around her hips.

Finally he backed away an inch, resting his forehead against hers. "That should see me through dinner," he panted, wiping his thumb along the side of her mouth. He kissed her once more, gently. "Don't forget your shawl."

With that he opened the morning room door and slipped into the hallway.

Alyse took a breath. He hadn't asked her for information. With a smile, feeling lighter than she had in a very long time, she hurried up to the attic for her wrap.

Chapter 18 _____

After dinner, everyone removed to the music room. It was upstairs, and again Phineas stood back while Andrews carried William and one of Donnelly's footmen toted the chair. His brother's flip answer about taking the waters at Bath bothered him. Had he attempted it? The restorative powers of the water were legendary, and even if they were exaggerated, it seemed at least worth an attempt.

A slender arm wrapped around his, disrupting the path of his thoughts. "Why did you let everyone think you're some kind of boor?" Beth asked, her hazel eyes searching his.

He would have given a great deal to be able to explain himself to her. "Because I am, Magpie."

"You wrote me entire letters in French to help me

with my studies. Now you say you only know the curse words—I don't understand, Phin."

"Color me however prettily you like, Beth, but I'm still a soldier. A killer for pay. They see me for what I am. I don't know why you don't."

She let him go. "You are a liar, Phin Bromley," she said in a low, shaking voice. "You are proud to wear that uniform. How dare you say otherwise."

"Beth," he began, but she walked away. *Bloody wonderful.*

"Entire letters, eh?" A smooth, low voice said from behind him.

Charles Smythe. The evening was getting better and better. Phineas glanced over his shoulder. "As long as no one compares the handwriting too closely," he muttered with a short smile.

"Who wrote them for you, then?"

"A gentleman doesn't kiss and tell. As I'm hardly half a gentleman, I'll give you her first name only. Marie."

With a chuckle, Smythe patted him on the back. Hard. It took every bit of hard-earned discipline Phineas possessed not to flinch in pain, but he managed not to. Clearly Lord Charles suspected him of being The Frenchman. The strategist in him considered whether that might actually not be a bad thing. It would certainly turn Smythe's attention from Quence to him. And unlike the rest of his family, Phineas was ready for trouble. He would welcome it, in fact.

Lady Claudia sat at the pianoforte to play. As everyone took seats to listen, he found Alyse—just in time to see Lord Anthony holding a chair for her and then sitting beside her.

Jealousy stabbed through him. Clenching his jaw, he

took a seat on the other side of William, reminding himself that satisfying as pummeling Ellerby might be, he had other things to consider tonight. And while Lord Anthony and his friends would be leaving at the end of the evening, he would be staying the night.

A footman offered him a glass of port, and he accepted it, downing it at one go and taking a second glass. That one would go into the potted plant beside him, but no one else need know that. Beth might not approve, but he didn't know yet whether Smythe was the only culprit. Being boorish and loud—being noticed—might keep his foe plotting to remove him from the equation, which he hoped would spare Quence and its inhabitants from further disaster.

"Phin, I've allowed you to live your life as you choose," his brother said, very quietly, "but I must ask that you comport yourself with more decorum this evening."

"You've 'allowed' me?" Phineas shot back, beginning to wonder whether simply shooting Smythe and turning himself in for a subsequent hanging might be less painful than allowing the slim remainder of his family's respect and hope for him to wither away and die.

"And you told me that you've changed. I'm beginning to think you can afford the words, but not the actions to prove that."

"And you should have assumed that chair years before I put you into it. Martyrdom suits you."

William slapped him.

It didn't hurt. Not physically. And it would still mark him for life, Phineas thought. Pasting a grin on his face that he hoped didn't look as ghastly as it felt, and ignoring Beth's horrified gasp, he eased to his feet. "Perhaps

I'd best sit over there," he said, moving to the far side of the room and sinking down on the couch beside Mrs. Donnelly.

Lady Claudia's playing had faltered, but at a look from Richard she resumed the piece. That should take care of it. No one in his right mind would assume that he was confiding anything in William now. In the morning he would wear his uniform again, to emphasize the idea that he was an outsider. He would have to send Gordon to fetch it.

"Alyse, sit beside me," Mrs. Donnelly commanded. No doubt she wanted some distance between herself and him. Considering that it brought Alyse next to him, Phineas wasn't about to complain.

She made her apologies to Lord Anthony and walked over to sit between him and her aunt. Phineas made room for her, grateful tonight for a friendly face who knew what he was up to and why.

"Alyse," he murmured.

"Don't talk to me," she returned in the same tone, not looking at him. "You're awful. I made a mistake, thinking you'd changed."

Phineas closed his eyes for a moment. He could do without respect, or pride, as long as he knew it was for his family's own benefit. Without Alyse, though, he suddenly felt denied hope. And that hope, he wasn't certain he could live without.

Even knowing he was doing what was necessary, that his behavior, while it might embarrass his siblings, could also save them from a game in which the players were now attempting to shoot one another, didn't make the evening pass more easily. Phin kept up the pretense, though, and accepted, with an inebriated humor he didn't feel in the least, Beth's unwillingness to kiss him good night before she went up to bed.

Finally he went upstairs to the bedchamber assigned to him, stumbled around loudly for a few minutes, and then put out the lantern at the bedside. Darkness suited his mood better, anyway.

Sitting on the edge of the bed, he shed his jacket and then his boots, moving his knife to his waistband. The Donnellys' private rooms were in this same part of the manor—with the notable exception of Alyse's one floor above—and he stood by his door, listening, until the house quieted into sleep.

Heavy footsteps creaked up to his door, then stopped. Silently Phineas slipped the knife from his waistband and tested the grip in his fingers. Those weren't a woman's steps, and William obviously wasn't walking. That left Donnelly. And—

The someone rapped softly on the door. With a scowl, Phin hid the knife behind his back and pulled the handle. And blinked. "Gordon? What—"

"I brought yer uniform," the Scot whispered, slipping past him into the room, a bundle in his arms.

"Thank you. And why are you still here?"

"Because I'm yer bloody valet. So ye keep tellin' me, anyway. I'm supposed to see ye to bed, am I not?"

"Yes, you are. But not after I've supposedly gone to sleep."

"I knew ye wouldn't be asleep. The servants here're talking a might nastily about ye, by the way. I nearly had to blacken that butler's eye."

"They've been talking nastily because I've been behaving nastily."

Gordon eyed him in the dim flicker of firelight. "An' why is that?"

"Beth mentioned that I speak French fluently. Smythe suspects me of being The Frenchman now, and I didn't want him thinking that my family is party to my masquerade. I want him—and whoever he's allied with—looking at me alone."

"And t'do that ye need yer family to hate ye?"

Phineas narrowed his eyes. "I needed to make our estrangement obvious to anyone looking."

"Why don't ye just kill this bloody Smythe an' be done with it, then?"

"Don't tempt me." Phin tucked the knife back into his trousers. "With the dogs gone, I have no proof of his involvement. And I don't know who's working with him. At the moment, he's more useful to me alive." To himself he could admit that if left with any choice at all, he wanted to find proof, because he wanted at least that much of a chance at redemption.

The sergeant gestured at his attire. "Ye ain't precisely dressed for bed," he noted. "If yer goin' huntin' for clues, then I reckon I got up here at just th' right time."

"No. You go downstairs and find a bed. Keep your ears and eyes open. In this house you have one duty, Sergeant—to make certain my family stays safe."

Gordon gave a crisp salute. "Aye, Colonel. With me last breath."

"Thank you. Now get going. And don't bloody anyone's nose."

Phineas waited another twenty minutes after Gordon left, anticipating the turmoil his valet was likely to cause with the belowstairs staff and giving them time to settle into slumber again. Then he opened the bedchamber door and slipped into the darkness of the hallway.

With every bit of bone and blood in him he wanted to

go upstairs to the attic, to find Alyse and explain to her that if he was a boor, it was an intentional one, and to tell her that he needed her, at least, to have some hope that he wasn't a complete failure as a friend, a brother, and a man.

That, though, would have to wait. He didn't know how much time he might have, and he needed to do a bit of hunting, as Gordon called it.

He had a target in mind tonight, as well: Richard, Lord Donnelly. Beth might consider him attractive, and William a brother to replace the useless one with whom he'd been burdened, but Phineas didn't believe it. Donnelly's life of charitable works had only begun once he'd arrived in East Sussex. And there had to be a reason behind it.

As of this moment he had little more than suspicions and a few oddly placed facts. Donnelly had arranged for the new irrigation dam to be put where it would annoy the rest of Quence's neighbors. He'd known about the dog attack and had claimed ignorance for no discernible reason. And largest of all, he was good friends with both Lord Charles Smythe and Lord Anthony Ellerby.

No, it wasn't much; not yet. But there was also a soldier's instincts. If they'd been on the battlefield, Phineas wouldn't have turned his back on the viscount. That was for damned certain. But he wanted proof. And he intended to remedy that shortfall tonight.

Moving silently, he slipped down the stairs to the ground floor. Donnelly's office and study lay down a side hallway at the front of the house, and he padded barefoot down the dark corridor until he reached the door.

It was closed . . . and locked. The sign of a guilty

mind? He didn't know that, but he did know that a lock wouldn't stop him. Pulling his knife free, he slid it between the door and the frame and pushed down. With a small click, the door swung open.

Simple enough. He made his way inside, closing the door behind him again. Donnelly had kept the huge inlaid mahogany desk he remembered from his youth, when Alyse's father had sat behind it. The windows took up most of the left hand wall, while directly behind the desk were two orderly bookcases, a third on the opposite wall.

Clutter would have been easier to sift through without the disruption being noticed, but he'd manage regardless. He began with the desk, pulling open each drawer in turn and examining anything interesting by the light of the nearly full moon. Estate account ledgers, correspondence from solicitors and friends, invoices—nothing out of the ordinary.

His frustration growing, he kept looking. Half the books on one shelf behind him seemed to be about the various Roman baths scattered about the south of England. Apparently Donnelly had an obsession. Of more interest was the map folded up between two pages of one of the books. He drew it out, unfolding it. The scale was one inch to a quarter mile—the same as the rice parchment he'd stolen from Smythe. A geological survey of Quence Park, noting elevation, vegetation, and water flow, along with markings he couldn't quite make sense of in the dark.

Anger coursed through him. However helpful Richard Donnelly might have been to Quence, he had no right to be making surveys of another man's property. Phineas pocketed the map. When he returned home he would make a little survey of his own, combining this map with the one he'd liberated from Smythe.

He flipped through the book, a history of the rediscovery and restoration of the town of Bath itself. Everywhere he turned tonight, Roman ruins, Roman baths—the last thing he wanted to think about. That was where he'd destroyed his brother, and himself. What the devil was the attraction?

Attraction. Something tickled at the back of his mind. Something they'd all been talking about during dinner. He reached for the map again.

The office door rattled and opened.

In the same heartbeat Phineas ducked behind the desk. Light glowed yellow—whoever it was had a candle.

"Phin?" Alyse's soft voice whispered.

Thank God. He started to his feet.

"Yes, Colonel Bromley," Lord Donnelly's voice returned.

Bloody— Phineas sank down again.

"Why in the world would you say such a thing?" Alyse asked. "Aside from the fact that Phin has spent the past ten years *fighting* the French, he came home to help William. Not to become a highwayman."

"He speaks French."

"So do I. And so does his sister. Does that make us The Frenchman's companions?"

"He's The Frenchman."

Trying to hide her discomfort with spinning lies, Alyse looked at her cousin as they entered his office. He seemed fairly confident that he was correct. And yet he hadn't chosen to confront Phin with his suspicions. That was all he had, then—suspicions. And he wanted her to confirm them. So Phin was probably enjoying a good night's sleep and she was supposed to betray a friendship that had become much more than that. No matter how . . . awfully he'd behaved tonight.

"Well?" Richard leaned one haunch against his desk and eyed her.

"What do you want me to say? It's ridiculous."

"I am in a position," her cousin said slowly, clearly choosing his words with great care, "that may soon see me with a great deal of money. Phin Bromley and his bumbling about could very well put that . . . endeavor at risk. I need to stop him. I will stop him."

Alyse took a breath. "And yet he's still fast asleep upstairs."

"I need proof. I need proof that he's riding about the countryside robbing coaches."

"Richard, why are you telling me this? I hardly have your confidence."

"Because the two of you used to be friends. If he talks to you, then you talk to me."

Alyse shook her head. "I couldn't do that. Friendship means more than that." And Phin meant much more than that.

Her cousin straightened again. "As I said, I have a great deal of money ready to flow into the family coffers. I would be willing to share some of it with you."

"Beg pardon?"

"You heard me. In fact, if you should happen to be in a position to aid me by providing me with that particular information, I would hand you ten thousand pounds, Alyse. For you."

She couldn't breathe. Ten thousand pounds? That was more than she would be able to liberate from her relations in a hundred lifetimes. She could purchase her own home, hire her own servants, never have to be anyone's companion again. The young men of her circle would abruptly find her acceptable again. A wealthy, independent heiress. Her.

"Consider it, my dear. And it's not as though you would be doing anything but good. Phineas Bromley is unwanted and unhelpful, especially to his own family. And if he doesn't stop, things could become worse. For everyone involved. Think on it."

With that he moved past her, blowing out the candle, and left the room. Alyse sat down hard in one of the guest chairs. Ten thousand pounds. And she already knew enough to earn it.

All she had to do was betray Phin. Phin had already asked her to betray Richard—or his friends, anyway. And he hadn't offered her anything in return. Nothing she could use to set herself free. Oh, she needed to think. And not in the middle of Richard's office.

She returned upstairs. When Phin had arrived this evening, she'd looked forward to nothing so much as having him steal up to her bedchamber sometime in the middle of the night. Then when he'd said those terrible things to William, she'd wanted him to come visiting so she could give him a piece of her mind. Now, though, she didn't know what she wanted.

Or rather, she did know what she wanted. All that remained uncertain was whether giving up one was worth the price of the other.

Chapter 19 _____

Alyse sat on the worn rug in front of her small fireplace. Resting her chin on her knees, her arms enfolding her, she gazed into the dying embers. Her mind raced in a hundred different directions, swooping toward possibilities and veering away again.

Her door opened almost silently and then closed again. It wouldn't be Richard; he'd already been there, and he'd knocked before he'd taken her downstairs and made her an offer that would have caused Judas to blush.

He—and she knew who it was without looking—sat on the rug behind her. Fingers stroked softly through her hair, sending a warm tingle down her spine. For a long moment he simply sat there in silence, playing with her hair.

"I'm sorry," Phin finally said, his voice low and quiet and intimate.

She kept her chin on her knees. "What are you sorry for?"

"Firstly, for being so . . . awful, as you put it. I had no choice."

"It's not me to whom you should be apologizing."

"Yes, I know that. Smythe suspects me of being The Frenchman, though, and I didn't want him thinking that William condoned—or even knew—what I've been up to."

"You've still hurt your family, when they've done nothing wrong."

"That's my hell, then. But I owe *you* an apology as well, Alyse."

She drew a breath, part of her wishing that daybreak would never come, and they could just sit like this forever. "Are you going to apologize for kissing me, or for . . . bedding me?"

"Neither. Everything since I've come home has been a surprise. You've been the best part of it."

If there had been anything that could make her feel worse and more conflicted than before, hearing him say that accomplished it. "I think you should go."

"I think you should confirm Richard's suspicions about me."

Alyse froze.

"What do you mean?" she stammered, not daring to look at him now.

"I was in Richard's office earlier," he returned. "Looking for anything that might explain this mess. I didn't mean to eavesdrop, but I didn't have much choice."

Her cheeks flushed. "If your plan was to be nice to me or to seduce me into keeping my silence, you shouldn't have said anything about that."

"I put you in the middle of this mess." He put a hand on her shoulder, gently turning her to face him. "I want to make it up to you."

"By having me turn you in? If you're concocting another game, at least make it believable."

"I'm serious. Ten thousand pounds, Alyse. No more doing the wash or mending socks for your damned aunt."

"And you hanged."

Phin shook his head, leaning in to softly brush his lips against her forehead. She liked the gesture; it was as though he couldn't help himself, that he simply needed to touch her. "It won't happen."

"So you'll flee back to the Continent? You'll never be able to return home." And that thought bothered her a great deal.

"I need to ask you for a few days before you tell Richard what you know. Will you give me three days?"

She eyed him. "You aren't going to ask for my help, or for me to tell you what I know?"

"I want to, but I won't. I have enough enemies, and I don't want to make one of you. Just give me three days, and I'll do the rest. Will you do that?"

It could be a ploy, she supposed, Phin's version of playing the compassionate friend in order to sway her decision. It felt different than that, though, and the look in his green-brown eyes was serious and troubled. "Tell me what you know," she said.

"Alyse, I've done badly enough by you. If you ask me, I'll tell you, but the more you want to be involved, the more I will involve you. Be careful what you ask for."

She searched his face for a long moment. He'd certainly given her a way out, had even removed a share of guilt from the equation. "I don't want to be used, Phin," she said quietly, holding his gaze.

"I underst—"

"If you want my help, ask me for it. No tricks, no seductions, and no lies. Just ask me. And tell me the truth."

To her surprise, he smiled—the open, genuine smile he'd had as a youth, before . . . before the scandal, before everything had gone wrong. "I won't promise not to seduce you, but I will swear that it's only because I can't keep my hands off you."

Oh, goodness. "I can accept that," she said unsteadily, heat starting between her legs.

"Good."

Phin tilted her face up and kissed her, softly at first, and then with more and more . . . need. He groaned against her mouth, sweeping his arms around her and lowering her onto her back.

"Aren't you going to tell me what you know?" she asked, then gasped as he opened the front of her night rail and reached in to circle his fingertips around her left breast, moving in closer and closer until he gently pinched her nipple between his thumb and forefinger.

"Later," he murmured, lowering his head. "I can't think at the moment." His mouth closed over her breast, sucking and pulling.

Her eyes rolled back in her head. She could certainly understand his inability to think. Nothing was supposed to feel this good. That was certainly why unmarried persons weren't supposed to indulge. Because if they did, then why marry at all?

"Phin," she murmured, lifting her hips as he tugged at the bottom hem of her night rail, pulling it up around her waist.

"Lift up," he ordered thickly, and pulled the gown off over her head.

His very capable mouth returned to hers, then trailed down between her breasts, lingered at her belly, tongue flicking, before he slipped down between her thighs. Panting breathlessly, Alyse tangled her fingers into his hair.

She felt on fire, flames sweeping around her and through her. This was Phin, her Phin, and he wanted to be with her. It was a powerful realization, that as seductive as he could be, as dangerous as he could be, he'd come here, to her.

Phin sat back a little, just enough to pull off his waistcoat and then yank his shirt off over his head. Someone had put a fresh bandage across his shoulder, she noted. Someone else had touched him. His valet, she hoped. "Come up here," he growled.

Alyse sat up, and he took her hands, guiding them to the fastening of his trousers. He watched her hands, his breath coming deep and fast. Running her tongue across her lips, Alyse brushed her fingers across the tented material at his crotch. Phin jumped, his eyes half closing. "This excites you," she whispered shakily.

"You excite me."

She unfastened the buttons as swiftly as her fumbling fingers could manage, then yanked down his trousers to his thighs. He came free, proud and erect. Alyse's mouth went dry. "Goodness," she murmured.

Phin grinned again. "Nothing good about it," he returned, pressing her back again and following her down with another heart-stopping, openmouthed kiss.

"What do I call it?"

"A cock," he said in his low drawl.

"That sounds wicked."

"Oh, it is."

He kicked out of his trousers, then wrapped his arms around her and twisted so that in a breathless whirl she ended up lying atop him. Phin reached up, pulling her face down to kiss her again, teasing at her mouth with his tongue until she opened to him. His tongue flicked along her teeth, shocking and intimate. His . . . cock pressed up between her thighs. She wanted it inside her, and lifted up.

"Phin, what—"

Reaching between them to guide himself, he drew her back down on him again with his free hand on her hip. As she sank down over him, on him, he sighed. The sensation as he slowly filled her was . . . indescribably satisfying and arousing. Alyse moaned shakily, curling forward over his chest.

"You're not going to faint, are you?" he asked, laughter in his deep voice.

"No."

"Good, because that wouldn't be seemly." He placed both hands on her hips, lifting her up and then drawing her down again, pressing up with his hips to match the motion.

"Like riding a horse," she gasped, repeating the motion as he pursued her again.

"A very naughty one," he agreed, plunging up into her as she lifted up and down, up and down across his hips.

They moved faster and faster, more and more urgently, until she drew so tight she couldn't even breathe. And then she shattered, collapsing against his chest. Phin surged up into her again, wrapping his arms around her to hold her as he moaned, shuddering, against her.

She lay across his chest, entwined with him, until her

breath and heartbeat steadied. Then she sat up a little. "How is your shoulder?"

"Hurts like the devil," he answered, reaching up to twine a strand of her hair around his finger. "What say we move to the bed?"

With a nod she reluctantly separated from him to stand, taking his good hand to pull him to his feet beside her. He'd been nearly six feet tall when he'd left, and he had to be several inches past that now. He was still lean, but more muscular and solid-looking than she remembered. And of course there were the scars.

"Keep looking at me like that, and we won't make it to the bed," he murmured, leaning down to kiss her once more. As he straightened, a lock of his brown hair fell across his forehead, making him look young and disheveled and devilishly delicious.

Alyse smiled. "Is your mind working again?" she asked, not bothering to dress again before she slipped between her sheets, shifting over to leave room for him.

"Barely functional." Shifting his trousers closer to the bed, Phineas lay down on his back, pulling her across his chest and helping her lift the blankets to cover them both.

"Who rebandaged your wound?"

"Gordon. My sergeant. My valet." Phineas, still filled with the need to touch her, rested his palm on her shoulder. "He said you did a sterling dressing, by the way, and he's patched me up enough to know the difference."

She chuckled, her breath soft along his chest. No tears, no panicking for Alyse Donnelly. She'd already seen what their world had to offer for those who . . . disappointed. And she continued to live her life as she chose, as best she could under her present circumstances. God, she was a brave soul. Braver than he was. If she wanted to know everything, he would tell her.

"I told you that I saw Smythe with the wolfhounds," he began quietly. "And he denied it again tonight."

"Yes. I noticed that. It's still just your word, however. Or rather, The Frenchman's word."

"I found a map in Richard's office that matches the one I liberated from Smythe. Take a look at this." Stretching to reach his trousers and trying not to wince, he pulled Donnelly's map from his pocket and unfolded it. "Smythe's drawing is back at Quence, but the center of attention seems to be those damned ruins."

"The old baths?"

"Mm-hm."

"Do you have anything other than a map with which to prove this?"

He eyed her. "What are you, a solicitor?"

"You're the one risking your neck. I'd like to believe that it's not because of some hunch or other."

"I see. You want to be certain I have a boat before you jump into the duck pond with me."

"A boat *and* oars."

"I'm not entirely certain what I have."

"Phin—"

"You asked me to be truthful. Smythe's drawing shows what looks like a fairly substantial road leading past the ruins, and several buildings adjoining them. Other than a handful of historians and landscape painters, I can't think of anyone who would be interested in making the journey to see them. And that's certainly not enough people to warrant a road, much less structures."

"No one can build a road or anything else on Quence property without William's permission."

"They can if William doesn't own Quence."

"What?"

"Quence has never been entailed; it can be lost, or sold."

Alyse shifted to rest her head on his good shoulder. He couldn't remember ever feeling so . . . comfortable with a lover before. But then, he and Alyse had known one another for years. "You think the dogs and the flooded pasture and everything have been for the purpose of forcing William to sell the property? To whom?"

He took a breath. For someone who claimed not to wish to be involved, she'd begun asking a great many pertinent questions. But he'd said he would be forthright, and so he would. Even if she decided not to help him, knowing that she at least believed him would mean . . . everything. "If I were William and facing the loss of Quence, I would want to sell it to someone I trust, a fellow who's already familiar with the workings of the property."

"Richard, you mean." She sat up, staring down at him.

"He did just tell you that he anticipates coming into a great deal of money. Having Quence would more than double his property in East Sussex."

She thought about that for a moment. "It's still a large step to go from thinking him helpful to a crippled neighbor to calling him a criminal."

"In your opinion." Unable to help himself, Phin reached over to cup her soft right breast. She half collapsed on top of him again.

"Stop that. This is serious."

"I know that. And I know he wants Quence, by purchase or by inheritance. I would imagine that courting

Beth is all part of his plan to ingratiate himself with William, as well. The only thing I can't figure is how he would have planned to bypass me. Surely, whatever happened between us, William would deed Quence to me before he would give it over to Beth's husband."

Her breath stopped. His soldier's instincts screamed that she knew something, but he kept his mouth shut. He'd said he wouldn't ask her to do anything but wait a few days before she told Richard what she knew. He wouldn't break his word, however much he wanted to.

"He didn't know about you," she said after a moment.

Phineas lifted his head to look at her. "He didn't know about me?" he repeated.

"When you first arrived he actually seemed a little angry with me, because I'd never mentioned a third Bromley sibling."

Now, this was interesting. "It made him angry, eh? That's good news, because I intend to make him even more angry."

"I . . . may know a bit more," she offered unexpectedly, "but I need to think about it first."

He kept his expression even. "Fair enough."

Alyse curled a fist and hit him in the ribs.

"Ow. What the devil was that for?"

"Why are you being so reasonable, Phin Bromley?"

"Because I've made my family dislike me, probably more than they did before I returned home. And I saw the way you looked at me in the music room. I want an ally. I . . . need . . . a friend." He drew a breath. "And now that I've found you again, I'm reluctant to lose you."

Alyse twisted, putting one hand on either side of his

head to look down at him. "You can, on occasion, be very nice," she whispered. "And you make me forget that I'm alone."

"You're not alone."

And neither was he. She sank down, touching her lips feather-light to his. He wanted to devour her, but let her set the pace, and the tone, and he softly kissed her back. As her hand crept down to curl around his stiffening cock, he groaned. Yes, a fellow could get very comfortable with this. If he didn't get himself killed first.

Chapter 20 _____

When Alyse awoke, Phin was already gone. She sat up. The only sign that he'd been there at all was the red rose he'd placed on the pillow beside her head.

With a smile she stretched, relishing in the feeling of her naked skin against the smooth sheets. He couldn't have been gone long, because the pillow where he'd rested his head still felt warm.

Goodness, she'd slept well, especially considering that after the offer Richard had made her last night she'd never thought to sleep again. He would have his proof—in three days, and after she'd had another chance to go over with Phin what he wanted her to say. It seemed she had chosen her side in this, however many questions she still had.

Her floor thudded. "Alyse!"

"Blast it all," she muttered, flinging aside the covers and racing naked to find her shift and a morning gown to wear. The Bromleys would be staying for breakfast and then returning home as soon as William felt able, and more for her own sake than her aunt's she wanted to be downstairs in time to dine with them. With Phin.

What a relief it had been to hear him say that he'd actually had a reason for distancing himself from his brother and sister. Because angry and disappointed as she'd been, neither had she felt ready to condemn him. After the night they'd spent, she had another reason to be pleased that he wasn't what he publicly made himself out to be.

Humming, she shrugged into her pelisse and hurried out her door. Downstairs she knocked at her aunt's door, then opened it at her summons. "Good morning, Aunt Ernesta, Harriet," she said, walking over to kneel at her aunt's feet and help her on with her shoes.

"What are you so happy about?"

"It's a pretty morning," she improvised, flattening out her smile a little.

"Pretty for you, perhaps. You had me up half the night with your thudding on the floor, right above my head."

Oh, good heavens. Hoping she wasn't blushing, Alyse folded her expression into a sympathetic frown. "I beg your pardon, Aunt. I spilled some water, and needed to sop it up before it soaked into the floorboards."

"You should be more cautious. I don't want your clumsiness giving me a damp chill. Or keeping me awake for hours and hours again."

"Of course I shall be. More cautious, I mean."

She and the maid pulled Aunt Ernesta to her feet so

she could make her way over to her dressing table for
Harriet to do her hair and rouge her cheeks. Restless
and wanting badly to head for the breakfast room,
Alyse swung her arms and wandered over to the door
and back. At the sound of heavy footsteps she pulled it
open and looked out. Phin's valet, the sergeant, walked
past the doorway.

"I'll be back in a moment," she said over her shoulder, and left the room, closing the door behind her.
"You. Gordon, is it?"

The valet turned around. "Aye, miss," he said in a
heavy Scottish brogue. "What can I do fer ye?"

"Is Ph—is Colonel Bromley still to bed?" she asked.

"No, Miss. 'E's down havin' breakfast. I'm t'pack his
bag."

She took a step closer. "You served with him on the
Peninsula, did you not?"

"Aye." He puffed out his stout chest. "Still do. An'
proudly. The colonel's a fine officer. The finest."

She'd meant to ask Mr. Gordon about Phin's character away from the mess in East Sussex, though he'd
answered that fairly clearly already. His words, though,
reminded her of something else entirely, and served to
return her floating feet firmly to the floor. "Has he said
when you'll be returning to Spain?"

"Not yet. Fairly soon, I imagine. 'E gets restless without a battle t'fight."

"No doubt." Alyse cleared her throat, fighting against
the sudden urge to cry. "I won't keep you from your
duties, then," she said, and turned around again.

Phin had said that she wasn't alone. He'd probably
meant to say that she had company—his—for that evening. Of course he would return to his regiment. He
would repair matters here, which would undoubtedly

entail shredding his relationship with his siblings beyond repair, and then he would leave again to fight his battles after he'd ensured that he could never return.

She would have her ten thousand pounds, more than enough to buy the silence of a discreet lover or two, if she should choose to pursue that path, but somehow last night when she'd imagined her future, Phin had been a part of it. *Stupid, stupid girl*, she muttered at herself, and returned to her aunt's bedchamber.

"Don't put much on your plate," her aunt instructed as they went downstairs. "I may not be able to stand that man's company, and it will appear rude if you leave with a full plate of food."

Alyse wanted to ask whether Aunt Ernesta would be eating lightly as well, but she had enough silver to help Saunders polish later without giving herself more trouble. So instead she nodded. "I shall sit between you, if you wish it."

"I do wish it. That man deserves a good dressing-down. He . . . Oh."

Aunt Ernesta's hesitation was understandable. As they walked into the breakfast room, Phin stood at the sideboard piling rolls and strips of ham onto his plate. His appetite hadn't been what had stopped her aunt in her tracks, however.

It was the uniform. He'd said he meant to wear it again, but she'd forgotten. There he stood, though, in his crimson coat with its blue facing, adorned with his rank and insignia and several important-looking medals, his breeches white and snug across the muscles of his thighs, his black Hessian boots polished to such a shine that they reflected her distorted face in them. *Oh, my.*

He nodded to them. "Good morning."

"Good morning." She waited, scarcely noting that Beth and Richard were already at the table. Then Phin's gaze met hers, warm and welcoming. In a heartbeat he looked away again, taking a seat halfway down the table. But in that second, he belonged to her, and she to him.

"What are your plans for today?" her cousin asked, his attention on Beth. Was his interest a ploy? Did he mean to use the seventeen-year-old to gain ownership of Quence Park? If so, he was more of a monster than Phin could pretend to be even on his darkest day. But it was all conjecture, and she had no idea how Phineas would ever find proof—and certainly not in the three days he'd asked for.

"I'll return home with William," Beth answered, "and then Lady Claudia and Janet Harving and I are going riding after luncheon."

"I hope you ladies will have an escort. There is a highwayman roaming the countryside."

"I thought he was dead," Phin commented.

Beth's smile was directed at Richard rather than her brother. "Are you volunteering, Richard?"

"I certainly am."

"Good. Then come by Quence at two o'clock."

"I shall be there promptly."

"You might have asked me, you know," Phin put in, around a mouthful of ham.

"No, thank you." His sister's smile froze in place, her voice sharpening.

William, his servant behind him, wheeled into the breakfast room. "Good morning, all," he said, his gaze skipping over Phin.

Oh, this was awful. If Phin was wrong about Richard and Lord Charles, wrong about the misfortunes that had befallen Quence, he would never be able to make amends to his family. And if he was correct, the prospects were even more worrisome. She had to wonder how far he would go to protect his family from a perceived threat. He was a soldier, and saw things in black and white. Life and death.

"You look very official, Colonel," Richard offered.

Phin nodded. "I'm going riding myself, this morning," he said. "I didn't want anyone mistaking me for that damned Frenchman and taking a shot at me."

All the blood left Alyse's face, and she sat down hard in her chair. If that had been any more direct, it would have involved slapping gloves and challenges to duels. And still Phin managed to look as though he'd just delivered a hilarious jest.

"A red coat and a yellow horse," she commented, forcing a chuckle. "You will definitely be noticeable."

"My intention precisely." He glanced at her plate, lying beside his. "No appetite this morning?"

She couldn't very well confess that she'd been forbidden to gather a full breakfast. "There were no strawberries left," she said instead.

"Ah. If you'll excuse me, I think I'll go find something with which to occupy myself. My man brought my horse, so I bid you farewell. *Adieu.*" With a last bite of his breakfast, he pushed away from the table and strolled out of the room.

"I apologize for my brother's behavior," William said to no one in particular, nodding his thanks as his valet brought him tea and two pieces of toasted bread. "He's having difficulty adjusting to civilian life, I think."

"That's understandable," Richard commented promptly. "He's served his country for the past ten years. There's no need to apologize."

Abruptly Alyse felt alone again, and trapped. They all disliked him and dismissed him—which was as he planned, but she didn't have the luxury of ignorance. Then she looked down at her plate. The half dozen strawberries that had been on Phin's plate were now on hers. The man had the skill of a master illusionist. And he'd been thinking of her, even with everything else he had to worry over.

Smiling, she bit into one of the sweet fruits. As she looked up again, William was gazing from her plate to her face. And she didn't think it was because he was hungry for strawberries. What *she* was hungry for was the man who'd given them to her.

"What're we lookin' at, now?"

Phineas closed his eyes for a moment. He should have done this on his own. Considering the location, he didn't precisely feel chatty. The soldier in him, though, knew there was a very good possibility he was being watched, if not hunted, and he wanted a second pair of eyes on his side.

"The ruins." He nodded in the direction of the shallow slope, down to the bottom of the meadow.

"Way down there?"

"Yes, way down there. I want to take a look at the perimeter."

"Ah. I don't think th' Romans're up fer a siege, then, if that's what's worryin' ye."

"You are an amusing fellow. Just keep your eyes open, Sergeant."

"Aye, Colonel."

He wanted to do a comparison of the terrain versus the notations on the two-part map, but not at the crest of the hill where anyone with a spyglass could see precisely what he was up to. It would have to wait until he descended into the meadow to the ruins themselves. The problem being, he didn't want to get any closer.

It was ridiculous. He'd faced down battalions of French soldiers, charging cavalry, lines of cannon. And none of them sent sick chills down his spine the way those ruins did.

Better to get the damned business over with. Phineas blew out his breath, squared his shoulders, and nudged Saffron in the ribs. They descended into the center of the meadow at a walk, Gordon and Gallant on their heels.

"This was a big place," the sergeant noted, leaning out to run his hand over one of the remaining standing stone pillars. "'N it's warm down here. Are th' hot springs still flowin'?"

"Yes." Phineas shook himself. "Watch the footing. It can get swampy there where the lilies are growing."

"Hm. Not too bad now. Probably durin' the winter. Did ye go swimmin' here as a lad?"

"Yes."

"The waters were probably good fer yer brother the viscount, weren't they? If ye could get 'im down here."

"William wasn't crippled then. He could climb down on his own."

Phineas dismounted, leaving Saffron standing while he walked over to a small tumbled wall away from the main part of the bath ruins. It had happened here. He supposed it would have been devastatingly poetical if he could imagine he still saw traces of the blood—but he remembered quite distinctly that there hadn't been any blood. None at all. Just William, lying there at a chilling angle, his face white and his mouth open as if he were screaming, though no sound emerged.

"Colonel? Colonel!"

He shook himself. "What?" he snapped, looking over at Gordon.

"Are ye well?"

"Yes. I'm fine. It's just that I nearly killed my brother right on this spot, and I haven't been here since that day." He felt the sergeant staring at him, but continued anyway. "I hate this place, you know?" he said half to himself, slowly circling the wall. "We used to play here all the time, and now I can't stand to be in sight of it."

"Then why're we here?"

"Because it's important." Still feeling almost . . . dazed, as though he'd walked into his own dream—or his own nightmare, more like—Phineas pulled the two maps from his pocket. Setting Richard's on the bottom, he lay Smythe's across the top.

It was a better match than the one at the surveyor's office, and more accurate. Or more recent, at least. The stream had moved its banks in the past few years, but its most recent track was carefully noted.

"You've done terrain mapping for me before, Gordon," he said. "Come take a look at this and tell me what you see."

The sergeant dismounted to join him at the wall. Phin handed him the maps, and he looked at them for a long moment. "This is definitely here," Gordon said slowly, turning with the maps in his hands. "But it's not."

"Why not?" Phineas had his own theory, but with so many people telling him he was creating havoc to suit himself, he wanted a second opinion.

"Th' ruins is gone," the sergeant said, scowling. "Part of 'em is. An' there's a new buildin' in their place. A grand one. An' another two 'r three over here, on top o' the hill. An' a road joinin' 'em all, heavy like th' one the engineers had t'put in for supplies last year at Salamanca." He looked up at the meadow, then down again. "Why would someone want t'build a house in the middle of a marshy hot springs?"

"It's not a house."

"Then wh—"

"It's a bath. And I would guess that those other buildings are inns, up where the ground is firm all year round and they'll have a view."

"What the devil is this about, Colonel?"

Phineas sighed, pushing back his growing frustration and anger. He knew how to harness those emotions, how to save them, nurture them, until they could be used—with withering results. "In my opinion," he returned, taking the maps back and folding them together, "this is the beginnings of the next city of Bath."

"Bath is past its prime, I thought."

"It is." Phineas faced south. Down in the meadow bottom all he could see was the rise of the slope, but at the top would be fields and trees and rivers, and beyond them, the sea. And Brighton. "Imagine a place to take the waters, located between London and Brighton. Not a place to settle in and play whist and grow old and senile, but to holiday for a few days or a sennight and then move on."

"Holy Jasus," Gordon breathed.

Here, unlike Bath, there would be a destination at both ends. Brighton was becoming hugely popular, thanks mostly to Prinny's obsession with building himself a palace there. And it also offered a launching place to the Americas, or to Africa or beyond, and back again.

"These plans," the sergeant said, gesturing at the map. "Yer brother th' viscount ain't a part of 'em."

"He doesn't know anything about them."

"This is Donnelly's doing?"

"It is beginning to seem so." Phineas pocketed the maps and strode back to collect Saffron.

"Why wouldn't he tell yer brother, and they could become partners?"

"Because the money's in the land."

The scope of what he'd begun to piece together stunned him. The Frenchman had snatched a few watches and snuffboxes, and it was a robbery. This, though, was a plan that, once begun, would take years to realize. No wonder Donnelly and Smythe had been content with a dog attack here and a pasture flood and cottage fire there. They could afford to be patient; once they secured the land there were still years of planning and building ahead of them.

"So d'we kill 'im?"

"Not yet. I can't kill a viscount, but I can kill a thief. Unfortunately, I have to prove him one, first." Of course, there was a second option; Phin Bromley might not be able to settle this with a pistol, but he knew someone who could. The Frenchman.

Satisfying as that might be, however, the part of him that wanted the respect of his family knew he needed to have proof. All he had at the moment was some talk about hot springs, some questionable mishaps, and a map. Hardly enough to drive Donnelly to ground and force him to confess.

They cantered up the slope and back toward Quence House. And then another thought occurred to him. Destroying Donnelly would save Quence, but he very much doubted that a disgraced and hopefully jailed viscount would be willing to settle ten thousand quid on his cousin, whatever agreement they might have made. Alyse would be left with nothing, again, or at best a position as companion to a woman with a jailed, disgraced son.

"Damnation," he muttered.

"What's got ye sour now?"

"A choice between two boxes. One holds a poisonous snake."

"An' t'other?"

"My damned conscience." It was more than that, but he didn't know how to put it into words. Everything was a damned muddle. The only thing he knew clearly was that he needed some help. Luckily he had some waiting close by.

Chapter 21 _____

Richard leaned into the morning room. "Alyse, will you come with me for a moment?"

Cold apprehension ran through her fingers, and she jerked too hard on the embroidery needle, putting a hole in the fabric. Blast it. With a quick look, she set it aside and stood. She could put a rose there, she supposed. "Of course."

"Fetch me a peppermint tea," her aunt said, returning to her correspondence.

"I'll have it brought to you," her son commented, backing out of the doorway and leading the way toward the stairs. "Saunders, have a cup of peppermint tea brought to Mrs. Donnelly."

"Yes, my lord. Right away." With a bow the butler left the foyer.

"Come along, Alyse." Richard gestured for her to follow him as he ascended the stairs to the first floor.

"I don't know anything yet, if that's what you're wondering," she blurted. "I only had breakfast to see him, and you saw how quickly he left. The—"

"I know, I know. No worries."

He left the stairs, walking down the west wing of the house where the bedchambers were. Uneasiness rippled through her. Richard had never shown any . . . amorous inclinations toward her, but if he was the villain Phin claimed he was, she supposed he could be expected to do anything. If he attempted an assault, though, he would discover that she hadn't been cowed quite as much as he thought.

When he stopped in front of one of the guest rooms, her pulse quickened, and she hung back from him. "What's this?" she asked, clenching her fists, ready to fight or flee.

"It occurred to me that offering a lofty prize for something is well and good, but it's rather . . . intangible." He reached back and turned the handle, opening the bedchamber door. "Come in."

"I—"

"My mother has your old room," he continued, as if she hadn't spoken, "but this one has a nice view of the garden and the meadow. What do you think?"

Frowning and cautious, Alyse followed him into the room. And stopped. All of her things were there—such as they were. Her mirror, her bedstand and quilt, mingled with the furniture already placed in the room. "What—"

"It's yours, if it pleases you. Your new room. Do you like it?"

"I . . . yes, I like it," she stammered. "But . . . why?"

"Call it an . . . advance. A gesture of trust." He started out of the room, then snapped his fingers and faced her again. "I nearly forgot. Mary will be assuming your duties with my mother, and she will be assisting you, as well. And I've instructed the grooms that the mare Snowbird is to be for your particular use."

Alyse felt her mouth hanging open, and she belatedly snapped it closed. "This is, ah, very nice," she said slowly, unwilling to relinquish her suspicions entirely. "But . . . what if it should come to pass that I can't prove anything about Phin? What if he isn't The Frenchman?"

Richard smiled, one hand on the door. "Then you will look back at your room in the attic and but wish it could be yours again. Have a rest. Enjoy your day." Softly he closed the door behind him, leaving her alone.

She stared at the door for a minute. His threat had left a great deal to the imagination, but she understood it. If she didn't or couldn't do as he asked, what came afterward would be worse than anything she'd yet experienced.

As she sat heavily on the bed, she noticed that it was much softer and fuller than the one in the attic room. Logically she didn't have to lose these unexpected gifts; Phin *wanted* her to give his secret to Richard. If it meant his arrest, though, she wasn't certain she could do it. It could cost him his life.

On the other hand, the unnamed things that were worse than an attic room could kill her. No home at all? Life on the streets of London? If her own family threw her out, no one would hire her as a governess or a companion. And the money she had to hand would only be enough to delay the inevitable, not prevent it.

She wanted to think that an alliance with Phin would help her, but she wasn't willing to wager her future on the idea of him abandoning the military for her sake. Alyse lay back on her new bed. If Phin had never returned home, none of this would have happened. She would still be in the attic, but she wouldn't have to worry about wintering in Covent Garden somewhere. She would have had the time she needed to make her escape on her own terms.

If she thought about it logically, then Richard was attempting to intimidate her. Did that mean he suspected that her loyalties had strayed? Or was he so desperate for the answer he wanted that he would push her to lie in order to get it? Hm. It helped, to look at this as a problem that could be solved rather than as a threat to her continued . . . what, happiness?

Except that she was happy now because Phin was home. She'd always relished his friendship, and had been angry when his actions, as well as her parents' warnings, had driven them apart. But now it was more than friendship. He felt like a part of her life. An important part. She wondered whether a share of ten thousand pounds could convince him to stay.

She could always ask him, she supposed. And somehow she needed to inform him that she was in a different room now before he came calling in the middle of the night and found her gone. Mary would have her attic room now, and that would be awkward. She stifled an unexpected smile.

Sitting up again, she looked out her window in time to see Richard riding off in the direction of Quence. So she could sit alone in her bedchamber and wish she could talk to Phin, or she could do something that might help him. He'd looked through Richard's office, he'd said, but that had been in the dark, and he'd obviously not had much time. She would have at least an hour.

If she was going to be thrown out of Donnelly House, it should at least be for something she'd done—not because she'd been unable or unwilling to take any action in this at all. Ignoring the hard, fast beating of her heart, Alyse stood and went to her door, then headed downstairs.

In the morning room she could hear Aunt Ernesta complaining to someone about a lack of gratitude and getting a swelled head, so she assumed herself to be the target. The fact that for the first time in almost two years she didn't have to sit and listen to it, though, was heavenly. If this was only a temporary reprieve and her life would return to the attic, she had this one thing for which to be grateful. She touched her lips as she slipped into Richard's office. She had more than one thing.

Silently she closed the door behind her. Where in the world had Phin been hiding last night? When her father had used this room it had been pleasantly cluttered, but now it was spotless. The only hiding place at all seemed to be under the desk. Heavens. He'd been that close, and she and Richard had never known it. Clearly he hadn't stayed alive through ten years of war by chance or by luck. Phin knew his business, and he knew it well.

Later, Alyse, she reminded herself, and sat at the desk. Slowly, careful to be silent, she pulled open the drawers one by one and looked through them. If her cousin caught her at this, she wouldn't have the chance to sleep a single night in her new bedchamber.

Nothing. Pursing her lips, she went to the bookcase behind her. Books on Bath and Roman history, the almanac, various books on planting and on architecture. Most of the farming books had belonged to her father, but the other ones must have been put there by Richard.

Her cousin did seem to have an obsession with Roman baths. First he'd gone all aflutter nearly two years ago when she'd mentioned that Quence Park had the ruins there. And then when he'd decided to reside at Donnelly Park rather than at Halfens in Devon, he'd mentioned his wish to see the ruins almost on a daily basis.

Alyse froze. It had just been a keen interest. Certainly Richard hadn't intended anything sinister when he'd settled himself and his mother here. This hadn't happened because she'd mentioned the bath ruins to him back when she'd resided with her horrid Great-Aunt Stevens in Hereford. Back when he'd first decided that she should be companion to his mother.

She shook her head, placing the books back on the shelf. No, no, no. It was merely a coincidence. The move here had had nothing to do with her, and nothing to do with anything on Quence property.

But did she want to tell Phin about these coincidences? He would certainly wish to know. If they weren't mere happenstance, however, then this could be her fault. The troubles at Quence, even Phin's return. She closed her eyes for a moment. If she'd caused Phin's return, she couldn't precisely regret it. Not that.

"I'll fetch her, my lord," came Mary's voice, followed by the sound of someone hurrying up the stairs.

Oh, good heavens. Richard couldn't be home already. *Blast it.* With a quick check to make certain she'd left the office tidy, Alyse inched open the door and peered into the hallway. She could just make out the foyer . . . and Lord Anthony Ellerby standing there.

There was absolutely no way she could leave the office without him seeing her. Alyse shut the door again and turned around. The window. Hurrying over, she unlatched it and pushed the heavy thing open.

Not taking the time to wonder if she could actually make it or not, she hiked her bottom onto the sill and swung her legs over. She pushed off and dropped to the ground. By reaching up she could just touch the bottom of the opened-out glass, and she shoved at both sides hard. With a creak they swung closed. It wasn't perfect, but it would serve for the moment.

Alyse hiked up her skirts and ran for the front of the house. Then she slowed and walked as calmly as she could up the front steps and pushed open the door. "Oh!" she exclaimed. "Lord Anthony! I was out walking in the garden. I had no idea you'd arrived."

With a smile, the light-haired duke's grandson took her fingers and bowed over them. "I'm only pleased you're here."

"I'm afraid Richard has gone out riding with your sister and Beth Bromley."

"I know. I was wondering if I might persuade *you* to go riding with *me*."

Alyse covered her quick frown. Did Lord Anthony know that she'd been granted some freedom? If he was part of this, perhaps he was to attempt to charm her after Richard had delivered his threats. Well, she could ask her own questions while she avoided answering his. "I would be delighted," she said. "Let me go upstairs and change."

"I'll attempt to entertain your aunt while I wait," he returned with his open smile.

Halfway up the stairs she nearly crashed into Mary, and put out her hands to stop herself. "Goodness."

"I was looking for you, miss," the maid said with a nervous curtsy.

"I was out in the garden. You should go see to Mrs. Donnelly before she becomes impatient."

Mary gave her a pained smile. "Thank you, miss."

So she'd earned some freedom, however temporary it might be, at another's expense. If she ended up receiving ten thousand pounds, she decided right then, Mary was coming away from this place with her. And so was Saunders the butler.

Her clothes had also been moved into her new quarters, and though they hadn't been made more fashionable by their trip down the stairs, she found that she minded their dated appearance a bit less. Swiftly she buttoned up the front of her sea-green riding dress, stomped into her boots, and hurried down the stairs again.

Lord Anthony was listening to a diatribe on joint stiffness when she swept into the room. "All ready," she said, smiling a little because she knew Aunt Ernesta wouldn't like her leaving the house without having first asked permission.

"Take a groom with you, for heaven's sake," her aunt said, scowling. "If you ruin yourself a second time, no one will wish anything to do with any of us."

Alyse settled for nodding, rather than pointing out that she had been ruined several times by Phin Bromley. "I'll be back soon."

"Yes, go. Ungrateful girl."

Winston saddled the white mare Snowbird and helped her up into the sidesaddle. She thought the mare had been purchased as a gift for Beth, but apparently hers weren't the only plans that were changing. After the head groom arrived outside the stable on another horse, Anthony gestured her to take the lead down the path that wound alongside the small lake.

"You ride well," he said after a minute, drawing even with her, while Winston fell in a good twenty yards behind. Goodness, it had only taken four years for her to warrant a regular chaperon again.

"Thank you. Until a few weeks ago, I hadn't had the opportunity to ride in quite some time."

"You've had a great deal of misfortune fall your way, haven't you, Alyse?"

"Some," she acknowledged, keeping in mind that they were both probably looking for information. "And some kindnesses, too."

"You mean Richard, taking you in."

"Yes."

"Have you thought about your future if Richard should ask for Elizabeth Bromley's hand?"

She knew what he meant; Beth would become the mistress of the household, and would likely become the companion of choice for Richard's mother. Poor Beth. That wasn't Lord Anthony's point, however. "I'm certain Richard would find a place for me in his household," she lied. "We are family, after all."

"Of course. Is it a place you would wish, however?"

Alyse looked over at him, tall and straight on his pretty bay hunter. "Why are you asking me this, my lord?"

"Anthony, please. We've become friends, don't you think?"

Not by her definition of friendship. "Yes, we have. Anthony, then."

He smiled. "Very good. So tell me, Alyse, what is your favorite bit of countryside?"

"I enjoy the lake very much. Have you visited the Jupiter's temple on the far side?"

"I haven't."

"It's very picturesque."

"I'm sure it is. Are there any Roman ruins on the Donnelly estate, or does Quence Park have the only remains in the area?"

Again the ruins were the topic of interest. Phin suspected Smythe and Richard. Was Lord Anthony interested merely because everyone else seemed to be, or was there a third member of Phin's conspiracy? "Only Quence Park, as far as I know. There are some old barrows on your grandfather's estate that might predate any Roman settlements."

"Yes, I've seen them. You know your ancient history, then."

"Only what we all learned as children after being caught pitching Roman coins into the old baths or jumping over the collapsed roofs." That had been Phin, actually, but she'd stayed about for the lecture and for the roasted quail served for dinner at Quence afterward.

"You were an adventurous child, then. Tell me about the condition of these baths. How many separate pools are there?"

"Haven't you seen them? I thought Richard must have taken you and Lord Charles riding across Quence."

"Oh, we've done our tour, but you actually *know* the place. I'm certain you have insight that none of us do."

"You might ask Lord Quence, or Beth, or Phin. The baths are theirs, after all."

A muscle beneath his left eye twitched. "If I didn't

know any better, I would say that you're avoiding the question," he said with a grin.

She met his gaze. "All I'm trying to avoid," she returned, "is discussing something about which I have very little knowledge. Ask me about Paris fashions or who's been portraying Ophelia and Hamlet onstage at Drury Lane, and I am all information."

Had she annoyed him? Or would he become suspicious that she did know more than she wished to say? Lord Anthony chuckled. "A fair riposte. Tell me this, then. As a longtime resident of East Sussex, who do you suspect of being our French highwayman?"

Oh, dear. She'd fallen out of the pot and into the fireplace. "I did grow up here, but before I returned with Richard I'm afraid I have to claim a nearly five-years' absence," she said easily, amazed at how steady her voice stayed. "I don't know of any Frenchman, but that doesn't mean there isn't one lurking about. If Lord Charles didn't kill him, as he claimed."

"Aren't you curious about his identity?"

"Only insofar as he has my pearls, and I would like them back. Otherwise, I would simply wish him gone from here."

"And that's all you have to say on the subject?"

"Yes, I'm afraid so. Do you have an idea who he might be?"

"I do indeed, but I prefer not to say without proof."

Her blood chilled. "If you know who he is," she returned, not having to pretend her frown, "then why are you asking my opinion?"

"You're a beautiful young lady who behaved foolishly, Alyse," he said quietly, reaching over to pull Snowbird up as he stopped beside her. "Under the right circumstances, you could be very useful to have about. As things are now, and as they could become, I suggest you not trifle with your betters." He released Snowbird's bridle again. "We could see to matters in the way we consider most efficient, so I suppose your moment to be most useful to the most people would be . . . now."

They would kill Phin. And perhaps William, too, and even Beth, if she wasn't willing to go along with whatever Richard might be planning for her. Alyse wanted to be ill. All of this over some ancient ruins? Why? She could scarcely believe such a thing. But it was their beliefs, and their intentions, that would count.

She drew a steadying breath. "Richard said specifically that he wanted proof. All of you threatening me will not gain you that. If you want proof, I need a few days. And perhaps time to spend going riding with Phin rather than with you, *Lord* Anthony."

"Ah, we're not friends now, then," he said easily. "Remain useful, Alyse, or we may be forced to find something else with which to occupy your time." His gaze lowered to her breasts. "There are many ways to be useful, I suppose," he mused.

Alyse turned Snowbird back toward Donnelly House. "Winston, Lord Anthony must leave us now. Please see me home."

"Of course, Miss Alyse."

What she wanted to do was go find Phin, but at the same time she didn't know where Lord Charles was, or what Lord Anthony might do now. If they thought she was telling Phin what was going on, they might simply put another ball through him. And this time he might not be as lucky. But she had very few options.

She couldn't send Phin a letter, because Richard would hear about it even if he didn't somehow manage to read it. Alyse frowned, looking over her shoulder to see Anthony Ellerby in the distance, riding at a canter back toward the Duke of Beaumont's estate.

"I've changed my mind, Winston," she said as soon as Lord Anthony vanished over the hill. "I'd like to ride to Quence and call on my friends there."

"Very good, miss." Winston fell in a little behind and beside her again. "And if I might say, it's nice to see you riding again these days."

"Thank you, Winston. It's nice to be riding again." For however long that lasted. Which would at least be until she managed to get to Phin.

Chapter 22 _____

Proof could be a damned elusive thing. In war, one didn't always have time for it. A preponderance of evidence would serve, or even a gut feeling if a decision needed to be made quickly. This, however, was a different sort of war.

Phineas leaned over the door of Ajax's stall and fed the black an apple. "I think we may get you some exercise tonight," he said, rubbing the big fellow's nose.

The level of proof he needed was directly opposed to the level of faith the people he needed to convince had in him. He therefore needed a great deal of proof. And at this particular moment he remained uncertain of how much he wanted to tell his family. William certainly wasn't up to a violent confrontation with anyone. And all that prevented him from taking matters in hand all on his own was the wish for . . . what, forgiveness? Acceptance?

"Colonel," young Tom said, skidding into the stables, "someone's riding in."

Handing over the remainder of the apple to Ajax, Phineas left the stables. As he entered the front court-yard, a white mare trotted into view, another rider be-hind. He recognized the mare's rider immediately, and his heart began bashing about in his chest. "Alyse," he said, walking forward to catch the mare's bridle.

"Phin," she returned breathlessly. "Help me down. I haven't much time."

Mindful that the courtyard was visible from most of the windows at the front of the house, Phineas placed his hands around her waist and lifted her to the ground. It took every bit of self-control he possessed not to pull her into an embrace and kiss her. "What brings you here?" he asked, noting that her groom was well within earshot.

"I've come to see your yellow horse again," she an-nounced. "I've become distressingly fond of him. Win-ston, remain here with Snowbird, if you please."

The groom tugged on the brim of his hat. "Of course, miss."

A few days ago Phineas wouldn't have dared allow her into the stables. Now, though, he didn't seem to have any secrets left at all where Alyse Donnelly was concerned. He offered his arm, trying to ignore the jump of his muscles as she slid her fingers around his sleeve. "Saffron will be delighted to see you," he said, for the groom's edification.

As soon as they were through the door of the stables he grabbed her shoulders, pushing her back against a support post and lowering his mouth over hers. "That's more like it," he murmured against her mouth. He craved her; there was no other way to describe it. And no cure but Alyse.

She slid her arms around his neck. "Good heavens," she whispered, turning her gaze beyond his shoulder. "He looks as though he might eat children and small animals."

Phin chuckled against her mouth. "That's Ajax," he said, knowing without looking what had her attention. "He's actually quite gentlemanly. Unless you're talking about me, in which case you'd best beware."

Alyse nuzzled her face against his shoulder, the desperation of her grip a bit alarming. "Can we speak here?" she asked quietly.

So she hadn't ridden to Quence just for kisses. Phineas took a steadying breath and backed away a few inches. "Yes, we can speak here."

"Some things have happened today." To his surprise a tear rolled down her cheek. She wiped it away swiftly. "I think this may be my fault," she continued at an unsteady whisper.

Phineas scowled. "What do you mean, your fault? That's ridiculous."

"I may as well just say it." She stroked a finger along the scar on his face, then curled her hand into a fist, withdrawing. "Richard came to see me when I was staying in Hereford. He mentioned that he was torn between settling at Halfens or at Donnelly House. Since I'd lived at both, he wanted to know which would suit him better. During the conversation I mentioned the Roman ruins at Quence. He was very interested. The next thing I knew, he'd whisked me away from Aunt Stevens to be companion to his mother, and we were moving to Donnelly." She sniffed. "He would never have known about the baths if I hadn't been trying so desperately to be interesting."

"It's not your fault, Alyse. For God's sake. You mentioned something of interest. Most people wouldn't have then taken on the idea of driving their neighbor off the property and turning the springs into a resort for all the aristocrats traveling between London and Brighton."

Her wind-reddened cheeks paled. "He means to do that?"

He nodded. "It's mostly putting those two maps together along with some logic and conjecture, but it makes more sense than anything else. All I need now is some bloody proof."

"That's what they want, as well."

Quietly and concisely she told him about her new bedchamber, the horse, the ride with Lord Anthony, and the threats. The blood left his face as he listened. The bastards could threaten him—even try to kill him—but no one—*no one*—was allowed to hurt his family. And that included his Alyse.

His Alyse. He didn't know when that had happened, but that was how he thought of her now. And of everything she'd said, the bit that angered him the most was Lord Anthony Ellerby's suggestion of ways she could be made useful.

"Phin?" She touched his arm.

He jumped. "What?"

"What are you going to do?"

"Go inside and get my weapons," he said shortly, moving past her.

"You can't kill anyone," she gasped, grabbing his wrist. "We have no proof, remember?"

"I won't kill Ellerby." He shrugged free. "I'll just make certain that the only way he can ever bed a woman again is in his imagination."

"And then you will go to prison, or be transported, or hanged. What will become of your family then?"

Phineas stopped. Facing the doorway, his jaw clenched, he worked on returning his breathing to normal. It hadn't even been his family he'd been thinking of in particular. It had been her. "I'll risk it."

"No! No. I won't allow it."

He whipped around, facing her. "You won't *allow* it?" he repeated.

"We still have a few days, Phin. Nothing has changed other than the fact that they've expressed some of their intentions aloud. That can only help us, yes?"

She had a point, damn it all. "At the least I don't want you going back there. You'll stay here."

"And forfeit both what little trust Richard has in me, and the ten thousand pounds? I don't think so."

"If I win, Alyse, he won't be in a position to give you anything."

For a moment she gazed at him. "I know that."

The pattern of his heartbeat changed. He could feel it in his chest, still beating, but . . . more alive. More fierce. More protective. And at the same moment, he knew why. And he wanted to tell her, wanted to say the words aloud. *I love you, Alyse. I love you, I love you, I love you.* "You are a very good friend," he said instead, his voice husky. "And I think it's time we stop waiting to see what they are going to do, and take the offensive."

She eyed him dubiously. "And how do we do that?"

"We use our highwayman," he said.

Alyse gasped. "Phin, they'll kill you. They won't have to prove you're The Frenchman, because they'll have your corpse there to show the world."

"It isn't my intention to die."

Walking back up to him, she grabbed his lapels in her hands. "Are you certain of that? Because it looks to me as though you've decided the only way you can make amends to William is to save Quence and be killed in the process."

That may have been how this began. She knew him devilish well. Phineas smiled down at her. "I've recently discovered that I have several things I wish to live for."

"Do you, now?"

He leaned down and touched his lips softly to hers. "Yes, I do."

She kissed him back. "Then don't attempt this alone."

"I make no promises, though I have a few ideas. I'll get word to you in the next few days. Try to keep my secret until then if you can. If . . . if it compromises your own safety to do so, then for God's sake tell them."

"I'm supposed to be winning your trust. I would suggest that you call on me."

Phineas grinned. "How can I refuse that invitation?"

"Humph. Snowbird and I had best return before Richard does, or he may think that Anthony panicked me, and I ran to you for help." She grimaced. "Which I did."

"You came here with information I needed. I've yet to see you panic."

Alyse lifted up on her toes to kiss him again. "I don't know whether you're good for me, but I certainly do enjoy being around you," she breathed, then released his coat and stepped back. "Please be careful."

"You be careful, Alyse. I'll see you tomorrow, if I can."

He didn't want to let her leave. Keeping her there, though, would do her more harm than good. And so he stood and watched as she rode back in the direction of Donnelly House. He had more than just the rescue of Quence Park to deal with. One thing at a time, though. Time to do as he'd told Alyse, and take the offensive.

When he returned to the house, Digby pulled open the front door for him. "Might I have some luncheon prepared for you, Master Phineas?" he wheezed.

"Is William eating?"

"Lord Quence has requested a pea soup, sir."

"I'll have some as well, then. Where is he?"

"In the library."

"My thanks, Digby."

Phineas trotted up the stairs and down the long corridor to the library. He'd never spent much time in there as a youth, and he certainly hadn't set a boot heel through the door since he'd returned. It seemed a good setting, though, since he was about to attempt to educate William, and hope to God that he didn't kill his brother in the process.

"Good afternoon," he said, strolling into the bright, window-lined room.

"Phin," his brother said, looking up from a book set in his lap and then returning to it.

"Andrews, give us a few moments, will you?" Phineas asked, looking at the valet where he sat in a windowsill. He couldn't remember ever seeing the man seated before, but he supposed that standing for the entire time William was awake each day would get a bit tiresome.

"My lord?" Andrews asked, not moving.

"See to having my luncheon brought up here, please."

"Yes, my lord." The valet stood and glided to the door.

"Mine as well, Andrews," Phineas put after him,

though the servant didn't acknowledge that he'd heard the request. "He's very loyal to you, that fellow."

"He's my legs," William said simply. "What do you want?"

Phineas went back and closed the door, then pulled a chair over to sit opposite his brother. "I need to speak with you."

"So I gathered."

William wasn't going to make this easy, then. After what Phineas had said to him last night, though, he could hardly blame his brother for being standoffish. "You're the patriarch of this family, and I—"

"I'm aware of my position."

Taking a breath, Phineas reminded himself that no insult William could hand him could possibly make them even. "You need to know what's been going on."

"Here?"

"Yes, here."

"Ah. And where have you been over the past ten years, that you are going to tell me what's going on here?"

"I know where I've been. But being here doesn't mean you've seen everything that—"

"You mean because I sit here in my wheeled chair looking through windows?"

Phineas gritted his teeth. "That is not . . . I've been in a unique position to see things from the outside. And th—"

" 'Unique.' That's one way of putting it, I suppose."

"The messenger isn't important. But the information—"

"Looking for sympathy now, are you?"

Phineas shot to his feet, his hands curling into fists. "Will you shut your bloody mouth for a damned minute and let me speak? For God's sake!"

William looked up at him. "It's about damned time."

"What?"

"I can't count the number of times you and I argued over the years, Phin. And ten years ago it became very evident that you would rather not speak to me, not contact me at all, if it meant the possibility of a disagreement."

"I don't have the right to argue with you."

"Why is that?"

"Because." Phineas drew a hard breath. He would rather talk about anything else than this. Anything.

"Because you knocked your mount into mine and I ended up breaking my back?"

"Yes."

"Sit down, Phin."

The muscles across his back so tight he swore he could feel them creaking, Phineas sat down again. "My . . . sins aren't what matter at the moment. You need to listen to me. And then when I finish this, I'll leave again. I've done enough damage to this family."

"You're one-third of this family. But your whereabouts aren't my decision. I won't ask you to stay, or to go."

"You may be calm and superior at the moment, William, but you had to hate me. You have to hate me still."

"No." William shook his head. "I was angry at you. You left us at the time you most should have stayed."

"I nearly killed you. Intentionally."

William eyed him. "Honestly, Phin, it hurt more that you gave up and fled when you could have stepped forward and become . . . the man we all wanted you to be. And I think we both know that if you'd wanted to kill me, I would be dead."

Phineas wanted to stand and pace, but he remained seated because William *had* to remain seated. "I didn't— I couldn't look at you. I ruined your life, William. I would never have let me back into this house."

"I was furious that you abandoned me with a broken back, a seven-year-old sister, and property that needed to be managed. But I have never hated you." He cocked an eyebrow. "I imagine you took care of that yourself. I was awake, you know, when you came in to see me the day you left."

God. Phineas dropped his head. "You sneaky bastard."

"Yes, well, my back was broken. I could be sneaky if I wished to."

"William, that—"

"You joined the army to get yourself killed. Suicide by Bonaparte."

"I don't want to talk about this. You need to know what I've found—"

"I want to talk about this," William said, only the slightest tremble in his voice giving away the fact that he might be less than calm, himself.

Phineas blew out his breath, pushing to his feet again.

"Don't you dare leave this room."

"I'm not. I need a bloody drink, damn it all." He strode over to the decanters on the writing desk and poured himself a whiskey. "How about you?"

"The same."

He poured a second glass and carried both to the chair, handing one to his older brother before he seated himself again. At the time he thought he'd run so that William wouldn't have to . . . set eyes on him ever again. The truth, though, was that he'd stayed away because *he* didn't want to think about what he'd done. As if he'd ever thought about anything else. "What would you like me to say?" he asked quietly.

"Why were you so angry? Before our race, I mean."

"That day, or in general?"

"In general."

Phin blew out a breath. "Shortly before our father died, I overheard him talking with Lord Donnelly. They were discussing their daughters, or some such thing. Father and Mother had wanted a son and a daughter. I recall very distinctly that Father said, 'We got what we wanted, with Phin in between. The boy's a bit useless, but he serves as a spare, I suppose.'"

"Phin, our parents loved you. They loved all of us."

"I know that. I was fourteen, and an idiot. But then they died, and every time I turned around I was living down to his expectations. It was . . . it was as though I'd fallen into some pit, and I couldn't get out. After a time, I stopped trying. It was easier to dig down than up." He sat forward, leaning his elbows onto his knees. "So you see, you're stuck forever in that chair for no reason at all." He took a long swallow of whiskey, savoring the burning sensation as it went down his throat. "Other than my general idiocy, that is."

William closed his eyes as he sipped at his own drink. Finally he opened them again. "You have no idea how long I've been wanting to hear that."

"But it's no excuse at all!"

"It's an explanation." His brother took another sip. "So what is this thing I need to hear?"

Phineas blinked. "That's all you wanted? For me to say that I had no reason for what I did?"

"For you to say something."

He would dwell on that later. At this moment, he

needed to be logical and composed, or William wouldn't believe anything other than that his younger brother was inventing excitement for himself. He'd as much as said that before. "I found a couple of things," he began, pulling the pair of maps from his pocket, "and I'd like your opinion of what they are."

He spread them out on the table, Smythe's over Donnelly's, and wheeled William over to where he could look at them. And then he told his brother about the conversation he'd had earlier with Alyse, though he left out how that had come about. He told his brother about Smythe owning the wolfhounds, and about his theories regarding the flood and the fire and the poisoned feed and about the monetary possibilities of locating a bath spa squarely between London and Brighton. And then about his suspicions regarding Donnelly's pursuit of Beth.

William didn't interrupt him, but spent most of the time running his fingers over the lines of the map overlay. "You neglected to mention how you acquired this," he finally said, looking up again.

"That's another story."

"Tell it."

"Damnation, William, I can't tell you everything."

"Today, you can. Out with it."

Phineas cursed. Slamming his glass on the worktable, he strode to the nearest window and glared outside. "Fine. I stole it. Both of them."

"You what?"

"I'm The Frenchman."

In the window's reflection he could see William staring at his back, see the color drain from his brother's already pale countenance.

"You're a highwayman."

"I didn't know how else to get the information I needed without putting you and Beth at risk."

"So you put yourself at risk. I knew you would. Damnation."

Phin cocked an eyebrow at him. "You knew what?"

"That if Beth wrote you about any of our troubles, you would throw yourself at it, full tilt."

"So you did suspect something," Phineas said. Beth had been correct. William had been worried about him.

"I suspected the ill luck was being helped along. But a highwayman, Phin? For God's sake, Smythe said he shot The Frenchman."

"He did. He's not the dead shot he claims to be, however."

Behind him a glass crashed to the floor. "Good God."

"I'm not dead, if you'll note," Phineas said, turning around and squatting down to pick up the spilled glass.

William looked at him. "Neither am I, if you'll note. Let's keep it that way for both of us, shall we?"

Andrew returned to the library with two bowls of pea soup and half a loaf of warm, fresh bread. As they ate, Phin couldn't help but note that his confessions of stupidity and the tale of the possible demise of Quence hadn't shaken William, while the mention that he'd been shot had unnerved his older brother.

Maybe there was hope for him after all. Maybe there was a chance for forgiveness.

Chapter 23 _____

When Phin sent over a note asking if she cared to go riding with him, Alyse knew that Richard had read it. Her cousin didn't even bother to disguise or explain his snooping. In fact, he was the one who handed her the missive.

"Spend the afternoon with him," her cousin said, joining Alyse and his mother in the morning room and opening his newspaper.

"She'll disgrace us, spending time with that madman," Aunt Ernesta grumbled. "I don't understand why things can't be as they were again. It was much more pleasant and proper."

"Yes, Mother," he said calmly, continuing to read.

"I suppose we'll ride for as long as he wants to," Alyse answered, only half paying attention to the conversation as she read the note. "I'll send him an answer."

"I already have." The paper lowered for a moment. "On your behalf, of course."

It was just as well. She couldn't say any of the things to Phin she wanted to in writing, anyway. And certainly not when she knew that other eyes would be reading her correspondence.

Richard had asked how her ride with Lord Anthony had been; he'd known the villain would come calling, then, and he'd very likely known what Ellerby would be discussing. Whatever gratitude she'd had for his initial rescue had fast faded to a barely tolerable loathing. Only the knowledge that Phin was hunting him made speaking with her cousin tolerable.

As soon as Richard returned to his newspaper and her aunt to her new embroidery project, Alyse allowed herself a smile. It seemed like ages, if ever, since she'd been able to do that in this household, much less in the presence of her relations. Phin might have taken her virginity, but he'd given her even more in return. He'd given her back her spirit. Her thoughts weren't only of fleeing, any longer; she wanted to strike back.

How, then, was she supposed to let Phin leave again? Not that she could do anything to stop him from going, but just the thought of him riding away to definite danger and probable death made her heart hurt. But if he hadn't come back at all—that would have been worse.

"What are you going to wear?" Richard asked abruptly, making her jump.

"To go riding? My riding habit, of course."

"The green one."

"It's the only one I own."

He regarded her, blowing out his breath as he did so. "You and Beth are of a size, I believe. You, Mary, go up to the green room and look in the wardrobe. There's a gold riding habit in the bottom drawer."

Mary stood up, somehow managing to curtsy at the same time, and hurried from the room. Alyse recognized both the maid's expression and the speed of her flight; poor Mary was miserable even after only one day of serving as Ernesta's companion.

"Are you certain you wish to be giving me all of Beth's gifts?" she asked, hoping this courage she'd found wouldn't serve her poorly.

"I trust you'll use them wisely," he replied, somehow able to make even such a benign sentence sound menacing.

"I agree with Alyse," her aunt interjected. "When you offer for Beth, you certainly don't wish to explain that your ruined cousin has borrowed all of the gifts you'd meant to shower on your betrothed."

Heavens. He did mean to offer for Beth. It would give him a stronger claim to Quence, but it didn't speak well at all for the continued survival of either William or Phineas.

"I will have a great many gifts for Beth, Mother. There's no reason to be uncharitable where my cousin is concerned."

Her aunt actually laughed. "You must be in love, Richard, to have become so generous with those less worthy."

Alyse stifled a sigh. It would have provided her with a little satisfaction to know that she had ten thousand pounds coming to her, and that she would never have to fetch anything for her aunt again. But the more she helped Phin, the less likely she was to receive anything from her cousin.

Perhaps she could demand a partial cash payment, so she could at least leave Lewes with enough funds to keep herself safe. Hm. As Phin had said, it was time they stopped following and instead began guiding the action.

Mary returned to the room, a riding habit draped over her arms. The color was lovely; Richard had elegant taste, if a poor way of going about getting what he wanted. "Thank you, Richard," she said, taking it from Mary.

"Go put it on. Mary, help her."

"Yes, my lord."

"Phin won't be here for nearly three hours, Richard," Alyse countered, curious about how far she could push his so-called generosity.

"Then you'll be ready when he arrives," he returned in the same easy tone.

"You're not hoping to match her with that . . . soldier, are you, Richard? His own family can barely tolerate him. There will be gossip again."

"He won't be in East Sussex long, Mother. And she'll show well in her new habit in the meantime. Perhaps she'll catch some shopkeeper's eye."

Show well—like a horse. Well, little did they know that Phin had already . . . ridden her. She snorted.

"Is something amusing to you, Alyse?" Richard asked, lowering the paper to gaze at her.

"It's only that I have a new dress. Thank you again." She rose, handing the dress back to Mary. "Shall we?"

Mary dipped another curtsy. "Yes, miss."

As soon as she buttoned up the front of the riding habit she realized what Richard had meant about her showing well. She'd never worn anything as snug in her life. So he meant for her to seduce a confession out of Phin.

"Goodness, Miss Alyse," Mary breathed, stepping back from pinning up her light brown hair. "You look beautiful."

Alyse spun a slow circle in front of her dressing mirror. "Thank you. I feel beautiful." With the low-cut neckline she also felt positively scandalous, and for anyone but Phin, she would have refused to wear it.

Now all she needed to do was wait for him to arrive, and then the two of them could figure out the best way for her to betray him.

Phineas left Saffron standing with a groom and topped the shallow front steps to Donnelly House. As Saunders opened the door to admit him, he felt rather like he was about to walk into the middle of French territory armed with only his wits. He hoped they would prove to be sharp enough to serve.

"The family is in the morning room," the butler intoned.

"Thank you, Saunders. I know the way."

"But I wish to announce you, sir."

Halting his advance midstep, Phineas looked sideways at the butler. The man had been at his post for at least the past thirty years, one of the few faces he recognized from his boyhood visits to Donnelly House. "How is Miss Donnelly this afternoon?" he asked.

"Very glad to see a friend, I would imagine, sir."

Phineas nodded. He recognized an ally when he saw one. "Announce me, then, Saunders."

"Very good, sir."

He waited outside the morning room door as the butler pushed it open and entered. "My lord, Colonel Phineas Bromley."

And so the next act of the play began. Phineas could

only hope it wasn't another tragedy. Gathering himself, he strolled into the room. "Good afternoon, Donnelly, Mrs. Donnelly, Miss . . . Donnelly."

Good God. If Alyse's attire had been meant to cause him to pop the buttons of his breeches, it very nearly succeeded. Gold and low-cut and nearly molded to her delicious curves, a flare at the hips that made his mouth dry, it was stunning. She was stunning. He had no idea how the devil he was supposed to ride now.

The other two Donnellys and their accompanying servants nodded and curtsied, though he hardly noted it. He couldn't remove his gaze from Alyse. In that attire she *could* have caught herself a duke. Or a prince. Or a king.

Slowly he began to catch bits of what Donnelly was saying, something about pleasant weather for going riding. Phineas shook himself. He was in the middle of bloody enemy territory. *Concentrate.* "Indeed," he said aloud, trying for something noncommittal. He cleared his throat. "Shall we?" he asked, holding out his hand to Alyse.

She glided forward to slide her fingers around his arm. "Yes," she returned softly, smiling at him.

The hairs on his arms lifted. What the devil was she doing, letting Donnelly know how close they were? She could be ruined. Phineas swallowed. "I'll have her back before dark," he said.

"Enjoy yourselves."

He waited until they were on horseback, a groom trailing them, before he spoke again. "Two questions," he said.

"I'm listening."

"Firstly, where the devil did you get that dress?"

"Don't you like it?"

"It's not a matter of liking it. It's a matter of how long I can keep my hands off you while you're in it."

She smiled, her cheeks flushing. "I shouldn't tell you, then, that Richard gave it to me."

His amusement dropped into something much darker. "What?"

"I mean he gave it to me with the intention that I should seduce your secrets out of you. At least I assume that's what he wanted. He did say that I would show well in it."

Despite the nastiness of her cousin's suggestions, the information actually left Phineas feeling better. He wouldn't tolerate poaching. Particularly not when it came from someone who had a large degree of control over Alyse's future. "How did he know I would ask you to go riding?"

"Well, this was actually supposed to be a gift for Beth. He wants his information, Phin."

That blackguard had purchased that dress for his little sister? Phineas drew in a hard breath through his nose. His private animosity toward Richard Donnelly could wait. Saving Quence, and Alyse, came first.

"My second question, then: Has he threatened you again?"

"No. Just more talk about how well I'd best do the task assigned me."

"Oh, you're going to do it very well."

"Do you have a plan, then?"

Phineas gazed at her. He imagined that most females who'd been through what she had wouldn't have hesitated to give him up in exchange for what Richard offered. Conscience notwithstanding, ten thousand quid would make for a warm blanket on any cold, sleepless night.

"What are you looking at?" she prompted. "I told you that the dress was not my idea."

"I'm not looking at the dress."

"Oh." She blushed prettily.

"I'm going to ask you to trust me," he said slowly.

"I trust you."

He smiled at that; he couldn't help it. If she knew how very much it meant to him to have someone—to have her—say that . . . *Later, Phin.* "Then there are parts of the plan I can't tell you."

She didn't like that; he could see it in her eyes as she glanced at him and then returned her gaze to the path. "Perhaps I should have thought to ask if *you* trust *me*," she said.

"I trust you with my life," he returned, hearing the shake of his words as he spoke. "And I swear that after this is over with, I will honestly answer any and every question you put to me."

"Every question?"

"Every question."

Alyse nodded. "Very well. I'm listening."

As he told her, Phin sent up a quick prayer. Most of this brilliant plan of his relied on two people who hadn't even arrived yet in East Sussex. And if they failed to appear in time, he was going to lose everything, including his life.

"What did he tell you?"

Alyse stopped halfway up the stairs as Richard leaned over the balcony railing above her. Her heart beat so hard and fast she was surprised everyone in the household couldn't hear it. What Phin had asked her to do felt . . . deadly, if not to her then to him, but she'd given her word. "Might we speak in private?" she returned, continuing her climb.

"He did tell you something, then."

"Richard, I—"

"Yes, yes, come into the library."

"I'd like to change my clothes, first." And to gather her thoughts for more than the time Phin had given on the ride back to Donnelly House.

"Later. We don't have all day to wait for you."

We. "Who else is here?"

As she topped the stairs, her cousin took her arm and half dragged her toward the library door. Oh, how she detested this man. She couldn't allow him to know that, however. Not yet.

Lord Charles and Lord Anthony were seated in the library, both smoking cheroots and looking terribly pleased with themselves. Alyse squared her shoulders. She could do this. Phin had faith in her, and he needed her to succeed.

"Gentlemen," she said, tugging her arm free of Richard's grip as he closed the door, leaving the four of them in private. As he did so, Anthony's threats about ways she could be useful trickled into her mind, sending a surge of uneasiness through her.

"What did he say?" Richard repeated, emphasizing each word and making it clear that he wasn't going to ask again.

"He didn't confess to being The Frenchman."

"Damnation," Lord Charles muttered. "What the devil good is she?"

"He did, however," she continued, "several times mention the ball at Roesglen evening after next. Then he rubbed his left shoulder and said he hoped you,

Lord Charles, would be coming by coach." She took a step forward. "I think you did shoot him, after all."

"I knew I had."

"Anything else?" her cousin asked.

"One thing."

"Out with it, then."

Alyse took a breath. Phin hadn't mentioned this part, but as far as she was concerned, she needed some incentive for turning on an old friend. "First I would like five thousand pounds."

Anthony stood up. "What?" he scoffed. "Are you joking?"

"No, I'm not. I . . . I would like some assurance that you won't simply take my information and forget that we had an agreement."

Richard narrowed his eyes. "Clever little bit, aren't you?"

"I won't end up begging in the street."

Shoving a cigar between his teeth, Richard pulled open the door and left the room. While the other two men gazed at her, making her feel completely naked and dirty as they took in the low-cut riding habit, Alyse kept her gaze, if not her attention, on the fireplace.

"How much more would we have to pay, do you think," Anthony drawled, "to put you on your back?"

"You don't have enough to tempt me," she retorted.

"Everyone's got their price, Alyse," Charles took up. "You just told Richard what yours is."

"I've been promised a great deal more," she stated, as Richard entered the room again. "This is just proof of your honorable intentions."

Her cousin dumped a bag into her hand. "Twenty-five hundred pounds," he muttered, leaning against the back of one of the chairs. "All I had to hand. Out with it, Alyse, or I'll let my friends here persuade you."

She closed her fist around the heavy bag. Goodness, it was a fortune compared to what she'd been able to hide away. "Phin returned my mother's pearls to me. The Frenchman took them, the night he stopped us."

Anthony clapped his hands together. "That settles it well enough for me," he said. "By God. We've got him."

Richard shook his head. "No. We'll have him after the Roesglen ball." He turned his head to look at Alyse. "Go count your money, Judas. We have things to discuss."

"When you've stopped him, I want the rest of what you promised me," she said, walking with as much dignity as she could to the door, considering that she wanted to run, to flee the room and the house and not stop running until she'd reached Phin.

"You'll have it. And just remember, Alyse. If you say anything to him, I'll make certain he knows all about our agreement."

Straightening her shoulders, she left the room and closed the door firmly behind her. Only when she'd made it safely to her new bedchamber did she let out her breath and sag onto the bed. Phin already knew all about her agreement with Richard. She only hoped that knowledge would be enough to keep him alive.

Chapter 24 _____

When Phineas arrived downstairs for a quick breakfast, he was surprised to see William there already. "This is early even for you, isn't it?" he asked, shoveling fresh bread and a stack of sliced ham onto his plate.

"I don't want you riding the property," his brother returned. "You've made yourself a target."

"Nothing else is going to be damaged at Quence while I'm here. Gordon's going to take the north and east of the property, and I'll take the south and west. I won't be alone; I hired some men to keep an eye out for any mischief."

"Just stay inside the house, Phin. Please."

"For how long?" He took the seat at his brother's elbow. "Smythe surprised me the other night because I was overeager. Now I know what they're willing to do, and I'll be ready." He flashed a smile. "I am a trained officer, after all."

"I would rather sell Quence to Richard today than have you risk your life," William said quietly.

"You are not doing any such thing. You may not trust me, but trust that I won't allow this to continue."

"And how do you intend to stop it, short of killing people?"

Killing people was beginning to seem a reasonable response. "I'll find proof. If I can't, then threats will have to do." He shrugged. "If they aren't sufficient, then—"

"For God's sake. Don't even say it." William shook his head. "How am I going to tell Beth to stay away from Donnelly?"

"I don't think that will be a problem."

"Why not? She's half in love with him already. Or she thinks she is. And I've encouraged it, damn it all."

"Help is on the way," Phineas finally said, though he'd been reluctant to do so until it actually arrived. It was already late.

"Help is here," a low drawl came from the doorway.

Phineas shot to his feet, his hand going to the pistol in his pocket before he recognized the speaker. With a grin he strode forward. "Bram."

Lord Bramwell Lowry Johns, black-haired, black-eyed, and black-clothed, ignored his outstretched hand and gripped him hard around the shoulders, one of the few times since Phin had met him that he seemed to show genuine emotion. "Welcome home, Phin."

"Thank you. Is Sul—"

"Right behind me," Bram interrupted, setting him loose and going around to the head of the table to shake William's hand.

With the timing of a clock, Sullivan Waring walked through the doorway, a tall, tawny-haired angel to Bram's devil. Grinning, he swept his arms around Phineas and lifted him into the air. "You shouldn't have waited so long to send for us," he said, setting Phin down again.

"You're just married," Phineas returned, more relieved than he could describe. Notorious gentlemen, fellow officers, friends, brothers. Help had indeed arrived. "I didn't want to take you away from your wife if I could avoid it."

"He's insufferably happy," Bram put in, avoiding the sideboard and instead calling for a bottle of whiskey. "Very annoying to witness, really."

"God, Bram, it's seven o'clock in the morning," Sullivan said, taking a seat at the table. "What do you need, Phin?"

"The sun hasn't risen," Bram returned. "It is therefore still last night. And I've been riding for the past six hours." He took a glass and the bottle from Digby and opened it.

"I'm in a bit of a spot." Phineas sat back in his chair again. "And so, my friends, I need you to be highwaymen."

Sullivan looked at him. "Beg pardon?"

Bram sank into a chair, toasting the room in general before he took a long swallow of whiskey. "Excellent. When do we begin?"

After an hour of discussion Sullivan was in agreement with some reservations, William was angry that others were going to take chances that he couldn't physically undertake himself, and Bram was wondering why they had to wait until tomorrow evening to begin. Phineas continued running possible scenarios through his mind—success or failure, it rested on his shoulders. And if anyone was hurt, that would be his fault, as well.

"William," Beth's voice came, as she pushed open the breakfast room door, "is it true that we have guests? I—" She stopped dead, then broke into a bright, excited smile. "Lord Bram! Sullivan! My goodness! Phin said you wouldn't be coming to visit him."

Sullivan made his way over to Elizabeth. "I'm here to visit you," he said with a smile, taking her fingers. "Didn't even know Phin was home."

Bram, on the other hand, looked as though he wanted to sink beneath the table. Phineas stifled a grin. The only thing in the world that Bram feared, it seemed, was the seventeen-year-old sister of a friend. In particular one who'd been mooning over him since his return from the Peninsula.

"The thing is, Beth," Phineas said, thumping Bram in the calf with his boot before he stood, "Bram's in hiding from his father."

"I won't tell a soul that you're here," she agreed. "But you must let me take you on a tour of the gardens."

Slowly Bram pushed to his feet. "I would be delighted," he muttered, not looking the least bit delighted.

"Take Jenny with you," William stated.

"William, why do—"

"Take Jenny."

Beth stomped one foot. "Oh, very well. I'll go fetch her." With a last glare at her oldest brother, she left the room to go find her maid.

"I came here to erase a few of the marks the devil has against me," Bram said darkly. "Not to help him begin a new chapter."

"I don't want her to know yet that we suspect Richard in all of this," Phineas said. "She's not very proficient at concealing her feelings."

"So I've noticed. Let Sullivan go touring with her. He's married. Practically gelded."

"Allow me to disagree," Sullivan commented with an amused scowl. "And I need to talk to Phin."

"Damnation."

William cleared his throat. "If you'll push, I'll join you in the garden."

"God, yes."

Phineas watched the two of them out the door. Bram might have thought William was being generous, but it likely had more to do with Bram's reputation and a very impressionable young lady. At least with Bram about, Richard's ultimate fate would trouble Elizabeth less.

"So you're keeping Beth out of this."

"As far as possible."

"But you've got Miss Donnelly in it up to her neck."

Phineas scowled. "I didn't have any choice."

Sullivan grinned. "Don't bite my head off. Bram said she got into some scandal or other a few years ago."

"And when did you two have this conversation?"

"Your note mentioned Donnelly House, and we spent most of the night on horseback getting here." Sulivan blew out his breath. "And you know Bram. If there's gossip, he's heard it."

"Apologies, then. It's just . . . she's been put in an untenable position here, and it's my fault."

He wanted to say more, to somehow explain how much Alyse had always meant to him even when he hadn't realized it. And how important she'd become to everything. Considering that he'd turned her into a spy against her own family and that he'd put her present well-being and her future at risk, calling himself in love didn't quite have the . . . depth to it that he felt.

Sully cleared his throat. "At least you've found a use for Ajax."

Phineas snorted. "Yes. He helped me launch my criminal career. I couldn't have done it without him."

"Having some . . . familiarity with legality's backside, Phin, all I can say is for God's sake be careful. You have a family, and they'll pay the price if you get caught."

"I know that. Why do you think I sent for the two of you?"

"About that. You know we'd both do anything for you, b—"

"As I would for you," Phineas interrupted, beginning to fear a retreat. Sullivan was newly married, though, and if he wanted to stay clear of this mess, no one would blame him.

"I know," Sullivan said, lowering his voice further. "Just keep an eye on Bram. He plays at wearing darkness, but lately those clothes seem to be fitting him rather comfortably."

He nodded. "Then I'll be thankful that he's terrified of Beth."

The breakfast room door burst open. "Captain Waring!" Gordon burst out, striding into the room. "By all th' holy saints!"

Sullivan grinned. "Sergeant Gordon. Still trying to keep Phin out of trouble, I see."

"Aye, and quite a task it's been."

"Gordon, I believe I've mentioned something about knocking. And decorum."

"Aye, aye, but it's Captain Waring! The most gifted soul on a horse since Hector himself."

"Yes, he has a stable in Sussex, breeding them. You know this."

"I was hopin' when we arrived here that we'd come to visit ye, but with all the trouble and the colonel moonin' after the Donnelly girl, there's—"

"Sergeant!" Phineas snapped.

The Scotsman reddened. "Aye. No gossip, either. I just come to tell ye that Saffron is saddled and ready for ye." Turning crisply on his heel, he marched out of the room.

" 'Mooning'?" Sullivan said distinctly.

"I've known Alyse her entire life. We're friends."

"Mm-hm. Are you certain there isn't something more you'd care to tell me?"

Phin looked at him for a moment. "Not before I tell her." Hell, he hadn't even figured it out himself.

"Fair enough. Why don't you show me those maps, and then we'll need to go over the local terrain to pick our point of attack."

Relieved at the change of subject, Phineas gestured for Sullivan to precede him out the door. They had a great deal to accomplish, and not much time to do it.

Even though she'd been waiting for it, Alyse couldn't help the stutter of her heart when one of the grooms, hat in hand, shuffled into the morning room shortly after breakfast. It had been two days since she'd seen Phin. She'd even left her windows unlatched and her door unlocked in case he came calling, but he hadn't made an appearance. The Roesglen party was this evening. And she was very, very worried.

"My lord," the groom said, staying close behind Saunders. "I beg your pardon, but you said you wished to be informed of any rumors about The Frenchman."

Richard snapped upright from the correspondence he'd been bent over. "What have you heard?"

"Peter Adams came by in his hay cart this morning, and he said that The Frenchman rode through Lewes last night, tossing coins onto the street. I know Lord Charles said he killed him, but Peter Jones swears it was him. Says he gave out near fifty quid."

"And did no one attempt to stop this coin-throwing highwayman?" Richard asked, scowling and clearly furious.

"There was a handful of soldiers in town on leave, but they couldn't catch that black monster he rides. They say it breathes fire and that The Frenchman's eyes glow red in the dark."

"That is nonsense. Get back to work. Saunders, give the boy a shilling for his troubles."

The groom grinned. "Thank you, my lord."

"Do you hear that?" Aunt Ernesta squawked. "That awful man is trying to turn himself into some sort of Robin Hood."

"It won't last, Mother. He's breaking the law, and he will be stopped."

Alyse noted that he said "stopped" rather than "arrested." None of the men had said anything directly, and she supposed they might very well think her stupid enough not to have realized, but she knew precisely what they meant to do to The Frenchman the moment they had the opportunity. They would kill him. Phin. Tonight.

She'd carefully hidden away her twenty-five hundred pounds in a place that Richard would never think to look. After all, she'd grown up in this house, and she hadn't told him everything about it. He'd promised her another seventy-five hundred pounds, but that prospect was beginning to look less and less promising. Two days ago he'd only had a relatively small amount of ready blunt to hand. And he hadn't gone to see any bankers or accountants since then, even though he meant to make full use tonight of the information she'd given him.

At the moment, his apparent willingness to cheat her actually made her feel a bit better. He wasn't a hero, trying to stop a villain. He was a villain, willing to do whatever was necessary to get what he wanted. And lying to his own cousin, who depended on him for food and clothing and shelter, didn't even cause him to blink.

"Do we dare go to Roesglen tonight?" her aunt continued with a shudder. "I have no wish to be stopped and robbed again."

"We are going tonight. Never fear; I mean to take precautions."

"I certainly hope so." She looked over at Alyse. "And I suppose you are going riding about the countryside again, showing off your borrowed clothes?"

"Alyse will be staying in today," her cousin answered, returning to his paperwork.

Of course she would be; Richard had barely let her out of his sight since the library. He wouldn't want to risk her warning Phin that a trap was being set for him. She turned the page of the book she'd deliberately chosen to read in her aunt's presence. Her aunt hated the sight of young women reading. It took every bit of self-control she possessed to keep from smiling. Because Richard's trap wasn't going to go as he expected. Not at all.

The only frustration was that she didn't know precisely what Phin did have planned. She understood why he hadn't wanted to tell her, but she also had a large suspicion that it would involve him risking his life yet again. And with the way she was beginning to feel about their . . . partnership, she supposed it was, the only thing worse than him returning to the war would be him dying.

Both the sun and every clock in the house seemed determined to crawl forward as slowly as possible. As the day progressed, Alyse for once wouldn't have minded having some mending to do; at least it would keep her hands occupied. Her mind flitted about like a hummingbird, refusing to light on any one subject.

Finally the sky began to darken and she could justify going upstairs to change into her evening gown. Then she had to sit through dinner and listen to her aunt lamenting their chances of remaining alive long enough for them to reach Roesglen. The woman was a small-minded tyrant, but at least she didn't seem to know anything of her son's dealings. It wasn't quite enough to make Alyse look on her kindly, but it did save her aunt from having ill wishes sent in her direction every few minutes.

"You look very fine this evening," Richard commented as he handed her into his carriage. "Green becomes you."

"Thank you."

He tugged on her hand, keeping her from stepping up. "If you say anything to him that looks the least bit suspicious, Alyse, you will regret it."

"What would I say to him, Richard? That I agreed to take ten thousand pounds if he would kindly hand himself over to the authorities?"

"I don't know what you would say. But I do know that you didn't pin up your hair for me. You've already chosen the money, my dear. And he is a very poor risk."

She pulled her hand free. "I told you what I know, Richard. Please don't threaten me again."

As they turned up the long drive twenty minutes later, every window at Roesglen seemed ablaze with light. Apparently the marquis' embarrassment at the hands of The Frenchman wasn't enough to keep him from throwing his doors wide open for his neighbors. Or perhaps he'd been so extravagant because he wanted his fellows to think of his ballroom rather than his misdeeds.

Alyse looked swiftly about for the Quence carriage, but she couldn't distinguish it amid the crush of vehicles crowding the top of the drive. "Heavens," Aunt Ernesta said, clutching on to her arm, "every member of the nobility in all of East Sussex must be here tonight."

"Lord Roesglen's parties are famous," she supplied. "He seems to outdo himself every subsequent year."

"And it's been several years since you've attended, hasn't it?" her cousin noted, as they joined the crush waiting to get through the front doorway.

He knew quite well that it had been over four years. "Yes," she returned. "So I have no idea what to expect."

"Expect a dance with me," Richard said, smiling as he handed their invitation over to the expressionless butler. "And I imagine Charles and Anthony will wish a turn or two about the floor with you, as well. You do look very nice this evening."

Was that part of their plan, to keep her surrounded by his cronies so that she had no chance to see Phin, much less dance with him? That might be the wiser course of action for her to take, but her heart said otherwise. Her heart wanted a waltz with Phin.

And then there he was, chatting with some of the other guests. For a second her breath caught. She'd half expected him to walk into Roesglen's ballroom dressed as The Frenchman, sporting his old-fashioned tricorne hat and brandishing pistols. Instead he wore a dark gray jacket and black breeches, with a cream-colored waistcoat and his polished black Hessian boots. He looked . . . magnificent. And from the glances he received from the other ladies in the room, both single and married, it was clear she wasn't the only one to think so.

His gaze roamed the room as he spoke, and then those hazel eyes found her. Warmth spiraled through her as he immediately excused himself and crossed the room to her side. "Alyse," he said with a smile, taking her hand and brushing her knuckles with his lips, "you teach the torches to burn bright."

"Ah, we're stealing from Shakespeare now, are we?" Richard said coolly, offering his hand.

Phin shrugged as he shook hands. "The man's dead. I don't think he minds."

Goodness. Alyse felt as though she were watching a duel right there in the middle of the ballroom. Next they would draw daggers or rapiers or something. "Did you come with William and Beth?" she asked, deliberately stepping between the two men.

Taking a quick breath, Phin smiled. "I did. Once you grant me a waltz, I'll take you over to see them."

"I—"

"I'm afraid the two waltzes are spoken for," Richard broke in. "They belong to myself and Lord Anthony."

"Well, this is a dilemma. A country dance or a quadrille, Alyse? Or perhaps a cotillion."

She smiled. "A country dance, I think. If you promise not to trounce on my feet."

"I make no promises I can't keep." He drew her hand over his arm. "My brother and sister are this way."

As soon as they set off through the crowd, Richard and Aunt Ernesta in tow, Alyse leaned a little toward Phin. "I don't know what they're planning, but it's—"

"No need to apologize for the waltz," he interrupted. "I'm certain I can find a partner or two with whom to amuse myself."

He sounded so . . . callous that for a bare moment she felt taken aback. When he glanced down at her, though, she saw nothing but affection and secrets in his gaze. Secrets for her. Alyse squared her shoulders. Very well. She'd said she would trust him, and so she would.

"If you get killed," she whispered, as he released her hand, "I am going to be very angry with you."

Phin squeezed her fingers for a heartbeat. "So will I be."

Chapter 25_____

If Richard felt it necessary to keep Alyse away from him, Phineas decided, then he would not risk raising her cousin's suspicions any further than they already were. Instead he joined in the conversation, adding a pointed jab in Richard's direction whenever he could manage it. He wanted the bastard's attention on him. Not on Alyse, and not on Beth or William.

A great deal of the evening's talk centered around The Frenchman. The women seemed to find him frightening but dashing, and surprisingly generous with the local townsfolk. The men, on the other hand, all had plans to shoot him between the eyes and otherwise teach him the perils of stopping the coach of an Englishman.

The main benefit of everyone's increased caution was

that it had become more difficult for anyone to unleash killer dogs or break open floodgates. That was something, but he didn't want a mere delay in the attacks. He intended to put a stop to them.

The Frenchman had helped him figure out Lord Donnelly's game, and now The Frenchman would, he hoped, serve to rattle all the players once more—and ideally in the process would gain him the missing pieces of information he still needed. He wrote his name beside the dance of Alyse's choice on her dance card, and then excused himself. The farther he stayed from her tonight, the better. And besides, he wanted to keep an eye on Smythe and Ellerby.

Before he could retreat more than a few feet, however, Beth caught his arm. "You are going to dance with me this evening, aren't you?" she asked.

"I thought you were angry with me."

"I am. I was. But I still wish to dance with you."

Grinning, he swooped an arm around her shoulders. "Does this have anything to do with my visiting friends?" he whispered.

She blushed. "Perhaps. I would have liked it more if they'd been able to attend tonight."

"Not while Bram's in hiding. And remember, not a word to anyone."

"Of course not."

"Then give me a waltz," he said, deliberately choosing the second one of the evening. Richard had taken the first one with Alyse, which left the viscount unable to waltz with Beth. And that suited Beth's brother quite well.

"B . . . He," she amended, "wouldn't say how long they mean to stay."

"I suppose that depends on his father. Levonzy's a bit

notorious with that temper of his." He stopped, the older brother in him warring against the soldier. "Beth, you know that Bram isn't the best company for you to be keeping."

"Oh, I know. And I know that I'm too young for his taste." She smiled coyly. "I do like to see him so skittish, however. It's a great deal of fun."

He relaxed a little. Thank God Beth had some sense. And even if Bram was a mere distraction from Richard, that was precisely what she needed. "Good. Terrorize him all you like. Just don't give him your heart."

"I would never be that foolish, Phin." She stood up on tiptoe and kissed him on the cheek. "I like it when you forget that you're supposed to be bad," she murmured. "I only wish you would tell me why you're doing this."

So much for fooling the infant. "I'll tell you when I can."

"You'd better."

He needn't have worried about keeping Donnelly's cronies in sight; they trailed about after him all evening. If this was the extent of their skills at subterfuge, he'd overestimated them. Then again, perhaps they weren't attempting to be subtle. He supposed they could be hoping to shake him, to cause him to make some mistake. Blurt out his identity, perhaps. He stifled a grin as he gestured for a glass of port. He didn't have to drink; he only needed to look as though he were overindulging.

Phineas spent the soiree dancing with women whom he'd once found fascinating, but whose names he now barely remembered. Even if the world knew he was in pursuit of Alyse he still wouldn't have been able to claim more than a pair of dances with her, but he wanted them all. All with her.

Approaching early to claim her for their country dance, Phineas had to content himself with glaring at the rotund young man twirling about her for the remainder of the preceding quadrille. Once the dance ended, he moved forward. "Shall we?"

"Beg pardon, but we ain't even left the dance floor yet," the balding fellow drawled.

Phin wasn't in the mood. "Who are you?" he asked.

The man blushed. "Henning. Francis Henning."

"Phin Bromley," Phineas returned. "And now that we're acquainted, you may step away from Miss Donnelly."

"Phin," Alyse chastised, tugging her fingers free from Henning's and placing them into his.

He shook himself. Simply because he was primed for a coming battle didn't mean he could attack everyone in sight. He nodded. "Apologies, Henning. Good evening."

"Ah. Good evening."

The country dance was torture. Donnelly, Smythe, and Ellerby all took the floor when he did, so any conversation, even banter, with Alyse verged on being impossible. Fingers touched and slid away again, when all he wanted was to sweep her into his arms and kiss her senseless. All he could do was keep repeating to himself that an evening's frustration was a small price to pay for setting everything right again. As soon as the dance was over he snatched up a glass of whiskey.

"Phin, is this truly necessary?" William asked, as Andrews rolled the chair up to him.

"Yes, it's necessary. Now go away. You're angry with me, remember?"

"Don't you dare take additional chances in order to protect me. It's my job to protect you."

As absurd as that should have sounded coming from a man denied the use of his own legs, coming from William it had both strength and dignity. "I won't risk anything unnecessarily," Phineas said. "But for God's sake distance yourself from me tonight. Yell at me for drinking. Something."

William scowled. "Bah," he summoned, and Andrews turned the chair back into the crowd.

Well, not as fine as the performances he'd viewed on the stage, but it would do for this evening. It would have been simpler if he could talk to Alyse and determine how much of an act he needed to put on, but he could manage it on his own. In truth, his reasons for wanting to talk to Alyse had little to do with her cousin or with Quence.

It was selfish and shortsighted, but he wanted just to be around her. To talk with her, to listen to the sound of her voice, to touch her soft skin. And then he spotted her making her way toward one of the privacy alcoves off the main room.

Swiftly he turned in the opposite direction, dodged through a doorway, and ducked out of sight of Donnelly's associates. They might be proficient at shooting pheasants, but they knew nothing about hunting a trained soldier.

"Alyse," he murmured, catching her arm as she left the alcove.

She pulled him back through the curtains with her. "What are you doing?" she whispered. "We already danced. And I thought you wanted to stay away fr—"

"Shh," he interrupted, and captured her mouth with his. He kissed her, then retreated, relishing in the way she pursued him, wrapping her arms around him and pulling her slim body hard against his.

His cock ached. God, he wanted to peel her out of that silky green gown and run his hands along her skin, bury himself in her again.

"I want you," he murmured, tilting her head back to run his mouth along her throat. "No more country dances. Only waltzes."

"Phin. Phin, stop it," she whispered huskily, still clutching her fingers into his shoulders. "If Richard finds us, he'll shoot you right here."

He didn't particularly care, but clearly she did. With a last rough kiss he broke away from her. "I know you would be safer if I kept my distance," he murmured, running a finger along her lips, "but I can't."

"Maybe staying away would have been safer when this first began," she returned, "but at the moment I much prefer being where I am."

"Thank you for that."

She touched his cheek, then with a sigh twisted out of his arms and reached for the curtain. "I made Richard pay me for giving him the information. He gave me twenty-five hundred pounds, and I don't think he intends to hand over any more than that."

"I want you out of that house tonight," he returned. "If he's willing to murder me, I won't risk what he might do to you."

"He wouldn't dare. He has an excuse for trying to stop The Frenchman. I would be much more difficult to explain."

Phineas sighed. "You are a very brave woman, Alyse."

"I'm not the one they are going to be shooting at."

He looked at her, just looked at her, for a long mo-

ment. "Let's get this damned thing over with," he muttered. "Offer to see William and Beth home, will
you?"

Alyse nodded. The way he'd gazed at her—she
couldn't even gather herself enough to speak. Silently
Phin kissed her fingers and then slipped away again.
She stayed where she was, concentrating on breathing
and trying to cool the heat in her cheeks. And then she
went to find Richard.

Phin was already there, standing not quite steadily
and facing his seated brother. "I told you," he said to
William in an overloud voice, "I have a head."

"Then go home," William snapped.

"I came here with you," Phin said, sneering.

The difference between the man who'd just been
kissing her and the one who stood there now was remarkable. And thank goodness she knew it to be a
ploy. "I'm certain we could see William and Beth home
later," she suggested. "Couldn't we, Richard?"

Her cousin pasted a smile on his face. "Yes, happily."

Phin made a show of hesitating, looking from his
brother to her cousin. Then he nodded. "Stuffed shirts,"
he muttered, then left the room, clumsily dodging the
other guests as he went.

Immediately after he left, Lord Charles and Lord
Anthony appeared on either side of Richard. Whatever
they were discussing, they didn't look pleased about
the developments. As she looked on, trying to appear
confused and finding it rather easy, William checked
his watch several times. After approximately ten minutes had passed, the viscount motioned to his valet and
approached the trio of men.

"I apologize," he said, keeping his voice low, "but

I hesitate to send my brother back to Quence without one of us there to . . . keep an eye on him. I hate to ask such a favor of you, Richard, but—"

"Say no more," her cousin interrupted. "Of course we'll see you home. Charles, Anthony, will you ride with us? I have no desire to meet up with The Frenchman tonight."

Lord Charles and Lord Anthony had both ridden to the ball on horseback. That worried her; she hoped Phin had anticipated that possibility. The Frenchman rode that monstrous black horse, but even he couldn't outrun an attack from three different directions. And he'd departed the soiree in a coach.

As their coach rumbled down the road, she looked through the curtains at the dark outside. In the dim light of the coach lantern she could make out Lord Charles a few yards to their left. As she watched, he pulled a pistol from his pocket to hold across his thigh. If they had the chance, they would never capture Phin for the authorities. They would kill him. Tonight. Now.

"Stand and deliver!"

On the echo of that shout, a single shot rang out. Alyse had to work not to clench her hands over her heart. *Please let him be well*, she prayed silently to herself. *Please let this go as he intends.*

"Oh, good heavens!" Aunt Ernesta squawked, grabbing at Richard's arm. "I knew we should have stayed at home tonight!"

"Hush, Mother." He pulled a pistol, and then a second one, out from behind the seat cushions.

"Is that necessary?" William asked. "I don't want to risk Beth getting hurt in a skirmish."

Lord Anthony yanked the coach door open, making Alyse jump. "It's not us," he barked.

"What?"

"He's stopped another coach just around the curve, the fool. Come on, and we'll have him surrounded before he realizes it."

Richard stood. "Wait here," he ordered the rest of the coach's occupants, and hopped to the ground.

Alyse stared at William. This was not what she had anticipated. Beth clung to her brother's arm, her eyes wide, and Aunt Ernesta continued to bemoan her fate from the far corner. And she was supposed to sit there as well, hands folded, while three men attempted to kill Phin.

She couldn't do it. Alyse lurched to her feet and scrambled out the door before William could do more than try to grab her arm. "Alyse, wait here," he muttered.

"I can't. I'll be careful."

The sound of angry shouting drew her forward, her heart beating so hard she began to worry that she would faint dead away on the road. As she rounded the bend, she stopped in her tracks.

Phin stood there, his fists raised, circling . . . The Frenchman? Blinking, wondering if she had fainted after all and was dreaming, Alyse gaped.

How long she would have stood there, dazed, she didn't know. At that moment she caught the glint of a pistol muzzle through the underbrush, and she rushed forward. "Richard!" she hissed, grabbing his arm. "Don't you dare! You'll hit Phin."

He shoved her away with his elbow. "What are they saying?" he demanded.

Both men were speaking French. The highwayman's partner still sat on horseback, his pistol aimed at the Quence coach's driver but his gaze on the sparring men.

"Alyse," her cousin muttered tightly.

She blinked. "Phin is ordering The Frenchman to surrender himself."

"And what's the answer?"

Alyse listened. It was something about Phin dancing in a pink dress. Her lips twitched. Whatever was transpiring, it seemed to be part of a plan. "He says that he'll never surrender," she improvised.

Phin leapt onto the highwayman. The two men hit the ground, rolling half under the coach. Fists swinging, they grappled across the roadway and into the shrubbery, leaves and dirt and curses flying.

It was mesmerizing. Even Richard seemed frozen, watching to see what might happen next. With difficulty she tore her gaze from the battling men to look at the second highwayman again. He was gone.

His scruffy bay horse still stood, calm as anything, but the man himself had vanished. She quickly looked away again so Richard wouldn't notice what had caught her attention. Abruptly her cousin stiffened.

"*Votre soeur est une guenuche*," came from directly behind him.

"Alyse," Richard whispered, his face going white as a pistol barrel rammed into his spine.

Obviously she couldn't tell him that his sister was a monkey. "He says to drop the pistol," she decided.

Her cousin's fingers flew open and the pistol dropped to the ground. "For God's sake, don't shoot me."

The highwayman glanced in her direction, eyes twinkling behind his mask. "Go," he said in accented English, prodding Richard forward. "*Et vous*," he continued, giving her a half bow.

She fell in beside Richard, and they stumbled into

the clearing. "*Dit à les outres idiots à nous joignez,*" the second highwayman continued in a carrying voice.

"He says to come out or he'll shoot Richard," she translated, very loosely. Calling Smythe and Ellerby idiots might make them a bit touchy.

"Show yourselves!" her cousin squeaked.

After a moment of muttered cursing, two pistols flew onto the road, hitting the soft ground one after the other. Then both Lord Charles and Lord Anthony came into view.

"*C'est une pitíe,*" the apparent highwayman commented.

The fellow's disappointment at everyone's cooperation notwithstanding, Alyse was grateful no one had yet been shot. "He says to sit down," she offered, and he glanced at her again.

Phin and The Frenchman tumbled past them, each commenting on the other's lack of virility and poor taste in liquor. It sounded vicious, though, which she supposed was the point. Throwing his attacker off, Phin dove for the two discarded pistols and came up with them. He fired one of them straight at The Frenchman—and somehow missed.

"Enough," he snarled, panting and with blood trickling from a cut on his forehead. "You've lost, you French swine."

Still muttering in French, this time about Phin's lack of hygiene, the fellow backed away a few steps. "You have won," he said in a heavy French accent.

"Then go back to France. We may meet again on the battlefield, where at least you can die with honor."

When The Frenchman started for his monstrous black horse, though, Phin stopped him. "I don't think so, my friend. You've forfeited your mount to me. You can ride with your companion."

Handing his pistol to Phin, the second highwayman climbed onto his scraggly bay. With a last rude gesture, The Frenchman swung up behind him. "*Adieu,*" he said, glancing over at her, and then they rode off into the night.

"Oh, heavens."

Alyse whipped around to see her aunt standing beside Beth as they clutched one another. And then Aunt Ernesta fainted dead away. Again.

When she looked back at the scene of the almost-robbery, Phin was walking up to her. "What are you doing here?" he asked.

She touched the cut on his head. "We were taking William and Beth home. Are you unhurt?"

"I'll live."

"I have to admit," she offered, glancing at her cousin as he and his companions climbed back to their feet, "there were a few times when I thought *you* must be The Frenchman."

"Understandable, I suppose," he returned, offering his arm to her, "since I hadn't been stopped by him."

"I thought you were feeling ill," Richard noted, not at all charitably.

"A bit of whacking, and I feel much better," Phin commented. "Why didn't you lot shoot them when you had the chance?"

"We didn't want to hit you by mistake," her cousin said flatly.

"I'll give you fifty quid for The Frenchman's beast," Lord Anthony said from the far side of the clearing, where he was running his hands along the black's withers.

"Thank you, no. I think I've earned the right to keep him," Phin returned, touching a free finger to his cut head and still keeping Alyse close by. "Well done," he murmured, as Richard finally went to see to his fallen mother.

"Who were they?" she whispered back.

"Later." Finally releasing her, he walked over to help Beth to her feet. "How are you, Magpie?" he asked.

She threw herself into his arms. "You were magnificent! I wish William could have seen it, but he said to let him stay behind with Andrews. I shall tell him all about your heroics." Belatedly she looked past him to where Richard stood, his moaning mother in his arms. "And you did admirably, as well," she said, then kissed Phin on the cheek.

Richard didn't look as though he would give himself the same halfhearted compliment. In fact, he looked furious. Alyse allowed herself a moment of satisfaction before worry took over again. Richard had been bested, and he wouldn't like that. Not at all.

But at least for tonight Phin was safe, and no one would suspect him of being a highwayman after this. Which only left saving Quence. And her, wondering how she would make do with twenty-five hundred pounds and the thought of him leaving again.

Chapter 26.

"Where are you going?" Sullivan Waring asked as Phineas strode over to the breakfast sideboard for a wedge of cheese and then started back out the door.

"I'm going out on my new horse, which I've decided to name Ajax, and see whether Alyse would care to go riding with me," he answered.

Bram stumbled through the door behind him and sagged into a chair. "Coffee," he mumbled, dropping his head onto his crossed arms.

"I didn't hit you that hard, Bram." Phineas stopped his retreat reluctantly; it seemed like days, rather than hours, since he'd last seen Alyse. He wanted to talk with her, to tell her what he hadn't been able to previously about the plan to be rid of The Frenchman. And he wanted to make certain she realized that this could very well force Donnelly and his cronies to further action.

"It wasn't the rolling about on the ground with you," the Duke of Levonzy's second son groaned. "It was the bottle of port I celebrated with after our return."

"Well, then it's your own fault, and I have no sympathy."

This time he made it all the way to the breakfast room doorway before William appeared to block it with his chair. "Where are you off to?" his brother asked.

"He wants to go riding with Alyse," Sullivan supplied before he could do so.

"Don't you think she's risked enough for you?" William asked, unmoving. "Richard doesn't like you, if you haven't noticed, and each time you speak with her, you're making her life more difficult."

"If you haven't realized," Phineas retorted, "we still need her help. The Frenchman's gone, and I need to know what course Donnelly will take now."

"And if you haven't realized, she's done enough. You can hardly expect her to take steps that would cause her to sacrifice the roof over her own head. Leave her be."

For a moment Phineas glared at his older brother. William was absolutely correct, and yet he still couldn't stop himself. He needed to see her. He couldn't expect them to understand it, because he barely grasped it himself. All he knew was that she'd become vital to him. "No," he snapped, pulling the arms of the wheeled chair forward until he could get past his brother and into the hallway.

As Phineas vanished, Bram lifted his head. "That, my friends," he drawled, "is a fool."

"A fool in love, I'd wager," Sullivan agreed.

William looked from one to the other of them. Though he hadn't precisely considered that his brother's feelings might run that deep, they could well be correct. What Phin needed to realize, however, was that he couldn't keep Alyse and his military career. Because over the past four years nearly everyone in Alyse's life had left her. He couldn't in good conscience allow Phin to do the same. Not for either of their sakes.

"How long do you stay?" he asked.

"I volunteered to remain until this mess is dealt with," Lord Bramwell said, lifting his head again as a steaming cup of coffee appeared in front of him, "but I think Phin worries that if we're seen, Donnelly might realize our ruse."

Sullivan was nodding, as well. "We thought to leave this morning, before we're spotted. But if you need us, William, for God's sake send for us."

"Does Phin know that you're going?"

"He knows," Bramwell supplied. "If he wasn't so moon-eyed over that Miss Donnelly, he'd likely have remembered to say goodbye. And to thank us again for our heroics."

Sullivan grinned. "I'd do it again just for the fun of it, thanks or not."

"That's because you've been domesticated, and your life is deathly dull."

"Mm-hm. Are you coming to visit on your way back to London?"

"Of course I am. But I'm damned well eating breakfast first."

Phineas stood in the foyer of Donnelly House, waiting for Alyse. Though he had no powers of mind-reading, he would say that the entire manor felt . . . tense this morning. And angry. And he imagined that that was due to Richard. He'd been bested. The question then became, what would he attempt next?

Donnelly entered the hallway, coming from the direction of his office. "Colonel Bromley," he said, giving a stiff nod.

"My lord."

"What brings you here this morning? Ah, Alyse, I imagine."

"We're going riding."

"Yes, well, enjoy it."

Phineas scowled, quickly covering the expression. "That sounded a bit ominous," he ventured.

"Did it? I only meant that Alyse has turned out to be a miserable companion to my mother. I can't very well afford to keep a useless relation living under my roof indefinitely. After all, while I believe in charity, this is becoming ridiculous. She's been through five households now, you know."

"Does she know that you're going to send her away?"

"Not yet. Perhaps you'd like to tell her. I'm sure you'll be more kind about it than I would be."

"Bastard," Phineas muttered.

Donnelly had the gall to smile at him. "Have a good morning," he said, and vanished down another hallway.

Phineas wanted to go after him, to give the viscount the pummeling he deserved. Being a damned gentleman, knowing that other people's reputations were tied up with his own, could be bloody tiresome.

"Ready?" Alyse said, as she appeared at the top of the stairs.

He shook himself. "Of course I am."

She'd worn the gold riding habit again, along with a warm smile that he knew was meant for him alone. Knowing what Donnelly had planned for her, he felt abruptly predatory and protective all at the same time. He wanted her, all of her, and he didn't want unhappiness or hopelessness or misery ever to touch her again.

Her smile faded. "Is something wrong?"

"No," he lied, taking her hand as she reached the foot of the stairs. "With your white horse and my black one, I'm just hoping no one thinks us pretentious."

She chuckled. "Eccentric, perhaps. Never pretentious."

Outside, he slipped his hands around her waist and lifted her into the sidesaddle. Every time he touched her, letting her go again became more and more difficult. Did she feel the same way? He'd certainly never been in love before, but he couldn't imagine that she didn't feel toward him at least part of what he felt for her.

As they left the drive, the groom trailing behind them, he belatedly remembered that Sullivan had said he and Bram would be leaving this morning. He'd been so occupied with thoughts of seeing Alyse again that he'd completely forgotten. *Damnation.*

Alyse glanced over her shoulder. "Can you tell me who your assistants were last night?" she asked in a low voice.

He nodded. "Two very good friends of mine. Sullivan Waring and Lord Bram Johns. We served together."

"Lord Bram Johns?" she repeated. "I've danced with him."

A stab of jealousy went through him. Phineas pushed

it back down. Of course they'd danced. Alyse had spent nearly three Seasons as the toast of London, and Bram had a fine eye for beauty.

For half an hour they chatted about nothing in particular. He needed to ask some questions, but they could wait a short time. If it was selfish to want to spend time with her for no reason at all, then so be it. And once he returned to current events, he would have to tell her what Donnelly planned for her future.

"It worked, I assume?" he finally asked, when he couldn't put it off any longer. "Our ploy?"

"Yes. Richard thinks you must have tricked them, but he seems to know that he'll never prove anything. He's very out of sorts today."

"So I assumed."

Brown eyes met his. "Did you speak with him?"

Damnation. As Donnelly had said, he would be kinder about it than her cousin would. Not that kindness would alter the circumstances. Phineas took a deep breath. He would rather face down a line of French cannon, but it had to be done. "He told me that he plans to send you away," he said quietly.

Her expression closed down. Alyse opened her mouth, then shut it again. "I can't say I'm surprised," she ventured after a moment, her voice quavering. A tear ran down one cheek.

"Alyse."

"It's silly, I know," she continued, another tear, then a pair of them, following the first, "since I don't even like Richard or Aunt Ernesta. But at least I got to come back here. I got to . . ." She cleared her throat.

"I love you."

He wasn't certain he'd spoken aloud, except for the

sudden surprise in her eyes. "Ph . . . Phin, you don't have to feel guilty about this. I knew what might happen."

Reaching over, he caught hold of Snowbird's bridle and pulled both horses to a stop. Still not speaking, barely able to think, his heart roared so loudly, he kicked out of his stirrups and jumped to the ground. "You, stay here," he ordered the groom as he walked around to Alyse's side and lifted her down. "You, walk with me."

She pulled against his hand. "Phin."

"I said, come with me." He pulled harder until she gave in and walked off the path with him. They continued on a short distance until he found a small glade carpeted with tiny white flowers. "No," he said, turning her to face him, "I did this to you, and I'm going to make it right."

"And how are you going to do that? Convince Richard to see the error of his ways?"

"Marry me."

That got her attention. She stared at him, openmouthed, for several hard beats of her heart before she stepped backward to sit down heavily on an overturned tree trunk.

He didn't know whether that reaction boded well or ill. "Well?" he prompted.

"You . . . you can't just do that."

"I can't ask you to marry me? I beg to differ."

"You just said that my predicament was your fault, and then in the next breath you ask me to marry you," she exclaimed. "It's noble, I suppose, but I certainly don't want you to be leg-shackled to me because you feel sorry for me. That's awful. It's the worst thing I can imagine. Especially when we both know that you mean to ride off to war again."

"Oh, well, thank you very much," he snapped, turning his back and striding to the edge of the glade and back, setting aside the abrupt . . . dismay at the thought of being separated from her again. "How am I supposed to help you, then?" he asked, stalking back.

"I don't know. I don't actually need your help. I have the twenty-five hundred pounds, together with the money I've been stealing from Aunt Ernesta. I—"

"What?" he interrupted, unexpected humor touching him.

"Whenever she sent me on an errand I kept some money back. I never meant to stay with them forever."

"Then why are you so upset at the idea of leaving now?"

"Why do you think?" she shot back. "I'll miss East Sussex."

"Ah." He watched her twisting her hands in her lap. "Would you marry me if Richard gave you all the money he owes you?"

She scowled. "What does one have to do with the other?"

"I don't know!" he shouted back. "I'm confused now!"

"Don't yell at me!"

"I'm not!" He paced again. "For God's sake, Alyse, I said that I love you, and now suddenly you're telling me that it's guilt and not love, and that you don't need me, and how the devil am I supposed to know what to do or say now?"

"Well, to begin with, you don't love me."

He faced her again. "I do love you."

"No, you don't. I'm a friendly face after ten years."

"There are quite a few people I haven't seen for ten years, and I haven't gone about telling all of them that

I love them. Nor have I slipped into their bedchambers at night."

She blushed. "We have a . . . connection. I'll grant you that. But—"

"But what? Did you know that before I left I'd begun riding past your window at night? And not just because I wanted to talk with you."

"I . . ." She cleared her throat. "You're a soldier, Phin. You left your own family ten years ago, and they were hurt. I saw it. I was hurt, too, but . . . that doesn't signify. I don't—I can't stand the thought of being left again. And especially not by you."

Phin knelt on the ground in front of her. "So you want me—or someone—for company. Like a dog."

"No! No, of course not."

"Then what is it, Alyse?"

More tears coursed down her soft cheeks. He hated the idea that he was making her cry, but he needed some damned answers. Any answers.

"Fine." She slammed her palm down on one thigh. "I don't want to be in love with you. I know you're going to hurt me, that you're going to leave again, and I can't help myself. I can't even . . . think of anything but you, and now you've asked me to marry you, and it's not even for the right reasons, and—"

He leaned up and kissed her. It was impossible not to. Her lips tasted of salt tears, and he kissed her again and again until her arms swept around his shoulders and she had lowered herself off the log and onto his knees, pressing herself against him. "We are good together," he murmured against her mouth. "You bring out the best in me."

"Phin, stop."

"No." He kissed her again.

"Phin, stop."

"No. I am n—"

"Look!"

Dazed, he lifted his face from hers. Her gaze was over his shoulder, and he turned around, half expecting to see Donnelly and his cronies bearing down on them, pistols at the ready. Instead, he saw a dark cloud above the trees. No, not a cloud. Smoke. Rising from the direction of Quence.

"God," he muttered, standing and pulling Alyse to her feet. "Come on."

They ran back to the horses. His heart seemed to have become a cold, frozen lump in his chest, and he couldn't breathe as he helped her into her saddle and then swung up onto Ajax.

"Stay with her," he barked at the groom, and sent Ajax into a dead run toward home.

The black pounded toward Quence, all sleek, lean power. Phineas bent forward along Ajax's neck, cutting the wind and urging him to go faster still. Beth and William were both home. Beth could get out, but he knew that she wouldn't leave her brother. With all his heart he prayed that Sully and Bram hadn't yet gone, that he and Alyse weren't the only ones to have seen the smoke, that the small household had found buckets and water and knew what to do.

As he topped the meadow and flew up the low rise, the smoke hung black and thick and heavy over the front of the house. A trio of horses crossed the corner of his vision, galloping down the main road and away from Quence. Donnelly and his friends.

This had been no accident, then. Black anger erupted

in his chest, but he shoved it back down. *Later*. They would pay for this later. First he needed to know that his family was safe.

From the drive he could see the smoke billowing through half a dozen windows on the ground floor at the front of the house. The main door was closed. Warner and Tom and a few others ran back and forth like ants, throwing bucketfuls of water at the broken front windows. He couldn't see anyone else through the haze of smoke.

Phineas jumped down from Ajax before the horse had even come to a stop. "Beth!" he bellowed, running for the front door. "William!" Coughing, he shoved on the door handle. It didn't budge.

"Phin!" Beth screamed from the far side of the door. "We can't get out!"

"Is it locked?" he yelled back.

"Phin!" Sullivan's deeper voice bellowed. "They nailed the doors shut!"

Backing up and waving his hands to try to clear the smoke, Phineas looked at the door. Right at the top someone had bolted a thick block of lumber over both doors. Not terribly noticeable to anyone coming across the wreckage later, but effective. Reaching up, he dug his fingers beneath it and pulled. It creaked, but he couldn't get enough leverage to pry it free.

"Sully," he yelled, "can Ajax kick?"

"Yes!"

Phineas ran to the black, who stood snorting nervously, shifting away from the house. He swung back into the saddle and urged the big fellow to the front steps. "Let's go, boy," he said, stifling another cough and trying to keep his voice calm.

With a whinny, Ajax clopped up the half dozen shallow steps to stand on the front portico. Phineas turned him so he faced away from the door.

"Stand back!" he called, then lifted up on the stirrups and swatted Ajax on the back haunch. "Hup," he commanded, thankful that he knew how Sullivan preferred to train his animals. "Hup, Ajax!"

Both back legs kicked backward with enough strength to disembowel a lion. The doors splintered top to bottom.

"Again, Ajax. Hup!"

The black kicked again. The left-hand door shoved inward, hanging off of the bottom hinge. Swiftly Phin urged Ajax back onto the drive and then swung off him again. As he reached the half-broken-in door, it ripped backward. Sullivan appeared in its place, Bram at his shoulder.

"Where's William?" Phineas asked, reaching in to grab Beth's arm and pulling her through the door's wreckage and onto the portico. "Go stand with Ajax," he ordered her.

"Back here," his brother called, coughing.

"Get him out!" Beth screamed, her voice shaking.

Together he and Bram shoved the second door out of the way, and he pushed inside. "Is everyone down here?" he asked, ducking beneath the thick smoke billowing from both the morning room and the front sitting room.

"I did a quick check," Bram said, coughing, his usual lazy drawl missing. "Didn't see anyone else."

Sullivan was helping the servants through the door, ordering them to get buckets and join the growing line of people dumping water through the windows. "I got the kitchen staff," he choked, "when I checked the back door. They nailed it closed, as well."

William, with Andrews as always standing behind him, sat a few feet behind them in the foyer. "You're next," Phineas said.

"My people first."

"No." Leaning down, Phineas pulled his brother into his arms and lifted him out of the chair. "Bring it," he instructed Andrews, and made his way through the milling servants to the door. He stepped through the mess and down the front steps.

A few feet away Alyse stood holding a full bucket of water. "Don't throw it at the wall!" she yelled, "get the water into the rooms!"

"Here, sir." Andrews set the chair down, and Phineas lowered William into it.

"Are you unhurt?" he panted, grasping his brother's shoulder.

"Just get everyone out."

"I will."

He charged back into the house, ripping the curtains off the foyer window and ducking into the morning room. With the lowering smoke he could barely see, but he managed to smother the fire out of the floorboards in one corner. Then he went to work throwing burning pieces of furniture through the shattered windows, pulling down flaming curtains, grabbing up buckets, and throwing water onto the pieces he couldn't move. Peripherally he noted that Bram was in there with him, as well, while through the foyer in the sitting room he could hear Sullivan and Gordon yelling.

Finally Bram grabbed his arm. "I think we've got it," he rasped, his face covered in soot, in places nearly as black as his hair. He bent over, coughing.

"Stay here and keep an eye out," Phineas instructed, his own voice hoarse from the thick smoke. He made his way through the smoking, soggy clutter to the room on the far side of the foyer. Sergeant Gordon lay on the floor, coughing, while Sullivan leaned out one of the windows. They'd gotten the fire out there, as well. "Anyone hurt?" he asked thickly.

"A few small burns," Sullivan said, wiping the back of his arm across his face. "And I think Gordon has a singed brow."

Phineas sagged against the doorframe and shut his eyes for a long moment. "Thank God you were here."

"First time I've ever heard anyone thanking God for me," Bram said from the doorway behind him.

"Phin? Phin?" Alyse stumbled through the wreckage at the front door and then flung herself against him.

His heart clenched and released again as he swept his arms around her, holding her close. "You were magnificent out there," he murmured into her hair.

"I knew you wouldn't leave the house," she returned, her voice muffled against his shoulder. "I didn't want you to burn. I love you."

He just wanted to hold on to her, let everything else slip away. She loved him. And at that moment, he felt as though he could accomplish anything.

"Is there something you haven't told us, Phin?" Bram asked, his sardonic drawl reappearing.

Taking a breath, Phineas looked from one friend to the other. "What, exactly, happened?"

"Two of them shoved into the breakfast room," Sullivan said, scowling. "We should have expected something, but—"

"*I* should have expected something," Phineas interrupted.

"Donnelly and Smythe," Bram contributed, wiping soot from his jacket sleeve. "They held pistols on us, probably while someone else nailed the doors shut, then locked us in. Less than a minute after that we smelled smoke. We were trying to decide how to get William out through the window when you arrived."

Phineas swore softly. "I expected their next move might be more direct," he grated, "but I thought it would be against me. They knew I would be out of the house, though." He looked at his friends, horror pulling at him. "They didn't expect you. And if you hadn't been here, I—"

"The question is," Bram interrupted, "how do you intend to respond to this little gesture?"

He knew how he *wanted* to respond. As he looked around the wreckage of the front room and at Alyse holding his hand, he knew how he *meant* to respond. "I'm finished with sneaking about and wearing disguises," he said, his voice shaking a little. "Gordon, I have an errand I need you to see to."

"Aye, Colonel."

"Sullivan, Bram, we're making a visit to Donnelly House."

Alyse kept hold of his arm. "What are you going to do?"

"I'm ending this."

Chapter 27 _____

"What are you going to do, murder him?" William demanded. "For God's sake, Phin, he's a viscount. You'll be throwing your future away."

"I'm going to stop him. I'll leave the method up to him." As he swung up on Ajax, he turned his gaze to Alyse. "And I'll leave his fate up to you."

She looked down for a moment. "I don't want him dead," she returned. "Mostly I just never want to have to see him or Aunt Ernesta ever again."

He nodded. "Done."

"Phin," William said in a more even voice, "don't feel that you have to sacrifice yourself to make things right. You don't owe us anything."

"Yes, I do."

Bram saluted the gathered onlookers. "Have luncheon waiting for us. I anticipate being famished."

The three friends set off for Donnelly House at a canter. William had hit on it, Phineas supposed. He did owe his brother and sister a good deed. He'd run out on them ten years ago, not because William couldn't stand to look at him, but because he couldn't stand to look at himself. It had been cowardly. For the past ten years he'd faced down armies, killed men, been shot at, and all through that time the most terrifying thing had been the idea of returning to Quence Park.

But then he had returned, and gradually both he and his siblings had begun to realize that he wasn't the same self-hating fool that he'd been at age seventeen. And Alyse—back then she'd been a fearless companion. Now she was a great deal more than that. He'd made her some promises, and he meant to find a way to keep them.

At the moment he had an advantage of sorts. If he'd gotten home a few minutes later, if Sully and Bram hadn't been there, his siblings would be dead. The thought brought the black anger coursing back up through him again, and this time he allowed it to flow into his fingers, through his veins, and into his muscles. Donnelly had meant to commit murder.

As far as the viscount knew, he *had* killed William and Beth—and everyone else in the manor. All Donnelly would need to do then to secure himself a damned good opportunity to take over Quence would be the death of the one remaining brother. They would be waiting for him, expecting him to be blind with grief and thinking of nothing but revenge. And they would expect him to be alone.

However badly he wanted to charge the house, pistols blazing, logic would serve him better. Donnelly had known that he wouldn't be at Quence when they

set the fire and bolted the doors. Which meant they
wanted to deal with him more directly. They wanted to
kill him up close.

And that, he could use. Just before the straight drive
up to the house the road curved inside a picturesque
stand of ancient oak and elm trees. He pulled Ajax to a
halt and dismounted. "Any preferences?" he asked, as
he freed the coil of rope he'd tied to the saddle and
slung it over his shoulder. "Other than Donnelly. He's
mine."

Bram checked his pistol before he replaced it in his
greatcoat pocket. "I've always found Lord Charles
Smythe's cologne annoying."

"Which leaves me with Ellerby," Sullivan murmured
with a grim smile.

"Try to keep them alive, if possible," Phineas said,
jamming a pair of pistols into his waistband. "I'd prefer
that they confess."

"Just once," Bramwell commented, as they moved
through the trees toward the cover of the formal garden, "it would be nice for the three of us to sit down
with a bottle, and no one shooting at us or trying to
burn us to cinders."

Sullivan chuckled. "Something to look forward to,
then."

They separated in the garden. Phin carried a second
brace of pistols in his greatcoat pockets, and whatever
he might have planned, he was perfectly willing to use
them. That gave him another advantage of sorts;
whereas Donnelly and his cronies had murdered their
share of pheasants and aimed a few shots at him in the
dark, for the past ten years he'd made killing his pro-
fession. And he was very good at it.

Keeping low, he left the trees and, using the shelter

of the low garden wall, made his way closer to the back of the house. He knew Donnelly House well, and had sketched it out in as much detail as he could for his friends. At the same time, he could only guess at how many weapons and how many eyes would be watching for him. The ones who concerned him were Ellerby, Smythe, and Donnelly.

From a defensive perspective, he would place two of them on the top floor, probably at opposite ends of the house. Bram and Sullivan must have been thinking the same thing, as Levonzy's son headed for the east wing, and Lord Dunston's son for the west. Unless he'd assessed Donnelly's character incorrectly, he would assume that the viscount would be on the ground floor, hoping for a finishing shot after one of the other two brought him down.

Using a tangle of vines for cover, he surveyed the windows that faced him. If they were counting on his fury, they might very well be concentrating on the front of the house. He supposed if they *had* managed to kill his family, he would have galloped straight up the drive.

He jumped the low fence, scrambling forward until he found more cover behind a marble statue of Aphrodite. A grim smile curved his mouth—the only thing he'd ever found that made him feel more alive than a good fight was Alyse. He could give up the fighting, but not her. It was as though he'd made the decision before he'd ever consciously asked himself the question.

Phineas moved forward again, angling his path toward the windowless kitchen. Once he reached the base of the house, he crept beneath windows until he spied one standing open an inch or so.

Moving swiftly, he glanced inside and ducked down

again. It looked to be one of the spare sitting rooms, and it was empty. He opened the window wider, slid over the sill, and made his way silently to the open door. As he moved, he pulled a pistol from his pocket, then stopped just short of the doorway. For a long moment he listened, pushing back his impatience. In this instance, time was his ally, and he would use it.

Silence. In a large, occupied house, the lack of sound and movement in the middle of the morning was rather disconcerting, but those he and his companions were hunting would have the same sensation. Slowly, placing his feet as carefully as he had the night he'd snuck in with a rifle ball in his shoulder, he made his way along the hallway, making certain no one was inside the small rooms on either side.

The house in between the corners of the west and east wings seemed to be utterly deserted. Donnelly had a definite mistrustful nature; it was entirely possible that he'd gathered his staff together in the cellar or the ballroom and locked them in. As for his mother Ernesta, given her past behavior she was probably in her bedchamber cowering inside her wardrobe. Unless she interfered, Phin would let her be.

He was halfway down the front hallway leading to the foyer and front rooms when he heard the viscount. "Any sign of the bastard yet?" Donnelly yelled from somewhere to the left of the main stairway.

Idiot. And considering that no one answered him, Phin had the signal he'd waited for. Time to move. He lifted a large glass paperweight off the hall table. Hefting it in his hand, he hurled it through the window of the room to the right of the foyer. Then he sank back into the shadow of the stairs as the crash of broken glass rang through the house.

"He's here!" Donnelly shrieked, and came running out of the morning room. "Get down here!"

Phineas aimed and fired his pistol. The viscount yelped as his own weapon went flying out of his hand and skidded against the front door.

"That's more like it," Phineas said, setting the spent pistol aside and stepping out of the shadows.

"Smythe!" the viscount screamed. "Anthony!"

"Apologies," Phineas returned, walking forward. "I'm afraid it's just you and me."

"You murderer!"

He lifted an eyebrow. "Me? And what precisely have you been up to this morning?"

"Nothing! You're the madman who's broken into my home and shot at me."

"I'm going to give you a chance," Phineas returned, shrugging out of his heavy greatcoat. "You can attempt to best me face-to-face. No sneaking about, no hurting innocent people to feed your own greed. Just you and me."

"What, so you can beat me to death?"

Phineas grinned darkly. "That is the idea."

"Never." Donnelly backed toward the front door. "I will have you arrested for breaking into my home and threatening me. You will go to prison, and I will be left with Quence Park."

"I don't think William would like that very much."

"W . . . William?"

Phin nodded. "He's recently become less fond of you. And I don't think he'll want you pursuing Beth any longer, either." He circled, cutting the viscount off from the door. "Did I forget to mention that you didn't manage to burn them to death, after all?"

"I . . . I have no idea what you're talking about. Clearly you've gone mad."

A high-pitched whistle sounded from beyond the garden wall. "You seem to have another guest, Donnelly," Phineas commented, unlocking and pulling open the front door. He whistled back.

"Leave, Bromley. I won't tell you again."

"I truly wish you would attempt to force me," he returned with a sigh. Fury still pulled at him. For the moment, though, he would let it pass. There were other things of more importance.

Sergeant Gordon walked up the front steps. "Everythin' well, Colonel?" he asked, sending Donnelly a suspicious look as he entered the house.

"That depends on whether your errand was successful."

"Oh, aye, it was." He leaned back out the front door. "This way, sir. If ye please."

Phineas took a moment to glance away from Donnelly as Gordon's errand entered the room. "Mr. Pepper," he said, offering his hand. "Thank you for coming."

"Your man here didn't leave me much choice," the solicitor returned, hefting the satchel in his other hand. "I was advising a client when he burst into my office and dragged me out. When I shared the ride to Uckfield with you, I didn't anticipate being kidnapped."

"I hope you'll find that the cause is worth the interruption. Let's adjourn to the breakfast room, shall we?" Phineas suggested, gesturing.

"I am not going anywhere," Donnelly snapped, his face red. "You will leave my ho—"

"I heard you before. Lord Donnelly, this is Mr. Malcolm

Pepper. Mr. Pepper is a solicitor in Uckfield. Mr. Pepper, Lord Donnelly."

"Ah, hello," Pepper said, clearly sensing the tension in the air.

When Donnelly continued to stand his ground, Phineas strode up to him, grabbed him by the lapel, and shoved him in the direction of the breakfast room. "Perhaps I didn't make myself clear," he said. "I gave you a chance to meet me face-to-face, and you declined. You, therefore, have lost. These are the consequences."

Once they reached the breakfast room, Phin pulled one of the pistols from his waistband and tossed it to Gordon. "Keep him here a moment. And Mr. Pepper, please begin drafting a confession. Sergeant Gordon here will help you with the wording."

He whistled up the staircase. Ellerby stumbled into view, Sullivan behind him. A moment later Bram appeared as well, dragging Smythe by the heels. "What?" the duke's son demanded. "He ran headfirst into the floor."

"Mm-hm. Bring them down here."

By the time they'd dragged Smythe and Ellerby downstairs and tied them to chairs in the breakfast room, Mr. Pepper had a fair quantity of the story down on the page. "I mentioned the ruins'n the dogs'n the flood, and, o' course, the fire," Gordon said.

"Don't forget the overturned carriage and the poisoned horses. I'm sure our Lord Donnelly had a hand in both," Phineas commented.

"Is all of this true?" Mr. Pepper asked, his expression going less uncertain and more grim by the moment.

"Those are only the incidents of which I'm aware," Phin answered. "I'm certain there are more, but these will suffice."

"You can't prove any of this."

Phineas ignored the protest. Once it was all was written out to his satisfaction, he set Mr. Pepper to work on a second document. "This one should be simple," he said. "Please write as follows: 'I, Richard, Lord Donnelly, do hereby agree to grant the amount of ten thousand pounds to my cousin, Miss Alyse Donnelly, the amount to be paid in full within forty-eight hours of this signing and to be used at her discretion.' We'll also need a copy of that one, for his lordship."

"I won't sign it. I won't sign anything."

"You will sign both of them, or I will kill you." Phineas leaned one haunch on the table. "I will tell you this. I will hand your confession, sealed, over to William. He will do nothing with it, on the condition that you leave Donnelly House and never return. Settle at Halfens or anywhere else you choose. If one more incident of ill luck befalls Quence Park or any member of my family, your confession will find its way to the chief magistrate of London."

Bram was nodding. "Tell him the other bit," he urged, rocking back on his heels.

"Oh, yes. Thank you, Lord Bramwell. Quence Park will be renovating the old Roman baths on our property. We've determined that they might prove popular for the gentry traveling between London and Brighton."

"I will not sign that ridiculous confession. You have no proof, or you would have gone to—"

Phineas pulled the second pistol from his belt and shot Donnelly in the leg. The viscount shrieked, and Mr. Pepper dove under the table. None of his own companions so much as blinked. "Did I mention that you courting my sister under false pretenses doesn't make me very happy?" he murmured. "Mr. Pepper, please show Lord Donnelly where to sign his confession. And then Lord Anthony and Lord Charles will witness it."

The solicitor scrambled out from under the table. Picking up his ink and pen and the papers, he brought them around to the whimpering, gasping viscount. "Here you are, my lord."

"You shot me!"

"That barely qualifies. There are three more pistols in this room, and you have three more limbs. Sign them."

His hand shaking, Donnelly dipped the pen into the inkwell, and with trembling fingers signed the documents, including both copies of Alyse's grant. Then the papers went around to Smythe and Ellerby, and Sullivan untied their hands so they could witness both. Only when Ellerby set down the pen did Phineas let out his breath.

"Now, Donnelly," he said, "I'm going to have my man here patch you up. After that, we will have no more contact with you, except for the men I send over to collect Alyse's things. Is that clear?"

"Yes, for God's sake. Help me before I bleed to death."

"If I see you again other than at some public gathering in London, we will have to finish this encounter. And I guarantee that you will not be pleased by the outcome. Agreed?"

"Agreed. Agreed. You blackguard."

Phineas stood again. "Oh, and you may send Alyse's funds to Quence Park."

"I already gave her—"

"Ten thousand pounds," Phineas repeated.

He waited as Gordon patched up Donnelly's leg, and then motioned the sergeant and Mr. Pepper out of the room. "This is finished, Donnelly," he said evenly, leaving one copy of Alyse's grant on the table and taking the rest of the papers with him. "It's not just me who knows what you've done." He sent a pointed glance in Bram's direction. Whatever his friend's reputation, as the Duke of Levonzy's second son, his word would carry weight. "No one else need be informed of any of this, unless you force my hand."

Only when they'd returned to the horses and started back for Quence did he begin breathing again. Now only one single thing remained.

Chapter 28

Alyse couldn't sit still. Phin had already been shot once. For heaven's sake, he didn't have to risk his life to set things right—except that he obviously thought he did.

"It's been two hours," Beth said in a small, worried voice. "I should have guessed about Richard. I only wanted Phin to come home. Now he's going to get killed, and it will be my fault."

"None of this is your fault, Magpie," William said from across the library. He'd had his valet wheel him to the window, and he hadn't moved since. "I don't know how I could have been so blind."

Alyse began yet another circuit of the room. William and Beth didn't realize that none of this mess would have happened if she hadn't been trying so hard to ingratiate herself with Richard. She'd been the one to tell him about the ruins. And now when she'd finally found Phin again, she was going to lose him.

"I see riders," William announced abruptly, a sharp, worried edge to his voice. "Four of them."

Please let one of them be Phin, Alyse prayed silently. *Please let him be unhurt. Let them all be unhurt.*

After a hundred hard beats of her heart, the library doorway abruptly filled. "Phin," she sobbed at the sight of his disheveled, soot-covered form, and threw herself at him.

He wrapped his arms hard around her, his face buried in her hair. It wasn't enough. She wanted to crawl inside him, to be part of him so that she could be certain he was there, he was real, and he was safe.

"Alyse," he whispered, so quietly only she could hear. "Alyse."

"What happened?" William's relieved voice came.

Goodness. She'd forgotten that anyone else was even in the room. She loosened her grip, but Phin didn't let her go.

"It's finished," he said roughly.

"Donnelly?"

"They're all alive," Lord Bram supplied as he entered the room, his tone somewhat regretful.

"And no permanent damage," Phin took up. "He'll be leaving Donnelly, I presume for Halfens. That was my suggestion, anyway."

"What's to keep him from attempting something else?" William asked.

Finally Phin loosened his grip on Alyse enough to pull a folded piece of paper from his pocket. "This," he returned, shifting to take her hand and then leading her over with him while he handed the paper to his brother. "I told him it would be sealed when I gave it to you, but he annoyed me. In any case, we're to keep it safe, and he will mind his manners."

William lowered his head as he unfolded it. His face paling, he looked up again. "There's blood on this."

Phin shrugged. "It's not any of ours. I needed to use a little persuasion."

His brother resumed reading, then slowly folded the paper again. "You did well, Phin," he said slowly. "Good God."

"I also informed Donnelly that *we* would be renovating the baths."

"I would love to. At the moment I . . ." His pale cheeks flushed. "It will take some doing to get the front rooms repaired. That has to come first."

"I have some funds at my disposal," Phin said, putting his free hand on his brother's shoulder. "And I think I may be looking for a change of career." He glanced at Alyse as he said that last part.

Beth swarmed up and hugged him. "Do you mean it? You'll stay? Truly?"

"If you want me to."

"For God's sake, Phin," the viscount whispered. "Of course we want you to stay."

Alyse tried to pull away. This was clearly a moment for the family, and that did not include her.

Phin, though, didn't release her. Instead he peeled off his sister. "Excuse us a moment, will you?" he said huskily. Without waiting for an answer he half dragged Alyse past Mr. Waring and Lord Bram and into the hallway.

"See to your family," she hissed at him.

"I'm attempting to. Stop fighting me."

She stopped struggling against his iron grip. "Fine. What is it?"

"First of all, I want to clarify something. I have always valued your friendship. Always."

Tears gathered in her eyes. "Phin."

"When I came back here, I expected to find resentment and skepticism, because I'd earned them. I didn't expect to find you, Alyse. You . . . you're not the only reason I want to stay. But you are the one I can't imagine leaving."

A tear overflowed and ran down her cheek. Phin caught it with his finger. "I know everyone in your life has left you or cast you aside. I will not do that. Not ever. I love . . ." He cleared his throat, his voice unsteady. "I love you, Alyse. I'm not a duke, and I'm certainly not a prince. But I am your friend. Forever."

She grabbed his lapels, twining her fingers into them so she could lift up on her toes. They kissed, though she couldn't say who'd begun it. It just was, like they were. "I love you," she whispered shakily. "I do love you."

"I'm going to ask you again to marry me," he murmured back. "But before you answer I want you to have this. I want your answer to be what you want, not what you think you might need."

Frowning, not having a clue what he might be talking about, she looked down as he pulled a second piece of paper from his pocket and handed it to her. Half her attention still on him, she opened it. In plain, direct lettering, signed by Richard and witnessed by his two friends, she was being given the ten thousand pounds she'd been promised. She gasped, having to read it again before she could believe what it said.

"Phin, how did you—"

"He laid out the conditions for the money, and you fulfilled them. It's your money. I only made certain he kept his word."

"This is . . . I can't believe it."

He smiled, the expression touching his hazel eyes. "Believe it." He touched her cheek, very gently, as though he thought she might break. "And now, Alyse, will—"

"Wait," she said, covering his mouth with her fingers. *Oh, could she? Why not?* It made sense. It made perfect sense. And she could be here. "Wait here."

Before he could answer, she slipped back into the library to find everyone clustered just behind the half-closed door. She ignored that, and instead approached William.

"I have a proposal for you," she said.

He looked truly startled, one of the few times she'd ever seen him surprised. "Yes?"

"I have just . . . come into a large sum of money. I would like to invest it in the restoration of Quence and the Roman baths."

"I—"

"Say yes," Phin said flatly from directly behind her.

"The—"

"Say yes," he repeated.

"Well, yes," William finally uttered. And then he smiled.

Phin yanked her back into the hallway. Before she could even gasp, he'd turned her to face him and covered her mouth with his. He kissed her with such . . . passion that it stole her breath. It stole her soul, it seemed.

"Marry me, damn it," he muttered against her mouth.

"I—"

He resumed kissing her, pressing her backward until she came up against the wall. Alyse groaned, wrapping her arms around his shoulders, pulling herself against his chest until no space remained between them.

"Marry me, Alyse," he repeated.

"Yes," she managed between kisses. "Yes, I will marry you. I love you, Phin. I love you so much."

"My dark-eyed Alyse," he breathed, laughter in his voice. He shifted to embrace her, lift her into the air, and spin a circle with her in his arms. "My dear, dear friend."

"My love," she returned, kissing the tip of his nose. "My highwayman. My Phin."

Dangerous Liaisons . . .

$\mathcal{W}$ho doesn't love a little romance tinged with a sense of danger?

In the coming months, meet four heroines who like to live on the edge with their deliciously wicked heroes . . .

Turn the page for a sneak preview of these exciting new romances from bestselling authors Jeaniene Frost, Loretta Chase, and a back-to-back appearance from Suzanne Enoch!

One Foot in the Grave

A Night Huntress Novel
by *New York Times* bestselling author
Jeaniene Frost

It's been four years and Cat is sure she's moved
on: there's a new man in her life and her vampire-
slaying is now government sanctioned. But it becomes clear that a hit has been taken out on Cat
and she must team up again with volatile and sexy
Bones as they track down the mole inside Cat's
organization, prevent her father from killing everyone, and try to resist their white-hot passion for
each other.

*L*iam Flannery's house was as quiet as a tomb, ap-
ropos as that may be, and it had been a long time
since I'd battled with a Master vampire.

"I believe the police told you that the bodies of
Thomas Stillwell and Jerome Hawthorn were found
with most of their blood missing. And not any visible
wounds on them to account for it." I said, jumping
right in.

Liam shrugged. "Does the Bureau have a theory?"

Oh, we had more than a theory. I knew Liam would
have just closed the telltale holes on Thomas and Jerome's necks with a drop of his own blood before they
died. Boom, two bodies drained, no vampire calling

card to rally the villagers—unless you knew what tricks to look for.

Flatly I shot back, "*You* do, though, don't you?"

"You know what I have a theory on, Catrina? That you taste as sweet as you look. In fact, I haven't thought about anything else since you walked in."

I didn't resist when Liam closed the distance between us and lifted my chin. After all, this would distract him better than anything I came up with.

His lips were cool on mine and vibrating with energy, giving my mouth pleasant tingles. He was a very good kisser, sensing when to deepen it and when to *really* deepen it. For a minute, I actually allowed myself to enjoy it—God, four years of celibacy must be taking its toll!—and then I got down to business.

My arms went around him, concealing me pulling a dagger from my sleeve. At the same time, he slid his hands down to my hips and felt the hard outlines under my pants.

"What the hell—?" he muttered, pulling back.

I smiled. "Surprise!" And then I struck.

It would have been a killing blow, but Liam was faster than I anticipated. He swept my feet out from under me just as I jabbed, so my silver missed his heart by inches. Instead of attempting to regain my stability, I let myself drop, rolling away from the kick he aimed at my head. Liam moved in a streak to try it again, but then jerked back when three of my throwing knives landed in his chest. Damn it, I'd missed his heart *again*.

"Sweet bleedin' Christ!" Liam exclaimed. He quit pretending to be human and let his eyes turn glowing emerald while fangs popped out in his upper teeth. "*You* must be the fabled Red Reaper. What brings the vampire bogeyman to my home?"

He sounded intrigued, but not afraid. He was more wary, however, and circled around me as I sprang to my feet, throwing off my jacket to better access my weapons.

"The usual," I said. "You murdered humans. I'm here to settle the score."

Liam actually rolled his eyes. "Believe me, poppet, Jerome and Thomas had it coming. Those thieving bastards stole from me. It's so hard to find good help these days."

"Keep talking, pretty boy. I don't care."

I rolled my head around on my shoulders and palmed more knives. Neither of us blinked as we waited for the other to make a move.

Your Scandalous Ways

An eagerly anticipated new novel
by *USA Today* bestselling author Loretta Chase

James Cordier had done a lot of things for his country, and when he's called for one last dangerous mission, saying no is impossible—especially when he sees his target. Francesca Bonnard, a beautiful and powerful courtesan, has many secrets, and how much she knows about a plot against the English government is just one of them. She has always been able to bend any man to her will, but the enigmatic stranger who moves in next door may be more than her match.

James's attention shifted from the golden-haired boy to the harlot beside him. They sat at the front of the box in the theater, Lurenze in the seat of honor at her right. He'd turned in his seat to gaze worshipfully at her. Francesca Bonnard, facing the stage, pretended not to notice the adoration.

From where he stood, James had only the rear view of a smoothly curving neck and shoulders. Her hair, piled with artful carelessness, was a deep chestnut with fiery glints where the light caught it. A few loose tendrils made her seem the slightest degree tousled. The effect created was not of one who'd recently risen from bed, but one who had a moment ago slipped out of a lover's embrace.

Subtle.

And most effective. Even James, jaded as he was, was aware of a stirring-up below the belly, a narrowing of focus, and a softening of brain.

But then she ought to be good at stirring up men, he thought, considering her price.

His gaze drifted lower.

A sapphire and diamond necklace adorned her long, velvety neck. Matching drops hung at her shell-like ears. While Lurenze murmured something in her ear, she let her shawl slip down.

James's jaw dropped.

The dress had almost no back at all! She must have had her corset specially made to accommodate it.

Her shoulder blades were plainly visible. An oddly-shaped birthmark dotted the right one.

He pulled his eyes back into his head and his tongue back into his mouth.

Well, then, she was a fine piece as well as a bold one, no question about that. Someone thought she was worth those sapphires, certainly, and that was saying something. James wasn't sure he'd ever seen their like, and he'd seen—and stolen—heaps of fine jewelry. They surpassed the emeralds he'd reclaimed from Marta Fazi not many months ago.

Bottle in hand, he advanced to fill their glasses.

Lurenze, who'd leaned in so close that his yellow curls were in danger of becoming entangled with her earrings, paused, leaned back a little, and frowned. Then he took out his quizzing glass and studied her half-naked back. "But this is a serpent," he said.

It is?

James, surprised, leaned toward her, too. The prince was right. It wasn't a birthmark but a *tattoo*.

"You, how dare you to stare so obscene at the lady?" Lurenze said. "Impudent person! Put your eyes back in your face. And watch before you spill—"

"Oops," James said under his breath as he let the bottle in his hand tilt downward, splashing wine on the front of his highness's trousers.

Lurenze gazed down in dismay at the dark stain spreading over his crotch.

"*Perdonatemi, perdonatemi,*" James said, all false contrition. "*Mi dispiace, eccellenza.*" He took the towel from his arm and dabbed awkwardly and not gently at the wet spot.

Bonnard's attention remained upon the stage, but her shoulders shook slightly. James heard a suppressed giggle to his left from the only other female in the box. He didn't look that way, but went on vigorously dabbing with the towel.

The red-faced prince pushed his hand away. "Stop! Enough! Go away! Ottar! Where is my servant? *Ottar!*"

Simultaneously, a few hundred heads swiveled their way and a few hundred voices said in angry unison, "*Shh!*"

Ninetta's aria was about to begin.

"*Perdonatemi, perdonatemi,*" James whispered. "*Mi dispiace, mi dispiace.*" Continuing to apologize, he backed away, the picture of servile shame and fear.

La Bonnard turned round then, and looked James full in the face.

He should have been prepared. He should have acted reflexively, but for some reason he didn't. He was half a heartbeat too slow. The look caught him, and the unearthly countenance stopped him dead.

Isis, Lord Byron had dubbed her, after the Egyptian goddess. Now James saw why: the strange, elongated green eyes . . . the wide mouth . . . the exotic lines of nose and cheek and jaw.

James felt it, too, the power of her remarkable face and form, the impact as powerful as a blow. Heat raced through him, top to bottom, bottom to top, at a speed that left him stunned.

It lasted but a heartbeat in time—he was an old hand, after all—and he averted his gaze. Yet he was aware, angrily aware, that he'd been slow.

He was aware, angrily aware, of being thrown off balance.

By a look, a mere look.

And it wasn't over yet.

She looked him up. She looked him down. Then she looked away, her gaze reverting to the stage.

But in the last instant before she turned away, James saw her mouth curve into a long, wicked smile.

Coming July 2008

After the Kiss

First in The Notorious Gentlemen trilogy
by *New York Times* bestselling author
Suzanne Enoch

The illegitimate son of the Marquis of Dunston, Sullivan Waring has made himself into a respectable gentleman, allowed into the fringes of Society, but never all the way in. If he resented his legitimate half siblings, he never let it show—until they stole what was rightfully his. Now he is determined to exact a little bit of revenge on the *ton* . . . except Lady Isabel Chalsey was never in his plans.

A woman stood between Sullivan and the morning room. At first he thought he'd fallen asleep outside the house and was dreaming—her long blonde hair, blue-tipped by moonlight, fell around her shoulders like water. Her slender, still figure was silhouetted in the dim light from the front window, her white night rail shimmering and nearly transparent. She might as well have been nude.

If he'd been dreaming, though, she *would* have been naked. Half expecting her to melt away into the moonlight, Sullivan remained motionless. In the thick shadows beneath the stairs he had to be nearly invisible. If she hadn't seen him, then—

"What are you doing in my house?" she asked. Her voice shook; she was mortal, after all.

If he said the wrong thing or moved too abruptly, she would scream. And then he would have a fight on his hands. While he didn't mind that, it might prevent him from leaving with the painting—and that was his major goal. Except that she still looked . . . ethereal in the darkness, and he couldn't shake the sensation that he was caught in a luminous waking dream. "I'm here for a kiss," he said.

She looked from his masked face to the bundle beneath his arm. "Then you have very bad eyesight, because that is not a kiss."

Grudgingly, though occupied with figuring a way to leave with both his skin and the painting, he had to admit that she had her wits about her. Even in the dark, alone, and faced with a masked stranger. "Perhaps I'll have both, then."

"You'll have neither. Put that back and leave, and I shan't call for assistance."

He took a slow step toward her. "You shouldn't warn me of your intentions," he returned, keeping his voice low and not certain why he bothered to banter with her when he could have been past her and back outside by now. "I could be on you before you draw another breath."

Her step backward matched his second one forward. "Now who's warning whom?" she asked. "Get out."

"Very well." He gestured for her to move aside, quelling the baser part of him that wanted her to remove that flimsy, useless night rail from her body and run his hands across her soft skin.

"Without the paintings."

"No."

"They aren't yours. Put them back."

One of them *was* his, but Sullivan wasn't about to say that aloud. "No. Be glad I'm willing to leave without the kiss and step aside."

Actually, the idea of kissing her was beginning to seem less mad than it had at first. Perhaps it was the moonlight, or the late hour, or the buried excitement he always felt at being somewhere in secret, of doing something that a year ago he would never even have contemplated, or the fact that he'd never seen a mouth as tempting as hers.

"Then I'm sorry. I gave you a chance." She drew a breath.

Moving fast, Sullivan closed the distance between them. Grabbing her shoulder with his free hand, he yanked her up against him, then leaned down and covered her mouth with his.

She tasted like surprise and warm chocolate. He'd expected the surprise, counted on it to stop her from yelling. But the shiver running down his spine at the touch of her soft lips to his stunned him. So did the way her hands rose to touch his face in return. Sullivan broke away, offering her a jaunty grin and trying to hide the way he was abruptly out of breath. "I seem to have gotten everything I came for, after all," he murmured, and brushed past her to unlatch and open the front door.

Outside, he collected his hammer and then hurried down the street to where his horse waited. Closing the paintings into the flat leather pouch he'd brought for the purpose, he swung into the saddle. "Let's go, Achilles," he said, and the big black stallion broke into a trot.

After ten thefts, he'd become an expert in anticipating just about anything. That was the first time, though, that he'd stolen a kiss. Belatedly, he reached up to remove his mask. It was gone.

His blood froze. That kiss—that blasted kiss—had distracted him more than he'd realized. And now someone had seen his face. "Damnation."

🌹 *Coming August 2008*

Before the Scandal

Second in The Notorious Gentlemen trilogy
by *New York Times* bestselling author
Suzanne Enoch

When Phineas Bromley returns home after ten years
of self-imposed exile, his world is thrown into a tail-
spin. More used to battlefields than ballrooms, the
adjustment to civilized life is not easy. But there's
nothing like a little mystery to liven up what seems
like an ill-timed return. Aware that someone is sab-
otaging the family estate, Phineas must come up
with a way to expose the culprits. His plan is risky—
but not as dangerous as his unexpected attraction
to Alyse Donnelly, the young lady next door.

Phin Bromley. Alyse Donnelly had never thought
to set eyes on him again. He was undeniably
taller, but he also seemed . . . larger. Not fat, by any
means, because he'd always been lean, but . . . more
commanding. Yes, that's what it was. And—

Richard jabbed her in the shoulder. "Who is he?" her
cousin hissed.

Alyse shook herself. "Their brother," she answered
in the same low tone he'd used. Either the footmen
knew already or they would soon, but if Richard didn't
want to be seen gossiping, she could understand that.
"The middle sibling."

"You never mentioned another brother."

"He's been away for a very long time. Ten years or more." She smiled a little, remembering. "I haven't set eyes on him since I was fifteen."

"Well, this could be an opportunity for you then, cousin, couldn't it?" Richard murmured. "After all, if there are things you don't know about him, then there are bound to be things he doesn't know about you."

Her face heated; she couldn't help it. After four years she should have been used to the insults, direct or implied, but obviously they still had the power to cut her. "Thank you, Richard," she said softly, "but I prefer to make his acquaintance first."

"I suggest you speak to your cousin with less sarcasm, Alyse," her Aunt Ernesta cooed. "You are not who you once were."

And no one in her family ever let her forget that fact. "I remember, Aunt Ernesta."

"Then have someone fetch me a blanket. My legs are cold."

Carefully hiding her annoyance, Alyse motioned to the nearest of the footmen and passed on her aunt's request. Things in the Bromley household might have taken a turn for the unexpected, but her life progressed with the predictability of a clock. An endlessly ticking clock.

The dining room door opened again. Lord Quence entered first, being wheeled in on his chair with a somber look on his pale face. Beth followed a heartbeat later, her expression tense. The door closed again, but Alyse kept her gaze on it.

Phineas Bromley. Phin. The last person she ever would have imagined joining the army, though he obviously had. She didn't know what the insignia on his shoulder meant, but he was clearly an officer.

A moment later he walked into the room, his gaze touching on the rest of the occupants, then finding her. Alyse blushed again at those clear hazel eyes, wondering what she looked like to him. Other than his eyes, she wasn't certain she would have recognized him. His dark brown hair was a little long, as though he'd been too busy to seek a barber, and his face leaner than she remembered. And a narrow scar dissected his right eyebrow, giving his appearance the rakish bent he'd always seemed to have inside.

"Alyse," he said, and took the seat across from her. "Miss Donnelly. William told me that your parents passed away. I am truly sorry."

"Thank you. It was . . . unexpected."

Richard leaned over to cover her hand with his. "I'm only glad that we've been able to give Alyse a place in our household."

Phineas glanced at her cousin, then back to her again. "Do you still like to ride?" he asked.

It felt odd to have someone pay attention to her these days. "I haven't had much opportunity," she hedged. "My aunt is unwell, and I sit with her a great deal."

"If I stay long enough, we should go riding," he pursued.

Alyse smiled. "I would like that."

"How long *will* you be staying?" Richard cut in again.

This time Phin glanced at his brother. "As long as I'm needed. I have several months of leave coming, if I require it."

"Where are you serving?" Alyse asked, disliking when that gaze left her.

"The north of Spain at the moment. I'm with the First Royal Dragoons."

"A . . . lieutenant, is it?" Richard asked, eyeing the crimson and blue uniform.

"Lieutenant-Colonel," Elizabeth corrected, pride in her tone. "Phin's received five field promotions."

"That's extraordinary." Richard lifted a glass, not in Phin's direction, but in the viscount his brother's. "You must be very proud of him."

"Yes," Lord Quence said, returning to his meal. "Very proud."

Clearly all was not entirely well at Quence Park, though Alyse had known that before. But for Richard to poke a stick into the tension—it was so unlike him in public, though in private he did little else. "When we were all children together," she said into the air, "we had the most hair-raising adventures."

Phineas sent her a short smile. "I can face cannons fearlessly after surviving the infamous pond-jump dares."

Alyse snorted, then quickly covered her mouth with one hand and made the sound into a cough. "You were fearless well before then."

Enjoy more love, madness,
murder and mayhem from
New York Times bestselling author

SUZANNE ENOCH

A Touch of Minx
978-0-06-087523-7

The Metropolitan Museum of Art wants Samantha Jellicoe's services as a private security consultant. She's only too happy to help, until she's targeted by a deadly adversary.

Twice the Temptation
978-0-06-123147-6

Two captivating tales of passion and peril—and one diamond that dazzles two women across the centuries.

Billionaires Prefer Blondes
978-0-06-087522-0

Samantha Jellicoe has promised her billionaire lover to walk the straight and narrow. But she certainly can't help it if trouble finds *her*.

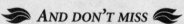 **AND DON'T MISS**

Don't Look Down
978-0-06-059364-3

Flirting With Danger
978-0-06-059363-6

Visit www.AuthorTracker.com for exclusive
information on your favorite HarperCollins authors.

Available wherever books are sold or please call 1-800-331-3761 to order.
SE 0508